A Harlequin

JANET DAILEY

Collector's Edition

Harlequin
JANET DAILEY
Collector's Editions

A Harlequin

JANET DAILEY

Collector's Edition

Harlequin Books

TORONTO • NEW YORK • LONDON
AMSTERDAM • PARIS • SYDNEY • HAMBURG
STOCKHOLM • ATHENS • TOKYO • MILAN

These books by Janet Dailey were originally published as
follows:

THE IVORY CANE
Copyright © 1977 by Janet Dailey
First published by Mills & Boon Limited in 1977
Harlequin Presents edition (#219) published
January 1978

LOW COUNTRY LIAR
Copyright © 1978 by Janet Dailey
First published by Mills & Boon Limited in 1978
Harlequin Presents edition (#302) published
August 1979

ISBN 0-373-80607-8
First edition May 1984
The Harlequin trademark, consisting of the word
HARLEQUIN and the portrayal of a Harlequin,
is registered in the United States Patent and Trademark
Office and in the Canada Trade Marks Office.

PRINTED IN U.S.A.

CONTENTS

THE IVORY CANE

"THERE'S NO NEED TO FEEL SHY AND SELF-CONSCIOUS."

Tentatively Sabrina began to explore Bay's face, as her initial resistance faded. Her fingertips searched the hard angles of his cheekbones and fluttered over curling eyelashes to thick brows. There was an arrogant curve to his Roman nose and gentle firmness to his lips. It was a masculine face, Sabrina thought in satisfaction.

A finger tucked itself under her chin and turned her head toward him. "I like your face, too," Bay murmured softly.

The warm moistness of his breath caressed her cheek before his lips touched hers. With expert persuasion, his mouth moved mobilely against hers until he evoked the pliant response he wanted.

And for a few fleeting moments Sabrina allowed herself to be a real woman and not just a pitiful blind woman.

CHAPTER ONE

OVERHEAD a sea gull screeched. The blustery wind off the Pacific Ocean swirled around the boats docked at the Yacht Harbor of San Francisco Bay. Distantly came the clang of a cable car, the one climbing the steep hill of Hyde Street.

A light blue Continental with a leather-grained top of dark blue was wheeled expertly into the parking lot in front of the harbor. The driver, a stunningly beautiful, titian-haired woman in her mid-thirties, braked the car precisely between the white parking lines and switched off the motor. As she reached for the door handle, emerald green eyes flicked to the silent girl in the passenger seat.

'It's quite chilly outside, Sabrina. It probably would be best if you waited in the car while I see if your father is back.' It was a statement, not a suggestion that the woman made.

Sabrina Lane opened her mouth to protest. She was tired of being treated as an invalid. With a flash of insight, she realized that Deborah was not concerned about her health as much as she was about spending some time alone with Sabrina's father.

'Whatever you say, Deborah,' she submitted grudgingly, her right hand closing tightly over the smooth handle of her oak cane.

The silent moments following Deborah's departure grated at Sabrina's already taut nerves. It was difficult enough to endure her own physical restrictions without having her father's girlfriend place others on her, regardless of the motive.

Her father's girlfriend. One corner of her wide mouth turned up wryly at the phraseology. Her father had had many women friends since her mother died when Sabrina was seven. But Deborah Mosley was not just another woman. If it had not been for Sabrina's accident some eight months ago, Deborah would have already been her new stepmother.

Prior to the accident, Sabrina had thought it was terrific that her father had found someone he wanted to marry. Deborah Mosley wouldn't have been Sabrina's choice, although she liked her, but that hadn't mattered not as long as her father was happy.

That was before the accident, when Sabrina had been totally independent. She had had a place of her own, a very small apartment, but it had been hers. She had had a career, not a lucrative one, but she could have supported herself.

Now—the word screamed with its own despairing wail. It would be a long time, if ever, before Sabrina could say any of that again.

'Why me?' a sobbing, self-pitying voice asked silently. 'What did I ever do to deserve this? Why me?'

Her throat tightened with pain at the unanswerable question. There was simply too much time to think. Too much time to think about the 'what-might-have-beens' and the 'if-onlys.' The damage was done and irreparable, as specialist after specialist had told Sabrina and her father. She would be incapacitated for the rest of her life and there was nothing, barring a miracle, that could ever be done to change it.

A seed of rebellion stirred to life. An anger seethed to the surface that she might forever sit in cars and stay at home while someone else decided what was best for her.

A sickening thought sprang to mind. Suppose, Sabrina thought, that Deborah's wish to be alone with her father was not prompted by a desire for some romantic moments but part of a plan to persuade him to send her away to that rehabilitation home? Rehabilitation—the word always made her feel like a criminal.

'Please, God,' Sabrina prayed, 'don't let Daddy listen to her. I don't want to go to that place. Surely there must be an alternative besides another school.'

She felt guilty praying to God for help. It hurt to need anyone to help her. She had always been so completely self-sufficient. Now she was constantly depending on someone. At this very minute, Deborah might be persuading her father to send her to another school and she was sitting in the car, accepting her fate by the very fact that she was not participating in the discussion but calling on someone else to intercede on her behalf.

Thousands of times Sabrina had walked from the parking lot of the harbor to the slip where her father tied his boat. It wasn't that great a distance. If she remained calm and took her time, there was no reason why she couldn't traverse it again.

Artistically long fingers tightened the cord of the striped tunic and adjusted the rolled collar of the navy dark turtleneck she wore underneath. The wind whistled a warning outside. She ran a smoothing hand up to the back of her head to be certain her mink-brown hair was securely fastened in its knot atop her head.

Taking a deep breath to still the quivering excitement

racing through her, Sabrina opened the door and swung her long legs on to the pavement. With the car door closed behind her and the cane firmly in her grasp, she moved slowly in the direction of the harbor fence. The icy tendrils of fear dancing down her spine added to the adventurous thrill of her small journey.

Emboldened by her initial success, Sabrina unconsciously began to hurry. She stumbled over a concrete parking stop and couldn't regain her balance. The cane slipped from her hand, skittering away as she sprawled on to the pavement.

Excitement disappeared immediately, leaving only black fear. Her shaking fingers reached for the cane, but it was out of her grasp. Except for the shock to her senses, there was no pain. She wasn't hurt, but how was she going to make her way to the dock without the cane?

'Damn, damn, damn!' Sabrina cursed her own foolishness for making the attempt in the first place.

If her father found her like this, it would only increase the apparent validity of Deborah's argument that Sabrina needed more professional help. Propping herself up on one elbow, she tried to check the rising terror that was leading her toward panic and think her way out of this predicament rationally.

'Are you all right?' The low, masculine voice offering concern was laced with amusement.

Sabrina's head jerked in the direction from which it had come, embarrassed red surging into her cheeks that a stranger should find her and humiliation that she was forced to seek his help.

The triangular line of her chin, tapering from prominent

cheekbones and square jaw, tilted to a proud angle. 'I'm not hurt,' she asserted quickly, then grudgingly, 'My cane, would you get it for me?'

'Of course.' The amusement disappeared.

The instant the cane was retrieved Sabrina reached out to take it from him, not wanting to endure the mortification of his pity and hoping a quick 'thank you' would send him on his way. As her outstretched hand remained empty, her cheeks flamed darker.

A pair of strong hands slipped under her arms and bodily lifted her to her feet before she could gasp a protest. Her fingers touched the hard flesh of his upper arms, covered by the smooth material of his windbreaker. The salty tang of the ocean breeze mingled with the spicy after-shave cologne and his virile masculine scent. Sabrina was tall, nearly five foot seven, but the warm breath from his mouth stirred the bangs covering her wide forehead, making him easily six inches taller than she.

Her cane, hooked over his arm, tapped the side of her leg. 'Please let me go,' she said crisply while her fingers closed over the cane and lifted it from his arm.

'Nothing sprained but your pride, is that it?' the man mocked gently, loosening his grip on her slim waist and letting his hands fall away.

Sabrina smiled tautly, keeping her luminous brown eyes that sometimes seemed too large for her face, averted from the man's face. His pity she didn't need.

'Thank you for your help,' she murmured unwillingly as she took a hesitant step backward.

Turning away, she waited for interminable seconds for him to continue wherever it was that he was going. She could feel his eyes on her back and guessed that he was waiting to be certain she hadn't hidden an injury from the fall.

Afraid that he might feel compelled because of her need for the cane to offer further assistance, Sabrina stepped out boldly. The shocking blare of a horn simultaneously accompanied by the squeal of car brakes paralyzed her. A steel band circled her waist and roughly pulled her back.

The husky male voice was still low, but there was nothing gentle and concerned about its tone as he growled in her ear. 'Were you trying to kill yourself? Didn't you see that car coming?'

'How could I?' Sabrina muttered bitterly, unable to tug the steel-hard arm from around her waist. 'I'm blind!'

She heard and felt his swift intake of breath a split second before he spun her around, her upper arms now prisoners of his hands. His eyes burned over her face. Her downcast chin was seized by his fingers and jerked up. Sabrina knew her sightless eyes were gazing into his face. For once she was blessedly glad she couldn't see. The pity that would be in his expression would have been unbearable.

'Why the hell didn't you say so!' There was a savage snap to his angry voice that caught her off guard. Anger she had not expected. 'And why the blazes isn't your cane white?'

Stung, Sabrina retorted in kind. 'Why am I supposed to have a white cane? Why am I expected to wear dark glasses? Should I run around with a little tin cup, too, crying "alms for the blind"? Why does being blind make me different from anyone else? Why do I have to be singled out? I hate it when parents point their fingers at me

14

and tell their children to let the blind lady go first. My cane isn't white because I don't want any special consideration or any pity!'

'And your abhorrence of white canes nearly got you killed,' the stranger said grimly. 'Had the driver of the car that almost ran you down seen a white cane in your hand, he might have taken extra precautions, slowed down to give you the right of way or perhaps honked his horn to be sure you knew he was there. You go right on being a proud fool. You won't live long. Just keep on stepping in front of cars and sooner or later one of them will hit you. It might not trouble your conscience, but I'm sure the driver who ultimately runs you down will have difficulty understanding the pride that kept you from carrying a white cane that could have saved your life.'

'It's not difficult to understand,' Sabrina replied in a strangled voice. 'If the man had ever lost his sight, he'd know how grating it is to advertise your blindness.'

'It's very obvious why you reject pity from others,' the man taunted. 'You're much too busy wallowing in a pool of your own self-pity.'

'Of all the arrogant—' Sabrina didn't bother to finish the statement as her hand accurately judged the distance and height before connecting with a resounding slap against the man's jaw and cheek.

The trajectory of her hand had not completed its arc when she felt a stinging hand against her own cheek. It was no more than a reproving tap, but her shock at his reaction magnified it tenfold.

'How dare you strike a blind person!' she exclaimed in an outraged whisper.

'I thought you didn't want any special privileges?' he

mocked. 'Or doesn't that extend to slapping another person, secure in the belief that he wouldn't retaliate against a blind girl? You'll have to make up your mind whether the kid gloves should be on or off.'

Sabrina gasped sharply, caught in the trap of her own words. 'You are insufferable!' she breathed, and turned away.

'Not so fast.' The hand digging into her shoulder and neck effectively halted her steps. 'You're worse than a toddler,' he muttered impatiently. 'Do you hear any cars coming? Do you know where you're going? Have you got your directions straight?'

'Just leave me alone!' Sabrina demanded. 'My well-being is nobody's responsibility but my own!'

'I'm sorry.' There was no apology in his harsh tone. 'But I was raised to believe that all of us are our brother's keeper, or sister's as the case may be. So, whether you like it or not, I'm going to see that you safely arrive at whatever destination you have. Go ahead and walk away.' Sabrina could sense his shrug of indifference. 'I'll be walking right behind you.'

She wanted to scream her frustration, but the stranger's unrelenting manner seemed to say that even that would be a waste of energy. She could not go on the docks, not with this man as an unwanted bodyguard. The last thing she wanted was to have her father feel that it wasn't safe to leave her alone even for a few minutes. The minute her father saw this man at her side there would be all sorts of questions and the entire embarrassing story would be told.

Reluctantly she turned back in the direction she had just come. 'You don't need to trouble yourself,' she said stiffly. 'I'm only going to the car.'

16

'And drive, I suppose.' Satirical amusement was back in the man's low-pitched voice.

Sabrina chose to ignore his laughing jibe. Embarrassment and anger had all but erased her sense of humor. She tried to step past the tall stranger, but he moved to block her way.

'Which car?' he asked softly.

'The blue Continental behind you in the next row.'

'That isn't where you were headed when I first saw you.'

She gritted her teeth. 'I had intended to go out on the docks to meet my father and Deborah. Since you insist on accompanying me, I prefer to wait for them in the car.' There was a saccharine quality to her carefully enunciated words.

'They're out sailing and left you here in the car?' His tone seemed to indicate that her father and Deborah possessed as little sense as she did.

'No, my father went sailing. Deborah and I came down to pick him up. She's somewhere out on the dock now and I was going to see what was keeping them,' Sabrina retorted.

'Deborah is your sister?'

'You seem determined to pry into my personal life,' she sighed impatiently. 'Deborah will quite likely be my new mother—if it's any of your business!'

His hand closed over her elbow, the firm hold guiding her steps in the direction Sabrina knew the car to be. Several steps later, the end of the cane clunked against the side fender of the car.

'Which slip does your father use? I'll go see what's keeping him for you,' the man offered.

'No, thank you,' she refused curtly. 'He's nearly

convinced already that I need a permanent baby-sitter. If you go carrying tales to him, I'll never be able to persuade him that I don't want anybody wiping my nose for me.' Exasperation ringed her voice. 'If I give you my word that I won't leave the car, will you go away and leave me alone?'

'I'm afraid it's too late to keep our meeting a secret from your father,' the man said.

'What do you mean?' Sabrina frowned.

'Is Deborah a redhead?'

'Yes.'

'Well, there's a man walking toward the harbor gates with a redhead at his side. He's looking this way with a rather anxious frown on his face,' was the reply.

'Please go quickly before he gets here,' she pleaded.

'Since he's already seen me, if I were your father I would be very suspicious if a strange man was talking to my daughter and left when he saw me coming. It's better that I stay,' the man stated.

'No.' Sabrina whispered her protest. With this man, words held little persuasion.

There was the clink of the harbor fence gates opening and closing. Time had run out.

'Stop looking as if I'd made some indecent proposition to you. Smile.' The sound of the man's low voice held a smile, warm and faintly amused at her apparent discomfort. Her reluctance was obvious as the corners of her mouth stretched into a slow smile.

'Sabrina.' Her father's voice hailed her, an undertone of concern in his otherwise warmly happy use of her name. 'Were you getting tired of waiting?'

Nervously she turned, trying to keep the faltering smile

in place, knowing how perceptively discerning the scrutiny of his hazel eyes could be.

'Hello, Dad.' She forced a casualness into her voice. 'Did you have a good sail?'

'What else?' he laughed his assertion.

Sabrina sensed almost the exact instant when her father's inquisitive gaze was turned on the man at her side. She had been so busy trying to get rid of him that she hadn't thought of a single excuse to explain his presence.

The problem was taken out of her hands. 'You must be Sabrina's father. She was just asking me if I'd seen the *Lady Sabrina* come in while I was at the docks. I have the ketch down the way from yours, *Dame Fortune*. The name is Bay Cameron,' the stranger introduced.

'Grant Lane,' her father countered, the vague wariness leaving his voice at the introduction.

Unconsciously Sabrina had been holding her breath. She let it out in a silent sigh. The stranger, now identified as Bay Cameron, could think on his feet, she decided with relief. Of course she was certain there wasn't another boat in the harbor named *Lady Sabrina*, but the man had been quick to put two and two together simply from her father's use of her name. And it sounded like such a plausible excuse for her to be talking to him.

Her father's hand touched her shoulder and she turned her face to him with an easy smile. 'You weren't worrying about me, were you, Sabrina?' he teased.

'Not a bit. Not a salty old sailor like you. Of course, you were minus the best deckhand you ever had,' she laughed.

'Yes, well—' His stumbling agreement made Sabrina wish she could bite off her tongue. She had not meant to remind him of the many hours they had spent together

19

sailing these very same waters before the accident that had left her permanently blind.

'Women always worry when their men are at sea,' the stranger named Bay Cameron filled in the awkward gap.

'It's our nature,' Deborah spoke up in her best purring voice. 'You men wouldn't like it any other way.'

'Quite right, Deborah,' her father agreed. 'Mr. Cameron, this is my fiancée, Deborah Mosely.'

'Miss Mosely, it's a pleasure, but I shouldn't keep you any longer. I'm sure you all have plans of some kind,' Bay Cameron responded.

'Thank you for keeping Sabrina company.' There was sincere gratitude in her father's offer of thanks.

'Yes, Mr. Cameron,' Sabrina added, reluctantly acknowledging the fact that he had not given her away. 'I appreciated your thoughtfulness.'

'Yes, I know.' Lack of sight made Sabrina's hearing more acute. She caught the mocking inflection in his words that quite likely escaped her father and Deborah's ears. He knew very well what she was thanking him for. 'Perhaps we'll all see each other again some time. Good afternoon.'

After their answering chorus of goodbyes, Sabrina listened to his footsteps fading away to another area of the parking lot. She wondered why he had not seen fit, in his arrogance, to tell her father the way they had really met. Pity, most likely, although he had certainly exhibited a remarkable lack of it earlier. In fact he had been downright rude and tyrannical.

The car door was opened behind her, bringing an abrupt end to her wandering thoughts as her father's guiding hand helped her into the back seat.

'I thought you were going to wait in the car,' Deborah said in a faintly reproving tone after they were all seated.

'It got stuffy, so I decided to get some fresh air,' Sabrina lied.

'It did put some color in your cheeks,' Grant Lane observed. 'You probably should get out more.'

Was that an innocent comment or a remark prompted by a discussion with Deborah concerning that new school for the blind she had heard about? It was impossible to tell. Sabrina crossed her fingers.

'This Mr. Cameron,' Deborah said, 'had you met him before?'

'No. Why?' Sabrina stiffened, vaguely on the defensive.

'It's not like you to talk to total strangers, that's all,' the redhead replied.

'You mean, not since I've been blind,' Sabrina corrected sharply. 'I've never been exactly shy. Besides, all I did was ask about Dad.'

There was a moment of uneasy silence. Her reply hadn't needed to be so cutting, but sometimes Deborah's air of solicitude and apparent concern got on Sabrina's nerves. For that matter, anyone's did.

'Do you suppose,' Deborah covered the silence, 'he's one of the real estate Camerons?'

'I can't visualize any other having a ketch in the Yacht Harbor,' her father replied. 'The Camerons are one of the founding families of San Francisco.'

A native San Franciscan, Sabrina was well aware of the city's colorful history. Until gold was discovered in 1849, it had been a nothing little settlement on San Francisco Bay called Yerba Buena, 'good herb.' The bay was a perfect harbor for the ships racing around the tip of South

21

America to join in the rush for California gold. The natural entrance into the bay truly became 'golden gates' for a lot of pioneers.

Few actually found the precious metal in any quantity, but the real treasure had been in the goods and services they brought with them. The great bulk of the gold was possessed by a very small number of men. The majority of it from the California and Nevada lodes built San Francisco, the City by the Bay.

The Cameron family was one of the less publicized of the original founders. It was laughingly said that they once owned all of San Francisco, and now they possessed only a quarter of the city. Hardly a step down in this day and age, Sabrina thought wryly, and it certainly accounted for the man's arrogance.

Oh, well, she sighed, what was the use in thinking about him? He was not the kind of man a person would run into very often, not with his background.

She had rather liked his voice, though. Sabrina qualified the thought quickly. She had liked it when he hadn't been dictatorially telling her what to do. The low baritone pitch had been warm and vaguely caressive, mature, too. She wondered how old he was.

That was one of the problems of not being able to see. She had to rely so heavily on the other senses to judge the new people she met. Still, she was becoming rather good at it. She began a quick exercise of the impressions she had gained in her brief meeting with Bay Cameron.

He was tall, over six foot by at least an inch. When he had pulled her out of the oncoming car's path, she had had the sensation of wide shoulders, a flat stomach and lean hips. Judging by the solidness of his muscles he was in excellent physical condition. The salty ocean spray that had clung to him at least verified that he often journeyed forth in the ketch tied up in the harbor and probably had that day since the scent had been predominant. That indicated an affection for the sea or at least, the outdoors, possibly both. His clean male scent and the fragrantly spicy after-shave cologne told her a bit about his personal habits.

At the time she had been too angry to appreciate his sense of humor, but she guessed it was there, somewhere beneath his amused mockery. His intelligence was in some ways measured by his educated manner of speaking and the quick thinking that had immediately assimilated the facts and come up with a reasonable excuse for her father as to why Sabrina had been talking to him. On the business side, he would probably be very shrewd and astute. The family fortune would be safe with him, if not increased.

She settled back into her seat with smug triumph. That was a great deal of information to glean from one meeting. There were only two things about him she didn't know. His age she could only narrow as being somewhere between thirty and fifty, judging by the maturity of his voice and his physical condition. The second was a detailed description of his looks—the color of his hair, his eyes, that type of thing. Sabrina was really quite pleased with herself.

For an instant she was motionless. There was one other thing she didn't know—his marital status. That was something she couldn't be certain of even if she could see, unless he was one of those men who faithfully wore his wedding ring. She couldn't recall the sensation of anything metal on his fingers.

Not that she cared one way or the other whether he was married or not. She had merely been conducting an exercise of her senses, a satisfactory one at that.

CHAPTER TWO

SABRINA licked the vanilla icing from her fingers, then painstakingly ran the knife across the top of every centimeter of the cake. No matter what kind of cake she made, her father invariably called it a fingerprint cake. Sabrina was never totally confident that the frosting covered the entire cake. The only way she could be certain was by feeling, hence the telltale impressions of her fingers across the icing.

Placing the knife on the formica counter, she set the cake platter toward the back, refusing to give in to the sensation that there was a gaping hole somewhere exposing the dark devil's food cake. Before the accident that had left her blinded, Sabrina had taken the simplest task in the kitchen for granted.

Now, washing dishes was a study in diligence, let alone cooking a meal. She had mastered nearly everything but eggs. There was only one type she could cook. Invariably they turned out to be scrambled omelettes. For the sake of their stomachs, breakfast had become the meal her father prepared.

Sunday was the day that Deborah did all the cooking, as had been the case this last weekend. She was a gourmet cook. Sabrina had always been mediocre at best, which made her doubly conscious of the occasionally charred or rare meals she placed on the table during the week compared to the perfection of Deborah's. Yet her father had never complained once, ignoring the less appetizing to compliment the good.

Except for a daily woman who came in twice a week to do the more thorough cleaning, Sabrina took care of the house herself, dusting and vacuuming. It took her longer than the average sighted person, but she had discovered that, with patience, there was very little she couldn't do. But patience was the key.

Without the benefit of sunlight, the passage of time was nearly impossible to judge. It seemed to slip through her fingers at times, five minutes turning out to be ten. Sometimes when the loneliness of her dark world caved in about her, the opposite was true. The empty, desolate sensation invariably occurred after a great surge of creative energy that she was unable to release.

Sabrina had learned to endure the myriad inconveniences that came from being sightless. She could even keep the bitterness in check until she thought about the career that had come to such an abrupt halt after the accident.

Since almost the first time a watercolor brush had been put in her hand, art and more specifically painting had been her special love. Her natural talent, enhanced by skill taught by some of the best teachers around, had made her a relatively successful artist at the early age of twenty-two, thanks to nearly fifteen years of training. Recognition had been achieved in portraits, not necessarily commissioned sittings but more often interesting faces she had seen along Fisherman's Wharf or Little Italy.

That had been the cruelty in the accident that had taken her sight. It had been a car accident. Even to this day Sabrina didn't know what had happened. She had been driving home very late at night after a weekend spent with a girl friend in Sacramento. She had fallen asleep at the wheel.

Looking back, her haste to return home seemed so senseless, considering the month she had spent in the hospital recovering from broken ribs and a concussion— not to mention the evident blow to her head that had irreparably damaged the optic nerves.

Giving her head a firm shake, Sabrina resolutely tried to push such memories to the back of her mind. Her survival lay in the future not in looking over her shoulder at the past. At the moment the future looked empty, but seven months ago Sabrina had not believed she would accomplish as much as she had.

Her next obstacle was walking from her home to the drugstore to buy a bottle of shampoo. It was only five blocks, but it was five blocks of San Francisco traffic and four intersections. Only in the last two months had she had sufficient confidence in her ability to attempt such a journey without accompaniment. Her pride always kept the humiliation of getting lost uppermost in her mind.

The pale green sweater jacket Sabrina took from the closet complemented the dark green of her slacks. She touched the handle of her oak cane in the umbrella stand, the smooth finish of the wood reminding her instantly of the arrogant stranger Bay Cameron that she had met at the Yacht Harbor last Sunday. She didn't care what he thought. She preferred the anonymity of a wooden cane. It was bad enough blundering about in her permanent darkness without drawing attention to her plight.

Entering into the stairway, Sabrina walked down the steps to the front door, carefully locking it behind her. The grillework gates just a few feet away creaked noisily as she opened and locked them. The sidewalk sloped abruptly downward. Sabrina counted the paces slowly, accurately turning at the front door of the neighboring Victorian house.

Pressing the intercom buzzer, she waited for her neighbor's response. As a precaution, her father insisted that she always let someone know where she was going and when she had safely returned, whether it was Peggy Collins, their neighbor for nearly fifteen years, or himself at his office.

'Yes, who is it?' a briskly sharp female voice answered the buzz.

'It's me, Sabrina. I'm on my way to the drugstore. Do you need anything?'

'How about three more hands? Or better yet, a plane ticket to South America?' the woman replied with amused exasperation.

'It's as bad as that, is it?' Sabrina laughed.

'Ken called me an hour ago and is bringing a couple of very important clients home for cocktails and dinner. Naturally there's not a thing in the house to eat and I'm also defrosting the refrigerator and have the contents of half the closets strewn through the house. It looks as if a cyclone had hit this place. Of all days to get ambitious, I had to pick today.'

'I'll be back in an hour or so.' Sabrina smiled at the intercom. There always seemed to be an impending crisis at Peggy's house that was invariably weathered with commendable aplomb. 'If we have anything you need—ice, drink, food—you just let me know.'

'My best solution is to find a husband with a better sense of timing,' Peggy sighed. 'Take care, Sabrina. I'll let you know if I need anything when you get back.'

Humming softly, Sabrina started out again. Her neighbor's droll humor had restored her somewhat dampened spirits. The trip to the drugstore became more of an adventure than an obstacle. There was a nip in the wind racing down the hill, but there always seemed to be a nip in the winds wandering through San Francisco.

There was no warmth on her cheeks as she crossed to the normally more sunny side of the street. The sun had evidently not burned through the fog yet. Instantly a vision of the fog swirling about the spans of the Golden Gate bridge sprang to her mind.

Her concentration broke for a moment and she had to pause to get her bearings. It was so difficult not to daydream. The end of her cane found the drop box for the mail and she knew which block she was on.

Crossing the street, she began counting her steps. She didn't want to walk into the barbershop instead of the drugstore as she had done the last time. A funny, prickly sensation started down the back of her neck. She ran a curious finger along the back collar of her sweater jacket and frowned at the unknown cause of the peculiar feeling.

'No white cane, I see,' a familiarly husky voice said from behind her. 'You're a stubborn girl, Miss Lane.'

A disbelieving paralysis took hold of her limbs for a fleeting second before Sabrina pivoted toward the male voice.

'Mr. Cameron,' she acknowledged him coolly. 'I didn't expect to see you again.'

'The city isn't as large as it seems. Here I am driving down the street and see a girl walking with a cane. I start wondering if you've been run down yet. Then, lo and behold, I realize the young girl with the cane is you. Are you in search of your father again?' Bay Cameron asked in that faintly amused tone she remembered.

'I was just going into the drugstore here.' Sabrina motioned absently over her shoulder in the general direction of her destination. 'You were driving?'

'Yes, I parked my car up the street. Do you live near here?'

'A few blocks,' she answered, tilting her head curiously and wishing she could see the expression on his face. 'Why did you stop?'

'To see if you would have a cup of coffee with me,' he replied smoothly.

'Why?' She couldn't keep the wariness out of her voice.

Bay Cameron laughed softly. 'Do I have to have an ulterior motive? Why can't it just be a friendly gesture on my part?'

'I just don't understand why you should want to have coffee with—' Sabrina nearly said 'with a blind girl'. The haughtiness left her voice as she ended lamely with '—me.'

'It seems to me, Sabrina, that you not only suffer from a persecution complex but a feeling of inferiority as well,' he suggested mockingly.

'That's absurd!' The sightless brown eyes that had been directed blankly at his face were sharply averted to the traffic in the street.

'Good.' Strong fingers closed over her elbow, turning her toward the drugstore. 'Where would you like to have the coffee? I know a little café in the next block we could go to.'

'I'm sure your wife would much prefer you spend your free time with her.' She made another feeble protest.

'I'm sure she would—if I had a wife.'

'I—I have an errand in the drugstore,' Sabrina protested again.

'Will it take long?'

Hopelessly she wished it would take an hour. She was simply reluctant to spend any time with him. That air of confidence that surrounded him did make her feel inferior.

'No,' she admitted with a downcast chin, 'it shouldn't take very long.'

'Your lack of enthusiasm isn't very flattering,' Bay Cameron taunted softly. 'Would you feel more comfortable if I waited outside for you?'

Just knowing he was in the vicinity unnerved her. Sabrina shook her head. 'It doesn't make any difference.'

'In that case, I'll go in with you. I need some cigarettes.'

She felt the brush of his arm against her shoulder as he reached around her to open the door. Her elbow was released and she entered the store more or less on her own. She tapped her way to the rear counter, sighing as she heard Bay Cameron's footsteps heading toward the tobacco section.

'Is there something I can help you find?' a woman clerk's voice asked.

Before Sabrina could reply, another gruffly happy voice broke in, male this time. 'Sabrina, I was beginning to think you had forgotten where my store was. I have not seen you in nearly two weeks.'

'Hello, Gino.' She smiled widely in the direction of the reproachful voice.

'It is all right, Maria, I will help Sabrina. You go see what that man at the prescription counter wants,' he dismissed the clerk that had initially approached Sabrina.

As the woman's footsteps moved away, Gino Marchetti whispered, 'Maria is new, a cousin of my wife's sister's husband. This is only her first week, so she doesn't know my regular customers.'

Those who worked in Gino's drugstore pharmacy were always related to him in some way, Sabrina had learned over the years. But she knew the information had been offered to gently apologize for the woman not knowing Sabrina was blind.

'She has a very nice voice. I'm sure she'll soon learn,' she replied.

'What is it that you need this day? Name it and I will get it for you.'

'Some shampoo.' Sabrina gave him the brand name she wanted.

While he went to get it, she carefully felt through the paper money in her wallet, marked by a certain fold to distinguish the denominations, for the amount she owed him.

As he was ringing up the sale on his old cash register, Gino Marchetti said, 'I still have the picture you painted of me hanging on this wall. People come in all the time and say, 'That looks just like you' and I say, 'Of course, it is me.' I tell them that the girl who painted it has come to my store since she was a little thing and that you painted it from memory and gave it to me on the anniversary of my twenty-fifth year in business. Everyone thinks it is a very fine gift to have.'

'I'm glad you like it, Gino,' Sabrina smiled wanly.

She remembered vividly how proud he had been that day she had presented the portrait to him nearly two years ago. It was that ever-present aura of pride that she had tried to capture in his likeness. It was a loving, generous pride and she had been relatively satisfied with the result. Now she would never know that sense of creative accomplishment again.

'Sabrina, I didn't mean—'

She heard the hint of regret and self-reproach in the elderly Italian's voice and guessed that some of her sadness had tugged down the corners of her mouth. She determinedly curved it upward again and interrupted him.

'It was really a very small gift, Gino,' deliberately misinterpreting the statement of apology he had been about to make. 'The painting was just a small way of saying thank you for all those peppermint sticks you gave me.'

The sensation of being watched tingled down her neck. Sabrina wasn't surprised when Bay Cameron spoke. Her sensitive radar seemed to be tuned to his presence.

'You did this painting?' he asked quietly.

'Yes.' She snipped off the end of the affirmation.

'It is very good, isn't it?' Gino prompted. 'I sold Sabrina her very first crayons. Then it was watercolors, then colored chalk. In my small way I helped her to become an artist, and she gave me this portrait as a present. She always comes to my store once, sometimes twice a week. That is, until her accident,' his voice became sad. 'Now she doesn't come as often.' Sabrina moved uneasily and Gino's mood immediately changed to a gayer note. 'Last week I saw her walk by my store and I wonder to myself where she is going. Then I see her walk into the barbershop next door and I say to myself 'Oh no, she is going to have that beautiful crown of hair on top of her head cut off, but she had only walked into the wrong store. She was coming to see me.'

'Do you know the very first time I saw her and that little knot of silky brown hair on top of her head, it reminded me of a crown, too.' There was a caressive quality to Bay Cameron's softly musing voice. Sabrina felt the rise of pink in her cheeks.

'I've taken up enough of your time, Gino,' she said hastily. 'I know you have work to do and other customers waiting. I'll see you next week.'

'Be sure it is next week, Sabrina.'

'I will. *Ciao*, Gino.' She turned quickly, aware of Bay Cameron stepping out of her way and following, although there was no guiding hand at her elbow.

'*Addio*, Sabrina,' Gino responded, not showing the least surprise that the stranger was with her.

'The café is to the left,' Bay instructed her as they walked out of the store. 'It's around the corner and down a short flight of stairs.'

'I think I know which one you mean. I haven't been there in several years,' Sabrina said stiffly.

They walked side by side down the sidewalk to the corner. He made no attempt to guide her, letting her make her own way without any assistance.

'That was a very good painting,' Bay ended the silence. 'Did you have training as a child?'

'I took lessons nearly all my life.' She swallowed the lump in her throat and replied calmly. 'It was my career. I was relatively successful.'

'I can believe it,' he agreed. 'You were good.'

'"Were" 'being the operative word,' she inserted with

faint bitterness. Then she took a shaky breath. 'I'm sorry.'

'Don't apologize,' he seemed to shrug. 'It must have been a doubly cruel blow as an artist to lose your sight. There's bound to be a feeling of injustice, otherwise you wouldn't be human.' There was a light touch on her arm to attract her attention. 'The iron banister of the stairs is on your left. You can follow it to the stairwell,' he instructed.

When her left hand encountered the railing, his own hand returned to his side. He had accepted the pain she felt at the loss of her career as a natural thing, hardly needing an explanation. There had been no empty words as others had offered that some day she would get over it. That Sabrina had never been able to believe.

At the base of the stairs, Bay reached past her to open the café door. A hand rested firmly on the side of her waist and remained there as a hostess showed them to a small booth.

'Let me take your cane,' he offered. 'I'll hang it on the post beside your seat so it will be out of the way.'

Sabrina handed it to him and slid into the booth, her fingers resting nervously on the table top. In the past she had avoided public eating establishments, too self-conscious to be at ease. She touched the edge of a menu and pushed it aside.

Their waitress had evidently appeared at the table because she heard Bay ask for two coffees before he addressed a question to her. 'They make their own pastries here. They're very good. Would you like any, Sabrina?'

'No.' In her nervousness she was too abrupt and she quickly added, 'No, thank you.'

'Would you like a cigarette?' he offered.

'Please,' She accepted almost with a sigh of relief.

The waitress arrived with their coffee just as Bay placed a lit cigarette between her fingers and slid the ashtray in front of her discreetly searching hand. Sabrina drew deeply on the filter tip of the cigarette, slightly amazed that she could feel the warmth of his mouth on the cigarette.

'Do you take anything in your coffee?' Bay asked.

'Nothing, thank you.' Sabrina exhaled the smoke from her mouth, blowing away some of her tension at the same time.

The heat from the coffee made the cup easy to find. The fingers of one hand closed around its warmth. A silence followed, one that Sabrina was pleasantly surprised to discover as comfortable. Her first meeting with Bay Cameron had been tainted by his apparent arrogance. It still existed, proved by the very fact that he had maneuvered her into this café, but it had somehow been tempered by his understanding.

In spite of that disturbing argument about the white cane, he seemed to approve of her desire for independence. The assistance he had given her had been unobtrusive. That coupled with his matter-of-fact comment about her loss of career made Sabrina wonder if she shouldn't re-assess her opinion of him. Bay Cameron seemed to be an unusual man. Sabrina wished she had met him before she lost her sight. He might have made an interesting portrait study. Then she sighed.

'What was that for?' he chided mockingly.

'Wishing,' Sabrina shrugged.

'A common pastime?'

'Only when I have nothing to distract me. Sometimes,' she ran a finger around the rim of her cup, 'I wonder when I'm alone if I wasn't given the gift of seeing people, places and things in minute detail early in life so I could store up a treasure of beautiful scenes to remember.'

'Do you believe in fate, then?' Bay asked quietly.

'Sometimes it seems the only explanation. Do you?' Sabrina countered.

'I believe we were given certain talents and abilities. What we do with them is the mark of our own character. I can't accept that I might not be the master of my own destiny.' His reply was laced with self-directed humor.

'I doubt there's very little you've wanted that you haven't obtained,' she agreed with a faint smile.

'Perhaps. And perhaps I've just been careful about what I wanted.' The smile faded from his voice. 'Tell me, Sabrina, how long has it been since you lost your sight?'

She was beginning to learn that Bay Cameron had a habit of coming straight to the point. Most of the people she knew or had met took special care to avoid any reference to her blindness and took pains that the conversation didn't contain words that referred to sight.

'Almost eight months.' She inhaled the smoke from the cigarette, wondering why his frankness didn't disconcert her. Maybe it was because he didn't seem embarrassed or self-conscious about her blindness.

'No days or hours?' There was the impression of a brow raised mockingly in her direction.

'I stopped trying to keep an exact count after the fourth specialist told my father and me that I would never see again.' Sabrina tried to sound nonchalant, but there was a faint catch to her voice.

'What happened?'

'A car crash. It was late at night. I was driving home from Sacramento and fell asleep at the wheel. I don't know

37

what happened.' Her fingers fluttered uncertainly in the air, then returned to grip the coffee cup. 'I came to in a hospital. There weren't any witnesses. A passing motorist saw my wrecked car in the ditch, the authorities estimate several hours after the accident.'

Sabrina waited for the supposedly bolstering comments that usually followed when she related the details of the accident, the it-could-have-been-worse and the you're-lucky-you-weren't-paralyzed-or-maimed sentences. But none of those trite words were spoken.

'What are you going to do now?'

'I don't know.' She didn't have the answer to that problem. She took a sip of her coffee. 'I've just been taking one day at a time, learning over again how to do all the things I used to take for granted. I was so positive that I was going to have a career in art that I never studied anything else but reading, writing and arithmetic. I'm going to have to make a decision about my future pretty soon, though,' she sighed. 'I can't keep being a burden for my father.'

'I doubt if he thinks of you that way.'

'I know *he* doesn't.' Unconsciously she put qualifying emphasis on the masculine pronoun.

Bay Cameron was much too observant to miss it. 'But someone else does, is that it?' he questioned. 'Is it your father's fiancée?'

Sabrina opened her mouth to deny it, then nodded reluctantly that he was right. 'I don't blame Deborah. She wants Dad to herself—' She hesitated. 'I don't want you to misunderstand me. I do like her. As a matter of fact, I'm the one who introduced her to him. She has a small antique shop here in San Francisco. It's just that we both know it would never work for the two of us to live in the same house. She wants me to go to some school she heard about where blind people are taught new skills, not basket-weaving or anything as humbling as that, but legitimate skills. They have a job placement program, too, when you've completed the term.'

'What does your father think of the idea?'

'I don't believe she's mentioned it to him yet.' A wry smile pulled her mouth into a crooked line. 'I think she wants to weigh me down with guilt so I'll be in favor of it when Dad brings up the subject.'

'Do you feel guilty?' Bay asked as she carefully stubbed out her cigarette in the ashtray.

'I suppose so. It's only natural, isn't it?' Sabrina spread out the fingers of her hands on the table top, looking at them as if she could see them. 'Everyone wants to think of himself as useful.'

'And you don't do anything that you consider useful?'

'I take care of the house and do most of the cooking. I could hardly keep doing that after Dad and Deborah are married. After all, it would be her house then.' She continued staring sightlessly at her long fingers. 'I know I could learn something.' She shook her head wearily, closing her hands around the coffee cup again. 'I'm still filled with too much pride, too much self-importance. My hands have always held an artist's brush. I guess it's just a case of not wanting to let go of that. Which is probably why I keep putting off the day when they'll have to do something else.'

'What does your boyfriend say to all this?'

'Boyfriend? I haven't got a boyfriend. A lot of men who are friends, but no boyfriends,' Sabrina denied firmly.

'You're a very attractive girl. I find it hard to believe that you didn't have a romantic attachment for someone,' Bay commented in a doubting voice.

'I always had my career,' she shrugged. 'I dated, quite often, as a matter of fact. I simply steered clear of any romantic involvement. Love and marriage were always something that would come somewhere in the future. I'm glad now that I did,' she added frankly. 'How many men would want to be saddled with a blind wife?'

'Isn't that a somewhat cynical view of the male sex?' he chuckled.

'Not really,' she smiled. 'It's not even a cynical view of love. It's just realistic. Being blind tends to make other people awkward and self-conscious. They're always trying to be so careful that they don't hurt your feelings by pointing out that there are some things blind people simply can't participate in, and that makes an uncomfortable relationship.'

'That's funny,' he mused mockingly. 'I don't feel the least bit uncomfortable, awkward or self-conscious, and I'm sitting here with you.'

For a moment, Sabrina was flustered by his observation. Mostly because it was true. There were no undercurrents of tension flowing around her.

'Actually I wasn't thinking about you,' she admitted. 'I was referring to some of my other friends, male and female. They all still keep in touch, the ones that count. They call or stop by to see me or invite me out, but it's not quite the same. With some of them our common link was art, so I understand why they don't like to bring up that subject in front of me. The others—there's just a vague uneasiness on both sides. With you,' Sabrina tilted her head to a curious angle, 'I don't really understand. I'm talking to you about things you couldn't possibly be interested in and I don't know why. Are you some kind of amateur psychiatrist?' A little frown of bewildered amusement puckered her brows.

'No.' Sabrina sensed his smile. 'And I wasn't at all bored. I imagine all of this has been building up inside you for some time. It's always easier to talk to strangers who don't have preconceived opinions. I happened to be an available stranger.'

'In that case, what wise advice do you have to offer me?' she asked with a pertly challenging smile.

'Strangers don't give advice. They only listen.' The laughter was obvious in his low voice as he dodged her question expertly.

Hurried footsteps approached their booth. 'Would you like some more coffee?' the waitress inquired.

'No more for me, thank you,' Sabrina refused. Her fingers touched the braille face of her watch. 'I have to be getting home.'

'Our check, please,' Bay requested.

By the time Sabrina had slid out of the booth seat, Bay was at her side, handing her the oak cane. His hand again rested lightly on the back of her waist, guiding her discreetly past the row of booths and tables to the café door. She waited there while he paid the check.

Once outside and up the stairs to the sidewalk, Bay asked, 'Did you say you only lived a few blocks from here?'

'Yes.' Sabrina turned her head toward him, the smile coming more easily and more often to her mouth. 'And it's uphill all the way.'

'Well, there's one consolation about the hills in San Francisco. When you get tired of walking up them, you can always lean against them.' Sabrina laughed at his amusingly accurate description. 'That's a nice sound,' Bay said lowly. 'I was beginning to think you'd lost the ability to laugh along with your sight. I'm glad you didn't.'

Her heart seemed to skip a beat for a few seconds. Sabrina discovered that she wanted to believe that was a personal comment and not a casual observation. That put her on dangerous ground, so she kept silent.

'My car is just around the corner,' Bay said as if he hadn't expected her to reply. 'Let me give you a ride home.'

It was past the hour Sabrina had told Peggy Collins she would be gone. That was why she agreed to his offer, giving him the address of the narrow Victorian house in the Pacific Heights section. The rush hour traffic had begun, so there was very little conversation between them in the car. Using the traffic at the intersections as a guide, Sabrina was able to judge when Bay turned on to the block where she lived.

'Our house is the dark gold one with the brown and white trim,' she told him. 'The number is difficult to see sometimes.'

A few seconds later, he was turning the wheels into the curb, setting the emergency brake and shutting off the motor. He had just walked around the car and opened her door when Sabrina heard her neighbor call out.

'Sabrina, are you all right?' The question was followed immediately by the sound of the redwood gate opening and Peggy Collins' footsteps hurrying toward them. 'I was just coming to see if you'd come home and forgotten to let me know.'

'I was longer than I expected to be,' Sabrina said, explaining the obvious.

'So I see.' The curious tone of voice also said that her neighbor saw the man Sabrina was with and was waiting to be introduced.

'Peggy, this is Bay Cameron. Peggy Collins is my neighbor,' she submitted to the invisible arm-twisting.

There was a polite exchange of greetings before Bay turned to Sabrina. 'It's my turn to say I'll have to be going, Sabrina.'

'Thank you for the coffee and the ride home.' She offered her hand to him in goodbye.

'My pleasure.' His grasp was warm and sure and all too brief. 'I'll see you again some time.'

The last sounded very much like a promise. Sabrina hoped that it was. His arrogance of their first meeting was completely erased. It was really strange how readily she had confided in him, she thought as she heard the car door open and close and the motor start. Not even to her father, who was very close to her, had Sabrina been able to talk that freely.

'Where did you meet him?' Peggy asked with more than idle curiosity.

'The other day at the Yacht Harbor when Deborah and I went to pick up Dad,' she explained, forgetting for an instant that her neighbor was standing beside her. 'I just bumped into him this afternoon—well, not literally,' Sabrina qualified. Her head followed the sound of the departing car until she could no longer hear it. She turned toward the older woman. 'Peggy, what does he look like?'

The woman paused, collecting her thoughts. 'He's tall, in his thirties I would say. He has reddish-brown hair and brown eyes, not dark brown but they are brown. I wouldn't call him handsome exactly. Good-looking isn't the right description either, although in a way they both fit.' There was another hesitation. 'He looks like a man. Do you know what I mean?'

'Yes,' Sabrina replied softly. 'Yes, I think I do,' guessing that his features were too strong and forceful to be classified in any other way.

'Good heavens!' Peggy exclaimed suddenly. 'I forgot to put the potatoes in the oven! I'll talk to you later, Sabrina.'

'Yes, all right, Peggy.' Her neighbor was already fast retreating to her door by the time Sabrina absently acknowledged her words.

CHAPTER THREE

'ARE you positive you want to walk out on the docks, Sabrina?' Deborah asked sharply.

'I would like to, yes,' she admitted. Unconsciously she raised her chin to a challenging angle. 'That is, of course, unless you want some time alone with Father.'

'It's not that,' the redhead sighed in frustration. 'Grant—worries about you so and there aren't any railings on the piers. He's naturally going to be concerned about your safety.'

'All parents worry, Deborah,' Sabrina said quietly. 'Father just feels he has more cause to worry than most, with justification, I suppose. I can't spend the rest of my life not doing things that might cause him to worry.'

'Believe me, if I could find a way to make him stop worrying about you, I would do it,' was Deborah's taut response as she stepped out of the car.

Sabrina followed, but more slowly, walking around the car parked in the lot of Yacht Harbor to the side of her father's fiancée.

'Has Dad said any more about setting the date?' Sabrina asked as they started toward the fence gates.

'No, and I haven't brought up the subject.' There was a pause before Deborah continued. 'A long time ago I recognized the fact that I'm a jealous and possessive woman, Sabrina. If I married your father while you were still living at home, it would create friction among all of us. You would be hurt; your father would be hurt; and I would be hurt. I'm quite aware that you're a very independent person and have no desire to be a burden to your father for the rest of your life.'

'Which is why you're pushing the idea of this school,' Sabrina breathed in deeply, knowing the vast amount of truth in the redhead's words.

'It may not be the answer, Sabrina, but it is a start,' Deborah suggested earnestly.

'I need more time.' Sabrina lifted her chin into the wind, letting the light ocean breeze play over her face. 'I keep hoping there'll be some other alternative. I don't know what, but something.'

'You are considering the school, though?'

'I have to consider it,' she sighed, 'whether I like the idea or not.'

'Thank you.' Deborah's voice trembled slightly before it steadied with determination. 'I like you, Sabrina, but I love your father. I've waited a long time to meet a man like him. So please, understand why I'm pushing so hard to get you out of the house.'

'I do.' The wooden floor of the dock was beneath her feet, the harbor gate closed behind them. 'If I loved a man, I would be just as anxious as you to have him to myself. But I won't be rushed into a decision, not unless I'm sure there isn't anything else.'

Deborah's guiding hand claimed her elbow. 'Turn left here,' she instructed.

The titian-haired woman was aware of Sabrina's stubborn streak. This was the time to let the subject drop when she had achieved a minor capitulation that Sabrina would consider her suggestion.

Sabrina guessed her tactics and willingly changed the topic. 'Is Dad in?'

'Yes, he's tying everything down now,' was the reply. A few minutes later, Deborah called out, 'Hello, darling did you have a good time?'

'Of course.' There was contented happiness in her father's voice that brought a smile to Sabrina's lips. 'Sabrina? I didn't expect to see you with Deborah.' A faint anxiety crept in.

'It was too nice a day to wait by the car.' She smiled away his concern. 'Don't worry, I'll be a good girl and not stray from the center of the dock.'

'I'll only be a few more minutes,' he promised.

'I'll get your thermos and things from the cabin, if you like, Grant,' Deborah offered.

There was hesitation before the suggestion was accepted. Sabrina knew her father was reluctant to leave her alone on the dock. His agreement was probably an indication that Deborah had given him a look that said he was being overly protective.

The creak of the boat was accompanied by the quiet lapping of the water against its hull. There was the flapping of wings near where Sabrina stood, followed by the cry of a gull. The ocean scent of salt and fish was in the breeze lifting the short hair on her forehead.

A tickling sensation teased the back of her neck. Instantly Sabrina was alert to the sounds of footsteps approaching, more than one set. Intuition said it was Bay Cameron and she knew all along that she had been hoping he would be there. But he was with someone, more than one, perhaps three others. The light tread of one pair of feet warned her that they belonged to a female.

'Are you calling it a day, Mr. Lane?' Bay Cameron's voice called out in greeting.

'Mr. Cameron, how are you?' her father returned with startled pleasure. 'Yes, this is all for me today until next week. Are you coming in or going out?'

'Out. We thought we'd take in an ocean sunset,' he replied, confirming that the other footsteps she had heard were with him. He had stopped beside her. Sabrina's radar told her he was only inches from her left side. 'How are you today, Sabrina?'

'Fine.' Her head bobbed self-consciously. She sensed the eagerness of the others to be on their way.

'I see you made it all the way on to the dock this time without mishap. Did you do it by yourself?' The words were spoken so soft and low that the light breeze couldn't carry them to anyone's ears but Sabrina's.

'No,' she murmured, barely moving her lips.

'Bay, are you coming?' an impatient female voice asked.

'Yes, Roni,' he answered. 'I'll see you again.' The ambiguous promise was offered as a goodbye. The raised pitch of his voice directed it to everyone and not Sabrina alone.

'Good sailing!' her father called out, but Sabrina said nothing.

A faint depression had settled in, intensified when the wind carried the woman's haughty inquiry as to who they were, but her acute hearing couldn't catch Bay's response.

Her fingers tightened around the curve of her oak cane. She was glad her cane was not white, identifying herself immediately to his friends as a blind girl. She could not have endured the sensation of their pitying looks. It was bad enough imagining the explanation Bay was giving them now. She wished she had not allowed him to bully

48

her into having coffee with him the other day, never poured out her troubles to him with such a complete lack of discretion.

'Are you ready yet, Dad?' she asked sharply, suddenly anxious to be gone, finding no more enjoyment in the scent and the sounds of the sea.

'Be right there,' he answered. 'Have you got everything, Deborah?'

'Yes.'

Seconds later the two of them were at Sabrina's side, her father's arm curving around her shoulders and guiding her back the way she had come. For once she didn't try to shrug away his assistance. She wanted the protective comfort of his arm.

She had tried to block out the memory of that Sunday, but it remained a shadow lurking near the edges of her already dark world. The melancholy violin strains on the stereo were not easing her depression. The position of the furniture in their house had long been memorized, and she walked unerringly to the stereo and switched off the music.

The front door bell buzzed loudly into the ensuing silence. With an impatient sigh at the unwanted intrusion, Sabrina continued to the intercom that linked the street level entrance next to the garage with the living area of the house.

'Yes. Who is it?' she inquired briskly after her searching fingers had found the switch.

'Bay Cameron.'

A surprised stillness kept her silent for ticking seconds. There was no warmth in her voice when she asked, 'What is it you wanted, Mr. Cameron?'

49

'I'm not selling brushes, insurance or bibles,' his amused voice answered. 'The only reason I can think of why I might be standing in front of your door is to see you.'

'Why?'

'I never did like talking to boxes. Will you come down?'

Sabrina sighed in irritation at the challenging tone. 'I'll be there in a minute,' she said, and flicked off the switch.

She opened the door to the stairwell that led from the second floor to the street entrance. There were two doors at the base of the stairs, one leading to the garage that occupied the ground floor and the second to the street sidewalk.

Opening the second door, Sabrina walked four paces and stopped. There was an iron grillework gate less than a foot in front of her, preventing direct access to the house from people on the street. Bay was on the other side of that gate.

'Now, what was it you wanted, Mr. Cameron?' she asked coolly.

'May I come in?' he asked in a mocking voice.

Her common sense lost its silent war. Angry fingers unfastened the lock, swinging the gate open to allow him admittance into the small detached foyer. Sabrina stepped back, clasping her hands in front of her in a prim pose.

'Why did you want to see me?' There was a vaguely haughty arch in her long neck.

'It's what a native would consider a most unusual day. There's not a cloud in the sky. The sun is shining. The breeze is light and warm. It's the perfect day for a walk,' Bay concluded. 'I stopped to see if you'd come with me.'

Sabrina doubted the sincerity of his words. She couldn't

believe that his motive for asking was a genuine desire for her company. He was feeling sorry for her.

'I'm sorry, it isn't possible,' she refused with honest cause.

'It isn't possible?' he questioned. Sabrina could visualize the arrogant life of his brow. 'Why?'

'I'm fixing a pot roast for dinner this evening. I have to put it in the oven in—'she touched the braille face of her watch '—forty-five minutes. So you see, if I went for a walk with you, we would barely be gone and we'd have to come back. An hour after that I'll have to be here to add the potatoes, carrots and onions.'

'Is that the only excuse you have?'

'It's a very legitimate one,' Sabrina returned firmly.

'If that's your only reason, we can soon take care of that,' Bay said complacently. 'Your oven has a timer. While you're getting the roast ready, I'll set the timer to turn the oven on in forty-five minutes. We can put it in now and have nearly two hours for our walk before you have to be back to add the rest of the items.'

'But—' She tried to protest, but her mind was blank.

'But what? Don't you want to go for a walk? It's too beautiful a day to stay indoors.'

'Oh, all right,' she sighed in exasperation, turning toward the door.

His throaty chuckle mocked her obviously reluctant agreement. 'I'm amazed at how graciously you always accept my invitations,' Bay taunted.

'Maybe it's because I can't help wondering why you make them,' Sabrina responded with faint acidity in her tone.

'I have the impression,' he reached around and opened

the door for her before her searching hands found the knob, 'that if you ever stopped being defensive over the fact that you're blind, you just might be pleasant company.'

Again Sabrina bridled silently at his implication that she spent too much time feeling sorry for herself. When her entire life and future had been based on the ability of her eyes to see the things her hands would paint, it was natural that she should feel bitterness at the injustice of her fate. Even Bay had acknowledged that. If he agreed, then what right did he have to condemn her?

Bay Cameron seemed to make his own laws, Sabrina decided. She ushered him silently up the stairs, through the dining room into the kitchen. By the time she had the meat seasoned and in the roasting pan, he had the oven ready.

'Are we ready to leave now?' Bay asked.

'I have to call my father.' She ran her palms nervously over the rounded curve of her hip bones.

'When Peggy Collins, our neighbor, is gone, he likes me to let him know where I'm going and when I'll be back.'

'In case some unsuspecting motorist runs you down?' he mocked.

Her mouth tightened into a mutinous line as she pivoted sharply away. 'You certainly have a thing about white canes, don't you?' she murmured sarcastically.

'I suppose so,' he agreed lazily. 'Go ahead and phone your father.'

'Thank you, I will, now that I have your permission,' Sabrina snapped.

The switchboard girl at her father's law firm put the call through to him immediately. She explained quickly that

Peggy wasn't home and that she had called to let him know she was going to be out for a while, not mentioning with whom.

'How long will you be?' Grant Lane asked.

'A couple of hours. I'll call as soon as I'm back,' Sabrina assured him.

'I know the weather is nice, but do you have to be gone that long? I don't like the idea of you wandering about the streets on your own,' he said.

'I'll be all right.' She was strangely reluctant to tell him she was being accompanied by Bay Cameron. 'Don't start worrying,' she laughed nervously.

A muscled arm reached around her and took the receiver from her hand. She tried to take it back, but her hand encountered the rock wall of his chest. Her fingers drew back quickly as if burned.

'Mr. Lane, this is Bay Cameron. Sabrina will be with me. I'll see that she's back in plenty of time so that your dinner won't be ruined.' Her father made some affirmative reply then Bay said goodbye and hung up the telephone. 'He asked me to tell you to have a good time.'

'Thanks,' she murmured caustically, and walked to the closet to get her lightweight coat.

Retrieving her cane from the umbrella stand, she heard Bay open the stair door. She walked quickly through the opening, listening to him lock the door behind him before following her down the stairs to the outer street.

'I thought we'd take the Hyde Street cable car down to Ghirardelli Square. Is that all right?' There was an underlying tone of amusement in his voice, suggesting that he found her sulking display of temper humorous.

'Whatever you like.' She shrugged her shoulders stiffly.

There was no mocking rejoinder at her less than courteous acceptance of his plan. In fact, he said not another word. If it hadn't been for the hand that took her elbow at the traffic intersections, Sabrina might have been walking the blocks to the cable car street alone. Except for a curt thank you when he helped her on to and off the cable car, she didn't address any remarks to him either.

'Are you finished pouting yet?' His question was heavy with concealed laughter as his hand firmly attached itself to her waist to maneuver them through the stream of summer tourists.

'I wasn't pouting,' Sabrina asserted coldly.

'You weren't?' Bay mocked.

'Maybe a little,' she acknowledged reluctantly, a trace of anger remaining. 'But you can be insufferably bossy at times.'

'I think you've just got your way too often lately. The people who care about you don't like to say "no," ' he observed.

'The same could be said for you.'

'I'm sure it's true.' Again there was a lazy acceptance of her criticism. 'But we weren't talking about me. You were the one who was pouting.'

'Only because you were taking over and running things without being asked,' Sabrina retorted.

'So what now? Do you maintain a state of war or take our walk as friends?' She could feel his eyes on her face. 'We didn't get along too badly the other day.'

Sabrina breathed in deeply, feeling herself surrendering to the invisible charm of his low voice. 'Friends,' she agreed against her better judgment.

Once she had succumbed it was easy to let herself be warmed by his persuasion as he gently steered the conversation to less argumentative topics. They wandered around the fountain in the center plaza of the old Ghirardelli Chocolate factory renovated into a shopping mall. They stopped at one of the outdoor cafés and sampled some of the thin delicious crêpes freshly made.

Their strolling pace took them by the windows of the multi-level shops in the buildings that made up the square. Bay laughingly challenged Sabrina to identify the type of store by sound and scent. She did quite well at the flower and leather shops and identifying what native cuisine was served at the various restaurants, but the jewelry, gift and import stores she missed entirely.

When Bay stopped in front of another shop window, she emitted a defeated sigh, 'I'm really out of guesses. Please, no more.'

'No, no more,' he agreed absently. 'It's a dressmaker's shop, more specifically labelled as Original Fashions by Jacobina. There's a dress in the window, and I'd swear it was made for you. Come on.' His arm tightened suddenly around her waist. 'We'll go in so you can see it.'

Instantly Sabrina strained against his arm. 'You're overlooking one pertinent detail. I'm blind. I cannot "see" the dress,' she reminded him sharply.

'I've overlooked nothing, my blind queen,' he replied patiently. 'So you can wipe that look of indignation from your face. Where's all that creative imagination you were bragging about the other day? I'm taking you into the shop and you're going to see this dress with your hands.'

Feeling roundly chastised, Sabrina mutely allowed

herself to be escorted into the shop. A tiny bell sounded above their heads as they walked in. Immediately footsteps approached from the rear of the store.

'May I help you?' a woman's voice inquired.

'Yes,' Bay answered. 'We'd like to look at the dress in the window.'

'We don't sell ready-made dresses here, sir,' the woman replied politely. 'It's a model from which we make another using the precise measurements of our customer.'

'Let me explain what I meant.' The velvet charm was very pronounced in his voice. 'Miss Lane is blind. I admired the dress in the window and wanted her to see it. In order for her to do that, she must touch it. Would that be possible?'

'Of course, I'm sorry. It will take me only a few minutes to remove it from the model,' the woman offered quickly and warmly.

Her words were followed by a rustle of motion and material. Sabrina shifted uncomfortably and felt the pressure of Bay's hand on her waist increase in reassurance. Short minutes later there was a silky swish of material in front of her.

'Here you are, Miss Lane,' the clerk said.

'Would you describe it for her?' Bay requested.

'Of course,' the woman agreed. 'Miss Jacobina calls this dress "Flame." Its ever-changing colors of red, gold, orange and yellow in irregular layered vees of chiffon curl at the ends like tongued flames.' Sabrina's sensitive fingers lightly traced the edges of the many layers. 'The neckline is vee-shaped but not plunging by any means. The illusion of sleeves is created by the cutaway vees of chiffon from the neckline, draping over the shoulders and the bodice.'

As the exploring tips of her fingers went over more of the dress Sabrina's mind began to form a picture with the help of the clerk's description.

'It's beautiful,' Sabrina murmured finally.

'What size is the model?' Bay asked. The woman told him. 'Would that fit you, Sabrina?'

'I think so,' she nodded.

'Can you stretch the rules to allow her to try it on?' he asked the clerk, again in that persuasive tone that Sabrina was certain no one could resist.

The woman took a deep breath, then laughed. 'I don't know why not. We have a changing room in the back. Miss Lane, if you'd like to come with me.'

Sabrina hesitated and Bay gave her a little push forward. 'Go on. Let's see what it looks like on,' he prompted.

'Why do I let you talk me into these situations?' she sighed.

'Because deep down, you enjoy it,' he teased. 'Besides, I bet you haven't bought any new clothes since the accident.'

'I haven't needed anything,' Sabrina protested weakly.

'When has that ever been a valid excuse for a woman?' Bay mocked. 'Now, go try that dress on. That's an order!'

'Yes, sir.' She didn't really have to have her arm twisted. The vision in her mind and the touch of the expensive material already had her excited about wearing it even if she couldn't see the end result.

Changing swiftly out of her sports clothes into the dress, she only required the assistance of the clerk with the zipper. With her hand resting lightly on the clerk's arm, she moved nervously to the front of the store where Bay waited.

'Well?' Sabrina asked breathlessly when the silence stretched to an unbearable length. Her head was tilted to one side in a listening attitude.

'You look beautiful, Sabrina,' Bay said simply.

'That's an understatement,' the clerk inserted. 'You're stunning, and I'm not saying that because I work here. The dress might have been made for you. The style, the color suits you perfectly. It's amazing, but you must have the same measurements as the girl who models it.'

Her fingers ran down the neckline of the dress, trailing off with a draping fold of the filmy chiffon. 'Could you—would you sell this one?' Sabrina asked.

'It's not customary,' the woman hesitated, then added with a resigned smile in her voice. 'Let me check.'

When the woman had left, Sabrina turned again to Bay. 'Are you very sure it looks right?' she questioned anxiously.

There was a click, then cigarette smoke wafted through the air to her nose. 'Are you seeking more compliments?' he asked.

'No,' she denied, nervously running her hand along the waist and glancing sightlessly at the floating vees of material cascading over her arm. 'It's just that I can't be positive—'

'Be positive.' With cat-soft footsteps he was at her side, lifting her chin with his finger. 'I told you the truth. You look beautiful in the dress.'

She wished she could see his expression. The sincerity

in his voice she didn't doubt, but there was an illusive sensation that he was aloof, withdrawn. The fringe of dark hair hid the tiny frown that knitted her forehead.

'Now what's troubling you?' Bay mocked.

'I—' Her chin was released as he stepped away. 'I was just wondering when I would ever wear this,' Sabrina hedged at the truth.

'Sometime there'll be an occasion when the dress will be just right for it. Then you'll be glad you bought it,' he replied in an indulgent tone.

'I never asked how much it is,' she murmured. Then an accompanying thought dropped her shoulders. 'I have hardly any money with me. Do you suppose I could give them some money to hold it and Daddy and I could come down later with the rest?'

'I could pay for it,' Bay suggested guardedly.

Sabrina bit into her lower lip, eager to possess the dress she wore but unwilling to obligate herself to a man who was neither friend nor stranger.

'If it wouldn't be too much trouble,' her acceptance was hesitant, 'you could write down your address and the amount. I'll have Dad mail you a check tonight.'

'You wouldn't consider accepting the dress as a gift?'

Sabrina drew back. 'No.' She shook her head firmly, ready to argue the point further if he should attempt to bully her into accepting it.

'I didn't think you would.' A rush of smoke was exhaled in her direction. He sounded vaguely angry. 'All right, I'll *loan* you the money for the dress.'

'Thank you,' breathed Sabrina, relieved the episode was not going to end on a quarrelsome note.

'Instead of your father mailing me a check, why don't I stop by your house Friday afternoon?' he suggested.

'If you like,' she frowned.

'I would like.' The smile was back in his voice and she gave him an answering one.

The sales clerk returned with the information that they would sell the dress model to Sabrina. The price of the garment was not as high as she had expected. While she changed into her denim slacks and top, Bay took care of the purchase.

Outside the store he gave her the unwelcome news that they had used up the two hours and it was time for him to take her back to the house. He suggested that instead of taking the cable car, then walking the several blocks to her house, that they take a taxi. At this point, Sabrina would have preferred to prolong the outing, but there had been a subtle change in his attitude, so she agreed to his suggestion.

'I'll see you Friday afternoon around two,' Bay repeated, stopping inside the iron gate but not following her into the stairwell.

'Would y-you like to come in for coffee?' she offered.

'I'll take a raincheck on that for Friday,' he refused.

'All right. Till Friday, then,' Sabrina agreed with a faint smile of regret.

CHAPTER 4

SABRINA touched the face of her watch. Two o'clock. She reached to be certain the check was still on the coffee table where her father had put it this morning. It was. She leaned against the cushion of the couch, rubbing the back of her neck to try to relax the tense muscles. It was crazy to be so on edge because Bay Cameron was coming over, she told herself.

The front buzzer sounded and she hurried to the intercom answering it with an eager 'Yes?'

'Bay Cameron.'

'I'll be right down.'

Recklessly Sabrina nearly flew down the stairs. A smile wreathed her face as she opened the door and walked to the gate.

'You're right on time,' she said.

'I try to be punctual.' The warm huskiness of his voice swept over her as she unlocked the gate, swinging the iron grille open to admit him.

'I have the coffee all ready if you have time to stay,' she offered.

'I have time,' Bay answered.

Leading the way up the stairs to the second floor living area, Sabrina motioned toward the living room. 'Have a seat while I get the coffee tray. The check for the dress is on the table in front of the sofa.'

Bay made no offer to help pour the coffee when she returned, letting her take the time to do it herself. He took the cup she held out to him, the almost silent swish of the cushions indicating that he had leaned back against the chair next to the sofa.

'You have a very nice home. The paintings on the wall, are they yours?' he asked.

'Yes,' she acknowledged carefully balancing a cup in her lap. 'My father likes landscapes, so he chose those for the house. Because of his love for the sea, they are actually ocean scenes.'

'Are these the only paintings of your own that you have left?'

Sabrina bent her head. 'No.' Her jaw tightened.

'May I see them later?' Bay requested with watching softness.

'I'd really rather not show them to you.' She swallowed, lifting her chin defiantly.

'If you'd rather not, I won't insist,' he shrugged. 'But I won't pretend that I'm not curious why. I've already seen several examples of your work. Why wouldn't you want to show me the rest?'

Sabrina fidgeted nervously with the handle of her cup. Trying to adopt an uncaring attitude, she set the cup on the table.

'I'll show them to you.' Not certain whether her change of mind had been prompted by the patiently humorous tone of his voice or an application of common sense. 'They're in the studio upstairs.' She rose to her feet, pausing to turn her head in the direction of his chair.

'Lead the way,' Bay agreed, now on his feet, too.

Climbing the stairs to the upper floor, Sabrina trailed her hand along the wall until she came to the second door.

62

The knob was cold beneath her fingers as she swung the door open. The lingering scent of oil paints whirled around her.

'The room isn't used—any more, so it might be a bit stuffy,' Sabrina explained self-consciously, halting against the wall just inside the door.

Bay didn't comment. It wasn't really necessary. She listened to the quiet sounds as he wandered about the room, pausing sometimes to take a closer look at something that had caught his eye. Other times she could hear him moving canvases to see the paintings behind them. A tightness gripped her chest with a painful hold.

'They're very good, Sabrina,' he said at last. Her head turned in the direction of his voice only a few feet from where she was standing near the door. 'It's a pity to keep them hidden in this room.'

'Dad and I have talked about selling them. We will some day.' Sabrina swallowed to ease the constriction in her throat.

'Did you ever do any modeling?'

'Modeling? No,' she replied, striving for a lightness even though she knew neither of them would be fooled by it. 'I was always the one painting the person who was posing.'

'I meant modeling in clay,' Bay explained. Quiet, unhurried footsteps brought him to her side. A hand lightly touched her arm to turn her toward the open door.

'Yes, when I was studying the different mediums of art,' Sabrina acknowledged with a slight frown. 'Why?'

'Have you ever considered taking it up now that you're blind?'

'No.' She shook her head.

Unconsciously she had allowed him to lead her into the hallway. His inquiry had been unexpected and it set off a chain of thoughts. The closing of the studio door brought her back to their surroundings.

The subject was not explored further as Bay let her descend the stairs ahead of him, deliberately allowing her to mull the idea over in her own mind without any attempt to influence her. In spite of an ego-born desire to reject the idea to do anything but her chosen field of painting, the seed had been planted in fertile ground.

The coffee Sabrina poured had grown cold. While she emptied the cups, there was more time to contemplate his indirect suggestion. She marveled that none of her art friends had mentioned it before. Perhaps the objectivity of a relative stranger had been needed.

'I meant to ask,' Bay said as Sabrina handed him his cup refilled with hot coffee, 'whether you and your father had any plans for tomorrow evening.'

Her own cup was half-filled, the coffee pot poised above it for a startled, split second. 'No,' Sabrina answered in a curious tone. 'Saturday afternoon and evening Dad spends with Deborah. Why?'

'I thought we could have dinner somewhere. It would give you an excuse to wear your new dress,' Bay answered smoothly.

'No, thank you,' she refused with cutting abruptness.

'Do you have other plans?'

'No.'

'Then may I ask why you don't want to have dinner with me?' he asked, completely unruffled by her cold rejection.

'You may.' With a proud set to her head, Sabrina replaced the coffeepot on the tray and leaned against the sofa, protectively cradling the cup in her hands. 'I simply don't eat at public restaurants. I have a habit of knocking over glasses and dropping food on the floor. It's embarrassing,' she concluded self-consciously.

'I'm willing to take the risk,' Bay returned.

'Well, I'm not.' Impatiently she took a sip of the hot liquid, nearly scalding her tongue in the process.

'If this is not a refusal of my company,' there was a hint of amusement in his voice, 'then would you consider a less formal suggestion? For instance, we could buy some shrimp and crab at the Wharf, sourdough bread and a salad of sorts, then have an impromptu picnic somewhere along the shore line of the Golden Gate Promenade.'

Sabrina hesitated. It sounded like fun, but she wasn't certain she should accept his invitation. In between the moments when she was angered by his arrogance, she had discovered she liked him. Yet she doubted if any enduring friendship would ever develop between them.

'Is it such a difficult invitation to accept?' Bay taunted.

His gentle mockery made her feel foolish. She was magnifying the importance of the invitation out of all proportion. A faint pink tinted her prominent cheekbones.

'It isn't difficult,' she murmured, bending her head toward the cup in her lap to hide the flush of embarrassement. 'I do accept.'

'Would six o'clock be all right, or would you rather have me come earlier?'

'Six is fine.' There was a thump from something falling to the floor. Her head jerked up with a start. 'What was that?'

65

'It's a little something I bought for you as a present,' Bay replied with studied casualness. 'I meant to give it to you earlier, but I got sidetracked. I had it propped against my chair and I accidently knocked it over. Here you are.'

A long, narrow box was placed on her lap after Sabrina had set her coffee cup on the table. Her hands rested motionless on the cardboard lid.

'Why did you buy me a present?' she asked warily.

'Because I wanted to—and please don't ask me to take it back, because I wouldn't have any use for it and neither would anyone else I know. I doubt if I can have it returned either,' he stated.

'What is it?' Sabrina tilted her head curiously to the side.

'You'll have to open it and find out for yourself,' Bay answered noncommittally.

With a trace of nervous excitement hampering her movements, Sabrina eased the lid off the box and set it on the sofa. She could feel his alert gaze watching her. Her pulse accelerated slightly. Hesitantly exploring fingertips encountered tissue paper. It rustled softly as she pushed it aside to find what it protected.

The object in the box was round and hard. Initially the cylindrical object was unidentifiable until Sabrina felt along its length. Her hand had barely curled around it to lift it out of the box and she replaced it, folding her hands tightly in her lap. A sickening sensation curled her stomach.

'It's a white cane, isn't it?' she accused tightly, a bad taste bitterly coating her tongue as she uttered the words.

'Yes,' Bay admitted without any trace of remorse. 'But I like to think it isn't an ordinary white cane.'

The box was removed from her lap. The action was followed almost instantly by the rustling of tissue paper, then the sound of the box being set aside. Her lips were compressed tightly shut in an uncompromising line while her hands maintained their death grip on each other. Bay's fingers closed over her wrist and firmly pulled her hands apart, ignoring the resistance she offered.

One hand he released. The second he held with little effort. The curving handle of the cane was pressed into her palm and Bay forced her fingers to curl around it.

Sabrina's first impression was of a smooth glassy surface, then her sensitive touch felt the carving. Almost unwillingly her fingertips explored the design. It was several seconds before she followed the intricate serpentine lines flanking the sides of the cane to the end of the handle. There she was able to identify the design of reptilian heads as those of a dragon.

'It's a cane carved out of ivory,' Bay explained. 'I saw it in a shop window in Chinatown the other day.'

'It's very beautiful,' Sabrina admitted reluctantly. The hand covering hers relaxed its grip, no longer forcing her to hold on to the cane. She held on to it for a few more exploring moments. 'It must be valuable,' she commented, and extended it toward him. 'I couldn't possibly accept it.'

'It's artistic in design but hardly an art object.' He ignored the outstretched hand with the cane. 'What you really mean is it's still white.'

Sabrina didn't deny his charge. 'I can't accept it.'

'I can't return it,' Bay replied evenly.

'I'm sorry.' She pushed the cane into his hands and released it. He had no choice but to hold on to it or let it fall to the floor.

'I know you were trying to be thoughtful, but you knew my views on the subject of canes before you bought it, Bay. The cane is unique and beautiful, but I won't accept it. I get along very well with the one I have.'

'Is that your final answer?'

'Yes, it is,' Sabrina answered firmly, resolved not to be bullied or made to feel guilty because she had refused.

'I suppose if I try to persuade you to change your mind, you'll go back on your agreement to go out with me tomorrow night,' he sighed with almost resigned acceptance.

'Probably,' she shrugged, hoping he wouldn't put her in such a position.

'Then I'll save my arguments for another time.' There was a rustle of tissue paper and the lid being placed on the box. 'Mind you, I'm not giving up,' Bay warned mockingly, 'just postponing the battle.'

'I won't change my mind,' Sabrina replied stubbornly but with a trace of a smile curling her wide mouth.

'I accept the challenge.' She could hear the answering smile in his voice. 'While we're still on speaking terms, may I have another cup of coffee?'

'Of course.' She held out her hand for his cup and saucer.

The subject of the ivory cane was not re-introduced into the conversation, but when Bay Cameron left a half an hour later, Sabrina made certain he had the box with him and did not 'accidentally' forget it.

It was not until that evening when Deborah came that Sabrina discovered the way Bay had tricked her.

'When did you get this, Sabrina?' Deborah asked in a voice that was at one and the same time curious and surprised.

Her fingers stopped their braille reading in mid-sentence as she turned her head in the direction of Deborah's voice 'What is it?'

'An ivory cane. The handle has a dragon design carved on the sides. I found it on the floor beside the chair. Were you hiding it?' The red-haired woman laughed shortly.

'No, I wasn't.' Sabrina's mouth thinned grimly.

'It's very elegant. Where did you find it?' Deborah murmured.

'Yes, where?' Her father joined in. 'I haven't seen it before. Is this something else you found the other day when you were with Bay Cameron?'

'You should know by now, Father, that I would never buy a white cane, much less an ivory one,' she retorted. 'It was a present from Bay. I refused it, of course. I thought he had taken it with him.'

'Refused it?' Deborah questioned in amazement. 'Why would you refuse something as lovely as this?'

'Because I don't want it,' Sabrina answered tautly.

The sofa cushion beside her sank as it took her father's weight. His hand gently covered the rigid fingers resting on the now closed cover of her book.

'Aren't you being a little foolish, honey?' The chiding question was spoken softly. 'We both know you didn't refuse it because you thought it was too expensive or because you didn't think it was beautiful. It's because it's white. And a white cane means that you're blind. You

69

can't escape the fact that you're blind simply by not using a white cane.'

'I don't wish to advertise the fact,' was her curt reply.

'People are bound to notice, no matter what kind or color of cane you have. There's no shame in being blind, for heaven's sake,' Grant Lane argued.

'I'm not ashamed!' Sabrina snapped.

'Sometimes you act as if you are,' he sighed.

'I suppose you think I should use it,' she challenged with a defiant toss of her head.

'I'm your father, Sabrina. Take the chip off your shoulder.' The mildly reproving tone of his voice lessened the jutting angle of her chin. 'You're too old for me to tell you what to do. You know what the right and wise thing to do is. Whether you do it or not is your decision.'

'Excuse me, I think I'll go to my room.' Sabrina set the book on the table and rose stiffly to her feet.

It was impossible to argue when her father wouldn't argue back. She hated it when he appealed to her logic. She invariably lost.

'What should I do with the cane?' Deborah inquired hesitantly.

'Put it in the umbrella stand for now,' her father answered. 'Sabrina can decide what she wants to do before Bay Cameron comes over tomorrow night.'

As Sabrina put her foot on the first step of the stairs leading to the upper floor and her bedroom, she heard Deborah ask, 'Bay Cameron is coming tomorrow night. Why?'

'He's taking Sabrina to the Wharf,' her father replied.

'You mean a date?' his fiancée asked with amazed disbelief.

'I suppose you could call it that. He called me yesterday afternoon at the office after he'd seen Sabrina to ask if I had any objection. I couldn't bring myself to ask him what his intentions were. It would have been too presumptuous when he's been kind to her.'

'Did he mention the cane?'

'No, it was a complete surprise to me,' he answered.

Well, Sabrina sighed in relief, at least her father hadn't been a part of any conspiracy with Bay Cameron. For a moment, she had been worried. She should have realized her father wouldn't do anything underhanded to trick her into making the decision he wanted. It was a pity the same couldn't be said for Bay Cameron.

Still, she had to concede that Bay had not forced her to accept the ivory cane. He had simply left it. And its presence had produced another dilemma, thanks to her father.

A few minutes before six o'clock, Sabrina sat on the sofa, nibbling on the tip of one fingernail. She absently reached out for the second time to be certain the hooded blue windbreaker was lying on the arm of the sofa. Then her pensive mood was broken by the front door buzzer.

Quickly she pulled on the windbreaker, stuffing the small clutch purse in its oversize pocket. A smoothing hand ran up the back of her neck, tucking any stray strands of hair into the knot atop her head. Her inquiry via the

71

intercom was answered, as she had expected, by Bay.

'I'll be right down,' she murmured.

Her hand closed over the doorknob, but she hesitated. Her sightless eyes stared at the umbrella stand. Her other hand was poised on the smooth oak cane. For several more seconds she remained immobile, then with a resigned sigh, she removed her hand from the oak cane and tentatively searched for the carved dragon heads of the ivory cane.

Slowly she descended the stairs, opening the outside door and locking it behind her. Squaring her shoulders, she turned toward the iron gates and Bay.

'You took your time,' he commented. 'I was beginning to wonder what was keeping you.'

'I had to put on my jacket,' Sabrina lied, waiting for him to comment on the ivory cane in her hand.

'My car is parked at the curb,' Bay said as she swung open the gates and joined him on the sidewalk.

The hand on her elbow firmly guided her to the car. The suspense of waiting for his expression of triumph began to build as he helped her into the car. When Bay had still said nothing after the car was started and turned into the street, Sabrina knew she could not continue waiting for a moment of his choosing.

'Well?' she challenged finally, turning her head toward him in a slightly defiant angle.

'Well what?' Bay countered evenly.

'Aren't you going to say anything about the cane?'

'What do you expect me to say?' The low, calm voice remained controlled and unruffled.

'I should think you'd be feeling pretty smug. After all,

you did leave the cane behind deliberately,' Sabrina accused.

'I gave it to you. It was a present, and I don't take back presents. It was entirely up to you what you did with it. I never insisted that you use it. I wouldn't have stopped you if you'd thrown it in the garbage,' responded Bay.

'Well, I have decided to use it,' she stated, facing straight ahead.

'I'm glad.' The car turned and went steeply down a hill. 'May we leave the subject of the cane behind now?'

Sabrina sighed, 'Yes.'

It seemed as if every time she thought she knew how he would react, Bay did not do the expected. He should have been triumphant or a little righteous. Instead he was so calm and matter-of-fact that it was impossible for Sabrina to feel resentment. She had made the decision to use the ivory cane, not Bay, and he knew it.

At the bottom of the inclining street, Bay turned the car again. 'I thought I'd park at the Yacht Harbor. We can follow the sea-wall by Fort Mason to Aquatic Park and on to Fisherman's Wharf. All right?'

'Fine,' Sabrina agreed.

Once the car was parked and locked, they started out at a strolling pace with Bay hooking Sabrina's left arm under his right. Gulls screeched overhead. As they passed Fort Mason and neared the docks of the fishing fleet, the heavier flapping wings of pelicans accompanied the soaring seagulls. The damp salt odor of the air was altered by a fishy smell.

Although the seafood stalls were their ultimate

destination, they mutually decided to walk farther and come back. The sidewalks were filled with tourists exploring the sights and sounds of the colorful area. A few were jostling and in a hurry but most took their time absorbing the atmosphere as Sabrina and Bay were doing.

The churning propellers of a tour boat indicated the start of another harbor cruise. The highlights would be a close look at the famed Golden Gate Bridge, the Oakland Bay Bridge and the former maximum security prison of Alcatraz. Now the island was a national park, only a mile out in the bay from the wharf.

At the end of the piers, they crossed the street to the rows of shops and started slowly back toward the seafood stalls.

Sabrina lifted her face to the breeze, salty and damp. 'Is the fog coming in?'

'Starting,' Bay agreed. 'It's just beginning to obscure the top spans of the Golden Gate and the Marin hills north of the Bay. It might get thick tonight.'

'In that case, I'll have to lead you back to the car,' she grinned impishly, and Bay chuckled. Sabrina tipped her head curiously toward him. 'Where did you get the name Bay?'

'My parents gave it to me—or didn't you think I had any?' he teased.

'Of course I did. Are they still living?' she asked, sidetracked momentarily from her original question.

'Last I heard they were. They're in Europe taking a second honeymoon.' His arm tightened fractionally in warning. 'You have to step down here.'

'Is Bay a family name?' Sabrina questioned again after negotiating the intersection curb.

'I wish it were. No, I was named after the obvious, the San Francisco Bay that my mother saw from the hospital window. She was born and raised here, so she'd seen it thousands of times,' he explained. 'What about Sabrina?'

'My mother liked the sound of it. She was very romantic.'

'And you're not?' he mocked.

'Maybe a little bit,' she smiled faintly.

'We've been walking for over an hour. Are you getting hungry?' Bay inquired with an easy change of the subject.

'Very close to starving.'

'You should have said something sooner.'

Sabrina shrugged that it didn't matter and breathed in the tantalizing aroma carried by the light breeze. 'It's just across the street, isn't it?' Then she laughed. 'All I have to do is follow my nose.'

'Are you certain you wouldn't rather eat in one of the restaurants here?' Bay checked her movement into the street and a car drove slowly by.

'Positive,' bobbing her head firmly.

At the long row of seafood stalls, Bay selected the cooked crab, including a round loaf of sourdough bread, a salad and cocktail shrimp to the order. Sabrina pressed a hand against her rumbling stomach. The delicious smells were making her all the more hungry. With the purchase completed, Bay handed her the bag and asked her to wait outside while he bought a bottle of chilled white wine to go with it.

Tingles ran down the back of her neck an instant before his hand touched her arm signaling his return. She decided that she must have telepathic powers that told her when Bay approached.

'Are you ready for our picnic?' he asked. At that moment her stomach growled the answer and they both laughed.

Taking the bag of food from her grasp, Bay added it to the one he already had in his arms. The hand she linked in his arm was not for guidance but companionship as they set out for the Yacht Harbor and the shoreline beyond.

They were on the edge of the harbor when Sabrina noticed the fine mist on her face had intensified. 'It's drizzling rain,' she moaned angrily.

'I was afraid it was an overcast more than fog,' Bay sighed.

'I suppose we could always take the food to the house,' Sabrina suggested.

'I have a better idea. My ketch is tied up here. We can eat aboard her. What do you say?'

'I say,' she smiled, 'that it sounds much more pleasant than my house.'

'Let's go!'

Bay had Sabrina wait on the dock while he stowed the food below. Topside again, his strong hands spanned her waist and lifted her aboard. He maintained the hold for steadying minutes, her own hands resting on the rippling muscles of his forearms. The dampness of the drizzling rain increased the spicy aroma emanating from his shaven cheeks and the heady male that enfolded her. The deck beneath her feet moved rhythmically with the lapping waters of the bay.

'It's been so long since I've been on the water,' Sabrina said with an odd catch in her voice, 'that my sea-legs are a bit shaky.' It seemed a reasonable explanation for the weakness in her limbs.

With an arm firmly circling her waist in support, Bay led her below deck. Making certain she had something to hold on to, he went down the steps ahead of her. Sabrina knew it was to catch her in case she fell. Once below he told her where the seats were and let her make her own way to them.

'Do you like sailing?' he asked. The rustling of bags indicated he was getting the food out to eat.

'Love it.' A wry grimace pulled down the corners of her mouth in a rueful expression. 'I used to go out every weekend with Dad.'

'You haven't been out since your accident? Why?' His low voice was honed sharp with curiosity.

'Oh, a couple of times, but I had to stay below. Dad can't swim. He was afraid I would fall overboard and he wouldn't be able to save me. I like to be on deck where the salt wind stings your face and the waves breaking over the bow sprays you. So I don't go out any more,' she concluded.

'And you aren't afraid of falling in?'

'Not really,' Sabrina shrugged.

A shrimp cocktail was set before her as Bay took a seat opposite her. For a time the conversation centered around sailing, then shifted smoothly to other topics of interest, mainly leisure activities, as they slowly ate their picnic meal.

'I used to really enjoy watching people, studying their faces.' She sipped lightly at the wine. 'Of course, I did it often in connection with my work. Most of my better characters came from the faces of people I saw on the streets. A great deal of a person's attitude toward life is written on his face. The grumpy look of a pessimist, the hardness of a cynic, the authority of a leader, the harried worn look of a man driven to succeed, an eagerness for life, the contentment of family and home. There are so many things,' Sabrina exhaled slowly. 'It's not so easy to do it with just voices, but I'm learning. It's difficult, though, to visualize a person's looks from their voices.'

'What have you learned about me?' Bay challenged mockingly.

'Well,' a hint of mischief tickled the corners of her mouth, 'you're self-confident to the point of arrogance. You're well-educated, accustomed to having authority over others. You obviously enjoy the outdoors and especially the sea. You have a quick temper, but you can be thoughtful when it suits you.'

'Have you put a face with my voice yet?'

Sabrina quickly ducked her head from his gaze self-consciously. 'Only a blurred image of strong features.' She pushed her plate away. 'That was good.'

'Why haven't you asked to look at me?' Bay asked quietly, ignoring her attempt to switch the subject to food.

'W-what?' she stammered.

'As you did with the dress,' he explained patiently.

78

Humor hovered on the edge of his voice after she had shifted uncomfortably in her seat. The thought of exploring his face with her hands was disturbing.

'I could fill in the blank spots for you. I have green hair and purple eyes, a long ugly scar down the side of my face. I keep it hidden with a bushy green beard. I have a tattoo of a skull and crossbones on my forehead—and I won't tell you what the picture is on my chest.' The spreading smile on Sabrina's face broke into laughter at his absurd description. 'Don't you believe me?'

'Hardly. Besides, my neighbor's already told me you have reddish-brown hair and eyes,' Sabrina laughed, her tension fading.

'Cinnamon, according to my mother,' Bay corrected. 'At least you were curious enough about me to ask.'

'Naturally.' She worked to make her reply sound casual and offhand.

'What else did she tell you about me?' he prodded.

'Peggy isn't very good at describing,' Sabrina hedged, unwilling to pass on the comment concerning his masculinity.

'All the more reason for you to see for yourself,' he challenged.

There was the clatter of plates being stacked, then movement as the dishes were carried away. Bay's actions gave her time to think of an excuse to avoid the exploration of his features that he had invited. Try as she could, Sabrina was unable to come up with one that did not reveal her inner apprehension at such intimacy.

When Bay returned, he did not take his former seat

across from her but one that placed him beside her. Before she could voice her half-formed protest, he had taken her wrists in a light yet firm grip and carried her hands to his face.

'There's no need to feel shy and self-conscious,' he scolded gently as she tried to pull away. 'It doesn't embarrass me.'

The hard outline of his powerful jaw was beneath her hands, pressed by his on either side of his face. As her resistance faded, he released his hold. The initial contact had been made and the warmth of his body heat eased the cold stiffness of her fingers. Tentatively Sabrina began to explore his face.

From the jawline, her fingertips searched over his cheeks to the hard angles of his cheekbones. Fluttering over the curling lashes of his eyes, she reached thick brows and the wide forehead. Thick, slightly waving hair grew naturally away from his face, maintaining a suggestion of dampness from the fog and the drizzle. There was an arrogant curve to his Roman nose and a gentle firmness to his male lips. After inspecting the almost forceful angle of his chin, her hands fell away.

It was a masculine face, Sabrina thought in satisfaction. There was no doubt about that. No one would ever refer to him as conventionally handsome, but he was certainly striking. Heads would turn when he walked into a room.

'What's the verdict?' Bay asked in a husky caressing voice like deep velvet.

She guessed her approval was mirrored in her expression. She averted her head slightly from the warm gaze she felt on her face.

'The verdict is,' she answered with false lightness, 'that I like your face.'

A finger tucked itself under her chin and turned her head back toward him. 'I like your face, too,' he murmured softly.

The warm moistness of his breath caressed her cheek a warning instant before his lips touched hers. Initial surprise held Sabrina rigid under his kiss, but the gently firm pressure of his mouth transmitted a warmness that seeped into her veins. Her heart seemed to start skipping beats. With expert persuasion, his mouth moved mobilely against hers until he evoked the pliant response he wanted. Then slowly, almost regretfully, he drew away from her.

Sabrina could still feel the imprint of his mouth throbbing on hers. She had to resist the impulse to carry a hand to her lips. A wondrously satisfying warmth filled her, leaving her bemused to its cause.

'Why the pensive look, Sabrina?' Bay's husky voice inquired gently.

'I've . . . never been kissed before,' she murmured, uncertain if that was the cause.

'Liar,' he mocked softly. 'That was no inexperienced maiden who kissed me back just now.'

'I—I meant,' crimson flames stained her cheeks, 'since I lost my sight.'

'That I will believe.' Bay took hold of her hand in a casual, not intimate grip. 'Let's go get ourselves a cup of coffee at a restaurant somewhere.'

Sabrina willingly agreed to leave his ketch. For some reason the floor beneath her feet didn't feel very steady. She wanted the security of solid ground beneath her.

It was a few minutes past ten o'clock when Bay parked the car in front of her house and walked her to the grillework gates. He didn't follow her inside the small enclosure and Sabrina turned to him hesitantly.

'I've had a wonderful time. Thank you,' she offered.

'So did I, therefore no thanks are necessary,' Bay said with a smile in his voice. 'I'll be in L.A. all of next week. I'll give you a call when I get back.'

'It isn't necessary.' Sabrina didn't want him to think that he was under any obligation to see her again.

'I know that,' he chided gently. 'Goodnight, Sabrina. I'll wait in the car until I see the light on upstairs, so be sure to turn it on, will you?'

'Goodnight, Bay,' she nodded.

He swung the iron gate closed and Sabrina locked it. She felt his gaze follow her to the door. Cinnamon brown eyes they were, to go with his cinnamon hair.

CHAPTER FIVE

THE switch on the stereo was snapped abruptly to the 'off' position. There was nothing soothing to the music as far as Sabrina was concerned.

What was there to do, she wondered tiredly. She did not feel like cooking or cleaning even if it was needed, which it wasn't. She was tired of reading. Besides, her fingers were still slow to read the raised braille letters, so the task required her total concentration. In this restless mood, she knew her thoughts would wander.

An inner voice unfairly blamed the mood on Bay Cameron. Although why his business trip to Los Angeles should affect her this way, Sabrina didn't know. These restless moods had been with her before anyway, even before her accident. Then she had channeled the surging energy into her paintings. Now there was no outlet.

'Have you ever done any modeling—in clay, I mean?'

Bay's voice spoke clearly in her mind as if he was standing beside her. The seed that had been planted several days ago began to germinate.

Walking to the telephone, Sabrina felt for the receiver, picked it up, then hesitated. Before she changed her mind, she dialed the number. Excitement pulsated through her veins at the sound of the first ring.

'Art Supplies,' a voice answered on the second ring.

'Sam Carlysle, please,' Sabrina requested. Her fingers nervously twined around the corkscrew curl of the telephone cord. A few minutes later a familiar male voice came on the line. 'Hello, Sam. This is Sabrina.'

'Sabrina, how are you?' he exclaimed in glad surprise. Then his tone changed immediately to contriteness. 'Listen, I'm sorry I haven't phoned or stopped by for so long, but what with one thing or another——'

'That's all right,' she interrupted quickly. 'Actually I was calling to see if you could do me a favor.'

'Name it and it's yours, Sabrina.'

'I wondered if you could send someone over today with some artist's modeling clay and an inexpensive set of tools?'

'Are you taking up modeling?' he asked in a stunned voice.

'I'm going to give it a try,' Sabrina acknowledged. 'That's why I only want the bare necessities to see if I'm going to like it or be any good at it.'

'I think it's a tremendous idea!' Sam enthused. 'A stroke of genius!'

'Can you send someone over?'

'I'd come myself if I could, but I'll have a delivery boy leave here in about ten minutes and I'll make sure your place is his first stop.'

'Thanks, Sam.' A contented glow spread over her face.

'Hey, listen, I'm just sorry I didn't suggest something like this to you before,' he replied, shrugging aside her thanks. 'I'll get this stuff out to you right away. We'll get together soon, okay?'

'Yes, Sam, soon,' Sabrina agreed.

Barely a half an hour had elapsed when the delivery was made. She had already cleared a small area in the studio where she could work, realizing that her father would have to give her a hand this evening with the heavier items. The delivery man had thoughtfully offered to carry the packages wherever Sabrina wanted them so she hadn't had to carry them to the studio.

After he had left and she had returned to the studio, a thrill of excitement danced down her spine. Her old smock was behind the door, smelling of oil paints and cleaning fluid. Soon, the odor of clay would wipe out that smell, she told herself gaily as she donned the protective smock and felt her way to the work table.

All conception of time vanished. She started out with simple shapes, using fruit she had taken from the kitchen for her hands to use as a guideline. Her name was called for the third time before it penetrated her concentration. It was another full second before she recognized her father's voice.

'I'm upstairs in the studio!' she answered.

She stepped back, wiping her hands on a rag as she listened to his hurrying steps up the stairs. A look of apprehension and excitement was in the expression Sabrina turned to the open doorway.

'I was getting frantic,' Grant Lane declared with an exasperated sigh. 'Why didn't you answer me? What are you doing up here anyway?'

'Working,' Sabrina replied softly, but she could tell by the tense silence that her explanation wasn't necessary. Her father had already looked beyond her and seen for himself. She waited interminable seconds for his comment. 'What do you think?' she asked breathlessly.

'I . . . I'm speechless,' he told her. 'How—when . . . ?'

Then he laughed at his inability to get his questions out and came the rest of the way into the room, throwing an arm about her shoulders and giving her a fierce hug. 'You are one fantastic little gal. I'm proud of you.' His voice was choked with emotion.

'Yes, but what do you think?' she repeated anxiously.

'If you're asking whether I can tell the apple from the pear, the answer is a definite "yes." I can even see that's a cluster of grapes you're working on now,' her father smiled. 'And I didn't need that assortment of real fruit spotted with clay to make the identification either!'

'Do you mean it?'

'I mean it,' he assured her firmly. 'Now how about an explanation? When did you decide to do all this? You never mentioned a word about it to me. Where did you get all this?'

'Last week Bay asked if I'd ever worked in clay. I guess that's when I started thinking about it, subconsciously at least. This morning I decided to try it and called Sam at the art supply store. He had this delivered for me,' Sabrina explained.

'This morning? And you've been working ever since? You must be exhausted!'

'Exhausted?' She turned her face to him, her wide mouth smiling broadly. 'No, Daddy, I'm alive. For the first time in a very long while.'

There was a moment of silence. Then her father took a deep breath. 'Just the same, you'd better call it a day. No sense in overdoing it. You clean up here and I'll see about the dinner you forgot,' he teased.

'All right,' she submitted.

For the rest of the week, Sabrina spent every waking minute she possibly could in the studio room. The end results were more often failures than successes. It didn't do any good for her father to insist that she couldn't expect to be perfect as a beginner. But Sabrina demanded perfection of herself. Nothing less would satisfy her.

On Sunday morning, Grant Lane ordered her out of the studio. 'For heaven's sake, Sabrina,' he declared, 'even God rested on the seventh day!'

The mutinous set of her chin dipped as she sighed her reluctant surrender to his logic. Her fingers ached to feel the molding clay beneath her hands, but she knew her father was right.

'I've got some work to do on the boat. Why don't you come with me this morning?' He suggested. 'Deborah is going to be busy in the kitchen. If you have nothing to do, I know you're going to sneak back up here the minute I leave.'

'I wouldn't do that,' Sabrina laughed softly.

'Oh, wouldn't you?' he mocked. 'You're coming with me.'

'I think it's awful that you don't trust me, your own daughter!' She clicked her tongue in reproval. 'But if that's the way you're going to be, I guess I'll have to go with you.'

'There's a pretty stiff breeze blowing in from the Pacific, so dress accordingly. But make sure it's something you won't mind getting dirty,' her father added. 'I thought I'd put you to work cleaning below deck.'

'That's why you want me to come along,' Sabrina nodded sagely.

'You don't think it was your company I was wanting, did you?' he teased, and walked to the stairs.

The wind was chilly, Sabrina discovered. It had not yet blown away the morning fog, so the sun had not warmed the air. Below deck, she didn't feel the cool breeze. Wiping the perspiration from her forehead that had separated her dark silky bangs into damp strands, she wished she could feel it.

She pushed up the sleeves on her navy blue pullover and set to work scrubbing the galley sink. The perspiration was making the wool blend of the turtleneck collar tickle the sensitive skin of her neck, but she couldn't very well scratch it with her soapy hands. As soon as she finished this Sabrina decided she would call her father down for a cup of coffee. From the sound of voices overhead, he was doing more chatting with fellow sailing enthusiasts than work.

Maybe she should take the pot of coffee and some cups on deck and offer it around. There was a waterproof tin of cookies in the cupboard. Then she smiled to herself. That would really make certain nothing was accomplished today!

The quiet step of rubber-soled shoes approached the steps leading below. Sabrina was rinsing the soap from the sink when they began their descent. She stopped, turning slightly in the direction of the footsteps.

'I thought I would bring some coffee up as soon as I finish here, Dad. I'll bring some extra cups if you think the others would like to join you.'

'That sounds fine.'

'Bay! You're back!' The exclamation of delight sprang unchecked from her lips.

'I got in late yesterday afternoon,' he acknowledged. 'I thought I might see you here today with your father. I never guessed he would make you a galley-slave.'

Sabrina smiled at the teasing voice. 'Did you have a good trip?'

'Yes. I had some investment property to check on and inspected some other land I've been interested in acquiring. I even ran into an old friend I went to university with. He's topside talking to your father. Why don't you come and meet him?'

She had half expected it to be a woman, and she wondered if her relief was reflected in her expression. She hoped not. She didn't want Bay to think she was jealous. They were only friends.

'I'll be through here in a minute,' she said. 'If you'd like, you can take the coffeepot on up. There are some mugs in the cupboard. I can bring the sugar and powdered cream.'

'All right,' Bay agreed.

A few minutes later, Sabrina joined the others on deck. The wind lifted her bangs and she turned her face into the cooling flow of air.

'Here, Sabrina, let me take those.' Her father took the tins of sugar and powdered cream from her hands and helped her on deck.

'This is Grant's daughter, Sabrina Lane,' Bay said. 'This is my old fraternity brother, Doctor Joe Browning.'

'You'd better watch who you call old,' said a gruff male voice in a mock serious tone. Then Sabrina's hand was taken in greeting. 'I'm more commonly known as Joe or Doctor Joe to my patients.'

Cold fingers raced icily down her spine. 'How do you do.' Her greeting was stiff. Since her accident and the string of doctors she had been to, Sabrina had developed an aversion to those in the medical profession.

'Joe, the name is Joe,' he said. 'Your father tells me you've been blind for only a year. You seem to be getting along rather well.'

'There really isn't much choice, is there?' she retorted.

'Of course there is. You could always get along badly.'

His nonsensical reply unwillingly brought a faint smile to her mouth. She had always expected that even at home doctors were somewhat staid and unemotional, spouting platitudes and doing charitable deeds. This one seemed to be different.

'I ran into my share of furniture and buildings in the beginning,' she admitted.

'Do you use a cane or do you have a seeing eye dog?' He didn't give her a chance to reply. 'I hear they're using standard poodles as well as shepherds and other breeds as seeing eye dogs. Can you imagine a poodle prancing down the street with its fluffy pompadour and that ball of fluff on his tail leading some blind man? It always seemed like the height of absurdity to me. Not that I have anything against the intelligence of poodles.'

Sabrina laughed at the image he had created in her mind. She liked his irreverent attitude and her wariness disappeared. The relaxed sound of her laughter began a natural flow of conversation among all of them. Doctor

Joe Browning dominated most of the topics with his dry wit.

Some time, Sabrina was not certain when, the subject became centered on her blindness, the accident, and the damage to her optic nerves that had resulted from the head injury. She was suddenly aware that the inquiries were not casual but had a professional undertone.

'Wait a minute,' she interrupted the doctor in mid-sentence. 'Exactly what kind of a doctor are you?'

'A very good one,' he quipped. 'A surgeon, to be specific.'

'What kind?' Then she raised her hand in a halting gesture, and accused angrily. 'No, let me guess. You're an eye surgeon.'

'You're right with the very first guess. Now that's the mark of a girl who pays attention,' Joe Browning replied without the least embarrassment.

'What have all these questions been? A subtle examination?'

'Yes,' he admitted simply.

Seething with indignation, Sabrina turned in the direction she knew Bay to be sitting. 'You put him up to this, didn't you, Bay Cameron? And you must have been in on it, too, Father.'

'It was my idea for you not to know the real reason why Doctor Joe was seeing you,' her father replied in a contrite tone. 'Bay did contact him originally, but the rest was my idea so you wouldn't have to go through the whole rigmarole again, maybe unnecessarily.'

'That's why you pretended,' Sabrina said tautly, 'that he

was an old school chum of yours, isn't that right, Bay?'

'No, that's the truth,' the doctor replied, 'and it's also the truth that we bumped into each other in Los Angeles. He had no idea I was there since I've been on the East Coast for the last few years. He mentioned you to me and professional curiosity took over.'

'I'm sorry, Sabrina,' Bay offered quietly. 'I knew you'd be upset when you found out.'

'Then why did you try to trick me?'

'I felt I should respect your father's wishes. And there was the likelihood that you wouldn't find out, not if Joe didn't think there was any hope that your vision could be restored,' he answered.

'And do you?' Her chin tipped proudly toward the doctor. The aura of pride was a defence mechanism to conceal any reaction to his verdict.

'I'd like to run some more tests in a hospital before I give you a definite answer, Sabrina,' he said honestly. 'I would guess you have no more than a ten per cent chance, if that much, that there's a surgical cure.'

'Four specialists told my father and me that I would never see again. What makes you think you can help me?' Sabrina challenged.

'I don't know that I can,' Doctor Joe answered, 'but I don't know that I can't either. On occasions, the body's natural healing processes repair some of· the damage, making a condition that was inoperable shortly after the injury operable a period of months later. It has happened.'

'I see,' she said tautly. 'And that's what you think has happened to me.'

'I don't know, but I don't think we should overlook the possibility,' he replied. 'To be certain, I'd have to admit you to a hospital and run some tests. I don't want to raise any false hopes, Sabrina. You have a very slim chance of having your vision restored, right next to none at all. The decision is yours.'

Not even the scent of roses that her father had brought could overcome the strong medicinal and antiseptic odor of the hospital. In the corridor, there were the hushed voices of a pair of nurses walking swiftly by her door. Sabrina listened to the even breathing of the female patient who shared her room.

Visiting hours were over. The lights were out. She knew that because she had heard the flick of the switch when the nurse left the room a few minutes ago.

Her dark world seemed blacker this night. She felt so very much alone and vulnerable. She was afraid to hope that the tests tomorrow would be encouraging. Yet it was impossible to be indifferent to the reasons she was here.

A hand doubled into a fist at her side. Damn Bay for running into his doctor friend, Sabrina thought dejectedly. She had accepted her blindness, stopped fighting the injustice of it and had started living with it.

Since Bay was partially responsible for her presence in the hospital, the least he could have done was come to visit her. But no, he had sent a message of good luck with Doctor Joe, passed on when Sabrina had been admitted.

A trembling shivered over her body and wouldn't stop. She hadn't realized she was so scared. Her chin quivered.

She wanted to break down and cry. The brave front she had worn was crumbling and she didn't care.

A swirl of air blew over her face. She had come to recognize that as the silent opening of the door to her hospital room. Someone was approaching her bed, and she had the sensation that it wasn't the nurse. A spicy scent of aftershave lotion drifting to her nose confirmed it.

'Are you awake?' Bay asked softly.

'Yes,' Sabrina whispered, pushing herself into a more upright position while trying to keep the flimsy hospital gown securely around her. 'Visiting hours are over. You're not supposed to be here.'

'If they catch me, they can ask me to leave, right?' he smiled with his voice. 'How are you doing?'

'Fine,' she lied. The edge of the bed took his weight. 'I thought Doctor Joe said you had to go to a party or something.'

'I did go,' Bay acknowledged, 'but I slipped away to see you. Is that all right?'

'It's all right with me as long as it was all right with the lady you were with,' Sabrina returned.

'What makes you think I was with anyone?'

'I certainly hope you were, because otherwise you're wearing some very expensive French perfume!' Her fingers clutched the bedcovers tightly. It was important that she maintain this air of lighthearted teasing so Bay would not guess her inner apprehension.

'Aha, the blind detective,' he mocked.

'Elementary,' she shrugged. 'After all, you were at a party. That makes it only logical to assume that you would turn your charm toward some attractive woman there.'

'Now that's where you're wrong.'

'Why?' Sabrina tilted her head to the side in mock challenge.

'Because I've been directing all my charms to a certain blind lady that I know, a very attractive one,' Bay responded lightly.

Her throat constricted. 'I find that difficult to believe.'

A hand warmly covered the hands clinging to the sheets. Gently he prised them free. 'Your hands are like ice, Sabrina. What's the matter?'

His frowning accusation set an uncontrollable shiver quaking over her shoulders. Emitting a shaky sigh, Sabrina admitted, 'I'm frightened, Bay—of tomorrow.'

He said nothing for a minute. She felt him shift his weight on the bed. Then his arm circled her shoulders and he drew her against his chest, the back of his hand cradling her head near his chin.

'Let's think about this,' he murmured calmly. 'It's not the thought of the tests Joe is going to do that frightens you. That only leaves two alternatives. One is that you're afraid to have your sight restored and the second is that you won't, right?'

Numbly Sabrina nodded her affirmation. The steady beat of his heart beneath her head and the protective circle of his strong arms was blissfully comforting.

'I know you can't be afraid of seeing again,' he continued. 'That result would have everyone rejoicing. That only leaves the second.'

'I——' she began hesitantly. 'I had accepted the fact

that I was blind. I've started working in clay, did I tell you that? I'm an awful coward,' she sighed. 'I wish I'd never agreed to these tests. I wish I'd never met Doctor Joe. I don't want to go through the agony of accepting all over again that I'm permanently blind.'

'Where is that gutsy girl who was always trying to thumb her nose at convention?' Bay mocked softly. 'You aren't a coward, Sabrina. A coward wouldn't be here in the hospital taking the slim gamble that Joe offered. If the tests prove negative, you aren't going to wail and pound your chest. The gutsy girl I know is going to shrug her shoulders and say, "Well, I gave it a go." ' She felt him smile against her hair. 'To borrow an old cliché, Sabrina, you have everything to gain and nothing to lose.'

'That's what I keep trying to tell myself,' she sighed.

'The secret is to stop saying and start admitting that it's true.' He didn't require a reply as he held her for more long minutes. The strength seemed to flow from the muscles in his arms into her, chasing away her unreasonable fears. 'Are you all right now?' he asked finally.

'Yes,' she nodded against his chin, and smiled faintly.

'Then I'd better be going before the nurse comes in and gets the wrong idea about what we're doing,' Bay teased softly.

Very gently he shifted her on to the pillow, tucking the sheet around her chest. As he started to straighten, Sabrina reached out for his arm.

'Thank you for coming, Bay,' she whispered tightly.

'Don't thank me for something I wanted to do.' Then he bent over her and there was a tantalizing brush of his mouth on hers. 'Goodnight, Sabrina. I'll be seeing you.'

'Yes. Goodnight Bay.'

There were soft footsteps, then the swish of air as the door opened and closed.

The hospital bed felt like a pincushion. Sabrina knew it was the waiting. Two days of tests were over, and Doctor Joe would be relaying the results any minute. The grimness that had been in his voice the last day had convinced Sabrina that the results thus far hadn't been encouraging.

Her father walked again to the window in her room. She knew he had no interest in the parking lot below, his patience giving way to restless pacing. She wished she could join him. In almost mid-stride he stopped and turned abruptly. A second later air from the corridor fanned her cheek and she turned toward the door.

'Good morning, Sabrina, Mr. Lane,' Doctor Joe Browning greeted each of them. His voice was professionally bright. 'It's really a lousy morning, but I suppose you San Franciscans are used to the fog.'

'Good morning, Doctor Joe,' Sabrina returned.

But her father skipped the pleasantries. 'Are all the results in?'

'Yes.'

The back of Sabrina's neck prickled. Unconsciously she called out hesitantly, 'Bay?'

'Hello, Sabrina,' he answered quietly.

'Don't tell me my patient has mental telepathy?' the doctor laughed shortly in surprise.

'A keen sense of smell,' Bay corrected in a smiling

voice. 'She probably recognized my aftershave lotion.'

Sabrina didn't correct him. She wasn't certain herself how she had known he was there and she couldn't be positive that she hadn't unconsciously caught a whiff of the spicy fragrance.

'Well, to get back to the business at hand,' Doctor Joe breathed in deeply, 'I've analyzed the test results twice.'

He paused and Grant Lane prompted, 'And?'

'We knew when we rolled the dice, Mr. Lane, that it was a long shot, not even house odds.' The grimness of his voice was all the warning Sabrina needed to brace herself for the rest of his answer. 'The dice came up snake eyes. There isn't anything that can be done. I'm deeply sorry that I put both of you through this.'

The silence from her father told Sabrina how much he had been praying for a miracle. So had she, for that matter, but she wasn't as crushed as she had been the other times that the verdict was pronounced.

She summoned a weak smile. 'We had to take the chance, Doctor Joe.' Her smile deepened as she remembered Bay's words that first night in the hospital. 'We had to give it a go.'

The doctor walked to the bed and clasped one of her hands warmly between his. 'Thank you, Sabrina.'

As Doctor Joe took his leave of her father, apologizing again, she heard Bay approach the bed. He stopped somewhere near the side. She felt his penetrating gaze run over her face.

'Are you all right?' he asked quietly.

'Yes,' she whispered, and she knew suddenly that it was the truth and not simply brave words.

'I knew that gutsy blind queen would resurface,' he told her.

'With your help, she did,' Sabrina answered.

'I can't take the credit for the strength you already possessed,' Bay denied, 'but we'll argue the point another time. How about Saturday night?'

'Saturday night?' she repeated.

'Yes, we can have dinner together. I'll pick you up around seven.'

There was a breathless catch in her throat. 'Is that an order or an invitation?' she asked unevenly.

'Both, depending on your answer.'

'I'd be proud to have dinner with you, Mr. Cameron,' Sabrina accepted with a demure inclination of her head.

More than proud, she added silently to herself. She found she was looking forward to Saturday night with uncommon eagerness.

CHAPTER SIX

SABRINA slowly descended the steps to the second floor, fingering the soft knit of her top uncertainly. A tiny frown of indecision pulled the arch of her brows together. In the living room, she could hear her father's and Deborah's voices. She walked to the open doorway and paused.

'Deborah, may I see you a minute?' Sabrina requested, a hint of anxiety in her voice.

'Of course.' Footsteps muffled by the carpet quickly approached the doorway where she waited. 'What is it?'

'This pant suit, is it too dressy?'

'I shouldn't think so,' Deborah frowned in confusion. 'Bay is taking you out to dinner, isn't he?'

'Not to dinner exactly,' Sabrina explained. 'We'll pick up something to eat at the Wharf like we did the last time and have a makeshift picnic somewhere. He's not taking me out to a public restaurant.' Her hand touched the camel tan slacks stitched in dark brown and the matching boat-necked top in the same brown. Over her arm, she carried a matching jacket and around her neck were progressively longer strands of gold chain. 'Maybe I should wear something simpler?'

'I don't think so,' Deborah decided after several seconds of consideration to the question. 'You may not be going out to a fancy restaurant to dine, but that isn't any reason why you have to look like an urchin. That pant suit is versatile enough to fit any occasion except the most formal one.'

'Good,' Sabrina sighed in relief. It was so difficult sometimes trying to judge by memory the clothes she wore. The front door bell rang. 'That must be Bay now.'

'Your purse is on the table,' Deborah stated. 'I'll tell Bay you're on your way down.'

Retrieving her purse, Sabrina slipped the ivory cane from the umbrella stand, hooked it over her arm and opened the stairwell door, calling a goodbye to her father before closing it. She darted eagerly down the stairs and through the street door to the gates.

'I'm ready,' she declared unnecessarily, unlocking the gates and walking through.

Bay's hand touched her arm in light possession as he directed her to his parked car. 'I was hoping you might wear that new dress tonight.'

Sabrina laughed softly. 'I'd look pretty silly wearing that to a picnic!'

'A picnic?' he repeated. 'We aren't going to a picnic. I'm taking you out to dinner, remember?'

'But——' she stopped short.

'But what?' He paused patiently beside her.

'You know very well that I don't eat in public places,' she stated, punctuating the sentence with an emphatic tap of her cane.

'Yes, I remember what you said.' His arm crossed her back and he forcibly moved her toward the car. The door was opened and Sabrina was helped and shoved inside. She fumbled for the door handle, only to find the door was locked. Before she could find the lock, Bay was in the car, his hand tightly closing over her wrist.

'You're not paying attention to me,' Sabrina accused.

'I can't give you all of my attention and drive too,' Bay countered logically, starting the car and turning it away from the curb with one hand. 'We're going to a nice little Italian restaurant. It doesn't look much from the outside, but the food is excellent.'

'I'm not going,' she declared.

'Sabrina, you can't keep avoiding things on the offchance that you'll do something embarrassing.' The firm tone of his voice said his patience was thinning.

'You're going to look pretty silly yourself dragging me into that restaurant,' she commented smugly.

'I hope you aren't counting on the fact that I won't, because if that's the only way I can get you in the door, I'll do it,' Bay stated.

In that flashing second, Sabrina realized that he meant it. No stubbornness or anger on her part would change his mind. He actually meant to get her in the restaurant one way or the other.

'You're a brute and a bully!' she hissed angrily. 'I don't know why I ever agreed to come with you tonight. I should have guessed you would do something like this.'

'You'd better be careful,' he warned mockingly. 'I could change my mind and take you to a Chinese restaurant and put a pair of chopsticks in your hand. I don't think you'd fare too successfully with those.'

The pouting line of her mouth twitched as her innate sense of humor surfaced. She covered her mouth with her hand to try to hide the smile that was breaking through. She had never mastered the use of chopsticks when she could see. Any attempt now that she was blind would be absurd.

'I see that smile,' Bay laughed softly. 'It's a decided improvement on that stubborn blind monkey that was sitting beside me a minute ago. You just keep wearing it. And don't be embarrassed if you spill something. Sighted people do it all the time.'

'Why can't I ever win an argument with you?' Sabrina sighed, but with humor.

'Because, my little blind queen,' he drawled, 'you always know that I'm right.'

Surprisingly, as far as Sabrina was concerned, the dinner was without mishap. The other times she had eaten out shortly after the accident, she had invariably tipped over a glass or dropped food on the table, but not this time. Bay had laughingly threatened to order her spaghetti, but it was a very excellent lasagna that she had received instead.

She leaned back in her chair, a hand securely touching the coffee cup so she wouldn't forget where it was. A tiny sigh of contentment broke from her lips.

'What was that for?' Bay inquired softly.

'For a very enjoyable meal,' she responded. 'Thank you for making me come.'

'I prefer the word "persuaded." ' Amusement danced in his voice.

'"Persuaded" me to come then,' she acknowledged with a dimpling smile.

'No depression because of the negative test results?' Despite the teasing tone, there was an underlying hint of seriousness.

'I wish it had been otherwise, of course,' Sabrina shrugged, 'but I don't mind as much as I might have. Partly because of the advice you gave me and partly because I'd already started working again, in a creative sense. My life as a blind woman was not without purpose when I went into the hospital this time. Before when the specialists gave me their verdict, I had nothing to look forward to but emptiness. Now, I have a goal.'

'You're referring to the modeling you've started in clay. When are you going to show me what you've done so far?'

'When I'm willing to stand some criticism,' Sabrina smiled ruefully.

'And you think my judgment would be critical?' Bay prompted.

'I don't think you're going to let me get by with mediocrity simply because I'm blind,' she acknowledged.

'I don't think you would lean on that crutch and lower your standards either,' he returned.

'I couldn't,' admitted Sabrina with a nod of her head. A fervent note crept into her voice. 'I want to be more than just good. I want to be great. It's the only way I'll be able to support myself with art as my career.'

'And that's very important to you, isn't it?'

'Yes. Not just for pride's sake or to be independent,' she went on earnestly, 'but because I don't want to keep being a burden to my father. I know he doesn't think of me that way, but I know that because of me he hasn't married Deborah. Only by having an independent income could I prove to him that I'm capable of living on my own.'

'You could always get married. That's a very excellent reason for leaving home,' Bay suggested.

'There happen to be two obstacles to that solution,' Sabrina laughed shortly, not taking his suggestion seriously.

'What are they?'

'First, there isn't anyone I happen to be in love with, and it would be pretty shallow to marry a man simply to get out of the house.'

'And the second?'

'The second is a very crucial one. There would have to be someone around willing to marry me.' There was a dubious shake of her head as if such a contingency would never occur.

'Is that so unlikely?' Bay asked with curious mockery.

'If they're sane, it would be.' She laughed quietly again.

'I've always considered myself to be sane. I guess that puts me out of the running, doesn't it?'

Sabrina felt his gaze searching her face, alert to her reaction. She was suddenly self-conscious about the subject they were discussing.

'It certainly would,' she answered firmly.

'I guess that settles that,' Bay stated. The nonchalance in his voice didn't match the sensation Sabrina had that he had been interested in her answer. Maybe he thought she wanted to take advantage of his apparent wealth. 'Would you like some more coffee, Sabrina, or shall we leave?'

'No more, thank you. I'm ready if you are.' Her hand found the ivory cane hooked over the arm of her chair.

After that first successful dinner, Bay took Sabrina out

several times during the following weeks. The restaurants he chose were seldom crowded but served excellent food.

The only twinges of self-consciousness she experienced came when friends of Bay's stopped at their table to say hello. She had sensed their surprise upon learning she was blind and guessed that they wondered why Bay was with her.

At odd times, she wondered why herself, but the answer had ceased to be important. It was enough to enjoy his company without constantly questioning his motives for being with her. In a way she didn't want to find out. She was afraid his reason might be a charitable one. Although she had come a great distance out of her shell, she was still averse to pity from any quarter and most especially from Bay.

Carefully she smoothed the arm of the clay figure, letting her fingers transfer the image to her mind's eye. A faint shiver of subdued elation trembled over her at the completed picture of a ballet dancer captured in the middle of a pirouette that her mind saw. With each passing week her hands had become more sure and more adept. The successes had begun to outnumber the failures.

Footsteps echoed into the studio from the stairway. Quelling her excitement, Sabrina stepped back from the work stand, a faint smile of triumph tickling the corners of her mouth. Wiping her hands on the towel, she turned slightly toward the door as the footsteps approached. An eagerness she couldn't conceal was in her stance.

'Come in, Dad,' she called when the footsteps paused at the door. 'I've finished the third. Come and see it.'

The instant the door opened, her head tipped sideways in a listening attitude. The person entering the room was not her father but Bay. She knew it instinctively.

'What are you doing here?' she breathed in surprise. 'You said you wouldn't come until seven. It can't be that late.' She had removed her watch so she couldn't check the time.

'It isn't. It's the middle of the afternoon.' Bay returned with faint amusement. 'Since you haven't extended an invitation for me to see your work, I persuaded your father to send me up here rather than have you come down.'

In an instinctive, protective movement, Sabrina moved a few steps to try to block his line of sight. Only her father and Deborah had seen the result of her many hours of labor in the studio. She was not yet ready for someone outside her family to see what she had done.

'That doesn't explain what you're doing here in the middle of the afternoon,' she murmured defensively.

'Doesn't it? I thought it did.' She could hear the smile in his tone. 'Actually you're right,' Bay conceded. 'I had another purpose for coming other than sneaking into your studio. I'm afraid I have to cancel our dinner date tonight—I'm sorry, Sabrina.'

'That's all right,' she shrugged.

It wasn't all right, but she didn't want him to realize how much she looked forward to an evening with him. She didn't like to admit it to herself. There was no future in it. The future was here in this studio with her work.

'I don't know whether I should be pleased or insulted that you've taken the news so calmly.' Sabrina sensed the

107

arching of a thick brow in her direction, faintly mocking and faintly curious. 'You might show a little regret.'

'I would have enjoyed the evening.' Pride inserted a slightly indifferent tone in her voice. 'Obviously whatever it is that's forced you to cancel our dinner together must be important or I don't think you would have canceled.' The intense scrutiny of his gaze was disturbing. Striving for lightness, Sabrina added with a taut smile, 'I certainly hope you've warned your jealous girlfriend that she doesn't need to scratch my eyes out. I'm already quite blind and disfigurement I don't need.' It was a facetious remark, not an expression of self-pity.

'What makes you think it's a jealous girlfriend who's changing our plans?' The inflection in his voice was mockingly amused, but Sabrina was still conscious of his penetrating look.

'I don't know that it is,' she answered with a teasing smile. 'But I certainly hope you don't expect me to believe that you're a celibate.'

'What makes you think I'm not?' Bay countered.

The virilely masculine face her hands had seen was immediately before her inner eye. The image made a mockery of his question. In too many little ways, Bay's actions in the past had answered his own question.

'A girl has ways of knowing these things,' Sabrina smiled complacently. 'A kind of female intuition, I suppose.'

'If you believe that about me, then what conclusion have you reached to explain why I haven't brought our relationship to a more intimate level?' he asked lazily.

'Really, Bay!' Sabrina laughed as if the question was ridiculous under the circumstances. 'We're friends, nothing more.'

'Strictly platonic, is that it?'

'Of course,' A tiny frown puckered her forehead at the faint harshness in his remark.

'In that case, when are you going to step aside to let a "friend" see your work? My view is somewhat limited with you standing in front of it,' he mocked.

Sabrina decided that she had imagined the sharpness in his previous question. She had only been stating the obvious and he had agreed in an indirect way.

For a hesitant moment, she remained where she was, wanting to know his reaction to her work but unsure yet of the extent of her own skill in this field of art. Almost reluctantly she stepped to one side, apprehension edging the corners of her bland expression as Bay walked forward for a closer look.

'S-some of my first attempts are on the side table,' she explained nervously. 'As you can see, they aren't very good, but I've slowly been improving. Right now I'm working on a series of ballet figures. I thought I'd do a small "corps de ballet" with the central model being a dancing couple. I'm only a third done with the secondary figures, though.'

The silence stretched seemingly without end. Sabrina thought she would burst with the suspense of waiting. Her hands were unconsciously clasped in a praying position.

'Have any of your friends seen your work?' Bay asked absently. 'Your art friends, I mean.'

Her throat worked convulsively as she shook her head in a negative answer before she could speak. 'Only Dad and Deborah.'

'I'm no critic, Sabrina,' he murmured. 'I only know what I like, and I'm impressed by what I see here. You've never done any extensive work in this medium before?'

'Never,' she breathed. 'Do you really think it's good? You're not saying it because I'm blind, are you?' She needed to hear his approval again.

'I haven't treated you with kid gloves since the first time I met you, and I'm not going to put them on now,' he answered seriously. 'You know that what you've done is more than good. I can see that it is. A professional is the only person who can tell you how good you are. If you want my suggestion, I think you should get hold of someone who can give you that answer.'

'Not—not yet,' Sabrina refused. Confidence in her own ability was not to the point where she could endure the scrutiny of her work by an art critic. 'I'm not ready for that. I need more time.'

'No one is ever ready to have anything judged by others, but you can't postpone it for ever.' His observance was gently understanding while reminding her of the practical need if she intended to make this her career.

'Not yet,' she repeated, running her palms nervously over the sides of her clay-stained smock.

'Cigarette?' Bay offered.

'Yes, please.' Sabrina accepted with a quaking sigh.

As the scent of burning tobacco reached her nose, she extended her hand for the cigarette, but Bay placed the filter tip against her lips, his fingers touching her mouth and sending a shiver of awareness down her spine. Invariably when she came in contact with him, she was intensely conscious of his maleness, the memory of that one fleeting first kiss haunting her again with its tender mastery and checked fire.

'There's coffee and cake downstairs,' she offered hesitantly. 'If you'd——'

'No, I'm sorry, I can't stay any longer,' Bay refused before she could complete the invitation. 'I won't be able to see you this coming week either. I do have a couple of tickets for the Light Opera's performance next Saturday if you're willing to accept that as a raincheck for tonight.'

'I would enjoy that,' Sabrina smiled.

'I promise I'll make certain I don't have to cancel that one,' he smiled. 'Oh, by the way, there's something I meant to give you as an apology for tonight.'

'Give me?' she frowned as she listened to him reach into his pocket and heard the faint rustle of paper. He placed a small, wrapped box in her hand, long and thin, similar in shape to a jeweler's box.

'Open it,' he ordered laughing at her hesitation. 'It's nothing expensive, if that's what's concerning you. In fact, you might decide to throw it in my face when you find out what it is.'

Curious and apprehensive, Sabrina began unwrapping the package. Removing the cardboard top of the small thin box, her exploring fingers touched a pair of tapering sticks. She turned a bewildered expression to Bay.

'Sticks?' she questioned in disbelief.

111

Bay clicked his tongue in mock reproval. 'Not just sticks,' he chuckled. 'They're chopsticks. I'm giving you a couple of weeks to practise before I take you to a Cantonese restaurant in Chinatown.'

Laughter bubbled in her throat and she bit into her lower lip to hold it back. With mock seriousness she replied, 'I suppose I should be grateful that you've given me advance warning.'

'Yes, you should,' he agreed in a tone of pseudo-arrogance.

'Even with practice,' Sabrina couldn't hold back the laughter, 'the only thing I'll probably eat is egg rolls, soup and fortune cookies. All the rest will end up on the floor or the table cloth.'

'I'll take the chance,' Bay smiled. 'As for next Saturday, I think the occasion will warrant the sophistication of that flame-colored dress.'

'Is that an order, too?' she laughed.

'If it is, will you obey it?' he countered.

'Yes,' she nodded, a wide smile spreading across her cheeks, softening her square jawline.

After Bay's approval of her work, Sabrina strove even harder for the perfection she demanded. This renewed vigor made the week pass swiftly. The performance of the Light Opera Company the following Saturday seemed a reward for her efforts.

The faint initial nervousness she had felt at the prospect of going to such a very public place vanished under the genuine praise from Bay at her appearance. She had taken extra pains, enlisting Deborah's aid with her hair and make-up. The two of them had got along much better since Sabrina had started working in the studio again.

No further mention had been made by Deborah of the special school she had thought Sabrina should attend. It was as if they were both counting on the efforts in the studio for the future happiness of each.

Sabrina had not intended to take her ivory cane, vanity not wanting her to be easily identified by the crowd attending the opera as being blind. However, Bay handed her the cane from the umbrella stand as they walked out the door of the house. She had known he would chide her reason for not wanting to carry it, so she had said nothing.

Now the cane was hooked over her arm as they stood in the foyer of the theater. It was intermission between acts. Had Sabrina been with anyone else she would probably have remained in her seat, but Bay had ushered her into the outer lobby.

Bay Cameron was not a man to be overlooked by those around him. His very stature would draw attention to him even if his male magnetism didn't. Thus Sabrina knew she was the object of many people's interest and curiosity, expecially once they saw the cane on her arm, because she was in his company.

Several people acquainted with Bay stopped, politely including her in their greeting. Bay did not encourage conversation with anyone and they gradually drifted away after the initial exchange. Sabrina wasn't certain whether it was because he was aware of her uneasiness with strangers or because he was self-conscious that she was blind. The last didn't seem to fit with his nature and she dismissed it.

'Bay Cameron!' an older woman greeted him effusively. Unconsciously Sabrina edged closer to be nearer his protection. 'I haven't seen you in ages!' the woman exclaimed. 'Where have you been keeping yourself? Is this the little lady I have to blame for your absence?'

His hand moved to rest on the back of Sabrina's shoulders, drawing her slightly forward as he introduced her. 'Pamela, I'd like you to meet Sabrina Lane. Sabrina, this is a very dear friend of mine, Pamela Thyssen. She tends to be a bit overpowering and nosy, but she has a gentle heart.'

'Don't you believe him!' the woman commanded gruffly, a raspy edge to her otherwise cultured voice. 'My bite is every bit as bad as my bark, so beware, Miss Lane. It is "Miss" Lane, isn't it?'

'Do you see what I mean, Sabrina?' Bay chuckled. 'She's a nosy busybody.'

'Yes, it is Miss Lane,' Sabrina confirmed with a faint smile.

She was beginning to agree that Bay's description of Pamela Thyssen was correct. Although curious and forceful, underneath the woman seemed to be kind.

'We single women must stick together,' Pamela Thyssen averred. 'Not that I intend to remain single. I've outlived two husbands, and they always say the third is a charm. And you, my dear, are you setting your cap for our Bay?'

114

Sabrina flushed deeply. 'Hardly, Mrs. Thyssen,' she denied vigorously.

'I guess that puts you in your place, Bay!' the woman laughed loudly.

'She's a very independent young lady,' he agreed with faint amusement, yet she sensed an inner displeasure in his tone.

'I must get to know Sabrina better. Bring her to my party after the performance.' It was a command, not a request, and the older woman bade them goodbye before Sabrina could prompt Bay into a refusal.

'You aren't actually intending to go, are you?' she said in a half-demand when they were alone.

'Why not?' he countered smoothly. 'Pamela's parties are quiet ones and friendly.'

'I'm uncomfortable with a lot of strangers,' Sabrina answered defensively.

'It's about time you got over that,' Bay responded, the hand on her back prodding her into movement. 'Now we only have a few minutes to find our seats before the curtain goes up.'

CHAPTER SEVEN

SABRINA curled her fingers into the soft rabbit fur of her black evening jacket, pushing the collar around her neck. The corners of her mouth drooped downward in frustration as she nibbled at her sensitive lower lip. The closed window of the car did not completely block out the sound of other cars exiting the theater lot.

'Why can't you take me home and go to the party by yourself?' The suggestion she made had a vaguely desperate ring to it.

'The invitation was for both of us,' Bay reminded her.

'Mrs. Thyssen doesn't know me. She wouldn't even miss me if I wasn't there,' Sabrina reasoned.

'Yes, she will.' A smile lightened the firmness of his tone. 'Especially since you were the one who prompted her to extend the invitation.'

'I did no such thing!'

'Let me rephrase it,' he said patiently. 'It was after meeting you and having her curiosity aroused that she invited us to her party.'

'She never gave us a chance to say whether we could come or not. We could have made other plans for all she knows,' Sabrina argued.

'But we don't have other plans, do we? There isn't any reason why we can't go to her party for a short while.'

'I don't want to go. That's a good enough reason for me.'
Her chin jutted out defiantly.

'No, it isn't,' Bay replied in a voice that said he would
not be swayed by any more arguments.

'You're a bully, Bay Cameron!' Sabrina accused lowly,
slumping in her seat.

'A gentle one, I hope,' he chuckled softly.

'A bully,' she repeated with no qualifying adjectives.

Bridling at the way Bay had maneuvered her again into
a situation not of her choosing, Sabrina couldn't
concentrate on the direction they were taking. She lost
track of the turns and eventually stopped guessing what
streets they were on. The absence of any heavy traffic
indicated a residential area, but she had no idea what
section of the city they were in.

The car slowed down and turned into the curb. 'Here we
are,' Bay announced, switching off the motor and opening
the door.

Sabrina said nothing, sitting in mutinous silence as the
door opened and closed on his side. In her mind, she
watched him walk around the car to her door, judging
almost to the second when he opened her door. Stubbornly
she didn't move.

'Are you coming in with me or are you going to sit in
the car and sulk like a little child?' Bay mocked softly.

'If I have a choice, I'll stay in the car,' she declared
coldly.

'Sabrina.' His sighing voice held indulgent patience in

its gentle tone. 'Are you really going to let some strangers intimidate you into staying in the car?'

'They don't intimidate me.'

'You're afraid to go in. What other word fits?'

'I'm not afraid,' Sabrina asserted forcefully.

'Of course not,' Bay agreed in a deliberately disbelieving voice.

'I'm not!' she repeated angrily.

'Whatever you say,' he agreed again with the same inflection. 'If you're going to stay in the car, I suggest you lock all the doors. I'll be gone about an hour.'

'You're not really leaving me here?' Sabrina frowned, tipping her head back, not certain any more if he was teasing or serious.

'You said you'd rather stay in the car,' Bay reminded her complacently. 'I'll put in my appearance and explain why you couldn't come.'

'You wouldn't dare tell Mrs. Thyssen that I'm sitting out here in the car?' she breathed. But her question was only met with silence, a silence that held an affirmative answer. 'You're completely without scruples,' she grumbled, turning to slide her feet out of the car, his hand reaching out for her arm to guide her safely to the sidewalk.

A maid admitted them into the house. The sound of warm, friendly voices filled the foyer entrance. It seemed to come from several directions, indicating that the party was larger than the small gathering that had been Sabrina's impression.

With her evening jacket in the maid's possession, Bay took her arm and led her in the direction where the

118

majority of voices seemed to be coming from. Her mouth tightened in a grim line.

'Smile.' Bay's order was whispered near her ear.

'No.' But the severe displeasure of her expression lessened.

Sabrina was unaware of the faintly regal tilt of her head, accenting the swanlike column of her neck as they entered the room. Her queenly posture and the softly molding flame-colored gown drew as much attention to her as was given to Bay. Since he was acquainted with most of the people there, the expressions of greeting were offered to him.

Stubbornly Sabrina didn't acknowledge any of them. Only the white knuckles of the hand clutching the ivory cane revealed the inner tremblings she felt at being in a roomful of strangers.

From their right, the instantly recognizable voice of Mrs. Pamela Thyssen called out to them. 'Bay—Sabrina! I'm so glad you could come.'

Sabrina's greeting when the woman was beside them consisted of only a polite 'hello.' She did not intend to lie by saying that she was glad to be there.

Bracelets jangled from the older woman's wrist. The hand that grasped Sabrina's free hand was heavy with rings, small and large. Her perfume was a comfortable, old-fashioned scent of violets.

'Bay, be a dear,' Pamela Thyssen commanded. 'Go and fetch Sabrina and me a drink. I'll take my usual and bring Sabrina the same.'

'Really, Mrs. Thyssen,' Sabrina started her protest,

but Bay had already moved away from her side, 'I don't care for anything to drink.'

'Neither do I. My usual happens to be iced tea,' the woman murmured in a confidential aside. 'That's a little secret between you and me. A hostess is expected to drink at her own parties or the guests don't feel free to imbibe. Iced tea looks sufficiently like drink to make the others feel at ease. So relax, my dear, I shan't attempt to free your tongue with intoxicating beverages.'

'I doubt if you could,' Sabrina answered almost beneath her breath.

'You have spirit. I like that,' Pamela pronounced. 'I'm Bay's godmother. Did he tell you?'

'No.' Was that the reason for the woman's apparent curiosity about her, Sabrina wondered to herself.

'His parents are in Europe on a second honeymoon. Louise, that's Bay's mother, and I grew up together. We've always been very close friends.'

'He mentioned they were in Europe,' she confirmed, since there seemed little other comment she could offer.

'I've been admiring your cane. It is ivory, isn't it?' There was no pause for a reply. 'It's a beautiful piece of workmanship, and so elegant as well. Where did you ever find it?'

'It was a gift—from a friend,' Sabrina added after a second's hesitation. Bay could tell the woman himself if he wanted her to know it was from him.

'A special friend?' the woman queried in a prompting way.

'A friend,' was the only explanation Sabrina offered.

120

'How long have you been blind, Sabrina?'

'Almost a year.' Her chin lifted fractionally as if to say she did not want any probing questions into her past.

'And how long have you known Bay?'

'About two months. Mrs. Thyssen——' Sabrina began, taking a deep breath in the hopes of switching the conversation to some other topic less personal, hopefully without offending the other woman.

'Speak of the devil,' Pamela Thyssen murmured, cutting her off in midsentence. 'That didn't take you very long, Bay. Thank you.'

The clink of rings against a glass accompanied the words. In the next instant, Bay's voice said, 'Here you are, Sabrina,' and a cold glass was placed in her outstretched hand. 'How have you two been getting along while I've been gone? I see by the queenly tilt of Sabrina's nose that you must have been prying already, Pamela.'

'Not prying, Bay,' Pamela corrected with a laugh. 'I was merely trying to find out more about her.' In absent musing, she added, 'She does have a queenly air about her, doesn't she?'

'Please, I——' Sabrina started another protest, but it wasn't allowed to be completed either.

'—don't like to be talked about as if you weren't here,' Pamela Thyssen finished the sentence. 'I know very well what you mean and despise it myself. But it was meant as a compliment. Sabrina and I don't need a referee, Bay. Why don't you go and circulate or something? Let me have her for an hour. I'll take care of her.'

Sabrina turned in Bay's direction, her lips parting in a

silent plea for him not to desert her. For a fleeting second she thought he was going to debate the other woman's request.

'You're in good hands, Sabrina,' he said quietly. 'Pamela won't let you fall. I'll see you later on.'

The line of her mouth thinned angrily as he moved away. First he maneuvered her into coming to this party attended by strangers, then he deserted her! Irritation seethed beneath the surface at her inability to escape from the situation on her own. Independence could only be attained to a certain point, after that she was at the mercy of those around her.

'Come, my dear,' Pamela Thyssen hooked her arm in Sabrina's, 'I want to introduce you around. I try to choose my friends carefully, so with luck we'll avoid meeting any snobs.'

Gritting her teeth silently, Sabrina was practically forced to accompany her hostess. The following flurry of introductions and new voices were difficult to assimilate and put the correct name to the appropriate voice.

There was not one condescending remark or patronizing comment regarding her blindness. The main topic of conversation was the performance that evening. Several of the people she met had seen her at the theater and inquired about her opinion. Everyone's interest in her seemed to be friendly without pitying overtones. Gradually Sabrina's defensive attitude relaxed.

'Tommy, why don't you let Sabrina sit in that love-seat with Mrs. Phillips?' Pamela Thyssen suggested in the firmly ordering tone. 'The armrest is just to your left, dear.'

The glass of tea, empty now, was taken from her hand as the searching tip of her cane found the front edge of the small sofa. Willingly Sabrina sat down. The obstacle course of strange names and voices was beginning to tire her and she guessed that the astute Pamela Thyssen had sensed it. She conceded, but only to herself, that Bay had been right when he said he was leaving her in good hands.

'That's an absolutely stunning dress you're wearing, Miss Lane,' the woman at her side stated, obviously the Mrs. Phillips that Pamela had mentioned. 'I noticed it in the theater.'

The compliment was followed by the woman's lengthy dissertation on the difficulty she had finding clothes to fit her properly and how uncomplimentary the present styles were to her figure. Sabrina listened, inserting a monosyllablic answer when she thought one was required but letting the other woman carry the conversation.

The sensitive area on the back of her neck began to tingle. Sabrina instantly guessed the cause. Bay Cameron had to be somewhere near. Her radar was seldom wrong where he was concerned. Pretending a concentration on the woman speaking to her, she strained her hearing to catch any sound that might pinpoint his location.

Then came the husky caressing sound of a feminine voice, vaguely familiar although Sabrina couldn't place it. 'Bay darling, I didn't expect to see you here.'

'It's a surprise running into you, too,' she heard Bay answer calmly. 'I thought you didn't care for Pamela's parties. I thought they were much too tame for you.'

'A girl can change her mind, can't she, darling?' the voice purred.

'And a man can always wonder why?' Bay countered.

'Actually a little bird saw you at the theater tonight and passed the word on to me. I took a guess that you might bring your little sparrow to Pamela's party.'

'Did you?' was his noncommittal reply.

'I don't think I'll ever understand that streak of charity you possess, Bay,' the silky feminine voice said. 'I mean, why do you have to take such a personal interest in the poor girl? Why can't you simply give her a bunch of money and be done with her? You certainly can afford it.'

Sabrina stiffened. She couldn't help it. The only saving grace in the whole situation was that she doubted anyone possessed the acute hearing that blindness had given her and Bay's conversation with the woman wasn't being overheard by anyone but herself.

'Would that be your solution, Roni?' he murmured in a low voice. 'Sometimes I think when they were handing out compassion, you went back to the line marked "passion." '

Roni. That was the name of the girl who had been with him that one day at the Yacht Harbor. Sabrina also remembered that Bay had said they were going to take in an ocean sunset, a romantic offer if she had ever heard one.

'Is it so bad,' the woman named Roni was speaking again, 'to be passionate, Bay?' Her voice was a caressing whisper that Sabrina could barely understand.

'Not in certain situations.' He sounded amused as if he

was remembering times when he had not felt the need to criticize Roni's passion. Sabrina's blood started to boil, temper bubbling hotly to her nerve ends.

'Tell me, darling,' Sabrina had the impression that the girl moved closer to Bay in an intimately confiding manner, 'you aren't trying to use that blind girl to make me jealous. Isn't that just a little ridiculous?'

'Why? She's a very attractive girl,' Bay stated, without denying the charge.

'But she's blind,' Roni reminded him. 'I know you must feel sorry for her. We all feel pity for those less fortunate than ourselves, but how cruel it must be for the girl when she eventually discovers that all the attention you've been giving her is because of pity. I don't think she'll thank you.'

'Knowing Sabrina, she would probably slap my face if——' Bay drawled.

But Sabrina didn't listen to the rest of his statement. She had heard enough. Her stomach was twisted into knots of tortuous pain. A black nausea attacked her head, swirling in sickening circles as she rose to her feet, unmindful of Mrs. Phillips' continuing voice.

'Excuse me,' she interrupted sharply. 'Mrs. Thyssen?' Her questing voice searched for the location of her hostess somewhere nearby.

'Yes, Sabrina.' Pamela Thyssen was instantly at her side, a curious note in the voice that answered her summons.

Sabrina swallowed, trying to calm her screeching nerves and make her voice sound as natural as possible.

125

'Would you please direct me to your powder room?'

'Of course. It's this way. Come with me.' A ringed hand guided her from the small group. 'Are you all right, Sabrina?' Pamela Thyssen asked in a concerned tone. 'You look pale. Are you quite sure you're feeling all right?' her hostess repeated.

'Quite sure,' Sabrina forced a smile of assurance.

Free of much of the party, they turned into what Sabrina guessed was a hallway. Her nerves were raw. The voices in the other room seemed to take on a higher pitch. Although she tried desperately, she couldn't block her hearing.

'Here we are,' Pamela stated. 'The door is directly to your left.'

Sabrina stopped, letting her cane determine the distance to the door before she turned to her hostess. 'Thank you, Mrs. Thyssen.'

'Would you like me to go in with you?' the woman offered hesitantly.

'No, that's not necessary.' Sabrina wanted solitude and quiet to get her chaotic senses back in order.

'I'll wait out here for you then.'

'No,' Sabrina refused swiftly, then drew a breath and made her voice sound calm. 'I can make it back on my own. I can't keep you from your guests. Just give me an idea of where I am and I'll find my way back. I'm really quite good at following directions.'

The older woman hesitated, then gave Sabrina a simple set of directions to follow back to the main party area. After thanking her, and assuring her again that she was all right, Sabrina walked unerringly to the door, aware that her hostess watched. Fortunately no one else was in the room and Sabrina had it to herself. The closed door reduced the voices to a low hum.

The exploring tip of her cane touched a chair leg. Sighing heavily, Sabrina sank on to the velvet cushion. A vanity table was in front of her and she rested her arms on its smooth top. But the silence didn't stop the racing of her mind.

She had always wondered—she had always questioned Bay's motive for seeing her. Secretly she had stopped believing it was because of pity. Bay had used the word compassion, but not even that less offensive word eased the stabbing hurt of the conversation she had overheard. And he was letting pity for her serve a twofold purpose. While he was charitably spending a night or two a week with Sabrina, he was trying to make this Roni jealous.

Her fingers balled into tight fists. Damn this acute hearing! She moaned silently. No, another voice inside remonstrated her, she should be glad she had discovered his real motive. She was lucky she had regarded him as nothing more than a friend and had found out the truth before she had begun to misinterpret his attention. How awful it would have been if she had started to care for him as a man!

The problem was—what was the next step? Should she confront him with what she had learned? That was what she wanted to do. She wanted to throw his charitable, pitying words in his face. But what good would that do? He would simply deny it as he had all the other times.

Bay Cameron was smooth and cannily intelligent—that was something Sabrina mustn't overlook. Look at the way he had maneuvered her first into accepting the ivory cane she used, then going out to dinner at a public restaurant and finally coming here tonight to this party of strangers. Well, the last had backfired. Now Sabrina knew his true colors.

The door opened and a woman walked in. Her voice as she greeted Sabrina was familiar, but she couldn't recall the woman's name. Self-consciously Sabrina smoothed the back of her hair, pretending that she was in front of the vanity table checking her appearance. With fingers crossed, she hoped the woman wouldn't tarry long. Unfortunately she did, and each passing second ticked loudly in Sabrina's head.

At last Sabrina knew she couldn't stay any longer without arousing suspicion. She had already been in the room a considerable time. She didn't want Mrs. Thyssen sending a search party for her. If only she could slip away from the house, she wished, as she rose to her feet. She didn't want to go back to the party. It was taking on the overtones of a nightmare.

But where would she go, she asked herself, pushing open the door to the hall. Even if she could sneak away unseen, there was little likelihood there would be a taxi cab cruising in this residential neighborhood. She doubted very much if she could hold her tongue during the long ride home with Bay.

Not concentrating on where she was going, she bumped into a small table sitting against the wall of the hallway.

Instinctively her hand reached out to prevent whatever was on the table from falling to the floor. A vase had started to tip, but she set it upright again. As she started to withdraw her hand, her fingers encountered a familiarly smooth object—the receiver of a telephone.

There was the answer! Not caring who might be observing her action, Sabrina picked up the receiver, her fingers quickly dialing Information and requesting the number of a taxi company. Without allowing any time for second thoughts, she dialed the number given her.

When the phone was answered on the other end, Sabrina said quietly, 'Would you please send a cab to——' She stopped. She didn't know where she was. Footsteps were approaching. 'Just a moment,' she requested the man on the other end of the line to wait. Taking a deep breath, she turned to the person coming nearer. She had to take a chance. 'Excuse me, please, but would you tell me what the address is here?'

'Yes, ma'am,' a courteous female voice replied, and gave her the address.

The studied politeness of the woman's voice prompted Sabrina to ask, 'Are—are you the maid?'

'Yes, ma'am,' the woman answered in a voice that said she had noticed the white cane in Sabrina's hand.

'Would you bring me my jacket? It's a black rabbit fur,' Sabrina requested.

'Right away, ma'am.'

At the departing footsteps, Sabrina removed her hand from the mouthpiece and gave the address to the man patiently waiting on the other end. He promised only a few minutes' wait. With the receiver safely in its cradle, Sabrina turned away from the table. The smell of success was intoxicatingly near.

Footsteps approached again from the direction the maid had taken. Sabrina could not tell if it was the maid and she held her breath, fearful that at any second she would be discovered by Bay or Mrs. Thyssen.

'Here you are, ma'am,' the maid spoke. 'Shall I help you on with it?'

'Please,' Sabrina agreed nervously.

The maid deftly helped her into the fur jacket. 'Shall I let Mrs. Thyssen know you're leaving?'

'No, that won't be necessary. I've already spoken to her,' she lied hurriedly. 'The cab will be here any minute. I'll wait outside. The front door, is it straight ahead down this hall?'

'Yes, ma'am,' the maid acknowledged. 'But the fog is rather thick tonight. It would be best to wait inside.'

'I'd prefer the fresh air. The smoke has got a bit thick in here.' She didn't want to risk being discovered when she was so near her goal.

'Very well, ma'am,' the maid submitted, and silently withdrew.

As quickly as her searching cane would permit, Sabrina traveled the length of the hallway to the front door. Her palms were perspiring with excitement as she opened the front door and stepped into the night.

The cool air was a soothing balm to her taut nerve ends. She moved away from the door, seeking the shadows she knew would be at the side of the entrance. The damp fog was heavy against her face. The thick walls of the house shut out the noise within. The sleeping night was profoundly still.

A smile turned up the corners of her wide mouth as she imagined Bay's confusion when he discovered she was gone. His overworked sense of pity would have him concerned for her safety, but she knew it wouldn't be long before the maid would be questioned. She would tell him that Sabrina had taken a taxi. He would be angry, but at this point Sabrina didn't care. Whatever debt she might have thought she owed him for his assistance and supposed friendship had been paid in full tonight.

Time went by slowly, but it always seemed to double its length when she was waiting anxiously for something. Sabrina remained in the shadows, hopefully concealed from anyone who might decide to leave the party early. Finally the steady growl of a car motor sounded down the street. She waited to see if it stopped at this house or continued past. It halted at the curb and a car door slammed.

As she stepped from the shadows, a man's voice asked curtly, 'Did you call for a cab, lady?'

'Yes, I did.' She walked as swiftly as she could toward him, victory lightening her step. A car door opened. She used the sound to judge the distance. The man's hand took her elbow to help her into the rear of the cab. 'I want you to take me to——'

Sabrina never got the address of her home out. The front

131

door of the house opened and the hairs on the back of her neck stood out, freezing her muscles into immobility. She had nearly made it.

Maybe she still could. There wasn't much time. Bay's long strides were already eating up the distance from the front door to the taxi.

As she tried to slip into the rear seat, an arm circled her waist, a hand spreading across the flat of her stomach and drawing her back to the sidewalk.

'Let me go!' She struggled against the steel band that held her mercilessly.

'Be still, Sabrina,' Bay ordered, only tightening his hold. There was the crisp sound of money being removed from his pocket. 'I'm sorry you were called out unnecessarily,' he was talking to the cab driver. 'I'll see her home.'

'I don't want to go with you,' she protested vigorously. The driver had not moved, and there was a chance he could be an ally. 'Please, tell this man to leave me alone.'

'Will you stop involving others in our quarrels?' Bay demanded curtly. The implication of his demand was that they were having a little spat, a ruse on Bay's part to assure the driver that his assistance was not really needed.

There was a crisp exchange of money before the man wished Bay good luck and Sabrina knew her means of escape was lost. For a deflated moment she stopped struggling to free herself from Bay's pinning grip while the cab driver closed the rear door and walked around to the other side.

Turning her at right angles, his hand shifted to the side

of her waist as he forced her to walk away from the departing taxi. Bay did not lead her back to the house but toward his car parked at the curb some distance down the street.

'Would you like to explain to me what's going on?' he requested grimly in a voice that was not at all amused.

'Surely it's obvious. I was going home,' Sabrina retorted.

'If you wanted to leave, why didn't you look for me? I never said we had to stay at the party until the last minute.' His fingers were biting into the soft flesh of her waist.

'I didn't want *you* to take me home, that's why!' she snapped.

'Then you should have left your cane behind. Maybe no one would have noticed you leaving if it hadn't been for that little white stick!' He was angry. It vibrated through his tautly controlled voice.

'If I'd given it a thought, I would have.' She refused to be intimidated by his tightly held temper.

'And why, after all this time, would you suddenly not want me to take you home?' Bay demanded.

'I don't need a reason,' Sabrina answered haughtily.

'Yes, you do, and before this night is out, I'm going to hear it,' he informed her with unrelenting arrogance.

Sabrina stopped shortly and Bay did likewise. 'Maybe I'm tired of your pity and your patronizing attitude!' she challenged boldly, tilting her head so he could see the dislike in her expression. 'I don't need you or anybody else to feel sorry for me!'

'What?' She could sense his frowning alertness.

133

'Go and join the Boy Scouts!' Her voice grew shrill. 'I'm tired of your good deeds!' There was a traitorous quiver of her chin.

'Pity! Is that what you think I feel?' The accusation exploded around her.

Sabrina opened her mouth to retaliate, and in the next instant she was jerked against him. The violence of his action sent her cane clattering on to the sidewalk. An arm curved punishingly between her shoulder blades. His hand gripped the back of her neck, forcing her head back while he drew her on to tiptoes.

Her startled cry was smothered by his hard mouth. Roughly, almost savagely he kissed her, not allowing her to draw a breath as he ground her lips against her teeth.

An elemental tension crackled in the air when he raised his head. His hands moved, closing over the slender bones of her shoulders, keeping Sabrina in front of him.

'You're a brute and a bully, Bay Cameron!' The hissing accusation was offered between gasps for air.

'Then I might as well be hanged for a sinner as a saint!' The harsh words carried the steel edge of sarcasm.

Again he gathered her to his chest, pinning her against the rock wall while the muscles in his arms rippled around her. Sabrina had not recovered from the brutal pressure of his first kiss when she was punished by the second. She strained against him weakly, her strength ebbing from the riptide of his embrace.

As her resistance faded, an angry passion was

134

transmitted to her by his demanding lips. A feverish warmth enveloped her and unwillingly her flesh began to respond to the hard commanding mouth that possessed hers.

Mindlessly her hands stopped pushing against him and her fingers curled into the lapels of his jacket. Through the rainbow explosion of her senses, Sabrina realized she was falling victim to the very virility she had warned herself against.

As suddenly as it all began, it ended with Bay firmly holding her an arm's length away. Her equilibrium was completely gone. Up was down and down was up. It was a topsy-turvy world, this midnight velvet blackness she lived in. And it was because of Bay and his punishing embrace.

'Get in the car!' The harsh command was like a physical slap in the face.

But even the abrupt jolt to reality couldn't prod Sabrina into movement. Finally Bay dragged, carried, and shoved her into the passenger seat. Her voice didn't return until he was behind the wheel and driving the car away from the curb.

'Bay——' Her weak voice was barely above a whisper.

'Shut up, Sabrina.' The terse, grating tone of his voice indicated that the words were drawn through clenched jaws. 'Maybe when I can think clearly, I'll be able to offer an apology. Right now all I want to do is wring your bloody neck!'

CHAPTER EIGHT

OBEYING his command, Sabrina had not spoken during that tense ride to her home. She had been too frightened to speak—not because she had thought he would carry out his threat or that he would subject her again to the punishment of his kisses. Sabrina had been frightened by herself. For a few fleeting moments in his arms, she had not been a blind woman, only a woman.

Her bruised mouth had retained the burning fire of his hard, demanding kiss. The racing of her heart had kept pounding in her ears as if she was on a runaway locomotive that she couldn't jump off. The impression of those muscled arms that had locked her in his embrace had still been felt.

Her breast and hips had remembered the solid rock pressure of his chest and thighs, implanting the hard male outline of his body so firmly in her mind that Sabrina thought she would never be able to uproot it. The scent of his maleness and spicy cologne had clung to her skin. Nothing had seemed to remove it.

What was worse, she didn't want to erase anything. That was why she was still frightened two days after the fact. Over and over again she had asked herself why he had kissed her that way.

Had the brutally volatile embrace been prompted by anger that she had found out his true motive? Could he have used her as an outlet for frustration because his plan to make the girl Roni jealous had failed? In view of the conversation she had overheard, it was the most likely explanation. Probably it was a combination of several things.

Sabrina would not consider the possibility that Bay had been prompted by any physical desire for her. Not that she believed that there would not be a time when she would meet some man who truly loved and wanted her. But visualizing Bay Cameron as that man was something she could not do. He had position, wealth, charm, and looks. There were too many other women he could have at his side in an intimate sense.

Her blindness had touched him. It didn't matter which noun was used to identify the emotion he felt—pity, compassion, sympathy. They were all one and the same thing.

Pain gnawed at her heart. Pride said that she couldn't regard Bay as a friend any longer. A true friend might commiserate, but he would never seek her company because he felt sorry for her. But Sabrina's heart honestly acknowledged the main reason why she must reject him. She was the one who had stopped regarding him as a friend and had started thinking of him as a man. For her, that was dangerously foolish.

A sob rasped her throat, choking her with its futility. Sabrina buried her face in her hands, letting the misery wash over her. For a little time in the solitude of this afternoon, she would feel sorry for herself and not regret it. She had earned the right.

Before the first tears slipped from her brown eyes, the

telephone rang. 'No!' Sabrina denied its call softly. But it persisted.

The urge was there to ignore it, to let it ring until the person on the other end gave up. Grimacing at the possibility that it was her father, she knew she had no right to cause him unnecessary concern. Reluctantly she rose to her feet and walked to the telephone.

'Lane residence,' she answered in a pseudo-calm voice.

'Sabrina.'

The sound of Bay's low husky voice nearly made her drop the telephone. It was as if a bolt of lightning had struck her. A weakness quaked her knees and she quickly sought the support of a chair.

'Are you there, Sabrina?' his frowning voice asked when she failed to reply immediately.

'Yes, hello, Bay.' Her reply was strained and unnatural, but it didn't matter any more.

'How are you?' It was not a casual question. There was too much guarded alertness in his tone.

'Fine. And you?' She was purposely distant and polite.

Bay ignored her aloof inquiry. 'You know why I've called, don't you?'

'How could I possibly know that?' Sabrina asked with cutting disinterest.

'Would you have dinner with me Saturday night?' A grimness changed the invitation into a challenge.

But Sabrina had guessed that if Bay did make any conciliatory gesture as he had indicated he might, it would be wrapped in a suggestion for a Saturday night date. She realized now that he always chose Saturday night because that was the evening her father devoted exclusively to Deborah and Sabrina spent it alone—at least, she had for the most part before she met Bay. Yesterday she had invited an old friend, Sally Goodwin, over on Saturday night.

'I've already made other plans,' she answered truthfully and a shade triumphantly.

'You have?' The mocking inflection doubted her statement.

'I do know other people besides you, Bay,' she retorted.

A tired yet angry sigh came over the wire. 'May I take a guess that you *arranged* to be busy on Saturday night?'

'You may guess if you want,' she shrugged, neither affirming or denying.

'May I also guess that because of my—indiscretion the other night, you've decided not to see me again?' He didn't let her reply. 'You didn't make any allowances for the possibility that I might have had the right to lose my temper because you walked out without even having the courtesy to leave a message that you were leaving? I probably should have turned you over my knee, but the other seemed more appropriate at the time.'

There was some validity to his argument, but Sabrina was not going to allow herself to be swayed. 'It's done. There isn't any point in discussing it.'

'Then that's your decision. You aren't going to see me again,' Bay stated with almost arrogant blandness. 'Those few moments of my anger wiped out all the memories of the hours, enjoyable hours I thought, that we spent together before. Is that right? They mean nothing to you?'

His challenge had to be answered. 'Yes, they did,' Sabrina admitted coldly, 'until they were tarnished by the discovery that you felt sorry for me. I told you once I don't need anyone's pity.'

'Who in their right mind would feel sorry for a pigheaded, spoiled brat like you?' he snapped. He drew a deep, calming breath. 'There are times, Sabrina, when you test a man's patience. How many times do I have to tell you that I don't feel sorry for you before you'll believe me?'

'Then explain to me why you see me,' she demanded defiantly.

'There has to be an ulterior motive, is that it?' Bay answered grimly. 'It can't be because I might—' he paused an instant, choosing his words '—admire you, your courage when you aren't being unreasonably stubborn. Let me put the question to you. Why do you go out with me? Am I a convenient means to get out of the house? Do you simply tolerate me because I take you places you want to go? What's your ulterior motive, Sabrina?'

'I . . . I have none,' she answered, taken aback by his counterattack.

'Come now. Surely you must,' he mocked derisively. 'You had to have a reason for going out with me.'

'No, I don't,' Sabrina insisted in helpless confusion. 'I simply enjoyed it. I had——'

Bay interrupted. 'Yet it's inconceivable that I might have simply enjoyed your company, too?'

'How could you?' she protested, seeking to regain the

140

offensive. 'I'm pigheaded and spoiled. You said so yourself.'

'So? I'm arrogant and a bully. You said so yourself.' He deflected her argument with mocking humor. 'That makes us equal with two flaws apiece.'

The corners of her mouth twitched in reluctant amusement. Her stand against him was weakening. She could feel the firm resolve crumbling under his persuasive charm and logic.

'You're smiling, aren't you, Sabrina?' he accused softly. 'Don't bother to answer,' Bay chuckled. 'I know you'll deny it. I won't ask you to cancel your well-laid plans for Saturday night but come sailing with me Sunday.'

'Sailing?' she echoed weakly. Of all the invitations Bay could have extended, her own love of the sport made this one she wanted least to refuse.

'Yes, sailing,' he repeated with amused patience.

'I——' Sabrina couldn't get the words of refusal to come out.

'I'll pick you up bright and early Sunday morning around seven. We'll spend the day.'

'I . . . I'll be ready.' Her words of acceptance stumbled over each other in their rush to get out before better judgment decreed that she change her mind.

'At seven Sunday a.m.,' Bay agreed, and hung up as if he had the same thought.

Sabrina didn't change her mind. She had a multitude of second thoughts, but none of them had lasted long enough to bring her to the point of canceling. Any thought that

141

her father might take the decision out of her hands had ended the same day Bay had called.

When she had told her father of Bay's invitation that evening, his reply had been: 'Yes, Bay called me this afternoon to be certain I had no objections. I don't, and I promise you I won't worry. You'll be in good hands. Besides, Bay can swim.'

Sunday morning, therefore, found Sabrina aboard his trim ketch *Dame Fortune*. Fog and dormant wind had delayed their departure for nearly an hour.

Now they were under sail, the stiff breeze ruffling the scarf tied around Sabrina's head, the salty taste of ocean spray on her lips. Passing under the rust-orange span of the Golden Gate Bridge, Bay had turned southward into the open sea, past Cliff House and Seal Rocks. He continued beyond the ocean beaches, the treacherous undertow in the area restricting their use to sunbathing and walking.

As always, Sabrina champed at the constricting life-vest tied around her even while she accepted the wisdom of the precaution whether for sighted or unsighted boaters. The deck was slanted sharply beneath her, heaving with each ocean swell, as Bay expertly took advantage of all the wind he could and still remain on course.

The billowing wind in the canvas, the ocean waves slapping the sleek hull, and the comfortable groans of a sailing ketch at sea were the only sounds around her. She had hardly exchanged five words with Bay since they had left the Yacht Harbor. Conversation wasn't necessary and would have been superfluous to the serene beauty of the moment. Each seemed to sense the other's deep pleasure and nothing needed to be said.

142

It was some time before Sabrina noticed there had been a change in their course. The sun was not in the place it normally would have been in their initial heading. Blocking out the song of sea and sail, she listened intently, trying to gauge by memory and sound their location and failing.

She turned to Bay. 'Where are we?'

'In the waters of Monterey Bay near Santa Cruz. Were you daydreaming?' he smiled with his voice.

Instantly she visualized his ruggedly forceful features, tanned by the sun and the wind, cinnamon brown hair dampened by the salt spray and tousled by the breeze. The sun was directly overhead. His light brown eyes would be narrowed against its brilliance, crinkled at the corners because of that flashing smile she had detected in his voice. It was disturbing how vividly clear her picture of him was, so vitally alive and masculine.

Her heart beat a rapid tattoo against her ribs. 'Daydreaming or sea-dreaming. I don't know which,' she murmured.

Again there was a change in the motion of the ketch. The wind was catching less canvas and their speed had decreased. The deck beneath her had begun to right itself.

'What are you doing now?' Sabrina asked.

'Taking her in close to shore. We just passed the natural bridges north of Santa Cruz. I thought we'd anchor south of Santa Cruz for lunch. There's a small quiet cove I know about that I hope no one else has discovered.'

Once anchored, with Sabrina giving what assistance she could, the only sound was the gentle lapping of the almost calm surf against the hull. She turned her head inquiringly

143

toward Bay and felt his gaze moving over her face. A fiery warmth started in her midsection. She was suddenly and intensely aware that they were alone, the two of them, a man and a woman. She put brakes to that thought sharply.

'I'll go below and fix lunch.' She pivoted abruptly away. 'What are we having?'

'Sandwiches, salad and the like. It's all fixed,' Bay answered. 'What about a swim before we eat? The water is warmer here than up the coast and there aren't any dangerous undercurrents.'

'Sorry,' Sabrina shrugged away his suggestion nervously. 'You didn't warn me to bring a swimming suit and I didn't.'

'That doesn't matter.' Bay dismissed her excuse. 'I always keep a few swimming clothes on board in case there's a spur-of-the-moment decision by one of my guests to take a dip in the ocean. I'm sure one of them will fit you.'

'But——' She hadn't been in any water other than her bathtub since before the accident.

'But what?' he prompted. 'You can swim, can't you?'

'Yes, I can swim,' she swallowed tightly.

'I'll point you in the right direction so you won't head out to sea if you're worrying about losing your reference points. Go and change.'

He told her which locker he kept the spare swimming suits and Sabrina went below. It was better to go swimming with the wide limits of the ocean and shore than remaining on the small deck alone with him.

144

Most of the swimsuits were two-piece outfits, some bare triangles of cloth. Sabrina chose the close-fitting knit of a one-piece with diamond cut-outs at the waist crisscrossed with ties. At least in it she felt less naked when she walked up on deck. Her long hair was let down and curling around her shoulders. The water would have pulled it free of its knot eventually, so she had done it first.

'I'm ready,' she said nervously.

Bay didn't comment on her appearance. 'I've put a rope ladder over the side.' He took her hand and led her to the rail. 'I'll go in the water first.'

When he released her hand after her silent nod of agreement, Sabrina tightened the hand into a fist to retain the warmth of his touch a while longer. It was a stupid thing to do. This was not a romantic outing but a friendly one—which was why the sensations she was feeling were troubling her.

The deck rocked slightly, followed by the sound of something slicing into the water, and Sabrina knew that Bay had not used the ladder but had dived into the water. A second later she heard him surface, turning her head in the direction of the sound. A few clean strokes brought him to the bottom of the ladder.

'Come on in. The water's fine,' he called to her.

While Bay held the ladder steady, Sabrina started down, her toes feeling for the rope rungs. In the water which was neither warm nor cold, Sabrina clung to the security of the ladder for a few minutes, adjusting to the eerie sensation of having nothing solid beneath her feet. The chattering of her teeth was from nerves and not the tepidly cool water.

'Are you ready?' Bay was still beside the ladder.

'I think so,' Sabrina answered, clenching her jaw so he wouldn't hear the clatter of her teeth.

He moved a few strokes from the ladder, then said, 'Swim toward my voice.'

Forcing her hand to release its death-grip on the rope, Sabrina took a deep breath and struck out toward him. At first she was hampered by nervousness and unco-ordination, but they soon faded as she became accustomed to watery environment. She could hear Bay's firm cleaving strokes keeping pace beside her and drew strength and assurance from his presence.

It seemed as if they had been swimming a long time. Sabrina had begun to get tired. Her reaching arms were beginning to feel heavy. She stopped to tread water and catch her breath, and Bay did the same.

'How much farther?' she asked as she swallowed down gulps of air.

'About another fifteen feet before we can touch bottom.' He sounded not at all out of breath. 'Can you make it?'

She didn't answer but started out again, maintaining a slow steady rhythm that would not wear her out too quickly. Surprisingly it didn't seem as if she had traveled any distance at all before a kicking foot scraped the sandy bottom. Sabrina righted herself quickly, wiping the salt water from her face and tucking her long wet hair behind her ears.

'You made it,' Bay spoke from somewhere near her left side. 'How do you feel?'

146

She smiled faintly. 'Exhausted, but good otherwise.'

'Let's go ashore and take a breather.'

Her hands were lightly resting on top of the almost chest-high water, letting the gentle swells roll over them. The waves would have told her which way the shore was if she had been in doubt, but Bay took her hand anyway and led her to the beach.

'This beach comes equipped with its own sunning rock,' he said as they waded on to the sandy ground, smooth and firm beneath her feet. 'It's a little hard, but it's better than the sand when you don't have a towel.' The pressure of his hand stopped her after they had gone a few yards. 'Here.'

Before Sabrina could protest, his hands were around her waist and he was lifting her on to the hard, warm surface of the stone. Her own fingers had automatically gripped the sinewy wetness of his arms for balance. Her flesh burned where his hands had covered the open diamond patches of the swimsuit waistline. It was several seconds before her racing heart settled to a more respectable pace. By then he was on the rock, too.

'Did you have a good time last night?' he asked after he had moved into a comfortable position. He was sitting. Sabrina could tell by the direction of his voice.

'Last night?' she frowned, and shifted more fully on to the rock. Then she remembered. 'Yes, I did.' Actually it had been a quiet evening. She and Sally had sat around and talked, listening to records part of the time.

'Where did you go?'

'Nowhere, Sally and I stayed at the house,' she

shrugged, turning her face to the warmth of the sun, letting it chase away the shivers on her damp skin.

'An evening of gossipy girl-talk, is that it?' There was a mocking smile in his tone.

Sabrina wasn't certain whether he was laughing at her uneventful evening or that she had chosen it over one with him. From what she knew of Bay, the first seemed more likely.

'Men gossip as much as if not more than women,' she replied.

He didn't argue the point. 'I suppose it's true of an equal number in each sex.'

An awkward silence followed. At least it was awkward for Sabrina. She was too aware of Bay, physically aware of him. She leaned back on her hands.

'The sun feels good,' she suggested.

'I think I'll stretch out and enjoy it,' Bay stated.

At the same time that he spoke, his movements were carrying out his words. And the silence that Sabrina had not wanted reigned, broken only by the slow rush of the ocean on to shore. There was little for her to do except to follow suit.

Her searching hands found a small, elevated hump in the rock behind her, a natural headrest, and Sabrina lay down on her back. For a long time she listened to the sound of Bay's even breathing. Her own was shallow, her chest muscles constricted with tension. Finally the heat of the sun and the rock coaxed her into relaxing.

Sabrina didn't fall asleep, but she did drift into that strange state of half-sleep. She was aware of her surroundings and the man beside her, yet deaf to them at the same time. Then something brought all of her senses alert. Her eyes blinked uselessly as she tried to determine what had disturbed her. She turned her head slightly in Bay's direction and accidently brushed his hand with her cheek. Then her sensitive nerve ends transmitted the message that he was holding a lock of her silky brown hair.

'Do you know this is the first time I've ever seen you wear your hair down?' he mused softly.

'I—I don't like to wear it down. It gets in the way.' There was an odd tremor in her voice as she guessed how close he was to her. She could almost feel the heat of his body stretched beside hers. His voice had come from a position slightly above her, indicating that he was possibly lying on his side, an elbow propping him up.

Bay didn't seem to pay any attention to her explanation.

'When you wear your hair up in that little topknot, you look poised and sophisticated, a well-bred young queen. With your hair down like this,' he twined the strand around his finger, 'there's a gamin vulnerability about you.'

A pulse was beating wildly in her temples. It was impossible to roll away from him. The edge of the rock was too near.

'Do you think we should be heading back?' Her throat was taut, making her voice likewise.

'What's the matter?' he mocked. 'Don't you like my comments on your hairstyle?'

'It doesn't matter.' Sabrina shook her head determinedly, loosing the lock of hair against her bare shoulder. 'I'm going to wear it up because it's the easiest to take care of, regardless of how you prefer it.' It was a challenging statement, but she didn't care.

Bay reached back and gave her hair a sharp tug. 'Then you'll probably be sorry to hear that I prefer that silky knot. The way it is now would be appropriate for the privacy of a bedroom.'

The sensual implication of his statement drew a sharp breath from Sabrina. Her heightened awareness of his masculinity made this type of conversation impossible. She wasn't capable of idle flirtation, this suggestive playing with words. She started to push herself back into a half-sitting position to escape his nearness, but Bay was already straightening to his feet.

'We'll head back,' he said as he towered above her.

Sabrina thankfully swung her legs to the edge of the rock. Bay was on the sand, his hands gripping her waist to lift her down before she could slide the short distance to the sand. Straining away from his unwanted assistance, her effort to keep from landing too close to him brought a heel down on a partially buried outcropping of the rock. The unexpected jarring pain sent her against his chest. His hold tightened to steady her.

'Are you all right?'

Her unspoken answer was negative. It couldn't be otherwise when the nakedness of his muscled torso and thighs pressed against her was playing havoc with her heart. Soft, curling chest hairs sensually tickled her palms. His head was inclined toward her, warm breath stirring a wing of her dark bangs.

150

The desire was strong to slide her arms around his broad shoulders and nestle her head against his neck. To resist the nearly overpowering impulse, she moistened her lips nervously and tipped her head back.

'I'm all right,' she assured him in a shaking voice. 'I stepped on a rock or something.'

A sudden breath of wind tossed a thin lock of hair across her face. It clung to the gleaming wetness of her lips. Sabrina started to push it away, but her hand was only part way there when Bay's fingers drew it gently away, pushing it back with the rest of her long hair.

His hand remained along the side of her face, his thumb absently caressing her cheekbone. She held her breath, motion suspended under the magical spell of his touch.

The heady warmth of his firm mouth was barely felt against hers before Sabrina sharply twisted her head away. Her defences couldn't endure a casual kiss.

'Don't, Bay, please!' she requested stiffly.

'I wasn't going to hurt you.' Her words brought a rigid stillness to his touch as he misinterpreted the reason for the shudders quivering through her.

'I simply don't want you to kiss me,' Sabrina stated, pulling free of his unresisting arms and taking several quick steps away until common sense warned her that she couldn't see where she was going.

She wrapped her arms tightly around her, trying to fight off the chill that shivered over her where the warmth of his body had been.

Bay walked over to stand beside her. She could feel his eyes boring into her. Her lashes fluttered downward in case her sightless eyes mirrored the heady sensations swimming in her mind. For an electric moment, she hardly dared to breathe.

'We'd better head back to the boat.' The savage bite of his words betrayed a tightly leashed anger. Sabrina couldn't tell if it was directed at himself or at her.

The hand that gripped hers and led her toward the water was cold and impersonal. Sabrina was glad when the water became deep enough to swim and he had to release her. She hadn't thought it possible that his touch, which usually started a fire, could chill her to the bone.

It was not a leisurely swim back. Sabrina set herself a pace that took every ounce of her strength to maintain. It was a form of self-punishment for being so foolish as to let Bay persuade her to come to this outing when wisdom had dictated that she stop seeing him.

She was completely spent when Bay reached out and pulled her to the rope ladder, but she climbed aboard without his assistance. She paused on deck to catch her breath.

'If we'd been anchored another ten feet away, you would never have made it. What were you trying to prove?' Bay snapped.

'Nothing.' Sabrina averted her head and self-consciously felt her way to the steps leading below deck.

'When you're dressed, you can get the lunch ready. I think you can find everything. In the meantime, I'll get us under way,' he ordered tersely.

'Don't you . . . Don't you want to eat first?' she faltered.

'I think we're both in a hurry to get back, aren't we?'

There was a derisive challenge in his voice that dared her to deny it. When she didn't reply, he added grimly, 'I'll enjoy the food as much as you once we're under sail.'

Actually Sabrina found the food tasteless. Most of it wanted to stick in her throat, but she forced as much of it down as she could. There was no atmosphere of friendliness on the return trip. Their mutual silence was brittle with tension.

Bay's acceptance of her polite words of thanks at the conclusion of the day was as cool and aloof as her offer had been. When the iron gate closed behind him, Sabrina knew why she was so totally miserable. She had plenty of time to ponder the reason on the way back. She had fallen in love with Bay Cameron. She was literally a blind fool.

CHAPTER NINE

BAY's last parting remark to her had been 'I'll call you.' In Sabrina's experience, those particular words had always signaled the end of a relationship. It was Friday night and he had not phoned.

Another tear slipped down her cheek. She wiped it away with her fingertips, leaving a streak of dark clay to smudge her face. Why couldn't her tearducts have been damaged as well as her eyesight? she wondered forlornly, then sighed. Perhaps it was better to have a way to release the pain.

There was a knock on the studio door. She had kept it closed this last week, not wanting anyone to pop in without at least the warning click of the doorknob. She had told her father it was because she wanted to block out any distractions. The truth was she could work in the middle of rush hour traffic. Lately, however, she had discovered herself simply standing and crying. It was this she didn't want her father or anyone else to see.

Sabrina took the hem of her smock and wiped her face carefully just in case there was a betraying tear she had missed. 'Come in,' she called in answer to the knock.

A cloud of perfume swirled into the room, a scent her mind labeled as Deborah's. The lightly graceful steps confirmed the identification.

'I came to remind you we would be leaving in an hour

so you would have plenty of time to clean up here and change clothes,' her future stepmother said brightly.

'I don't think I'll go,' Sabrina murmured, centering her attention on the partially completed clay bust on the work pedestal.

'Grant has been looking forward to the three of us dining out tonight,' Deborah reminded her.

'I know, but I'd rather keep working a while longer. I'm right in the middle of this piece. I want to keep going while the concept is still fresh in my mind,' she lied

'Are you sure?' came the slightly troubled question.

'I've just really grasped the form, and I don't want to lose it,' Sabrina assured her.

'I didn't mean about the work,' Deborah said hesitantly.

'What did you mean, then?' Her hand was poised along the half-formed ear of the bust. Was Deborah's womanly intuition at work?

'I . . . I wanted to be sure you weren't refusing because of me. I don't want you to think you would be the superfluous third tonight,' the attractive redhead explained self-consciously.

'No, Deborah, it wasn't because of you.' Sabrina expelled a silent sigh of relief. 'We'll go out another night. I probably shouldn't have started this so late, but now that I have, I must work a little longer.'

'I understand. I know how important this is to you. And don't worry, Sabrina.' There was the warmth of a smile in her voice. 'I'll explain to Grant.'

'What were you going to explain to me?'

'Grant!' Deborah exclaimed in a startled voice. 'You shouldn't sneak up on a person like that.'

'I didn't sneak. You simply didn't hear me.' There was the faint sound of a kiss exchanged. 'Now, I repeat, what are you going to explain to me?'

Sabrina answered for Deborah. 'I've decided to stay and work tonight instead of going out to dinner with you two.'

'The two of us were going out to dinner with you, not the other way round,' her father frowned.

'Then we'll go out another night,' she shrugged, determined not to let him change her mind.

'No, we'll go out tonight.'

'Grant!' Deborah interjected a silent plea into his name.

'Dammit, she's working too hard, Deborah,' he declared forcefully. 'Look at the dark circles under her eyes and the hollows in her cheeks. She doesn't sleep. She doesn't eat. All she does is work from dawn to dusk, or more aptly midnight.'

'Dad, you're exaggerating,' Sabrina sighed. 'Besides, my work is important to me.' It was the only thing that kept her sanity. Without it, the emptiness of a life without Bay would be more than she could stand. 'I promise as soon as I can leave this piece I'm doing I'll fix myself something to eat and go straight to bed. How's that?'

'I think that's a fair bargain, don't you, Grant?' Deborah murmured.

'I——' He took a deep, angry breath, but arguing with the two women he loved was not something he enjoyed. He sighed heavily. 'All right,' he surrendered. 'You can

156

stay home this time. But next week we're all going out together, with no excuses. Now, why don't you let me have a peep at this work of art that is too important to leave?'

Sabrina stepped to the side as he walked closer. 'I only have it roughed in right now. I'm doing the head and shoulders of Gino Marchetti as he was in his youth. Over a year ago, he showed me a picture taken at his wedding. I had intended to do a painting, but——' She left that unfinished for obvious reasons. 'He looked very Roman, very proud and very strong.'

'Gino, the druggist?' Grant Lane repeated with a hint of disbelief.

'It's only rough,' Sabrina defended.

There was a moment of silence as he studied the partially completed head of the bust. Then he turned suddenly, 'Deborah, who does it look like to you?'

'Well——' Her hesitation was pronounced. 'I don't know Gino very well.'

'I've known him for years. I'm sorry to be the one to tell you, Sabrina, but that doesn't look like him at all, not even when he was younger,' he said emphatically.

'When it's finished——' Sabrina began.

'It will look exactly like Bay Cameron,' her father finished the sentence for her.

'You must be mistaken,' she responded evenly, but she clenched her hands tightly together until they hurt, punishing them for having betrayed her. 'It doesn't look at all like Bay, does it, Deborah?'

157

'It does bear a slight resemblance to him,' the other woman admitted reluctantly, 'but as you said, it isn't finished.'

'The man has an interesting face. If you could see it, Sabrina, I know you would have had the urge to put it on canvas. But nevertheless, I'm not going to argue with you. You're the artist not me. If you say it's Gino, it's Gino. I suppose there's Roman characteristics in both of them.' He put his arm around her shoulders and gave her a reassuring hug. 'Now if you two ladies will excuse me, I came up here to shower and change.'

After bestowing a light kiss on Sabrina's cheek, he left the room. Sabrina stared sightlessly at the mound of clay on the work pedestal, her heart crying with pain. For a moment she had forgotten Deborah was still in the room, until the faint click of a heel reminded her.

'Sabrina, about Bay——' The gentle voice paused.

'What about Bay?' Sabrina challenged, her tone cold and aloof.

'You aren't becoming . . . too involved with him, are you?' Deborah faltered as if sensing she was trespassing on private territory. 'I mean, I admire him very much, but I don't think you should——'

'——take his attentions too seriously,' Sabrina finished for her. 'I'm well aware that he only sees me to be kind.' She couldn't bring herself to use the word pity.

'I'm glad.' There was a faint sigh of relief in the redhead's statement. 'I'm sure he likes you, Sabrina. I just don't think it would be wise if you became too fond of

158

him. After all you've been through, it wouldn't be fair.'

'I am fond of him,' she asserted. 'He helped me a great deal. Bay was even the one to suggest that I try working in clay.' Silently she admitted that it wasn't a fair trade to give away her heart for a career, but when was anything connected with love classified as fair? 'But don't worry, Deborah. I haven't misinterpreted his motives.'

'You always seem to have your feet on the ground,' was the faintly envious response.

Only this time my head was in the clouds, Sabrina thought to herself. She mumbled an absent reply when Deborah said she would leave Sabrina to her work.

As the studio door closed behind her father's redhaired fiancée, Sabrina's hands reached tentatively toward the bust, lightly exploring the roughed-in features, confirming for herself that indeed it was Bay. A cold anger pervaded her body.

Destroy it! Smash it! her mind ordered. Turn it back into an ordinary lump of clay!

Her hands rested on either side of the face, but they couldn't carry out the order. One tear fell, then another. Finally silent sobs racked her slender form, her shoulders hunching forward at the excruciating pain in her chest.

But her hands didn't remain immobile. Shakily they began working, painstakingly defining each detail of his face in the molding clay. It was a labor of love, and what pieces of her heart she hadn't given to Bay went into the soft clay.

Later, Sabrina wasn't conscious of how much time had

159

passed, her father knocked once on the door and opened it. She didn't have time to wipe the river of tears from her face, so she kept her back to the door.

'We're leaving now,' he told her. 'Don't forget your promise. Eat and straight to bed.'

'Yes, Dad,' she answered tightly. 'Have a good time.'

The interruption checked the onslaught of tears. She suddenly realized how drained she was, emotionally and physically. When the front door leading to the stairwell to the street closed, signaling the departure of her father and Deborah, Sabrina sank on to the work stool. She tiredly buried her face in her hands, not wanting to move or expend the energy to breathe.

A pounding began. For an instant she thought it was coming from inside her head. Then she realized it was coming from the stairwell door downstairs. She grimaced wryly as she rubbed her cheeks dry.

'Dad must have forgotten his key,' she muttered aloud, and slipped off the stool.

Her legs refused to be hurried as she made her way out of the studio and down the stairs to the second floor. The knocking continued, more demanding than before.

'I'm coming!' Irritation raised her voice and the sound stopped.

The muscles at the back of her neck had become knotted with tension and she rubbed them wearily as she turned the automatic lock and opened the door.

'What's the matter? Did you forget your key?' She tried to make her voice sound light and teasing, but it was a hollow attempt. Her greeting was met with silence.

Sabrina tilted her head to the side in a listening attitude. 'Dad?'

'Did you know there's a smudge of clay on your cheek?'

Sabrina recoiled instinctively from the sound of Bay's voice. Her hand moved to shut the door, but he blocked it effectively and stepped into the room.

'How did you get up here? What do you want?' she demanded angrily.

'I met your father and Deborah on their way out. He let me in,' he explained calmly.

'Why?' She pivoted away, unable to face him, a hand nervously wiping the clay from her cheek.

'Why did he let me in?' Bay questioned. 'He said something about you working too hard.'

'Well, I'm not!' she said emphatically. 'And I meant why did you come?'

'To ask you to have dinner with me.'

'No.' Sabrina tipped her head back, her lashes fluttering down in a silent prayer to be left alone.

'I won't accept that,' he stated. 'You have to eat, and it might as well be with me as alone.'

'You'll have to accept it, because I'm busy. It doesn't bother me in the least to eat alone.' A solitary meal was something she had better get used to, she told herself.

'Sabrina, stop being stubborn,' Bay admonished calmly. 'There's no need to change clothes. Just take off your smock and go as you are. We'll eat and I'll bring you directly back here to finish your work, if it's essential it be done tonight.'

'I'm not going to be talked into going,' she warned.

161

With a fluid step, Bay reached out and untied the sash of her smock. Quickly she tried to tie the bow again, but his fingers closed over her wrist to prevent it.

'You are not going to bully me this time, Bay Cameron,' Sabrina muttered, straining to free her wrist from his grasp.

He held it easily. 'It's going to be a long night, because I'm not leaving here until you agree.'

It was not an idle threat. He was just arrogant enough to carry it out. The fire spreading through her arm was a second threat, a threat that she might not be able to hide her feelings or hold her tongue if she tried to outwait him.

Sabrina closed her mouth tightly for a moment. 'If I agree to this blackmail of yours, do I have your word that from now on you will accept my decisions about going with you as final?'

Her request was met by guarded silence for long seconds. 'You have my word, if,' there was an edge of fine steel in his voice, '*if* you will agree that we will discuss the reason for your sudden animosity.'

'I don't know what you're talking about,' she said coolly. Her heart started pounding frantically.

'Your word, Sabrina,' Bay ignored her denial.

The sigh she released was a well disguised checked sob. 'All right, you have it. Now let go of me.' Her wrist was freed. She rubbed the tender area unconsciously. 'But I still don't know what you're talking about,' she lied.

Her attitude toward him had changed, but not for anything did she want him to discover why. Pity because she was blind was one thing, but pity because she loved him was something she refused to tolerate.

162

'We'll see,' Bay murmured quietly.

How she hated his air of confidence! Sabrina flung her smock in the general direction of a chair and stalked to the umbrella stand to get her cane, the ivory cane that Bay had given her.

'Let's go, so we can get this over with,' she declared.

'Aren't you forgetting your bag?' he mocked. 'You might need your key to get back in unless—you plan to spend the night with me.'

'Perish the thought!' Sabrina spat.

But the thought was pure torture stabbing into her heart as she hurried up the stairs to her room. It hurt that Bay could joke about making love to her, especially when it was something that she wanted so very much.

Downstairs with her purse in hand, she brushed past him through the door, ignoring his mocking, 'Are you ready now?'

Her continued silence in the car was for her own protection, not a desire to be rude. She couldn't begin to guess Bay's reasons for not speaking. He was an enigma. She didn't understand why he did anything he did. For instance, why did he want her company when she had made it obvious that she didn't want his?

Poignantly Sabrina realized that this was probably the last time she would be with Bay, if he kept his word. It was really impossible and impractical to keep going out with him when she knew the truth of her feelings. It would only bring more pain.

She knew he hoped to change her mind and persuade her to continue their relationship. He had succeeded the last time when she hadn't been aware of her love.

Naturally he was sure that he could do it again—why, she didn't know. She had to guard against his charm. She mustn't prolong the time when they separated.

Her thoughts were centered on the man behind the wheel. Nothing else around her penetrated her consciousness. She couldn't hear the traffic. Up or down a San Francisco street, it didn't matter. She could not care less where he was taking her, although at some future time she would probably think of the restaurant with pain.

'Sabrina.'

The faint command for her attention drew her out of the sheltering cocoon of her misery. She sat up straighter, realizing with a start that they had stopped. The engine had been turned off. Pink heightened her cheekbones, but she knew the dimness of the car concealed it.

'Are we here?' She tipped her head to a haughty angle.

'Yes,' Bay answered.

Her fingers closed tightly around her cane while she waited for Bay to walk around the car to open her door. The serpent heads carved into the ivory handle left an imprint in her fingers. Since she didn't know where she was going, she had to accept the guidance of his hand at her elbow. Several paces farther, he opened a door and ushered her into a building.

Footsteps immediately approached them and a woman's voice greeted them in pleasant surprise. 'You're here already, sir. Let me take your coat.'

Bay shrugged out of a light topcoat. 'Yes, it didn't take me as long as I thought, Mrs. Gibbs. Mrs. Gibbs, I'd like you to meet Sabrina Lane. Sabrina, this is Mrs. Gibbs.'

164

'How do you do, Mrs. Gibbs,' Sabrina greeted the woman warily, her ears straining to hear the sounds familiar to a restaurant.

'I'm pleased to meet you, Miss Lane.' Then the footsteps retreated.

'What kind of a restaurant is this?' Sabrina whispered, not certain if anyone could overhear.

'It's not a restaurant.' His hand was at her elbow again, leading her forward.

'But——' Sabrina frowned.

'This is my home, Sabrina,' Bay stated calmly.

She stopped abruptly. 'You said you were taking me out to eat,' she accused.

'But I never said to a restaurant.' He released her elbow and curved his arm around the back of her waist, propelling her forward. 'And you never asked.'

Sabrina twisted away from his arm. 'You've tricked me for the last time, Bay Cameron.' Her voice trembled with emotion. 'You can just turn around and take me home right now.'

'I gave Mrs. Gibbs a list of your favorite things. She's gone to a great deal of trouble to cook a meal you'll like. She'll be very disappointed if you don't stay.'

'You were never concerned about my feelings,' she reminded him sharply. 'Why should I worry about hurting hers?'

'Because essentially you're a gentle and sensitive woman and because,' his low voice became ominously soft, 'you gave me your word.'

'And I'm supposed to honor it even when you don't

keep yours.' Sabrina swallowed back a helpless sob of frustration.

'I've never lied to you.'

'No, you've only tricked, maneuvered and bullied me into doing what you want, but after all, you are Bay Cameron. You can make up your own code of ethics, can't you?' she snapped sarcastically.

'Shall we go into the living room?' A fine thread of cold steel ran through his voice and Sabrina knew her barbs had pricked.

Paradoxically she felt remorse and satisfaction at hurting him. She loved him desperately, but she hated him, too, for seeing her only as an unfortunate blind girl and not as a woman with physical and emotional needs. She didn't oppose the arm that firmly guided her forward. They turned at right angles and his steps slowed.

'Why did you bring me here, Bay?' Sabrina challenged coldly.

'We couldn't spend the evening in the hallway,' he answered, deliberately misunderstanding her question.

'You know very well I was referring to your home,' she accused.

'It offered privacy for the talk we're going to have.'

'Privacy could be obtained in your car, or for that matter at my house,' Sabrina reminded him.

'They wouldn't do. In a car, you could lose your temper and possibly jump out the door before I could stop you and be run down by some passing motorist,' Bay explained logically. 'Your home wouldn't work either. You know it better than the back of your hand. As stubborn as you can be sometimes, I would probably have found myself talking to the door of some room you'd locked yourself into. Here, in my home, you don't know which way to move without running the risk of falling over furniture or banging into a wall.'

'And you wonder why I've suddenly begun to dislike you!' Sabrina protested, spinning away, but unable to move with any swiftness.

He had laid the trap too cleverly. The end of her cane raced out to search for any obstacles in front of her and banged against a solid object.

'The sofa is directly in front of you. There's a chair to your right,' he said. 'Take one step backward and turn to your right and you'll avoid the chair.'

'What's in the way after that?' she asked caustically.

'Why don't you see for yourself?'

Slowly Sabrina followed his instructions, putting distance between them as she crossed an empty space with the aid of her cane. Finally the ivory white tip touched what appeared to be a table leg. She carefully sidestepped around it only to find the table had been sitting against a wall. Or at least, it was something solid, maybe a door. Sabrina reached out with her hand to investigate, and sheer filmy curtains met her fingers.

'The window overlooks San Francisco Bay.' His voice came from the center of the room. 'There's an unobstructed view of the Golden Gate and the Harbor.'

Sabrina didn't know what she had hoped to discover, a way out, possibly. Frustrated, she turned away from the window and partially retraced her steps, stopping before she came too near the area she guessed that he would be.

'Bay, take me home, please,' she asked softly.

'Not yet.'

The carpet was soft and thick beneath her feet. She wondered at its color, the type of furnishing that surrounded her. There was a desire to explore this place where he lived and slept. She shook her head firmly. She mustn't think about that.

'If you don't take me home, I'll just call a cab.' She raised her chin defiantly.

'Where's the telephone, Sabrina? Do you know?' mocked Bay. Averting her face from the watchfulness of his eyes, she released a frantic, sobbing sigh. 'What's troubling you, Sabrina?'

'You're virtually holding me prisoner in this house and you have the nerve to ask why I'm upset!' she cried angrily.

'There's more to it than that and I mean to find out what it is.'

His voice was moving closer, the plushness of the carpet muffling his steps. Sabrina turned to face him, trying to use her sensitive radar to pinpoint his location.

'Maybe I'm tired of being treated like a child,' she suggested icily.

'Then stop acting like one!' Bay snapped.

With a start, she discovered he was closer than she had realized. His hands touched her shoulders, but before his fingers could dig into her flesh, she shied quickly away.

'For God's sake, Sabrina, why are you afraid of me?' he demanded. 'Every time I come near you now you tremble like a frightened rabbit. You've been like this ever since Pamela's party. Is that what upset you? Why you're afraid to let me near you?'

Her breathing was shallow and uneven. 'It didn't inspire me to trust you.' Sabrina lashed back, unable to explain that it had precipitated the discovery that she was in love with him.

'I was angry. I never meant to frighten you,' Bay said forcefully. This time his hands closed over her shoulders before she could elude them. His touch was firm but not bruising.

'Isn't it a little late to be regretting it now?' She lowered her chin so he couldn't see into her face as she made the sarcastic retort. 'We can't be friends, Bay, not any more.'

'Then I'll undo the damage,' came his low, clipped response.

He pulled her toward him. Her hands automatically pushed against the solidness of his chest. It was the last resistance Sabrina offered as his mouth closed over hers. It took all of her strength and will to keep from responding to the persuasive mastery of his kiss. At all costs she had to prevent him from discovering the effect he had on her. He mustn't know the fiery leap of desire in her loins that nearly made her limp in his arms.

The kiss seemed to go on for ever. Sabrina didn't know how much longer she could hold back the raging fire Bay had started. Before the shuddering sigh of surrender escaped, he dragged his mouth from her throbbing lips.

'Sabrina.' The husky, whispering tautness of his caressing voice was very nearly the final blow.

169

Her heart had a stranglehold on her throat, but she forced the words of rejection through. 'Now, will you let me go?' she demanded in a strained voice.

'What is it, Sabrina?' he asked guardedly. 'My kiss doesn't frighten you, nor my touch. I don't think you're frightened of anything, but there's something wrong, some explanation why you don't want to continue to see me.'

She stood silently for a minute, realizing he was not going to free her immediately. Sabrina took a deep breath and tossed back her head. She was about to make the biggest bluff in her life and the most important.

'Do you want the truth, Bay?' she challenged boldly. 'Well, the truth is that when you first met me I was lost and lonely. I was nothing and my destination was nowhere. You pushed me out of my shell and gave me companionship. More important, you gave me back a chance for a career in a field I love more than anything else in the world. I'll always be eternally grateful to you for that.'

She paused for an instant, feeling his stillness. 'I wish you hadn't forced me to say this, Bay. I don't mean to be unkind, but I'm not lost or lonely any more. I have my career and a goal, and that's all I ever wanted in life. I've enjoyed the times we spent together. But you tend to dominate and the only thing I want to dominate my life is my work. To sum it all up in one sentence, I simply don't need you any more.'

'I see.' His hands fell away from her shoulders as he stepped away. His voice was cuttingly grim. 'I don't think you could have put it more clearly.'

'It was never my intention, consciously or unconsciously, to use you, I hope you'll believe that,' Sabrina explained. 'About two weeks ago I realized that I wanted to devote all of my time to my work, but I didn't know how to tell you that without sounding ungrateful for all you'd done. All you were asking in return was a casual friendship, and I was too selfish to even want to give you that. So I tried to pick a fight with you, thinking that if you became angry, you might be the one to break it off. I'm sorry, Bay.'

A tear slipped from her lashes at the magnitude of her lie. Nothing was further from the truth, but his silence told her that he believed her.

'Would you mind taking me home, Bay?' she requested, her voice choked with pain.

'I don't think either one of us has much of an appetite,' he agreed bitterly. 'It really isn't very surprising.'

An impersonal hand took her elbow. Not another word was spoken. Bay made no comment on the tears that ran freely down her cheeks. He didn't even tell her goodbye when he saw her to the door, but his sardonic 'good luck' echoed in Sabrina's ears all the way to her room where she sprawled on to the bed and cried.

CHAPTER TEN

'SABRINA! Would you come downstairs a minute?' Grant Lane called from the base of the stairs.

She sighed heavily. 'Can't it wait?'

'No, it's important,' was the answer.

Reluctantly Sabrina covered the lump of clay just beginning to take shape. If she had persisted, she probably could have persuaded her father to postpone whatever it was that was so important, but she was simply too tired to argue. In the last two weeks, she had worked hard and slept little.

'I'll be right down,' she said as she forced her legs to carry out her statement. 'What did you want, Dad?' Halfway down the stairs, she felt a prickling along the back of her neck. For a few steps, she blamed the sensation on strain and tired nerves. She stopped abruptly on the last step, her head jerking towards the stairwell door.

'Hello, Sabrina. I apologize for interrupting your work.' The sardonic derision in Bay's tone cut her to the quick.

Blanching slightly, Sabrina dropped her chin, taking the last step and shoving her trembling hands in her pocket. 'What a surprise, Bay,' her own voice sounded anything but delighted. 'What brings you here?'

'Bay stopped to——' her father began to explain.

'You might call it my last good deed,' Bay interrupted blandly. 'I want you to meet Howell Fletcher, Sabrina.'

'This is the young lady you've been telling me about?' a

cultured, masculine voice said, stepping forward to greet her. 'Miss Lane, I hope this is a pleasure, for both of us.'

Bewildered, Sabrina offered her hand. It was gripped lightly by smooth fingers and released. 'I'm sorry, I don't think I understand,' she apologized.

'Howell is here to see your work and give his considered opinion on your talent and potential,' Bay explained. The total lack of warmth in his voice almost made him seem like a stranger. There was none of the gentle mockery or friendliness she was accustomed to hearing.

'I don't think——' Sabrina started to protest stiffly that she didn't believe she was ready to have her work criticized by a professional.

'You might as well find out now whether or not you're wasting your time or building false hopes,' the man identified as Howell Fletcher stated.

'Good deed'—that was what Bay had said his motive was. Sabrina couldn't help wondering if he wasn't wishing she would fall flat on her face.

'I keep all my work in the studio upstairs.' Her chin lifted proudly. 'Are you coming, Bay?'

'No, I won't be staying.' The outcome apparently mattered little to him as he took his leave of her father and Howell Fletcher. Sabrina he ignored.

Robotlike, Sabrina led Howell Fletcher to the studio. The man spoke not one word while he slowly studied each piece, but she didn't mind. Strangely she didn't care what his opinion was. There was only one man who mattered, and Bay had walked in and out before her broken heart could start beating again.

173

Her work was a way of filling the empty, lonely hours, providing a challenge and a reason to get up each morning. Some day, she hoped her labors would allow her to be independent of her father. She wanted him to marry Deborah and be happy. It was only right that one of them should have the person they loved. She would never have Bay.

'How much of this work have you done since you became blind, Miss Lane?' the man asked thoughtfully.

'In clay? All of it,' she answered absently. 'The paintings were done before my accident.'

'I understood that you've only known Mr. Cameron for a few months,' he commented.

'Yes, that's right.' Sabrina wearily rubbed the back of her neck.

'How did you manage to do this bust?'

A wry smile curved her mouth. 'A blind person sees with their hands, Mr. Fletcher.'

'You haven't asked what I think yet. Aren't you curious, Miss Lane?'

'It's always been my experience that criticism comes without asking and compliments come without,' she shrugged dryly.

'You have a remarkable amount of wisdom,' he commented.

'Not in all things.' Not in loving wisely.

Then Howell Fletcher began to talk, more correctly to criticize. He didn't temper his words but sliced them into her, uncaring that it was her future he was cutting away. He dissected each piece. Every flaw, no matter how minute, was called to her attention. Each object was pushed into her hands so she could examine it for herself.

On and on the cultured voice droned until Sabrina wanted to cry out for him to stop. The weight of failure began to hunch her shoulders, trying to ward off the final, crushing blow. Her face, already haunted by the torture of unrequited love, became bleaker. Pride kept her chin up as the last piece was disposed of with the same analytical surgery as the others. A heavy silence followed his statement.

'Well,' Sabrina breathed in deeply, 'I never realized I was such an incompetent amateur.'

'My God, child,' the critic laughed, 'you're not incompetent nor an amateur. Some of the pieces are clumsy, the inanimate ones that need work on the flow of their line. But the others are stunning. The pride and power that you've stamped in Bay's face is unbelievable. The pathos of the madonna-like figure is touching in the extreme. Like your paintings, your talent lies in people. You bring them to life, heighten the qualities that attract people.'

'Then,' she couldn't believe she was hearing him correctly, 'you think I should keep working?'

'If you can keep up this pace and this standard, I can promise you a showing within six months,' Howell Fletcher declared.

'You must be joking,' Sabrina breathed.

'My dear, I never joke about money. And if you'll pardon me saying so, your blindness is going to attract a great deal of beautiful publicity. What we will do is combine a display of your very best paintings with the very best clay models and start out with an invitation-only showing for all the "right" people——' The plans continued to spew forth long after the shock of his announcement wore off.

'You aren't saying this because of Bay, are you?' Sabrina interrupted, suddenly afraid that Bay had exerted his influence to arrange this.

'Are you asking me if I was bribed to tell you this?' he demanded, sounding indignantly affronted. She nodded hesitantly. 'Bay Cameron did apply pressure to bring me here today, but I would never risk my reputation for anyone! If you had neither talent nor potential, I would have told you so in no uncertain terms.'

Sabrina believed him. The victory cup of success was within her grasp. She let the man issue forth his plans, knowing that the nectar from the cup did not taste sweet because she couldn't share it with the man she loved. The triumph was as hollow as she was.

A private show within six months, Howell Fletcher had declared. After careful consideration, he had pushed the date ahead to the first week of December, timing it for the holiday season and loosened purse strings. Sabrina had silently realized that his appreciation of art went hand in hand with his appreciation of money.

'I think you've done it, Sabrina,' her father murmured so he couldn't be overheard by the people milling about. 'All I've heard is one compliment after another.'

Sabrina smiled faintly, not at his words of success but at

the deep pride in his voice. She could imagine the beaming smile on his face.

'Words of praise are cheap, Mr. Lane,' Howell Fletcher put in from the other side of Sabrina, but there was triumph in his tone. 'You're a success, my dear Sabrina, because our guests are putting their money where their mouth is, to put it crudely.'

'Thanks to you, Howell,' she said softly.

'Always the diplomat,' he chided. 'It took both of our talents, as you very well know. Now, I must circulate. You stay here and look beautiful.'

'Sabrina.' A warm, female voice called her name, followed by the floral scent of violets. 'It's me, Pamela Thyssen. You were at my home some months ago.'

'Of course, Mrs. Thyssen, I remember you very well.' Sabrina extended her hand and had it clasped by beringed fingers. 'How are you?'

'A little upset, if you must know,' the woman scolded mockingly. 'It was dreadful of you not to volunteer any information about your remarkable talent. And wait until I get my hands on Bay. I'll teach that godson of mine a lesson or two for keeping me in the dark.'

'At the time, there wasn't anything to tell.' She swallowed nervously. Every time his name was mentioned her heart started skipping beats and an icy cold hand would close around her throat.

'I should think Bay would be here tonight, helping you to celebrate your success. Surely he could have cut short his sailing trip to Baja for an occasion like this,' Pamela stated.

177

'Oh, is that where he is?' Sabrina tried to sound unconcerned. 'I haven't seen him lately. I've been so busy getting ready for this show and all.'

Pamela Thyssen obviously wasn't aware that she and Bay had parted company several months ago. Sabrina didn't intend to enlighten her either.

'The bust you did of him is positively stealing the show. Everyone is talking about how remarkable the likeness is,' the woman observed in a faintly curious tone. 'Howell must have realized how successful it would be, judging by the price he put on it.'

'I'm merely the artist,' Sabrina shrugged to indicate that she had nothing to do with the price of the items.

She had not wanted to exhibit the bust at all, but Howell had been adamant in his arguments, insisting that she could not allow sentiment to color her judgment. When she had finally given in, it was with the proviso that the bust would not be for sale.

That was when she learned that Howell Fletcher's shrewdness was not limited to money and art. He had asked if she wanted to raise speculation as to why it wasn't for sale. It would be better, he suggested, to put an exorbitant price tag on it, too high for anyone to purchase it. Sabrina had finally agreed.

'What was Bay's reaction when he saw the model you did of him?' Pamela inquired.

One of the other guests chose that moment to offer his congratulations and comments and Sabrina was able to ignore the question. A few others stopped after that. Eventually Pamela was sidetracked by someone she knew and Sabrina was able to escape the question completely.

'It's stunning, Miss Lane,' a woman gushed. 'Absolutely stunning. . The paintings, the statues, they're all so breathtakingly real.'

'Thank you,' Sabrina nodded politely, not knowing how to counter the effusiveness of the woman's praise.

'Excuse me, Mrs. Hamilton, but I must steal Sabrina away from you for a moment,' Howell Fletcher broke in, a smooth hand tucking itself under Sabrina's elbow.

Sabrina offered her apologies to the woman and gratefully allowed Howell to guide her away. The ivory cane tapped its way in front of her. She had learned that Howell often forgot she was blind and let her run into things.

'Who are you spiriting me off to see this time?' she asked, wiping a damp palm on the skirt of her black dress.

'I don't know how to tell you this exactly, Sabrina.' Apprehension echoed in his cautious statement. 'We have a buyer for the bust, and he wants to see you.'

'A buyer?' She stiffened. 'You know it's not for sale.'

'I tried to explain that you were very reluctant to part with it, that its real worth was something less than the price. I couldn't very well tell him how much less for fear the information would get around and the other prices would be questioned,' he replied defensively.

'I shouldn't have been persuaded to display it in the first place. You guessed how I felt about it,' she accused.

'Yes, I did,' he agreed quietly. 'Perhaps you can appeal to his better nature and persuade him to choose something else. He's waiting in my office. It will afford some privacy for the discussion.'

'I'm not going to sell it,' Sabrina stated emphatically as they left behind most of the guests to enter a back hall. 'I don't care what the repercussions are.'

Howell didn't comment, slowing her down and turning her slightly as he reached around to open the door. She walked into the room with a determined lift of her chin. There was a quietly murmured 'good luck' from Howell and he closed the door. She turned back, startled, expecting to have his support.

Then she heard someone rise to his feet. She had been in the office many times and knew the potential buyer had been sitting on the Victorian sofa against the left wall. Fixing a bright smile on her face, she stepped toward the sound.

'How do you do,' Sabrina extended a hand in greeting. 'I'm Sabrina Lane. Howell told me you were interested in purchasing a particularly favorite piece of mine.'

'That's right, Sabrina.'

The voice went through her like a bolt of lightning. Her hand fell to her side as she fought to remain composed. The floor seemed to roll madly beneath her feet, but it was only her shaking knees.

'Bay—Bay Cameron,' she identified him with a breathless catch in the forced gaiety of her voice. 'What a coincidence! Pamela Thyssen was just telling me a few moments ago that you were on a sailing trip somewhere around Baja, California. It must be difficult to be in two places at once.'

Howell, that traitor, why hadn't he warned her that it was Bay who was waiting for her? No wonder he had sneaked away, leaving her alone!

'It was a natural mistake for Pamela to make. I hadn't planned to return for some time,' he replied in that impersonal tone that made her feel cold. 'Tonight you've achieved the success you wanted. How does it feel?'

Miserable, her heart answered. 'Splendid,' her voice lied.

'You're looking very chic and sophisticated in your dress of mourning black. The single strand of pearls around your long neck is a nice simple touch. The two make your complexion pale and hauntingly beautiful as if you've suffered great tragedy and risen above it. The press must be having a field day with your story,' Bay commented cynically.

She longed to tell him that her tragedy had been in losing him and not her sight, but she kept silent, trying not to hear the sarcasm underlining his voice.

'I would have thought by now you would have discarded the cane in favor of another.' The reference to the ivory carved handle in her hands made her grasp it more tightly as if afraid he would try to take it back.

'Why should I? It serves its purpose,' she shrugged nervously.

'I wasn't going to accuse you of attaching any sentimental importance to it,' Bay responded dryly. 'Although when I saw the bust you did of me, I was curious to find out if you look back on our association with fondness.'

'Naturally.' Her voice vibrated with the depth of her fondness. 'Besides, I told you once before that I liked your face. The features are strong and proud.'

'Howell did tell you that I'm going to buy it, didn't he?'

'Yes, but I never realized you were an egotist, Bay.' Her laughter was brittle. 'Imagine buying an image of yourself!'

'It will be an excellent reminder for the future.'

'Bay, I——' Sabrina pivoted slightly to the side, feeling the play of his eyes over her profile, cold and chilling. 'Th-there's been a mistake. Howell came to get me because . . . well, because it isn't for sale.'

'Why not?' He didn't sound upset by her stammering announcement. 'I thought the purpose of this show was to sell what was on display.'

'It is, but not this piece,' she protested. 'That's why we put the price so high, so no one would buy it.'

'I'm buying it,' Bay answered evenly.

'No! I'm not letting you have it!' She lashed out sharply in desperation. 'You've taken everything else from me. Please let me keep this!'

'Taken from you!' he laughed harshly. His hand snaked out to wrap his fingers around her wrist. 'What have I ever taken from you? Aren't you forgetting that I'm the one who was used? Why not take my money? You've taken everything else of value I had to give!'

'Pity? Sympathy? Charity?' The end of her cane tapped the floor sharply in punctuation to her angry words. 'When were those humiliating things ever of value? And to whom? Certainly not to me! You never cared about me! Not really! I was only a charity case to you!'

'You don't still believe I felt sorry for you?' A weary sigh came from deep within.

182

'You certainly don't love me,' Sabrina sniffed.

'And if I had,' his hand closed firmly on the back of her neck, turning her stiffly composed face toward him, 'would it have made any difference?'

If only he hadn't touched her, Sabrina thought, a fiery trail racing down her spine, maybe she could have withstood the agony tearing at her heart. Now she felt herself go limp inside, pride unable to support her, and she swayed against his chest.

'If you'd loved me just a little, Bay,' she sighed wistfully, inhaling the spicy fragrance clinging to his jacket, 'I might not have minded loving you so desperately. But what girl wants to be with a man who only pities her because she can't see?'

'You are blind, Sabrina,' he said. A great weight seemed to leave his voice. The hand slipped from her neck to the back of her waist while the other hand gently stroked her cheek. 'I never pitied you. I was too busy falling in love with you to waste time with that emotion.'

'Oh, Bay, don't tease me,' she cried in anguish, twisting free from his tender embrace. 'Haven't I shamed myself enough without having you make fun of me?'

'I'm not teasing. Believe me, the hell I've been going through these last months hasn't been funny at all,' Bay stated.

'I'm blind, Bay. How could you possibly love me?' she pleaded with him to stop tormenting her.

'My brave and beautiful blind queen, how could I possibly not love you?' His tone was incredibly warm and

183

caressing. The sincerity of it almost frightened Sabrina.

'You aren't trying to trick me again, are you, Bay? Don't do this to me if all you want is the bust I did of you. I'll give it to you gladly if it will make you stop lying.'

A pair of hands closed over her shoulders and she was drawn against his chest. He placed her hands on his heart, rapidly thudding against her palm. Her own heart had to race wildly to keep in tempo. Cupping her face in his hands, Bay bestowed soft kisses on her closed eyes.

'Being blind doesn't make you feel less of a woman when I hold you in my arms, darling,' he whispered tightly.

'You never let me guess, not once,' Sabrina murmured, leaning her head weakly against his heart.

'I wanted to a hundred times in a hundred ways.' Strong arms held her close as if afraid she would try to escape again. 'I loved you almost from the beginning. Maybe it started that night we took refuge from the rain in my boat. I don't know. But I told myself I had to take it slow. You were proud, stubborn, defensive and very insecure. I didn't try to convince you in the beginning that I was in love with you, because you wouldn't have believed me. That's why I set about trying to help you build confidence in yourself. I wanted you to learn that there was nothing you couldn't do if you set your mind to it. Arrogantly I thought after that was accomplished I would make you fall in love with me. You can imagine what a blow it was to my self-esteem when you informed me that you didn't need me any more.'

He smiled against her temple and Sabrina snuggled

closer. 'I needed you. I wanted you desperately,' she murmured fervently. 'I was terrified you would guess and feel even sorrier for me.'

'I never felt pity. Pride, but never pity.'

'Pride?' She turned her face toward him, questioning and bewildered.

'I was always proud of you. No matter what challenge I made, you always accepted it.' Lightly he kissed her lips.

'Accepted with protest,' she reminded him with an impish smile.

'No one could ever accuse you of being tractable. Stubborn and independent, yes, but never tractable. You made that plain the first time we met and you slapped my face,' Bay laughed softly.

'And you slapped me back.' Sabrina let her fingertips caress his cheek. 'It made me angry. Eventually it made me love you.'

His fingers quickly gripped her hand and stopped the caressing movement, pressing a hard kiss in her palm. 'Will you tell me now why you ran away from me at Pamela's?' he demanded huskily. 'The truth this time.'

Her heart skipped a beat. At the moment she didn't want to talk, not after the sensually arousing kiss in her sensitive palm.

'I heard you talking to a girl named Roni. She said you'd brought me with you because you felt sorry for me and because you hoped to make her jealous. You didn't deny it, Bay. I kept hoping you would at least say I was your friend, but you just let her keep rattling on about me being a charity case and a poor unfortunate. I thought she was telling the truth. That's why I ran away,' she admitted.

She heard and felt the rolling chuckle that vibrated from deep within. It was throaty and warm and strangely reassuring.

'One of the first things I'm going to have to remember when we're married is how acute your hearing is,' Bay declared with a wide smile of satisfaction against her hair. 'If you'd eavesdropped a little longer, you would have heard me tell Roni to take a flying leap at the moon and that I didn't appreciate her comments about the woman I was going to marry.'

'Bay!' Her voice caught for a moment on the tide of love that welled in her throat. 'Are you going to marry me?'

'If that's a proposal, I accept.'

'D-don't tease,' she whispered with a painful gasp.

His mouth closed over hers in a tender promise. Instantly Sabrina responded, molding herself tightly against every hard male curve. Hungry desire blazed in his deepening kiss as he parted her lips to savor every inch of her mouth. His love lit a glowing lamp that chased away all the shadows of her dark world.

Long heady moments later Bay pushed her unsteadily out of his arms. She swayed toward his chest rising and falling so unevenly beneath her fingers. His hands rigidly held her at a distance.

'Darling, I love you so,' Sabrina whispered achingly. 'Please hold me a little while longer.'

'I'm not made of iron, my love.' The sternness of his

voice only indicated the deepness of his love. 'A little while longer would be too long.'

The corners of her wide mouth were tugged upward in a tiny smile of immense pleasure. 'The door has a lock, Bay.'

'And there's a horde of people who must be wondering what's happened to the star of the show,' he reminded her tersely.

'I don't want to be a star,' she answered.

'Your work—' Bay began.

'—will fill the moments you are away from me. That's all it will ever do for me,' Sabrina declared in a husky murmur.

'You're not making it easy to be sensible,' he growled, letting her come back into his arms.

'I know,' she whispered in the second before his mouth closed passionately over hers.

LOW COUNTRY LIAR

"I'M NOT CONVINCED THAT I NEED YOU."

"Yes, you are," Slade countered. "It just sticks in your craw to admit it."

There was no mistaking the complacency in his tone, and Lisa wished there was an easier way to get the information she was seeking. "You're very sure of yourself," she commented sharply.

"No." Slade's thumb and forefinger captured her chin. "I'm sure of you."

Slade bent his head toward her, then stopped as if waiting for a protest from Lisa. When she made not the slightest sound to stop him, he closed the distance between them. Lightly he explored her lips, sensually feeling his way until she tingled with pleasure from his caressing kiss.

"It's crazy," she murmured when he raised his head. "I don't even like you."

"Yes," he said. "I know."

CHAPTER ONE

WITH A RELAXED SIGH Lisa Talmadge leaned against the curling backrest of the chair. It was a beautifully restored antique, reupholstered in a patterned brocade of rust, orange and brown. It complemented perfectly the solid rust-colored chair her aunt sat in.

Lisa felt she had been talking nonstop since she arrived, bringing her aunt up-to-date on the latest family happenings. Soon it would be time to get down to the true reason for her visit, which was more than just a wish to see her favorite aunt. Her aunt seemed to be of the same mind.

"We've gotten rid of the preliminaries, Lisa, I now know you've had a safe trip from Baltimore. Both your parents are fine. Your brother is having girl problems as usual. You have a drink in hand to loosen your tongue, so why don't you tell me what really brought you to Charleston?"

At fifty-two, Miriam Talmadge was warm, vivacious and darkly brunette. The latter fact Lisa would never have questioned her hairdresser about. She knew that Mitzi, as Miriam Talmadge was affectionately known by those who loved her, would grow old as gracefully as she stayed young at heart.

It had been several years since Lisa had last spent any time with her aunt. Not since Mitzi had moved back to her home town of Charleston, located on the southern end of the coastal flatlands that were known to all South Carolinians as the Low Country.

Lisa didn't try to hide the smile her aunt's pointed question had prompted. "Believe it or not, Mitzi, *you* brought me to Charleston."

"Me? Goodness, that's quite a burden." A wry smile deepened the corners of her mobile mouth. "I hope you haven't sought me out about man problems. Considering the mess I made of my marriage, I'm the last one to run to for advice."

"You can't claim sole responsibility for the failure of your marriage. Uncle Simon had a part in it somewhere." Lisa dismissed the statement with a shake of her silver blond hair, a gold hooped earring glittering through the long silk strands.

"That's what Slade says, too," Mitzi Talmadge sighed.

Quickly Lisa lowered her head, her jaw tightening at the name. Her aunt had just put a name to the reason Lisa had come. For the time being, however, that was Lisa's secret until she could find out what was really going on.

"But you must remember," Mitzi was continuing, and Lisa concentrated on what she was saying, "that I was raised in an era where divorce was a scandal and a woman was supposed to make the marriage last no matter what. It's understandable, I suppose, that I should have guilt feelings regarding the failure of mine. Simon and I just weren't suited at all." There was a reflective look in her dark eyes as she smiled, her cheeks dimpling. "I married him because he was so quiet. And I divorced him because he was *so* quiet,"

192

she laughed. "Which proves what an eternal romantic I am at heart, doesn't it? I was all caught up in the image of the strong, silent type when that wasn't what I really wanted or needed. Poor Simon didn't get any bargain with me either. I was so disorganized when it came to anything outside of my writing that it drove him to distraction. He wanted the unobtrusive, home-making kind of wife who always had a delicious meal ready at promptly seven o'clock. I could barely boil water without a crisis. Ours was a very sad mismatch, but I'm glad he had a few happy years with his second wife before he died," she concluded.

"What about you, Mitzi? You've had time to meet somebody new?" The question was put innocently, but there was a sharp edge to the look in Lisa's olive green eyes. "Tell me about the men in your life."

"Men in the plural? You make me sound like a femme fatale. At my age!" Mitzi shook her head laughingly, a bright twinkle in her eyes. "You're going to be awfully good for my morale, Lisa. And exactly how did the subject get around to my love life when I asked about yours?"

"I thought I'd dodged the question rather expertly." Lisa smiled broadly. "The fact is at the present time I don't have a love life."

"I find that extremely hard to believe. You've grown into a beautiful woman, Lisa Talmadge, with your mother's cheekbones and her blond hair. Those green eyes are definitely from the Talmadge side, outlined with sooty lashes just the way Simon's were. They're definitely your most striking feature. But you're side-tracking me again," Mitzi scolded with mock reproof.

"Now why have you come? Did you break up with some special man?"

"No. There isn't anyone 'special.'" Lisa raised her hands, making mock quotation marks with her fingers. "I'm escaping from nothing but work," she insisted.

"And that young man you were engaged to?" Mitzi prompted, tipping her head slightly downward to watch Lisa's expression closely.

"Michel? That was over three years ago when I graduated from college." Lisa picked up her cocktail, touching a forefinger to the lime wedge floating on top and watching it bob in the liquid.

"What really happened between you two?"

"A conflict of careers. He wanted a country-club wife and I wanted to work—that's why I'd got my degree. He didn't see it that way. To him, my education was supposed to be just a safeguard for my future in case anything ever happened to him. In the meantime he wanted me home taking care of him and raising a family." Lisa shrugged. The bitterness had long since fled. "I didn't object to that as much as I objected to him telling me that was what I wanted. It's just as well, because it would never have worked between us."

"You're not sorry, then?" Mitzi prompted.

"Not a bit," Lisa returned without any regret. "Now I just steer clear of the strong, masterful types like Michel with their super male egos that constantly have to be fed."

"You said you were escaping from your job. Hasn't it turned out to be what you wanted?" The older woman relaxed in the cushioned chair, its rusty orange a pleasant contrast to her dark coloring. "Your last letter seemed filled with complaints about staff and management."

"I think you can mark that up to almost a year and a half without a vacation rather than the job," Lisa stated, following her aunt's suit and leaning back in her chair. "Since the television station gave the go-ahead on the new show a year ago, it's been hectic, to say the least, but very rewarding and satisfying. I'd only worked as an assistant on other shows. This is the first one I've produced myself, so I put in a lot of hours to prove myself, postponing my vacation, certain the show would fall apart without me. Finally I realized I would fall apart if I didn't get away for a while."

"So you came here." Mitzi's curiosity over Lisa's choice was still evident.

"I couldn't think of a better place than Charleston. Time seems to pass so leisurely here. Plus, I have you for company," Lisa concluded, keeping to herself the other very pertinent reason for her choice.

"For whatever reason, I'm glad you're here for a few weeks. I only hope you don't find it too boring after the exciting life you've been leading working in television." Before Lisa had a chance to refute her aunt's statement, Mitzi Talmadge made one of her lightning changes of subject. One thought often triggered off another in Mitzi's mind; it was a trait that was characteristic of her personality. "Do you remember the letter you wrote me when you first went to work for the broadcasting company? I can't help laughing when I think about it. You'd put in your application and were so irate when they called you back to hire you as their weather girl."

"At the time, I was a very militant feminist," Lisa

agreed with a laughing smile. "I hope I've mellowed with age."

"Mellowed with age—and you're all of twenty-four," her aunt mocked.

"You don't know how vocal a Women's Libber I was," Lisa declared. "When I think of the lecture I gave the company about their weather-girl job, I wonder why they ever hired me!"

"That's what Slade said. I told him about the incident when I heard you were coming for a visit."

The mention of his name set Lisa's teeth on edge. She attempted a bright smile. "I'm dying to meet this paragon you call Slade Blackwell. You've mentioned him half a dozen times in your letters." A half a hundred would have been closer.

"I would have invited him to dinner this evening, but because it's your first night here, I thought it would be best with just the two of us. I promise you that you'll meet him soon. Maybe tomorrow night," suggested Mitzi Talmadge as the idea began to form in her mind.

"I believe you said he was the son of an old family friend?" Lisa's tongue felt almost honey coated as she made the casual inquiry—too sweet to be sincere—but Mitzi didn't seem to notice.

"Mmm, yes," Mitzi sipped her drink, replying absently. "I met him quite by accident shortly after I moved back here to Charleston when my divorce from Simon was final. If you remember, my mother died soon after my divorce, so I really had a very trying few months."

"I can imagine," Lisa murmured.

"But Slade was wonderful," Mitzi continued, not

hearing Lisa's low comment. "I never had a head for business—not that I'm as stupid as some people, but I just find it very tedious and dull. Anyway, things became quite complicated with the divorce and the settlement of the family estate. Slade simply took over for me and handled everything. You know how I loathe details, Lisa," Mitzi smiled at herself. "Now that Slade is looking after everything I don't have to be bothered with them. He makes out all the checks and all I have to do is sign them."

With sinking heart, Lisa felt as if her worst suspicions had been confirmed. How could her aunt be so gullible? Her letters this past year had been filled with "Slade said," "Slade suggested," or "Slade told me." He had been quoted as a veritable authority on anything and everything.

It was at Slade Blackwell's instigation that Mitzi had reopened the family home in Old Charleston. Lisa remembered that it also had been the interior decorator he had recommended who had been given the task of renovating the mansion.

Her green gaze swept the living room with its high ceilings and rich cypress woodwork. Lisa was unable to find fault with the completed product. The decor was a smooth mix of antique and modern. It invited a guest to sit back and relax, instead of giving a museum effect that said, Fragile, Keep Off.

Yet it grated, just as it grated to know that Slade Blackwell had suggested the landscape architect for the walled garden outside the colonnade portico. In the waning hours of a March dusk, it was ablaze with spring flowers—azaleas and camellias and the magno-

197

lia trees budding, the scent of honeysuckle drifting in the air. Magnificent spreading oaks dominated it all with their elegant draping of silvery beardlike moss.

The same company that designed the garden still maintained it. Lisa couldn't help wondering what kind of a kickback Slade Blackwell made out of the deal. Those two items were just the obvious ones; she guessed there were many other small deals as well. Now Mitzi had informed her that Slade Blackwell made out the checks for her signature. Lisa doubted if Mitzi even verified what she was signing. The man was probably stealing her blind.

"Does this Mr. Blackwell handle all your money?" There was a faint challenge in Lisa's question. She simply couldn't keep it out even though she tried.

"All except some that I keep in an account of my own. I call it my mad money." An impish smile made the woman appear even younger.

Heaven only knew how much was in that account! Heaven or Slade Blackwell—Lisa wouldn't even hazard a guess. She did know that her aunt had received a considerable amount from Simon Talmadge when they had divorced. Lisa's father had understood that Mitzi's mother had been quite wealthy and Mitzi had been an only child.

Plus, there was the income Mitzi made writing romance mysteries. The latter wasn't a large sum, but combined with the other, it was probably a sizeable amount that Mitzi Talmadge was worth.

"Aren't you worried that you're a bit too trusting, Mitzi?" Lisa set her glass on the ornate coaster sitting atop a marble inlaid table, trying to disguise the sharpness of her tone.

"Do you mean where Slade is concerned?" There was faint surprise in the woman's answering question. Then she laughed, a gay melodious sound. "A more honest, dependable man couldn't be found. You haven't met him yet, but when you do, I know you'll like him." Mitzi hesitated, her gaze sharpening. "On second thought, maybe you won't."

"Oh?" Lisa was instantly alert. "Why?"

"You said a moment ago that you have an aversion for the strong, masterful type. I'm afraid those adjectives would fit Slade. Of course, he can be very charming and gracious, too."

When it suits him to be. Lisa added the qualification silently. An older woman probably seemed an easy target to Slade Blackwell. Mitzi didn't have any close family—her parents dead, no aunts or uncles living, the husband she had divorced gone, too. What money he didn't steal from her while she was alive he probably hoped to inherit on her death.

"What did he say when he learned I was coming for a visit?" Lisa asked.

"I don't recall that Slade said anything in particular except that he was glad Simon's family hadn't forgotten me."

"We didn't forget you," Lisa protested quickly. Anger against this Slade Blackwell slowly began to grow hotter. No doubt he wanted Mitzi to be isolated and totally dependent on him.

"I didn't mean to imply that you had," her aunt hastened with a dismissing laugh. "But you must admit it was awkward when Simon was alive. After all, he was your father's brother and we were divorced. I couldn't very well be included as if nothing had changed. I wouldn't have wanted it that way if your parents had tried."

"Well, as far as I'm concerned, you are still part of my family," Lisa stated emphatically, "regardless of any divorce."

"God love you, Lisa," Mitzi laughed. "I still think of you as my niece, too. That's why I'm so glad you've come for a visit." Just as quickly, she became thoughtful. "There's only one thing I regret in my life. Oh, not the years I spent with Simon," she assured Lisa hastily. "But the fact that we never had any children and that Simon wouldn't adopt any. You seem like my own daughter, though, and Slade my son."

"Is Slade Blackwell related to you?" Lisa questioned. It suddenly occurred to her that he might be some distant relation.

"No," Mitzi denied somewhat ruefully. "His father once proposed to me, though, many years ago. Sometimes, when I'm in a really sentimental mood, I start thinking that if I'd married him instead of Simon, Slade would be my son. But of course, I didn't and he isn't and it's all water under the bridge." She dismissed the subject with a wave of her hand and a smile. "Tell me what you would like to do while you're in Charleston."

"Don't worry about entertaining me." Lisa folded her hands in her lap, relaxing more fully into the cushioned chair. "I know you're in the middle of a book. You just keep right on writing and I'll wander around on my own. I have a couple of people I want to look up while I'm here."

"College friends?"

"More or less," she answered without lying.

But her true plans were just beginning to take shape. One of the very first things she was going to do was meet this Slade Blackwell and find out what his game was. She was determined to accomplish her plan without her aunt present.

If there was one thing she had learned producing the local affairs show, it was how to handle people. And more importantly, how to ask the questions that would reveal a person's true stand, either by doing it herself, or having a reporter do it for her. Slade Blackwell was going to have quite a few questions to answer.

Mitzi glanced at her wristwatch. "Goodness, it's past seven!" She frowned and looked toward the dining room with its small teardrop chandelier suspended above a gleaming white-clothed table. "Mildred usually serves promptly at seven. I wonder what's wrong."

As if on cue, the housekeeper-cook and general dogsbody appeared. There was an exasperated thinness to the line of her mouth, a grimness to her features that said she had put up with more than her share of troubles.

"As near as I can tell, dinner is going to be about thirty minutes late tonight. The oven is on the blink again," she announced, her tone saying it was just about the last straw.

"Oh, no!" Mitzi echoed the housekeeper's sentiment, plus an additional note that indicated she didn't want to be bothered with the problem. "Didn't Slade say that he knew—"

"I've already phoned Slade," the housekeeper

replied, using his given name calmly. "He'll have the man out first thing in the morning. But in the meantime, dinner will be late."

Lisa waited until the housekeeper returned to the kitchen before asking, "Couldn't you have called your own repairman, Mitzi?"

"I suppose so," was the answer, as though it hadn't occurred to her before Lisa suggested it. "But it's so much easier to call Slade. He always knows a reliable firm to send."

Yes, Lisa thought cynically, one that will be certain to reward him for passing on business. And a house as old as this was costly to maintain. Several trades would be involved. It seemed to Lisa that what had begun as merely a suspicion against Slade Blackwell was proving to be a well-founded one.

"It isn't that difficult to find a reliable company," Lisa insisted. "It would require a few phone calls and some checking, but you could do it and not have to rely on someone else."

"Oh, I could do anything if I set my mind to it," Mitzi agreed with an expansive wave of her hand. "The trouble is that I am so lazy."

"I find that hard to believe. Look at your writing schedule," she argued.

"Ah, but that is something that I enjoy doing. It isn't work. As far as anything else goes, I don't want to be bothered," she said with an uncaring shrug. "If I didn't have Slade to turn to, I probably would take care of these routine matters. But I do have him. He spoils me outrageously and I love it."

What could she say to that, Lisa wondered. Her

202

aunt was an intelligent woman. Why couldn't she make her see that she was vulnerable? Or, perhaps the word was gullible?

Dinner was eventually served about a quarter of an hour later than Mildred had thought. The evening passed quite pleasantly despite the prolonged serving time. The conversation was filled with reminiscences of old times and gossip about family. The only irritant Lisa found was the way Slade Blackwell's name kept cropping up.

Mildred plodded into the living room to the low, marble-inlaid table in front of the sofa. She picked up the empty coffee service as if it weighed a ton and started to leave. At Mitzi's chair, she paused.

"Will you be wanting anything else tonight, Mitzi?" But she didn't give her employer an opportunity to answer. "If you don't, I'll be turning in now." Her heavily intoned words implied that she was on her last legs, and any further requests would be a severe strain on her health.

"I am sure there is nothing else we will need," Lisa's aunt responded with a sympathetic smile. "Have a good night, Mildred."

"I'll try," was the sighing reply as the housekeeper shuffled out of the room. She made it appear that it was too much of an effort to pick up her feet.

When the housekeeper was out of sight, Mitzi's twinkling gaze slid to Lisa. "Isn't she a character? She could do the work of an army, but she gives the impression that the smallest task is too much for her. Bless her grumbling soul. I don't know what I'd do without her. Slade found her, of course."

"Of course," Lisa echoed dryly and tried to swallow a yawn, but she couldn't.

"You're tired, aren't you? I had forgotten how exhausting it is to travel. I'll bet you'd like to have an early night."

"Oh, no, really," Lisa started to protest.

"Don't argue. You are tired. We'll have plenty of time to talk in the next two weeks. There isn't any need to try to do all our talking in one night," Mitzi insisted.

Lisa *was* tired and didn't object at all to having her arm twisted. "If you are sure you don't mind...."

"I don't mind. Do you remember which room you have?" Her aunt rose and Lisa did likewise.

"Yes, I remember. Turn right at the top of the stairs and it's the second room," she recalled.

"That's it. I'll be turning in now, too. I'll be rising with the sun to work on my novel, but you sleep as late as you wish," her aunt instructed. "Remember, you're on vacation."

"Which means not dashing about to get to work," Lisa smiled. She started toward the foyer and the stair-case leading to the second floor. Over her shoulder, she added, "And thanks for letting me spend my vacation here."

"Thanks aren't necessary. I am proud to have you here. Good night."

"Good night, Mitzi," Lisa waved as she rounded the opened double doors into the foyer.

The staircase of heavily carved and polished cypress made a lazy circle to the second floor. Lisa climbed its carpeted steps, a hand sliding along the smooth wood of the carved banister to the top. The plaster walls of the upper-floor hallway were painted a pearl white. The color gave light to the high-ceilinged but narrow corridor.

Turning right, Lisa entered the second room. Her previous inspection of the room had been a cursory one, a hurried tour on her arrival, cut short by her desire to return downstairs to visit with her aunt. Now she let her gaze wander around the room.

Mitzi had said she had specifically chosen that guest room for Lisa because it seemed to be "her." The walls were a rich jade green, accented by woodwork painted ivory. A small alcove held a sofa decorated in vivid greens and golds. The silklike material of the drapes was of ivory to match the bedspread on the canopied bed. The area rug was patterned in an Oriental design that incorporated the green and off-white colors with a vivid yellow.

The sight of her suitcases standing at the foot of the bed reminded Lisa that she hadn't yet unpacked. She sighed tiredly, then noticed her nightgown and robe lying across the bed. She picked up one suitcase. It was light as a feather. Setting it back down, Lisa walked to the closet. All her clothes were there, neatly hung on wire hangers. The rest of her things were in the drawers of a Provençal-styled dresser. The housekeeper had obviously unpacked the suitcases for her.

"Bless her grumbling soul." Lisa repeated her aunt's earlier comment about Mildred, murmuring it in all sincerity.

Kicking off her shoes, she walked to a second ivory-painted door. It opened into a private bathroom where her cosmetics were arranged neatly on the counter in front of a well-lighted vanity mirror. There wasn't anything left for her to do.

Lisa glanced at the large porcelain bathtub with its gold fixtures and green and gold shower curtain, but the bed looked infinitely more inviting at the moment. Closing the bathroom door, she changed into her nightclothes.

Climbing between the clean-scented sheets of the bed, she switched off the light on the stand beside the bed. Lisa stared at the pale silk of the canopy above her head. Tomorrow she would be meeting Slade Blackwell. She wanted to be very well rested for that. She closed her eyes.

As Lisa followed the descending rail of the spiral staircase the next morning, she could hear the staccato tapping of typewriter keys coming from the downstairs study. Smiling to herself, she knew she wouldn't have to make any explanations to Mitzi. Her aunt was hard at work on her new novel.

At the bottom of the stairs, Lisa paused in front of the large oval mirror to make a last-minute inspection of her appearance. The loose-fitting waistcoat-type jacket gave height to her average build, the skirt long enough to be fashionable while revealing the shapely curve of her legs. The waistcoat and skirt were spring green in color over a complementing brightly printed blouse with long sleeves.

Hats had become her passion in the last year and Lisa wore one now, a matching green turban that gave a touch of sophistication to the overall effect. A silkily blond wisp of hair had escaped the hat, trailing the curve of her neck. Lisa tucked it beneath the hat and adjusted the large gold stud of her earring.

Satisfaction sparkled in her eyes, their color enhanced by the green of her outfit. She liked the image of the woman looking back at her, professional yet definitely feminine. Her gaze slid to the bone-colored handbag in her left hand. Inside was a slip of paper with Slade Blackwell's business address.

Lisa had no doubt he would see her this morning, regardless of whether or not she had an appointment. He wouldn't turn away the niece of Mitzi Talmadge. Once she was inside the door, he would not find it so easy to be rid of her.

"Would you like breakfast now, miss?"

Glancing toward the sound of the voice, Lisa saw the long-suffering Mildred standing just inside the doorway and smiled. "No, thank you, Mildred. I function much better on an empty stomach."

"Beg pardon?"

"It doesn't matter." Lisa didn't bother with an explanation of her statement and ran a smoothing hand over her hip. "If Mitzi asks where I am, tell her I've gone to see an old friend."

As often as she had heard Blackwell's name in the past twenty-four hours, it did feel as if she had known him a long time and disliked him for an equal length.

"Will you be home for lunch, then?" Mildred inquired in a voice that was wearily patient.

Lisa hesitated. "No," she decided. "I'll be back sometime in the afternoon. What time is Mitzi generally through for the day?"

"It depends, miss. It depends," was the answer, indicating that anything more definite was quite beyond her.

Concealing the amused smile that tugged at the

corners of her mouth, Lisa wished the housekeeper a good day and walked out of the ornately carved front door into the midmorning of a March day. The air was balmy, the sun bright, not a hint of a blustery March wind to be found.

The lovely old mansion was narrow and long. The house didn't actually front the narrow street in Old Charleston; its entrance door opened onto the portico running the length of one side. Lisa's heels clicked noisily on the smooth stone as she walked to the false house door opening onto the street from the portico.

Closing it behind her, she heard the rumble of carriage wheels and the steady clop of horses' hooves. Lisa paused to watch a horse-drawn surrey around the narrow street corner, its fringe waving with the motion.

Tourists sat in the seats behind the guide, taking a carriage tour of Old Charleston. They had obviously seen her coming from the mansion, Lisa realized, and they stared openly. She smiled and waved, knowing they believed she was a full-fledged Charlestonian instead of a tourist like themselves.

The carriage ride looked like a fun way to tour Old Charleston, whose history encompassed the Southern manner of gracious living, the sad days of the Civil War, and beyond that, the era of Colonial America. Lisa glanced around the immediate neighborhood. Magnolia trees and massive oaks, with their leaves and branches draped by Spanish moss, towered beside and above fine old homes. The colorful splash of flowers seemed to be in every lawn and garden, creeping along fences and spouting from stone urns.

Lisa squared her shoulders. There would be time enough to do some sight-seeing later on. For the time being, she couldn't be distracted by the beauty around her, not until after she'd had her confrontation with Slade Blackwell. The click of her heels made a purposeful sound as she started out.

It was a short walk along the stagecoach-wide street to Meeting Street, where Lisa was able to obtain directions to the law offices of Courtney Blackwell & Son. Slade Blackwell was, of course, the "Son." The office, too, was located in Old Charleston, in an old merchant building with ornate cornice trim around the roof.

The instant Lisa entered the offices she had the impression of a small, exclusive practice. Richly paneled walls, their wood gleaming with the patina of years, emitted a studious air, while antiques and plush leather furniture added intimacy to the overall atmosphere.

The receptionist was an older woman with sleekly coiffed gray hair. She wore glasses with half lenses which she peered over at Lisa. Yet she managed to exude an attitude of polite deference.

"May I help you?"

"I'm here to see Mr. Slade Blackwell." Lisa didn't bother to inform the woman she didn't have an appointment nor that he didn't know her.

Surprisingly no questions were put to her as the woman nodded her head toward a set of carved oak double doors. "His office is through those doors."

This was going to be easier than she had thought. No preliminary introductions to be forwarded to him. No explanations as to why she was there. Slade Blackwell was proving to be much more accessible than she had believed.

The doors opened to a small office, complete with desk, typewriter and filing cabinets. Obviously it was supposed to be manned by his private secretary, but there was no one in sight to greet Lisa. Closing the doors, she walked into the office, deciding it had been partitioned from a larger room.

An overstuffed leather armchair was in a corner with an old wooden magazine rack and smokestand beside it, but Lisa didn't take its invitation to sit and wait. Instead she walked to the vacant secretary's desk. Except for an opened appointment book, it was tidily swept clean of any papers.

She glanced cautiously toward the door leading to Slade Blackwell's private office. There were no sounds coming from it, but the walls of the building were thick. Carefully she slid the appointment book around to peep at his day's agenda.

Without warning the door was opened, and Lisa nearly jumped out of her shoes. She quickly concealed her start of guilty surprise to inspect the man confronting her. His tall, leanly muscled build was clothed in an impeccably tailored suit of oyster gray, complete with waistcoat.

There the lawyer image ended and the man began. And he made an immediate physical impact on Lisa. The breath she had been holding she released slowly, then seemed unable to take another. Every nerve in her body quivered with the alertness of an animal scenting danger.

This was Slade Blackwell. Lisa needed no introduction. If she had expected the suave image of a Southern gentleman, chivalrous and courtly, charming a rich widow with his pearly smile, she would have needed to make an immediate reassessment. Somehow, though, Lisa hadn't got as far as picturing her opponent.

Strong and masterful, Mitzi had described him. Meek words, Lisa concluded silently. Belligerently male, he was as hard as a piece of granite that had somehow managed to come to life. He exuded an air of vitality that seemed to smother, a sensual power that was overwhelming. At least, Lisa felt its suffocating force.

Raven-black hair grew thickly away from his forehead, seeming to appear waywardly casual in its style. His eyes were the color of his hair, burning like black coals yet possessing the sharpness of an eagle. No gentle spaniel-brown eyes for Slade Blackwell.

Tanned lean cheeks, faintly hollowed, accented the angular slant of his jaw to a thrusting chin. There was an unyielding firmness to his mouth that seemed to suggest a latent ruthlessness in getting what he wanted. Dark, thick brows managed to appear finely drawn. One was arched slightly higher than the other now in arrogant censure.

"It's about time you arrived." His voice was low pitched. It might have been pleasant had his tone not been sharpened by tightly leashed impatience. "The agency had assured me they would have someone here by nine-thirty. It is now half past ten. There are some important letters that need to be out right away. They're on the dictaphone. I presume you do know how to operate a dictaphone?"

On the last dryly sarcastic note, he pivoted on his heel and reentered his private office.

211

CHAPTER TWO

THE SHARP CLICK of the closing door snapped Lisa out of her daze. Her mouth opened. The words formed to call him back, her hand raised uselessly. Then she hesitated, her hand coming back to her mouth as she began to thoughtfully nibble a fingernail.

Why not? a mischievous little voice inside her demanded.

Obviously Slade Blackwell was expecting a replacement for his regular secretary and had mistaken Lisa for that replacement. Why should she bother to tell him differently? A private secretary would have access to all the files. If she wanted proof to confirm or denounce her suspicions, what better way than through his own records?

It was a heaven-sent opportunity. She would be a fool not to take advantage of it. True, Lisa admitted, she wasn't trained as a secretary, but she could type, not very speedily, but at least it wasn't the hunt-and-peck method. She knew the rudiments of dictaphone use. With any luck she could bluff her way through what other skills might be necessary.

With the decision made, Lisa quickly stepped behind the desk, slipping her bag into a lower drawer. The first thing she had to do was cancel the order for a secretary. She had no idea which agency had been contacted and couldn't very well ask. That meant going down the list of agencies in the telephone book and calling every one until she found the right one. Luckily, she reached the right agency on the third call.

One more phone call. She looked the number up in the directory and dialed it quickly. Her fingers drummed the desktop impatiently as she listened to the ring on the other end.

Finally it was answered. "Talmadge residence," came the world-weary voice of the housekeeper.

"Mildred, this is Lisa." She hurried her words, speaking softly and quickly. "I'm just calling to let you know my ... my friends and I are going to make an afternoon of it. Tell Mitzi I'll be back shortly after five o'clock."

"Did she tell you?"

Lisa frowned at the receiver. "Tell me what?"

"That Sl—Mr. Blackwell is coming for dinner tonight." The housekeeper immediately corrected herself to refer to their guest formally.

"Good lord," Lisa muttered to herself, seeing all sorts of complications setting in. "What time is he to be there?"

"He usually comes for cocktails around six," was the reply.

"I'll be there by then." An irritated "damn" slipped out as Lisa replaced the receiver on the hook.

But there wasn't time to dwell on her ultimate unmasking. She had to start transcribing the letters on the dictaphone before Slade Blackwell became suspicious about the silence in his outer office. It took a few minutes to find the stationery and carbon paper, and another few minutes to figure out how to operate the dictaphone before she was finally able to start.

On the first letter, the spacing and margins were all wrong. The result was decidedly amateurish and Lisa had to do it all over again, interrupted by phone calls that she had to transfer to Slade Blackwell. The metal cabinets kept beckoning Lisa to investigate their files, but she remembered his statement that the letters were important. She didn't want Slade Blackwell coming out to discover her going through the files when she should be typing.

Working on the fourth—and what she hoped was the last—letter, Lisa heard the connecting office door open and mentally tensed as Slade Blackwell stopped at her desk. Her cool green eyes slid a brief glance in his direction as he picked up the letters she had finished. She tried to increase her typing speed to an efficient rate—a mistake, as she misspelled a word by reversing the letters. She reached quickly for the liquid paper to correct it.

The longest letter of those she had completed was tossed back to her desk. "The word is 'guaranty,' not 'guarantee,' Miss—?"

"Mrs. Eldridge." The false name came so quickly to her tongue that Lisa was slightly astounded. Quickly she used her little finger to turn the birthstone ring on her left finger around so a plain gold band showed. "Mrs. Ann Eldridge," she carried her lie further, using her middle name in place of her first.

"The word is repeated several times in the letter, Mrs. Eldridge. You'll have to retype it," he declared with cutting indifference.

"Of course," Lisa agreed with a nod of deference, but she was actually gritting her teeth. He seemed to be waiting for an explanation for her error, and Lisa grudgingly gave him one, masking it in sweet politeness. "Unfortunately I'm not familiar with the 'to wits' and 'whereas' and the other legal terminology, Mr. Blackwell."

"I specifically requested a legal secretary," he stated.

"The agency didn't have anyone available with legal experience. I'm sorry."

She didn't dare look at him as she made the false apology. Lisa knew the glint in her eye was anything but apologetic. She could feel his sharp gaze studying her and tried to ignore the uncomfortable sensation it aroused.

"Do you always wear a hat when you work, Mrs. Eldridge?"

Her hand lifted to her head in surprise, her fingers touching the green turban covering her silver blond hair. She hadn't completely forgotten about it, and a germ of an idea immediately took hold.

"Only when my hair is a mess, Mr. Blackwell." This time she met his arrogantly appraising look, smiling faintly with a touch of challenge.

One corner of his mouth quirked as if he found some cynical form of amusement in her answer, but he made no further comment about the hat.

"I have a luncheon appointment. I'll be back around one o'clock," he told her, and walked to the double doors leading to the reception area.

Waiting, Lisa listened for the opening and closing of the outside door before she darted from the desk to the metal filing cabinets. Alone at last, she had her first chance to investigate the files. She tried not to think

215

about how unethical her search was, if not downright dishonest.

Filing systems were beyond her experience, but luckily the drawers seemed to be labeled. Quickly Lisa began looking for the one that might indicate that it contained her aunt's records. The door to the reception area opened and Lisa stared visibly again.

"Hello." A man walked in, shorter than Slade Blackwell but in his age group of the late thirties. He wore glasses and his brown hair was combed forward across his forehead; Lisa suspected it was to conceal a receding hairline. "You must be Mary Lou's replacement."

"Yes, I am." Lisa heard the nervous tremor in her voice and tried to return the man's broad smile naturally. She glanced toward the connecting door to Slade Blackwell's office. "I'm sorry, but Mr. Blackwell has just left for lunch."

"Yes, I know. I saw him in the reception area before he left," was the answer, but the man made no move to leave.

Her fingers were resting on the handle of one drawer. The metal felt almost hot to the touch. It was so obvious that she was looking for something that she couldn't move away from the cabinets. She silently cursed the inner sensation of guilt that made her so uncomfortable.

"Was there something I could help you with?" she asked politely, wishing he would go.

The man was staring at her, his expression making it plain that he liked what he saw. Her prodding question seemed to awaken him from his silent study.

"Yes," he walked quickly towards her. "I came to get the Talmadge file."

"The what?" Lisa breathed weakly.

"Talmadge, Miriam L.," he repeated, not apparently noticing the way the color drained from her face.

She turned away from him, mentally grasping for straws. "I'm sorry, but these are Mr. Blackwell's files. I couldn't possibly—"

"Good heavens!" he interrupted with a laugh. "I didn't introduce myself, did I? I'm Slade's assistant, consultant or whatever label you want to pin on me." He extended a hand to Lisa. "The name is Drew, as in Andrew, Rutledge—unfortunately no relation to the Charlestonian Rutledges of yore. And you are?"

"L—" Inadvertently she almost gave him her real name and caught herself just in time. "Ann Eldridge. Mrs. Ann Eldridge."

When Lisa had first placed her hand in his, he had seemed inclined to hold it. He released it on hearing her marital status, a faintly rueful smile curving his mouth.

"Divorced? Widowed?" Drew Rutledge inquired with mock hopefulness.

Lisa had to add another lie to the rest. "As of this morning when I left the house and kissed my husband goodbye, I was neither of those."

"Isn't that just my luck?" he grinned. "The first attractive secretary we get in this place turns out to be married. Happily, I suppose?"

"Very happily married," Lisa lied again.

"Pity," Drew sighed mockingly, and shook his head. "I guess I'll have to retreat to the ranks of the confirmed bachelors with Slade."

"Mr. Blackwell isn't married?" Somehow she had never assumed that he was. Now it was confirmed.

"No. We've had a standing bet since our college days as to which of us gets married first, and we've both had our share of close calls."

"Haven't we all?" Lisa agreed dryly, thinking of her abortive engagement to Michel, but her remark drew a curious look from Drew. She had to cover the slip quickly. "But once you meet the right person you don't want to settle for a close call."

"So I've heard," he smiled, the curiosity leaving his hazel eyes at her reply. "Well, I suppose I'd better let you get back to work."

"Yes." She tried not to show her relief. "I have a lot to do."

"I'll get out of your way and let you get at it, as soon as you hand me the Talmadge file," he agreed.

Her hope that Drew had forgotten the reason he had come in faded with his statement. She hesitated. "I really don't think I should—"

"You guard the files more jealously than Mary Lou does," he laughed.

Lisa seized on that comment instantly. "If that's true, then that's all the more reason for me not to give it to you." The main reason, of course, was that she wanted to look at it herself. "If it's not common practice to let the files leave this office, I shouldn't give it to you."

"I have work to do, too, but I can't do it without the file," he insisted patiently, amused by her reluctance.

"Listen, I'm just a temporary," Lisa pointed out. "Maybe you should wait until after lunch when Mr.

218

Blackwell comes back." That would give her an opportunity to look at the file's contents before she handed it over to him.

"He's the one who sent me in here to get it," Drew replied. "He would have mentioned it to you, I'm sure, if he'd known you were going to turn into a green dragon guarding the file cabinets." His gaze flicked briefly and mockingly to the green suit she was wearing.

There weren't any more excuses left. She had used them all. Inwardly she railed against the fates that had brought him in here for the Talmadge file and no other. Here she was with the ideal chance to do some undercover work and the object of her inquiry was being removed.

"I promise I won't let the file out of my sight and return it the minute I'm through." Drew raised two fingers. "Scout's honor."

"All right," Lisa agreed very grudgingly. She looked at the metal cabinets and found herself back in the same dilemma. Which drawer was it in? "Do you know where it's filed? I don't know this system." Or any system, other than the helter-skelter one in her own office in Baltimore.

"I'll find it," Drew offered, and Lisa stepped aside. He opened the very drawer her hand had been resting on and flipped through the alphabetical index to the T's. "Here it is."

Lisa had a fleeting glimpse of her aunt's name on the tab before he tucked it under his arm and closed the drawer. It was frustrating to know how close she had been to it and to see it being taken away.

"Don't look so upset," Drew teased. "I'll have it back first thing tomorrow. I hope," he tacked on as a qualifying afterthought.

"I'm not upset. Not really." Lisa composed herself quickly. "I was just wondering if anyone else would be coming in asking for files." She latched on to the first excuse that came to mind.

"No need to worry," he assured her. "There's only myself, Slade and Ellen Tyler at the reception desk. Bob Tucker, the other assistant, consultant, whatever to Slade, isn't here. He should be back this weekend, although Mary Lou took a two-week leave of absence."

"Mary Lou? Mr. Blackwell's secretary, the one I'm replacing?"

"She's also Bob's wife. There was a death in her family," Drew explained. "After two weeks here, you'll know your way around the office and filing system like a pro."

"I may not be here for two weeks." *Not when Slade Blackwell discovers who I really am*, Lisa thought.

"Why not?" He cocked his head curiously, his eyebrows puckering together.

"I'm not a trained legal secretary. The agency didn't have one available when Mr. Blackwell called. They'll be replacing me with someone more experienced."

Her gaze kept darting to the file under his arm. Lisa turned away to walk back to her desk before Drew noticed her preoccupation with the folder.

"I'll put in a word with Slade to keep you on until Mary Lou comes back. Experience doesn't count for all that much in this place. Slade likes things done his way, which is not necessarily according to the book."

I can believe that, Lisa thought cynically, but she kept her opinion to herself.

"That's kind of you," she said aloud instead, "but Mr. Blackwell might have his own opinion."

"I know what he'll say." Drew nodded positively. "He'll tell me the same thing his father always tells me—that I'm a sucker for a pretty face."

"His father? The Courtney Blackwell of Courtney Blackwell & Son?"

"That's right, the old man himself."

"Has he retired?" Lisa asked. "You didn't mention him when you ran down the list of people in the office."

"He retired within a year after Slade got his law degree." Drew walked to Lisa's desk, leaning against the edge, hooking a knee over the corner so he was half sitting on the top. "He didn't like practicing law, said he was a farmer at heart, but there's been a Blackwell practicing law in Charleston for years. When Slade qualified, the tradition was carried on through him and Court moved out to the country."

"He's farming, then."

"Yes, he bought what was the old Blackwell plantation that the family had lost after the Civil War. The original house was still standing, but one wing was beyond repair and had to be torn down. They've restored most of it, though. It's quite a place," he smiled. "You should see it."

"Sounds interesting." But Lisa was wondering if Slade Blackwell was contributing Mitzi's money to the restoration.

"Is your husband the jealous type?" Drew asked unexpectedly.

"Burt?" Lisa was stunned. She couldn't believe the

221

way these lies and fake names were springing from her tongue. She just hoped she could keep them all straight. "No, he's not particularly jealous. Why?"

"I'd like to take you to lunch tomorrow. I'd make it for today, but I have this—" he touched the folder under his arm, "—to work on. Which means I'll have to settle for Ellen bringing me back a sandwich." He noticed her hesitation and teased, "Come on, Ann. I'm harmless. Just look at me—I wear glasses, I'm short, or at least shorter than Slade. But I have a great personality. Perfectly harmless, I promise."

"I'll bet you are," she laughed with mocking skepticism.

"What do you say? Is it a date?" Drew wasn't put off.

"Ask me tomorrow." *If I'm here,* Lisa added to herself.

"I'll do that." He started to straighten from the desk, glancing at the watch on his wrist. "Talking about lunch, if you want yours today, you'd better be leaving. Things get pretty hectic around here in the afternoons."

Lisa looked at her own watch, realizing how swiftly the time had fled since Slade Blackwell had left. It was nearly noon and her stomach was beginning to protest its hunger after skipping breakfast that morning. Mentally she thumbed her nose at the unfinished letter in the typewriter carriage and opened the lower desk drawer where she had put her purse.

"That's a good idea," she told Drew. "I think I will leave now."

Later, sitting alone in a booth at a nearby small restaurant crowded with lunch-hour patrons, Lisa

222

stared at the few crumbs left that had been her lunch. She had had time to think while she was eating and she was just beginning to recognize what a very complicated and potentially embarrassing situation she had got into with her lies.

Drew Rutledge had the folder Lisa wanted to read and he wouldn't return it before tomorrow. Which was too late. That left her with two choices. The first was to go back to the office and tell Slade Blackwell who she really was before he discovered it for himself.

But how could she possibly explain why she hadn't done it before? Lisa didn't think he had all that great a sense of humor to laugh off her masquerade.

The second alternative was to continue the deception until she could get her hands on the records concerning her aunt and take the risk of being unmasked before she could succeed. The only way she could do that was by avoiding meeting Slade Blackwell as herself, Lisa Talmadge.

Considering her aunt had invited him to dinner this evening, that was already impossible. He would recognize her instantly. Then she would have to be the one who did all the explaining instead of the other way around.

Sighing, Lisa glanced out the restaurant window. The sunlight hit the glass at just the right angle to reflect her own image. Her green eyes focused on the blurred reflection of the green turban on her head. Slade had made a reference to the hat earlier. The idea that had germinated at his mention of it now began to grow.

In flashback, she remembered the mailman who

stopped at the television studio practically every day for the past year. Yet when she had seen him off work in a store without his uniform, she hadn't recognized him.

The wheels began to turn inside her head. A disguise was the answer, a very subtle disguise. Lisa Talmadge had shoulder-length silver blond hair. Mrs. Ann Eldridge, whose hair had not been seen, thanks to the turban, would have—Lisa thought for an instant—red hair.

It would be a perfect foil for her fair complexion and green eyes and such a startling contrast to the true color of her pale hair. With luck, Slade Blackwell would never compare the two women.

Within seconds, Lisa was at the cash register, paying for her meal and inquiring where the closest wig shop was located. She was told a boutique three blocks away carried a small selection. In all it turned out that the shop had no more than a dozen wigs in their inventory. One was red, a shade of flaming orange, cut short, styled in a pixieish bob. Lisa hardly recognized herself when the saleswoman helped her put it on.

"That's it," she declared, and walked out of the store moments later wearing it, carrying the green turban in her hand. A brighter shade of lipstick glistened on her lips.

On the way back to the office, Lisa passed a jewelry store and remembered the "Mrs." part of her disguise. She hurried inside and bought the first inexpensive plain gold wedding band she saw. Outside the shop, she slipped off her birthstone and slipped on the wedding band.

At ten minutes past one she was rushing toward the

Blackwell office. Aware that she had taken longer than she should, she crossed her fingers and hoped that she could make it back before Slade Blackwell did.

After going through all of this, she didn't want to give him cause to dismiss her and have the agency send him someone else. Not when she hadn't accomplished her objective.

Unfortunately her wish wasn't to be. Approaching the office entrance from the opposite direction was Slade Blackwell. His long strides brought him to the door three steps before Lisa reached it. He waited for her, his dark eyes making a sweeping appraisal of her.

"I'm sorry I'm late," Lisa murmured hastily. Self-consciously she raised a hand to the red wig. She wondered if he was astute enough to recognize it as a wig. "I stopped at a salon during my lunch hour and had my hair washed and blown dry."

His gaze flicked to the green turban in her hand. There was nothing in his carved features to indicate he didn't believe her story. "Because of my comment about your hat?" he questioned, opening the door and holding it for Lisa.

"Well, yes," she admitted, glad she wasn't Pinocchio or her nose would have been six feet long by now.

The hard line of his mouth curved faintly. Lisa saw the suggestion of a smile an instant before she walked ahead of him into the office.

"I didn't intend to sound critical, Mrs. Eldridge. I was merely curious. Women so seldom wear hats nowadays," he remarked.

"I don't generally, either." Lisa Talmadge wore hats, not Ann Eldridge. She would have to remember that.

"Tell me, do you have a temper to match it?" The amusement in his low voice was unmistakable.

"Everyone has a temper, Mr. Blackwell. Some people have a lower boiling point than others," she replied. "That's the only difference."

"Is your boiling point low?" he mocked.

"Well, well, well!" The exclamation from Drew Rutledge allowed Lisa to ignore Slade Blackwell's taunting question. "If I'd had any idea your hat was hiding that hair, I would never have let you lunch alone!"

"She's married, Drew," Slade pointed out dryly, not pausing in his walk toward his own office.

"I know." Drew winked at Lisa as if there was a secret between them. "But just because she's married doesn't mean she has to eat alone or that I must deprive myself of an innocent hour of her beautiful company."

"You'll have to forgive him, Mrs. Eldridge." There was friendly indulgence in the look Slade Blackwell gave his assistant. "Drew has a weakness for redheads."

"That's right," Drew agreed as Lisa's shorter steps carried her toward the double doors Slade was holding open for her. "Slade gets the blondes and I get the redheads."

What happens when you have both in one? Lisa thought, her cheeks dimpling faintly at the unspoken question. But that was her secret and she hoped it would stay that way. She had barely walked around the desk to sit in her chair when Slade Blackwell's curt voice wiped the trace of a smile from her face.

"Haven't you finished those letters yet, Mrs.

Eldridge?" His dark gaze dwelt pointedly on the partially complete letter in the typewriter.

"Not yet," Lisa defended herself instinctively. "Shortly after you left the office, Dr—Mr. Rutledge came in to ask me for the Talmadge file. I'm not familiar with your filing system and it took me some time to find it." Another lie, since Drew had been the one to locate it, but she doubted that Slade Blackwell would ever question him about it.

"It's a standard system," he replied automatically. The hint of asperity in his tone indicated that he found her excuse inadequate. Almost instantly a preoccupied light entered his eyes. "The Talmadge file," he repeated in a thoughtful murmur.

"Yes, the Talmadge file," Lisa affirmed. "He assured me that he had your permission to take it from the files. If you want me to, I'll go and get it and bring it back." Gladly, on winged feet, she would go after it.

"That's not necessary." Slade Blackwell dismissed the suggestion without hesitation. "Get Mrs. Talmadge on the phone for me. Her number is in the directory on your desk."

"Yes, sir." Lisa hid her dismay and quickly flipped through the telephone listings until she found her aunt's number. Her pulse was hammering in her throat as she dialed it and listened to the ring.

"Talmadge residence," Mildred answered on the fourth ring.

"One moment." She couldn't disguise the pitch of her voice, not with Slade Blackwell standing beside her desk. "Did you want to take the call here or in your office?"

"In my office." He started to turn, then stopped, his

gaze narrowing on her. "A piece of advice, Mrs. Eldridge. If encouraged, Drew will find many excuses to distract you from your work."

Lisa stiffened. "I'll remember that, Mr. Blackwell. But, as you also pointed out to Mr. Rutledge, I am married so he's unlikely to receive any encouragement from me."

"I hope not."

Fuming silently at his cynically skeptical reply, Lisa glared at the retreating set of broad shoulders as he walked to the connecting door to his inner office.

"He is insufferable!" she murmured aloud before hearing Mildred's impatient voice in the receiver. Lisa removed her hand from the mouthpiece and said huskily, "Please hold the line for a call from Mr. Blackwell."

"Slade? Well, tell him to hurry. I can't stand here all day," the housekeeper grumbled.

There was the telltale click of another phone being picked up. As Lisa replaced the receiver, she heard the echo of Slade Blackwell's voice on the line.

What did he want to talk to Mitzi about? The impulse was strong to listen in, but Lisa knew she didn't dare. She turned her swivel chair to the typewriter and picked up the earpiece for the dictaphone.

She tried desperately to concentrate on the letter she had to finish, but she kept watching the small telephone light out of the corner of her eye. Her typing was not the fastest to begin with. The distraction of watching the telephone made it even slower. It didn't improve until the light went out.

That letter was finished and another begun when the

telephone rang again; a business call for Slade. She transferred it to him and went back to the letter. She wanted them all done and ready for his signature when he asked for them, which she guessed would be soon.

Despite numerous interruptions—phone calls, clients, and instructions from Slade to make notations of appointments with various people—Lisa completed the last of the dictation an hour and a half later. She had it all stacked neatly on her desk and was looking apprehensively through the papers in the tray that needed to be filed. Any filing system was a mystery to her, whether it was a standard system as Slade had informed her, or not.

The door to his private office opened and Slade walked out. "Have you finished those letters yet, Mrs. Eldridge?" His attitude indicated that he expected a negative answer.

"They are right here, sir." Lisa wasn't able to keep the ring of triumphant satisfaction out of her voice as she gathered the papers together.

He took them from her without making a complimentary remark. As before, he skimmed through the contents as if expecting to find something to criticize. It irritated Lisa, mostly because she was afraid he would find something. Apparently satisfied with what he found, he turned and started toward his office. Pausing, his dark, impersonal gaze swung to her.

"I have dictated some legal briefs I would like typed. They are filled with 'to wits' and 'whereas' and 'parties of the first part.'" His mouth quirked, a dry humor surfacing to her surprise. "Do you think you can do them?"

229

The prospect of spending the rest of the afternoon pounding at the typewriter was depressing. It brought her no closer to the purpose of her masquerade. But she really had very little choice.

"I . . . can try." She smiled in an attempt to hide her lack of enthusiasm.

"Very well. I'll bring them in to you." The instant he disappeared inside his office, Lisa took a deep breath and exhaled it angrily in a sigh.

Almost as quickly, Slade was back and Lisa had to fix an interested and studious look on her face. He briefly went over the contents with her and explained the form he wanted the material to take. He was all business, very professional, yet patient with her ignorance. Grudgingly Lisa gave him credit for that. She couldn't accuse him of being a tyrannical employer.

After he'd left so she could begin typing, Lisa wished she had not taken advantage of his mistaken identity of her. It was proving to be a lot of work. Surely there must have been an easier way to get the information she was seeking. But she couldn't think of a single one as she put the paper and carbons in the typewriter.

CHAPTER THREE

A BLOCK FROM HER AUNT'S HOUSE the street was empty of cars and pedestrians. Lisa paused to pull the red wig from her head and free her blond hair from its confining pins. Stuffing the wig in her handbag, she briskly ruffled her hair to rid it of that matted look.

Some vacation, she thought wearily. Her arms, neck and shoulders ached from the unaccustomed time she had spent at the typewriter. If this was what it was like to be a secretary, she decided that she was going to recommend Donna, her production staff secretary, for a raise when she got back to the Baltimore television station.

A car turned onto the street behind her, and Lisa cast a frightened look over her shoulder. Before leaving the office, she had heard Slade Blackwell mention to Drew that he was going straight from the office to Mitzi's house. She expected him to overtake her any minute. Not this time, though, as the car drew level with her and Lisa saw the driver was a balding, middle-aged man.

But the scare prodded her into walking faster. She had to reach the house before Slade Blackwell or all her plans were for naught. The wrought-iron gates blocking the driveway entrance at the sidewalk were closed when Lisa reached the house. She didn't breathe easy until she was inside. Her plan to rush immediately to her room and change clothes was thwarted by her aunt, who appeared almost the second Lisa closed the entrance door behind her.

"You made it back without getting lost, didn't you?" Mitzi's wide smile of greeting was swiftly replaced by a look of concern. "You look exhausted, Lisa."

"It's been a long day." The muscles in her arm protested achingly as she tried to brush the hair away from her face.

"If I'd known you were going to overdo it your first day here, I would have waited till tomorrow to invite Slade for dinner. As it is, it's too late. He'll be here any minute," her aunt apologized.

"I'd better run upstairs and change, then."

"There's no need to," Mitzi insisted. "From the looks of you, you'd do better to sit down and put your feet up and maybe have a relaxing drink." It sounded like a heavenly suggestion to Lisa, even though she knew she couldn't accept it. "Besides," Mitzi continued, "the outfit you're wearing is very attractive. You don't have to change it."

But that was precisely the point. She did have to change it. Slade Blackwell had seen her in it practically all day, but Lisa couldn't very well tell her aunt that.

"I think I would rather, Mitzi. A wash and a change of clothes will make me seem like a new person." *I hope,* Lisa thought.

"You do what you think is best," her aunt conceded.

Lisa started to hurry towards the stairs. "If your Mr. Blackwell arrives before I'm down, make my apologies, will you?" she tossed over her shoulder. Pausing at the stairs, she added, "I noticed the driveway gates are closed."

232

"That's all right," Mitzi waved aside the comment. "Slade will probably walk. He usually does."

Suppressing a shudder that he might have been only a block or two behind her all the way from the office, Lisa darted up the stairs. As she reached her room, she heard the opening of the entrance door downstairs. Another minute and her deception would have been uncovered before she had had a chance to make it work.

Her bedroom was spacious, decorated in vivid greens and golds. An alcove of the room was designed as a mock sitting room, complete with sofa, chair and an antique secretary desk. What had once been a dressing room off the bedroom had been remodeled into a bathroom. It was to the latter that Lisa hurried.

She would have loved to take a quick shower, but there wasn't time. So she settled for washing and splashing lots of cold water on her face to rinse away the weariness. From the closet, she chose a creamy blue dress. Its simple lines flowed smoothly over the bodice to her waist before flaring into a full skirt. Its style and color made her look petite and dainty, an appearance of fragility that was deceiving and a definite contrast to the bold outfit she had worn earlier.

Reapplying her makeup, Lisa was adding the finishing touches of mascara to her lashes when she noticed the way the blue color of her dress accented the green of her eyes. Only last night Mitzi had made the comment that her eyes were Lisa's most striking feature.

Two women with the same unusual shade of green eyes would definitely be noticed by Slade Blackwell.

But how on earth could she change the color of her eyes, Lisa wondered frantically.

Breathing in sharply, she dropped the mascara wand on the dressing table and raced into the bedroom proper. Her bag was on the bed where she had left it. Lisa opened it and dumped the contents, wig and all, onto the bedspread, scattering them around until she found her sunglasses.

Quickly she slipped on the large, wrap-around glasses and dashed back to the mirror. The lenses didn't conceal her eyes with the reflecting ability of some mirrorlike sunglasses, but the smoky-blue tint did mask the color of her eyes.

"Praise be," Lisa murmured in satisfaction.

Dressed and with every potential problem countered, she had no more reason to linger in her room. At the top of the stairs she hesitated, hearing the low voices coming from the living room. She pressed a hand against her jittery stomach, trying to quiet the butterfly sensation.

Her palms were clammy with nervousness. She couldn't put off the moment of truth. Fighting the traitorous weakness in her knees, she descended the stairs and entered the living room.

"There you are, Lisa. I—" Mitzi's bright exclamation ended abruptly as a frown dressed her forehead. Lisa was conscious of Slade Blackwell courteously rising to meet her, but she kept her attention on her aunt. "Why are you wearing sunglasses at this hour?" Mitzi queried with astonishment.

"Working so much of the time in the television studio around all those bright lights, my eyes have become sensitive to too much light. After being in the sun all day, my eyes started to bother me." Lisa was becoming certain she was a natural-born liar. "A specialist recommended that I wear sunglasses whenever that happened."

"You never mentioned it," her aunt queried.

"It isn't a serious problem. More of an inconvenience than anything," Lisa assured her, and turned to meet Slade Blackwell. She had been covertly watching him ever since she entered the room, but she had not detected any glimmer of recognition of her as Ann Eldridge in his dark gaze. "You must be Slade Blackwell." A full smile parted her lips as she walked toward him, extending a hand in greeting. "I'm Lisa Talmadge, Mitzi's niece."

"So I guessed." He returned her smile with one of his own.

The warmth it gave to his hard features was astounding. It seemed to slowly draw her breath away. Lisa realized how very potent his charm could be when he turned it on, as he was doing now. Her hand was lost in the firm grip of his, being held longer than was necessary. It created a disturbing sensation in the pit of her stomach.

"Mitzi described you perfectly as a beautiful, intelligent blonde, but she didn't mention that you had cold hands," he mocked, the velvet quality of his voice taking any sting from his comment.

"Cold hands, warm heart," her aunt quipped from the side.

"I think it's a sign of poor circulation," Lisa denied her aunt's allegation, and determinedly withdrew her hand from his warm grasp.

She had feld herself beginning to warm to him.

Seeing this side of him, she could well understand how her aunt, who was so sentimental and romantic, had been taken in by Slade Blackwell's charm. The secret, Lisa believed, was to stay out of range of that magnetic forcefield radiating around him. His physical attraction was a bit overwhelming at close quarters.

That was something she hadn't noticed about him at the office where Slade Blackwell had kept himself aloof and impersonal, crisply professional except for that one taunting remark about her red hair. Correction—Ann Eldridge's red hair.

"May I fix you a drink, Lisa?" Slade Blackwell asked smoothly, not faltering even slightly over the use of her given name.

"Lisa drinks gin," Mitzi Talmadge inserted, turning to Lisa to add, "Slade has a bartender's touch with mixed drinks."

"Gin?" Slade looked at her, waiting for a confirmation of her choice.

"No, I think I'll just have some juice." As tired as she was, Lisa knew the last thing she needed was an alcoholic beverage to muddle her thinking.

"Are you sure?" He gave her a chance to change her mind.

"Quite sure," Lisa nodded positively.

He walked to an ornate wooden trolley cart that was used as a serving bar. "There's tomato and orange juice in the icebox," he said without looking. "Which would you prefer?"

"Tomato." Lisa watched him pour the tomato juice over the ice cubes in a glass, add a dash of tabasco sauce and a wedge of lemon. Never once did he falter over the location of an item. "You know where everything is, don't you?" she commented, letting an inflection of sarcasm creep into her voice.

"I drop in quite often." He shrugged offhandedly, carrying her drink to her, but his dark gaze was probing her expression for the reason she had used that tone.

"But not often enough to wear out your welcome." Her tongue seemed to be running away with her, maybe because she had held it in all day.

"I hope not." But this time his smile didn't reach his eyes, eyes that had gone blank and shuttered.

"You couldn't possibly do that, Slade," Mitzi laughed, missing or overlooking the tiny barbs in Lisa's remarks. "Mildred and I love having you here. You couldn't come often enough. I would be delighted if you looked on this as your second home. You should. After all, you're responsible—directly and indirectly—for all that's been done here."

"Of course, how could I have forgotten?" The words were out before Lisa could check them.

She seemed bent on a course of self-destruction, making Slade an enemy and arousing his suspicions. Maybe it was true that those who do wrong really want to be caught.

Lisa only knew she had gone too far to reverse direction now. "Mitzi told me that you persuaded her to reopen the house and supervised the remodeling and redecorating. Naturally you would be familiar with everything, wouldn't you?"

"A house in this neighborhood of Old Charleston is an investment. Besides, it would have been a shame to

237

let this beautiful home become a derelict of the past," Slade replied.

"I agree with you completely," said Mitzi. "In fact I did the first time you suggested it, Slade, but I would never have attempted it on my own. Not that I couldn't have done it, but it's so time-consuming. You know how I dislike details, Lisa," she laughed at herself. "If Slade hadn't intervened to take charge of the workmen and various trades, I doubt if I would have fixed the old place up simply because I don't like the hassle that's inevitable."

"Yes," Lisa agreed. "You were lucky to have Slade take care of all that." She turned to him, a saccharine smile curving her mouth. "Ever since Mitzi has moved back to Charleston, all her letters have been singing your praises. You've become quite indispensable to her."

"I think Mitzi and I have become good friends. The purpose of friendship is to help each other when help is needed." There was a challenging set to his jaw although his voice remained quite calm and steady. "Now that Mitzi's on her own, without a man to look after her, I try to do what I can to help."

"I'm sure you do," Lisa taunted softly, and his gaze narrowed with piercing thoughtfulness.

"Believe me, I appreciate it," Mitzi stated. "I'm not interested in business and finances. I don't want to be bothered with investment credits and capital gains and stock dividends. It's a relief to turn it all over to Slade. I'm afraid I've rather taken advantage of his good nature, though."

"It must be wonderful to have someone you can

trust so implicity." Lisa thought the real point was who was taking advantage of whom? "It must be an awesome responsibility for you ... Slade—" she hesitated a bare second over his Christian name "—to have virtually sole control of someone else's money."

"Yes, it is," he agreed.

Lisa saw his mouth tighten and knew her gibes had to be getting close to their mark. She really should keep quiet, but she was deriving such fiendish delight out of antagonizing him.

Her subconscious seemed to have come up with a daring battle plan. While Lisa Talmadge attacked him boldly headon, Ann Eldridge could sneak up on him from behind.

"Lisa thinks I'm too trusting," Mitzi sighed in amusement. "But I'd rather be that way than the reverse. And of course, she doesn't know you as I do."

The invisible darts Lisa had been tossing hadn't escaped her aunt's attention. Neither did she seem upset by them. Yet, in the acknowledgment, there was a hint for a truce, however temporary.

"You're too trusting," Lisa reaffirmed, but gently and with affection. "It would be too easy for someone you like to take advantage of you."

Her subtle accusation against Slade Blackwell had been made, but not in a way that he could take open offense. He didn't like it—Lisa could tell by the hardening of his dark features.

"May I fix you another drink, Mitzi?" Slade rose from his chair, carrying his emptied glass.

"I don't believe so." Mitzi swirled her drink, ice cubes clinking against the side with the agitation of the liquid. "I still have some left, but help yourself by all means."

"I think I will," he said grimly, walking to the trolley cart. "In one way or another, it's been a long, tiring day."

You can say that again, Lisa thought, remembering the chaos in the office that afternoon.

The telephone had hardly ever stopped ringing, and clients kept stopping in expecting to talk to Slade whether they had appointments or not. It had taken forever to finish typing those letters, or so it seemed. The legal briefs weren't even half-completed.

"I never did have a chance to ask you how your day was, Lisa," Mitzi turned to her, curious and interested. "You left a message with Mildred that you were going to visit some friends. Did they take you sightseeing?"

"We were going to go after lunch," Lisa lied again, "but we got to talking. One thing led to another and before I knew it the afternoon was gone."

"I wasn't aware that you had friends living here in Charleston," Slade commented.

"College chums," Mitzi inserted.

"Yes, Susan, Peg and I were roommates in college." Lisa hoped that wherever they were, they didn't mind her using them in her story. "We're planning to make a day of it tomorrow since they're on vacation, too," she said, establishing a reason for her absence tomorrow.

"You must invite them over some time. I'd like to meet them," her aunt suggested.

"I'll do that," Lisa smiled. What else could she say?

From the archway came the sound of someone clearing her throat to attract attention, and Lisa glanced over her shoulder to see the unsmiling face of the housekeeper framed in the opening.

"If you'd all come into the dining room, I'll dish up the soup," she announced gruffly.

"We're coming," Mitzi agreed, and Slade was at the older woman's side when she rose from her chair.

"Did you fix my favorite, Mildred?" There was a teasing lightness to Slade's question.

Lisa was surprised to see the housekeeper flustered by his inquiry. There was a definite pink in her cheeks, which she tried to hide by turning away.

"It's she-crab soup, if that's what you're asking," she retorted.

Not only was her aunt under his spell, Lisa realized, but the housekeeper was as well. Lisa had not thought anything or anyone could pierce that armor of weary indifference that Mildred wore. The more she thought about it, as they followed the housekeeper into the dining room, the more logical it became that Slade Blackwell should cultivate the housekeeper's affection. Plus Slade was the one who had hired Mildred. She would naturally feel a certain sense of obligation and loyalty to him for obtaining this position. He would want an ally in the household to keep him informed. Mildred was being used as surely as her aunt was. The man was completely without scruples. But Lisa was determined that things were not going to go his way any longer.

The dining room was a formal, yet comfortable room. There were three accesses to the room: a set of double doors that opened into the living room; another set opening into the hallway; and a third door

241

to the kitchen. The rich luster of the woodwork and furniture was enhanced by the subtle pattern of the embossed wallpaper, a shade of peach. The crystal teardrops of the chandelier cast refracted light rays on the high beamed ceiling.

The leaves had been removed from the carved oak table to seat the three of them comfortably without a long stretch of white linen tablecloth to separate them. As Slade courteously held out the chair at the head of the table for Mitzi, Lisa walked around them to sit on her aunt's right.

Reaching for the carved wood of the chair back, her hand instead touched the back of his. Lisa drew it back in surprise, as if encountering a hot flame. Slade was directly behind her, an arm curved around to pull out the chair for her. She glanced at him, his dark eyes taunting, and an inner radar system seemed to clang in alarm at his closeness.

A built-in defense mechanism made Lisa step quickly aside to elude the force of his male presence. "Thank you," she murmured tightly as he held out the chair for her. Her shoulders felt the brush of his hard fingers through the thin material of her dress, her nerve ends quivering in reaction.

It was purely a physical response, regardless of the fact that she disliked him intensely. Lisa recognized that and hoped that forewarned was to be forearmed. She had never been accused of being a prude. She was well aware that she possessed a passionate nature.

In the past, she had met men she found physically attractive but for one reason or another had not liked personally, and she had always managed to control her reactions. She could do it again. She would not be ensnared by his sex appeal and lose sight of what he was as a man.

He was seated across the table from her, and she realized she had been staring at him quite openly, a fact he was well aware of as he watched her with masked alertness. For a panicked second, Lisa thought he could tell what she had been thinking. More than once she had been informed that her expressive green eyes revealed what she was thinking and feeling. Stormy green when she was angry, sparkling with a million tiny lights when she was happy, a murky green when she was troubled, a mysterious clear green when she was fascinated with something or attracted to someone.

But that wasn't the case this time, she remembered thankfully. The smoke blue sunglasses hid her thoughts. He didn't know of her vulnerability to him physically. But it was something Ann Eldridge would have to watch, since she didn't have the benefit of sunglasses.

"You were saying you had a rough day at the office, Slade," Mitzi commented, making the opening gambit of table conversation. "You were busy?"

"No more so than usual," he replied, and Lisa didn't think that augured well for tomorrow. "It's just that both Bob and Mary Lou are gone, which puts an extra workload on the rest of us."

"Vacation?" Mitzi leaned back in her chair as an unhurried Mildred began serving the aromatically steaming cups of soup.

"No, Mary Lou's parents were in an auto accident,"

Slade explained. "Her father was killed outright and her mother is in very serious condition in the hospital. So I'm stuck with a temporary girl as my secretary, which louses up the office routine even more."

"That's hardly her fault." Lisa instinctively defended her own inadequacies in the position.

"I didn't say that it was her fault," he corrected with dry sharpness. "But it would have been considerably easier on all of us if I could have obtained some trained help instead of this secretary who's virtually a novice."

"Trained help?" Lisa bridled at the term. "You make it sound as if she's supposed to be a trained dog that jumps through hoops on your command. You should give her credit for doing the very best she can."

A dark brow quirked in arrogant speculation. "Are you always so quick to defend people you've never met?"

Lisa realized she had been too vocal in her defense of the supposedly unknown secretary. She quickly dipped her spoon in the soup to conceal the intensity of her interest.

"Let's just say that I always support the underdog, especially if she's a woman." But the words came out sharp and argumentative despite her desire to sound casual and offhand.

"Are you one of those feminists?" There was dry laughter in his voice and the glitter of mockery in his eyes.

Stiffening, Lisa returned his look coldly. "Are you one of those chauvinists?"

"I guess it was too much to hope for that you two wouldn't clash," Mitzi sighed, glancing from one to the

244

other. Her expression was a mixture of regret and amusement.

"We aren't clashing, exactly." Lisa regretted her challenging outburst, but only because it had been issued in front of her aunt. "We simply have different points of view."

"Perhaps not as different as you think." His tone suggested some mysterious message that Lisa was supposed to understand, but she didn't.

And she said so. "I don't think that's true."

"You indicated that you don't believe I'm giving this temporary girl a chance, when the opposite is true, especially if she continues to show a willingness to learn. But I certainly can't be blamed for saying that it's inconvenient in the meantime to have inexperienced help," Slade concluded, so reasonably that it set Lisa's teeth on edge.

Lisa doubted that he really meant a single word he said and had only made the remark for Mitzi's benefit. Chameleonlike, he would change his stand on anything to one that her aunt would approve.

"Tell me about Mary Lou's replacement," Mitzi requested, "What is she like? She seems to have impressed you even though you claim she's a novice."

"She's young." His gaze flicked briefly to Lisa, and she held her breath, knowing he was making a fleeting comparison between herself and her alter ego, Ann Eldridge. "In her early twenties, about Lisa's age, I would guess. She has bright red hair, very attractive and eyes the color of—"

"Isn't that typical?" Lisa rushed to interrupt him, fearful Mitzi would make a comment about her own green eyes if Slade mentioned Ann's. "You ask a man to describe a woman and immediately he gives a physical description, judging a woman on her looks instead of her ability. They'll forgive a lack of brains if a woman is beautiful."

"Lisa!" her aunt admonished softly.

"That's quite all right, Mitzi. I understand what Lisa is saying." Slade dismissed the need for reproof. The look he gave Lisa was one of an adult indulging in the temper tantrum of a child, which did little to improve her disposition. "This new secretary happens to have brains as well as beauty. The reason I didn't boast about her skills is because she doesn't have any. I would be surprised if she can type thirty-five words a minute."

"Then why keep her on?" Lisa challenged. It was pure bravado since she might be providing him with the thought of firing Ann Eldridge and that would be cutting her own throat.

"Because she has a remarkable ability to handle several things at once without ever becoming distracted or flustered. That's a valuable asset," he stated. "When Mary Lou does return, she'll probably have a backlog of correspondence to type, but at least I don't have to be out there holding the new girl's hand."

"If she's as attractive as you say," Mitzi teased, "maybe that's unfortunate."

"Sorry," Slade smiled, "but she's married. Very happily, I understand."

"That's a pity," her aunt responded. "It sounds as if that was one girl who might have kept up with your many and varied interests."

"I guess that's something I won't find out." He shrugged. "How's the new novel coming along?"

"Marvelously!" her aunt declared enthusiastically, and the topic of conversation was switched.

As far as Lisa was concerned, the dinner was spoiled by Slade's presence. She took little part in the discussion, a fact that Mitzi didn't seem to notice as she warmed to the subject of her latest book. Slade pretended to concentrate on what her aunt was saying, but Lisa was intensely conscious of how often his piercing gaze was focused on her. It was disconcerting, like being under a microscope.

"Mildred, we'll have our coffee in the living room," Mitzi informed the housekeeper when they had finished dessert. "That way Slade can add a little brandy to his." She laughed briefly, and changed the subject, hardly drawing a breath in the transition.

"I wanted to show you the review of my latest book, too. It's in my study."

"I'll get it for you," Lisa volunteered quickly, eager for a few minutes alone.

"Would you mind?" The absent question by Mitzi was answered by a shake of Lisa's head. "It's in the pile of papers on the right-hand side of my desk. Somewhere in the middle, I think."

"I'll find it," she assured her aunt, hastily retreating while Mitzi and Slade started for the living room.

Study was a loose term since there wasn't anything about the room that resembled a study with the exception of the abundance of books. In this room, the creative side of Mitzi's personality surfaced amidst a clutter of papers, notes, books and magazines.

Yet it was definitely a feminine room, painted a bright, cheery yellow. A flowered sofa repeated the color. In a corner by a window sat a small, round table, painted white with a white cane-backed chair beside it. It was where Mitzi had her coffee and noon lunches.

There were no shelves of books, as such. They were stacked in every corner and scattered on every piece of furniture along with scraps of paper. A typewriter was on a long counter-style table. The table's surface was buried beneath papers, pencils, carbons and more books. There was a desk in the room, but its use seemed to be confined to being a catchall for more material.

There were three stacks of papers in all shapes and sizes on the right-hand side of the desk. Naturally Lisa found the newspaper clipping in the last stack she went through. Restoring the stack to its former ordered disorder, she turned to leave.

The study door opened as she made her turn and Slade walked in. For an instant, Lisa was too surprised to react. She stood in front of the desk, holding the paper and staring.

The click of the door latch closing seemed to suddenly isolate them from the rest of the house. Her pulse rocketed in alarm. The muscles of her throat constricted and she couldn't speak as he pinned her with his gaze.

"Did Mitzi send you in here?" She swallowed tightly, not certain why she was afraid.

"No, I came on my own." There was hardly a crack in his granite-hard features as he spoke.

"There was no need." Lisa raised her chin in a

gesture of defiance, her shattered poise beginning to piece itself together. "I found the clipping finally."

"So I see," Slade nodded, his gaze darting indifferently to the paper clutched in her hand.

A nervous hesitation quivered through her in the ensuing silence. There was something ominous in the crackling tension that made her doubly uneasy.

"Now that I've found it, I'd better take it in to Mitzi." Lisa realized she was rattling on like a clucking chicken, but she couldn't help herself.

Slade stood in front of the door, barring her way, but Lisa took a step forward anyway, expecting him to open the door for her. He didn't move.

"You aren't leaving yet," he told her in no uncertain terms.

Lisa stopped short. "What do you mean?" she breathed, caught between anger and dread.

"You are not leaving until you explain to me what's going on," he stated.

And Lisa felt a cold chill dancing down her spine. She had thought she had fooled him, that he hadn't recognized that she and Ann Eldridge were one and the same person. But obviously she had been kidding herself. She had underestimated him. How foolish! And how dangerous.

CHAPTER FOUR

PALING, LISA FELT the confidence draining from her as rapidly as the color receded from her face. Slade Blackwell had seen through her ruse. If only she had seen the file, obtained some proof to back up her suspicions. As it was, she had nothing with which to confront him. And how could she explain the deception?

"What's going on?" she repeated with false blankness.

"That's right." The line of his mouth was thin, harsh and forbidding.

"I don't think I know what you mean," Lisa stalled.

"Don't you?" Slade taunted with arrogant challenge.

A step in front of the door, he had not moved since entering the study. Yet he seemed to fill the room, intimidating Lisa until her legs felt like two quivering sticks of jelly. She wanted to sink into the nearest chair and confess her misdeed. But that would be too much like admitting guilt when he was the unscrupulous one who should feel guilty.

"Your question is confusing." Why was her lying tongue failing her now? "What's going on where?"

At his step forward, Lisa wanted to retreat. She had the eerie sensation of being stalked, but the large desk was directly behind her. There wasn't anywhere to run even if she could make her legs move.

"Your pretended innocence isn't fooling me, Lisa." His voice was smooth and controlled. She wished for a measure of his calmness. "I dislike people who sneak around."

Lowering her chin, she stared at her hands and the fluttering paper in the trembling fingers. "Sneak around?" She swallowed to rid her voice of its betraying tremor. "How could I be accused of sneaking around? Mitzi sent me in here."

"You know damned well that's not what I mean." Despite the imprecation, his tone of voice didn't change.

"Then you'll have to be more explicit with your questions." Lifting her head to challenge him boldly, Lisa clung to her false ignorance, hoping her racing brain would come up with a plausible reason for her deception—a reason other than the truth. "I'm at a complete loss to understand your meaning."

His gaze narrowed, impaling Lisa on its thrusting point. "I'll make myself clearer. Mitzi may believe that nonsense about personalities clashing and chemistries being wrong, but I don't buy it."

Lisa breathed in sharply. He didn't know! He didn't know she was Ann Eldridge! The knowledge sang through her veins, warming her with victory. She wanted to laugh wildly with delight.

"You don't?" she drawled. A suggestion of dimples dented her cheeks as she tried to conceal the bubbling smile tickling her mouth.

"No, I don't," Slade answered flatly. "I believe in neither love at first sight nor hatred at first sight. And your dislike of me borders on hatred, even though you've just met me."

"Hatred is a harsh word." Lisa was brimming with confidence now.

"It's a harsh emotion," he retorted. "You've been sniping at me all evening, and I want to know why."

Lisa's battle plan called for a frontal attack. She took a deep breath and plunged forward. "It's very simple. Unlike my aunt, I don't trust you."

His jaw hardened. "You made that obvious to Mitzi."

"Did I? Good." A smile accompanied the honey-coated comment.

"What's your game?" His dark head was tipped to the side, the angular planes of his face severely controlled to remain expressionless and cold.

"My game?" A delicate winged brow arched above the frame of her sunglasses. The question momentarily threw her off balance. "You ask *me* that?"

"Don't look so indignant, Lisa." One corner of his mouth curled upward in a jeer. "It isn't convincing."

Her temper flared. "And your apparent interest and concern for Mitzi is downright sickening," she seethed. "She must have seemed easy prey for you—divorced, alone, seemingly without any close relatives. And let's not leave out wealthy! You could even claim old family ties."

"The key word here is wealthy, isn't it?" he mused.

Her anger didn't seem to worry him. Slade was closer now, looming in front of her. His height seemed to dwarf her, forcing her to tilt her head back to meet the black glitter of his gaze. Warily she was conscious of his muscular physique and the blatant virility that was such an overwhelming part of him.

"Yes," she agreed, "the key word here is wealthy.

252

You've gone to great lengths to make yourself indispensable to Mitzi. You must be laughing up your sleeve at how gullible she is!"

"Are you?"

Slade Blackwell was clever. Lisa knew it would take a great deal to provoke him into admitting anything. But she could be cunning, too. Hadn't she already fooled him once?

"I don't find it at all funny!" she retorted. "She trusts you, and you're stealing her blind. It must be a rude awakening for you to discover that she isn't quite as alone in the world as you thought. Regardless of the fact that she and my uncle were divorced, my parents and I still think of her as part of our family. And we're certainly not going to let some cheap, money-grubbing lawyer take advantage of her!"

"Oh?" Slade seemed coldly amused by her threat. "What are you going to do about it?"

"I'm going to make her see what a conniving thief you are," she declared angrily.

"Then what?" He eyed her steadily, obviously confident that she wouldn't succeed, but he didn't know about Ann Eldridge.

"What do you mean?" Lisa frowned, not seeing the relevance of his question.

"What are you going to get out of it?" he elucidated calmly.

"The satisfaction of Mitzi seeing you for what you really are," she retorted.

"That's all?" Slade smiled with arrogant skepticism.

"What do you mean?" She was beginning to feel like a broken record, but she was puzzled by his attitude.

"You seem intent on getting me out of Mitzi's life

and her affairs," he replied. "Would that be because once I'm gone, you can step in?"

Lisa tensed, reading the implication he had intended her to find. "What are you getting at?" she demanded.

"That you aren't any blood relation to her. She has none left." His sharp gaze never left her face. "Admittedly you're her favorite niece, but the relationship is based on a marriage that has since been terminated."

"That's only a technicality." She defended her status in the household.

"My profession deals in technicalities," Slade reminded her with a trace of sardonicism. "Another interesting fact is that Mitzi has lived in Charleston for several years now, yet this is the first visit you've made."

"It's the first chance I've had to come," Lisa argued.

"Or the first time you thought there was reason?" he countered.

"Reason?" She drew herself up to her full height that still left her several inches shorter than Slade. "What are you saying?"

"That your motive for being here isn't as pure and lily white as you pretend." His gaze raked her with sweeping disdain.

"My motive?" Lisa repeated incredulously.

"It seems to me that you scheduled this visit after you became aware of how often my name was mentioned in your aunt's letters. Until then, I think you were too certain of Mitzi's affection for you to bother about visiting an elderly relative when you could be having fun with friends your own age. Money brought you here, Lisa Talmadge, Mitzi's money," he concluded.

"Are you accusing me of—" Lisa began in outraged anger.

"I'm saying that you dislike me because Mitzi had turned to me for advice in money matters and you see that as a threat, not to Mitzi but to yourself." Slade studied her with contempt.

"That's absurd!" Lisa bristled. "I don't care what Mitzi does with her money or who she gives it to! I certainly don't expect to receive a dime of it!"

"How very nobly spoken," he taunted. "Mitzi is fond enough of you to believe that. Personally I find it pathetically phony—as false as your concern for Mitzi's welfare."

Incensed, Lisa reacted blindly, words failing her. Her palm swung in a lightning arc, striking a leanly hollowed cheek with a resounding slap. His face was as hard and unyielding as it looked, and her hand tingled painfully from the impact.

But she didn't have time to dwell on it. She was too aware of the primitive anger darkening his features. She doubted if anyone had slapped his face in a long while, especially a woman.

A deadly silence filled the room. Lisa could hear the wild racing of her pulse pounding in her ears. Her hand had left a pale imprint on his tanned cheek, and the proud flare of his nostrils said it was a mark that would not go unpunished.

"I have never hit a woman in my life." His voice was a low, savagely growling sound, drawn through teeth clenched in anger. "But you're sorely tempting me to change that."

"Don't let the fact that I'm a woman stop you," Lisa bluffed recklessly.

An ominous fire blazed in his eyes. He seemed to move closer to her and she took a hasty step backward, bumping sharply into the desk. Thrown off balance, she wavered unsteadily for a second. Before she could regain her equilibrium on her own, steel fingers had clamped around her elbow to steady her.

"Take your hand off me!" Ice dripped from her voice.

Only after she had spoken did Lisa realize that his supporting hand had been an instinctive reaction on his part. Slade would have released her instantly if she hadn't demanded it. She tried to twist free.

"Let go of me!" This time there was a trace of desperate anger in her demand.

She struck at him again with her free hand, but this he was prepared, capturing her wrist and yanking her roughly against his granite length. Strong fingers wound around a handful of silver blond hair, tugging at her tender scalp.

Lisa breathed in sharply with pain. It was the last movement she was permitted as his mouth crushed her lips. Her arms were trapped uselessly between their bodies, unable to wedge even the slightest space, his strength easily overpowering hers. Lisa reeled under the bruising pressure of his mouth.

The touch, smell and taste of him was a physical assault on her senses. Her mind could register nothing but his complete domination, making a response as impossible as resistance. She was certain the fierce mastery could continue forever, that she would be locked eternally in the steel embrace of his arms. The very instant the thought crossed her mind that she would be endlessly condemned to this punishment, the brutal force smothering her mouth was retracted.

Numbed and without strength, she couldn't move. The hand pulling at her hair no longer forced her head back, but she couldn't raise it upright. As the constricting band around her relaxed its hold, her hands clutched at the sleeves of his suit jacket for support, feeling the fluid steel of his muscles rippling beneath the material.

With an effort, Lisa opened her eyes to gaze at him through the smoke blue lenses of her sunglasses. Dark, ruthless male features filled her vision. There was only one weapon left that she possessed in any appreciable amounts, and she resorted to it, however ineffectual it might turn out to be.

"Is your male ego satisfied?" Her voice was unbelievably husky, trembling as violently as she was inside. "Or did you intend to rape me?"

The hand that had been at the back of her hair slid to the side of her neck. The body heat it emanated burned her sensitive flesh as his thumb roughly trailed from the point of her chin to the hollow of her throat. It pressed lightly on her windpipe as if Slade was considering strangling her.

"If that's what I intended, you wouldn't still be standing up," he said grimly.

There was a smudge of dusty-pink lipstick at the corner of his mouth, the only evidence she could see in the hard, male features that Slade had been the one to administer the punishing kiss. Lisa felt branded by it.

Her lips throbbed, her smooth skin rasped by the

faint stubble of his beard, barely noticeable by sight, but definitely by touch. Her heart was pulsing chaotically, her cheeks flushed.

"Will you please let me go?" she requested tightly.

"Not until we come to an understanding," Slade answered unequivocally.

"An understanding?" she repeated angrily, and tried to push away from his chest, but he simply tightened his hold. "I'll make no bargain with you!"

"You'll make one and like it," he snapped. "I'm going to say this once and only once. You're going to keep your nose out of things that don't concern you—and that includes Mitzi's life!"

"Her life concerns me," Lisa protested.

"All you are is her nice little niece from Baltimore. Keep it that way."

"While you keep stealing her money—not a chance!" she retorted.

"I—" But Slade didn't have a chance to finish what he was going to say. Three light raps sounded in swift succession was warning only a second before the study door opened and Mitzi's dark head peered around the door.

"You two have been in here so long I was certain you'd gotten into a scrap and needed a referee," she said. Slade was slow in releasing Lisa, despite her angry attempt to twist free. A knowing smile spread across her aunt's face. "But it wasn't that kind of a scrap that you got into."

"Yes, it was." Lisa fired a venomous look at his unruffled exterior, trembling with violent hatred. "Your Slade Blackwell was molesting me, Mitzi."

He glanced at Mitzi and drawled lazily, a hand lifting to the cheek Lisa had slapped, "I kissed her, but only after she'd practically invited me to do it."

"What he means is I slapped him," Lisa translated.

"For heaven's sake, why?" Mitzi laughed, not entirely sure how much of what was being said was the truth and how much playful exaggeration.

"Because—" Lisa began.

"Because I was criticizing her for letting so much time go by without visiting you," Slade inserted swiftly. "But it really wasn't my place to say anything, and I apologize." He turned to Lisa, his dark eyes offering a silent challenge. "That's about what happened, isn't it? Or did you want to add something?"

He was daring her to accuse him of stealing her aunt's money. But it was something Lisa wouldn't do, not until she had some proof to back up her claim.

"I can't think of anything that needs to be added," she agreed. "Not for the time being."

There was a complacent twist to his mouth. "You have quite a niece, Mitzi. She's really very stimulating. I think she intends to keep me on my toes while she's here."

"I intend to try," Lisa retorted. The review clipping had fallen to the floor. She stooped to pick it up and walked to her aunt. "I'm afraid the clipping is a little bit worse for the wear. It was caught in the middle of our confrontation."

"It's a little wrinkled," Mitzi agreed, smoothing the paper in her hand, "but not hurt. The coffee is still in the living room if you two are still interested."

Slade pushed aside the cuff of his jacket to glance at his watch. "It's getting late for me. But to show you how much I enjoyed the dinner and the company tonight, I'd like to return the hospitality by taking you and Lisa to dinner tomorrow night. If you're free, of course," he added mockingly.

"I'm never free where you're concerned," Lisa snapped.

Without blinking an eye, Slade faced her. "Then how much will it cost me?"

"You know very well that's not what I meant!" Lisa flashed, and longed to slap that complacent look from his face.

"Then you are free?" he taunted.

"But not easy." If he seemed to be determined to issue innuendoes, so would she.

"It's rare that anything worthwhile is easy." The look on his saturnine features seemed to take up the challenge she had inadvertently made.

Lisa had to clamp her mouth tightly shut to keep from telling him exactly what she thought of his chances. There had been enough arguing in front of Mitzi. The time for taking a stand against Slade Blackwell hadn't come, not until she had something to back up her suspicions.

"It's settled, then." Slade turned back to Mitzi. "Dinner tomorrow evening. I'll pick the two of you up at seven."

"No!" Lisa snapped, and received a piercing look of inquiry from him.

"She's just being stubborn." Mitzi seemed to be amused by their cutting byplay. "Of course we'll have dinner with you, Slade. I want Lisa to have a few nights out in Charleston while she's here and you know all the good places."

"No," she refused again.

"Lisa," Mitzi said in a cajoling voice.

The tiredness of Lisa's bones and muscles was making her doubly irritable. She felt at her wits' end trying to cope with this intolerable situation.

Slade must have sensed that she didn't want to bring everything out in the open yet and was backing her into a corner. Tomorrow was going to be another trying day, and she simply couldn't face the thought of seeing him tomorrow night.

"Mitzi, I'm going to be out all day tomorrow with Peg and Susan," she reasoned. "I'm not going to feel like going out tomorrow night."

"We'll make it Thursday, the day after," Slade suggested.

"Yes." By then, Lisa intended to have all the information she needed to convict Slade Blackwell beyond Mitzi's reasonable doubt.

"I'll look forward to it," he said with a maddening smile, and took his leave.

"He's an infuriating man," Lisa muttered as the study door closed behind the arrogant set of his shoulders.

"But he is a man," Mitzi observed with a bright twinkle in her eye. "If I were your age—"

"If you were my age, you'd be welcome to him." She turned away from the door to face her aunt. Her lips still felt tender from his bruising kiss. "I told you once that I don't care for the strong, masterful type. He leaves me cold."

"Cold?" Mitzi raised an eyebrow, amusement evident in the action. "I think hot is more like it."

"Please, Mitzi." Lisa lifted a warning hand of protest. "At the moment, Slade Blackwell is a very volatile subject as far as I'm concerned. And unless you want me to explode, you'd better drop it."

There was a heavy sigh of agreement from her aunt. Lisa knew she was hurt by the veiled animosity between two people she liked, but she also knew that Mitzi was going to be even more hurt when she found out the kind of man Slade Blackwell really was. In the long run it would be best, though.

Mitzi wisely didn't introduce Slade's name into the conversation again. Despite that, neither the incident in the study nor the man himself was far from Lisa's thoughts.

By ten o'clock a mental and physical exhaustion began to set in. Lisa was grateful when Mitzi suggested that it was time they went to bed. Upstairs in her room, Lisa ignored the bed in favor of the bathroom where the shower spray massaged the aching muscles of her shoulders and neck. She tumbled into bed and turned off the light. In the darkness, she wondered if thoughts of Slade and how she would unmask him, would keep her awake. That was the last thing Lisa remembered thinking.

The study door was open when Lisa came down the spiral staircase a little after seven the next morning. The typewriter was silent.

"Is that you, Lisa?" her aunt called and appeared in the doorway an instant later. "Gracious, but you are up early this morning. And all dressed, too."

"I decided that I didn't want to sleep my vacation away," Lisa lied, preferring to be snugly asleep in her canopied bed.

"Come in and join me for coffee. Mildred just brought me a fresh pot," Mitzi invited.

"I wouldn't want to disturb you. I know you're working." Her finger clutched her large purse, its sides bulging with the red wig she had crammed inside.

"Nonsense. You aren't disturbing me," her aunt insisted. "I was just taking a break before I began the next scene."

"I'd love to have coffee with you, but I'm afraid I can't." Lisa glanced at her watch. The minutes were ticking away. She needed the early start to work so she could make the transformation into Ann Eldridge before reaching Slade's office.

"Are you going somewhere at this hour?" Mitzi frowned in astonishment.

Poor Peggy and Susan, Lisa thought, they might never know how useful they had been to her since she arrived in Charleston.

"I'm meeting Sue and Peg for breakfast." She hated deceiving her aunt this way, but it was for her own good. "Since we didn't get any sight-seeing done yesterday, we thought we'd get an early start at it today."

"Oh, I see." But something in Mitzi's tone indicated that she thought they had taken leave of their senses. "What are you planning to see today? There is a tour boat that takes you to Fort Sumter where the first battle of the Civil War took place. It's really quite fascinating to wander about the old battlements and listen to the park ranger explain about the long Union siege of the fort. The South never lost it in battle. They ultimately abandoned it toward the close of the war, but it was never taken from them."

"Actually I'm not sure where we're going today," Lisa explained. "The girls know their way around better than I do, so they are making all the plans."

"Be sure to have them take you to Fort Sumter."

"I'll tell them," she promised with fingers mentally crossed. "I'd really better be going, Mitzi. I'll see you tonight."

"Have fun."

"I will," she returned and nearly dashed out the door.

Her heels clicked loudly on the paved sidewalk as she hurried along the street. At least this time she wouldn't have to stop to ask directions to Slade's office. Lisa glanced at her watch. It was nearly seven-thirty. She quickened her pace.

Using the ladies' room of a restaurant to change, she donned the flame-colored wig, outlined her lips with a coral gloss and replaced her birthstone with the wedding band. She smiled secretly to herself as she emerged, wondering if anyone had noticed the blonde going in and the redhead coming out.

When Slade arrived at the office, she was hard at work, busily transcribing the legal briefs from the dictaphone. Nodding an indifferent "good morning," he picked up the few phone messages from her desk and went directly into his own office. Lisa hoped that he hibernated there. Now that he had met Lisa Talmadge, she didn't want him noticing similarities to Ann Eldridge.

At each sound coming from the outer reception area, Lisa glanced expectantly toward the door. Drew

264

was supposed to return her aunt's file this morning, and she desperately needed to get her hands on it. She couldn't hope to fool Slade indefinitely. The sooner she could get her hands on the information she needed the better.

Half the morning was gone before Drew appeared. Lisa was on the telephone when he walked in. She smiled a greeting, her eyes lighting up when she saw the folder in his hand.

It added a special glow to her smile that she was unaware of and caused Drew's quick intake of breath. While she transferred the phone call to Slade, Drew sat on the edge of her desk, gazing at her silently.

"It's a crime for someone so beautiful to be married," he declared when the transfer had been made.

"My husband doesn't think so," she smiled faintly, concealing her impatience to take the folder from his hand.

"Oh, yes," Drew nodded ruefully, then frowned. "What's his name again?" Lisa drew a complete blank. She couldn't remember the name she had given her fictitious husband. "Burt, that's it." Fortunately he supplied it. "Lucky Burt."

"Yes." But Lisa wanted to get off that subject before she buried herself in lies. "I see you brought the folder back safely."

"Yup, it's all here intact," he assured her, depositing it on the desk top. Lisa's fingers inched to open it and peruse the contents. It was an almost uncontrollable urge that she checked with a great deal of effort. "What about lunch today?"

"I'll have to take a raincheck," she refused, knowing

exactly how she intended to spend her lunch hour—glued to the folder.

"Come on, have a heart," Drew coaxed. "Make a poor bachelor happy for an hour."

"Sorry." Her mind wasn't going to be changed by any amount of flattery. "I'm behind with a lot of correspondence. I'm going to do what you did yesterday—have Ellen bring me back a sandwich to eat here."

"Okay," he capitulated unexpectedly. "If that's what you want, I'll buy the sandwich and we'll have a little picnic right here in the office."

"No," Lisa protested instantly, then tried to temper the sharpness of her refusal. "If you join me, then we'll talk and I won't get anything done, which would defeat my purpose for not going out to lunch. Let's just make it another day."

"I suppose I'll have to console myself with the knowledge that you didn't turn me down flat." Drew gave an exaggerated sigh.

"Exactly," she laughed briefly. "Now run off so I can get some work done." Her hands inched toward the folder as he straightened from her desk.

"You're a worse slave driver than Slade," he joked. "But a beautiful one."

With a wink and a wave of his hand, he left, and Lisa's hands greedily snatched up the folder, flipping it open to briefly scan the contents. The very first document caught her attention. It seemed to be a power of attorney.

Before she had a chance to examine it, there was the alerting sound of a doorknob being turned. She barely had time to close the folder when Slade walked in, aloof curiosity in his dark eyes at her guilty start.

"Is something wrong, Mrs. Eldridge?" His hard, handsome mouth softened slightly as if bemused by her reaction.

"No, I—I just didn't hear you, that's all." Her fingers tightened nervously on the stiff cover of the folder.

His dark gaze slid to the folder. "What do you have there?"

"Oh, er, this?" Damn, Lisa thought, she had to stop stammering like an errant child. "It's the Talmadge file. Drew just returned it, and I was just going to put it back in the cabinet."

"There's no need." He held out his hand. "I'll take it. There's a couple things in there I want to look over."

No, she cried inwardly, her fingers tightening convulsively on the folder. Aloud she murmured a hopeful, "Now?"

"Of course now." There was a humorless, silent laugh in his voice.

It had been a ridiculous question. Grudgingly Lisa handed it to him, unable to argue her right to keep it. "Was there anything else?" she asked, reverting to a taut, professional tone.

"No, nothing else." His gaze narrowed briefly on her before he shifted his attention to the folder in hand reentered his office.

Twice the file had been in her grasp and twice it had been taken from her. Frustration was beginning to set in.

Her assertion to Drew that she was going to have lunch at her desk trapped Lisa into spending the noon

267

hour in her office. Although Slade had taken her aunt's file, she was determined all this time wasn't going to be wasted. Perhaps she could find some incriminating evidence in the files of the decorators, carpenters, and landscape company Slade used.

The trouble was that she didn't know their names and she wasn't any nearer to understanding the filing system. Her own code of ethics wouldn't permit her to examine a file unless something in its title had reference to the type of firm she was seeking. This seemed to eliminate the bulk of the folders.

Before the lunch hour was over, Lisa knew how a spy felt. Every creaking floorboard in the old building made her jump. Voices filtering in from the street had her looking around in alarm. Snooping was an unpleasant occupation, especially when one came up with zero results.

The sound of Slade's voice in the outer reception area sent her scurrying to her desk. She was bent over the paper in her typewriter when he walked into her office. Lisa pretended an absorption in her work rather than look up.

"Have there been any calls for me?" He stopped at her desk.

"No, sir." She made an unnecessary erasure of a word she had typed much earlier and blew the erasure dust from the paper.

"I'm expecting Clyde Sanders to stop by. When he arrives, send him into my office," Slade instructed.

"Yes, sir." Lisa nodded her compliance and sighed with relief when he walked into his private office and closed the door.

CHAPTER FIVE

By the end of the day, Lisa was engulfed in frustration. She had kept waiting and waiting for Slade to return her aunt's folder so that it could be filed . . . after, of course, she had looked through it. But he hadn't.

Shortly after three that afternoon, Slade had left the office on an errand. Desperate, Lisa had sneaked into his office to see if he had left the folder behind. She couldn't find it among the papers on his desk. One drawer of his desk had been locked and he had taken his briefcase with him. Lisa had presumed it was in one of the two places.

This deception was threatening to last much longer than she had ever intended. The longer it continued, the greater became the risk of being unmasked. Lisa knew she had to take advantage of every opportunity. If an opportunity didn't present itself, she would have to try to arrange one.

A few minutes after five, Lisa was still at the typewriter. Her plan was to keep working until after Slade had left and hopefully find the folder in the briefcase he had brought back with him. Slade was in his office with a client. No matter how tired she was or how much her body ached, Lisa was determined to outwait him.

Her patience was rewarded five minutes later when

she heard the connecting door open to Slade's private office and the voices of the two men talking as they came out. Her fingers continued tapping at the typewriter keys.

Lisa faked a concentration in her task and hoped Slade would leave with the man. But he walked with him only as far as the door to the reception area and bid him goodbye. When the client was gone, Slade turned. Lisa felt his gaze rest on her. Her skin prickled with her awareness of it, sensitive nerve ends reacting. But she tried to give no sign that she knew he was looking at her.

"It's after five, Mrs. Eldridge," he spoke, not allowing Lisa to ignore him any longer. "You should have left twenty minutes ago."

Her fingers paused on the keys as she gave him a preoccupied glance. "I'll be leaving shortly," she assured him with vague indifference.

"You do realize your children will be home from school by now."

His statement paralyzed Lisa. He said it as if she had children. Among all the lies she'd told, had she claimed to have children? She searched her memory. Unless it had failed her, Lisa was positive that she hadn't.

"I don't have any children, Mr. Blackwell," she corrected that impression. "My husband and I have decided to wait a few years before beginning a family."

"Regardless, your husband will be home expecting his dinner."

Lisa seethed at that typically male statement, but as Ann Eldridge, she didn't dare voice her feminist views on the subject of equality of sexes, nor her opinion that

270

a husband could start dinner if his wife worked late. So she had to find another plausible reason why it wasn't essential for her to be home immediately.

"Undoubtedly my husband is working late, too," she said.

"Oh? What does he do?" Slade asked.

"He's in construction. When the weather is as beautiful as it is today, he gets in a lot of overtime. I'll be home before he is, even if I stay until six." Lisa shrugged her unconcern.

"There isn't any need for you to stay late."

"I want to finish this. You can go ahead and leave." *The sooner, the better,* Lisa added to herself. "As soon as I'm through here, I'll be going home, too, but I know how important it is—"

"Nothing is so important that it can't wait until tomorrow," Slade interrupted. "Your attitude is very commendable, Mrs. Eldridge, but unnecessary."

"But I don't mind staying," Lisa protested.

A dark eyebrow lifted at her persistence. "I said it wasn't necessary. Cover your typewriter and clear your desk. This is an order, Mrs. Eldridge," he stated.

"Very well." Lisa should have been grateful for his thoughtful consideration, but he had thwarted her attempt to stay late. She was frustrated once again.

Slade stood by her desk for several more seconds. Lisa shook out the plastic cover for the typewriter and draped it over the machine. The action apparently satisfied him that she intended to comply with his order and he returned to his private office.

Lisa took her time clearing the desk and putting things away. She used every excuse to linger, sharpening pencils and arranging the articles on her desk in a precise order. There was still a chance Slade might leave before she did. Ten minutes later, she was straightening a stack of papers in her file tray as Slade walked out of his office.

His gaze narrowed on her sharply, his features lean and hard. "Are you still here, Mrs. Eldridge? I thought I told you to go home."

"I was just straightening my desk." She took the blank stationery paper from beside the typewriter and returned it to its proper desk drawer. "I'll be leaving in a few minutes."

His mouth thinned as he turned and walked to the file cabinet. The hope that he might be on his way home, died as he removed two folders and returned to his office. There was nothing Lisa could do but leave and hope for better luck the next day.

Walking the blocks to her aunt's house, Lisa tried to formulate some plan of action, but she was too tired and vaguely dispirited to think. The wig in her purse seemed to weigh a ton. She had barely entered the house, the door not yet closed, when Mitzi's questioning voice sought her out.

"Lisa, is that you?" She came sweeping out of the living room into the foyer. "Gracious, I was about to send out a search party for you."

"I'm sorry I'm late," Lisa apologized, a faint, tired sigh in her voice. "I didn't mean for you to worry."

"You look exhausted. Sightseeing all day must have worn you out." A sympathetic smile curved her aunt's mouth. "Did you try to see everything in one day?"

"Something like that," she hedged and arched her

back to ease her cramped and sore muscles. "Right now the only thing I want to see is a tubful of hot water."

"A nice hot bath works wonders. You go soak for a while," Mitzi instructed. "Later you can come downstairs and join me in a relaxing drink before dinner."

"I'll do that," Lisa agreed and climbed the spiral staircase to her room.

While the bathtub was filling with water, Lisa undressed. Halfway to the bathroom she remembered the wig was still crammed in her purse. She took it out and hid it in the rear of a dresser drawer. She followed the scent of the fragrant bubble bath to the tub, turned off the faucets and climbed in. Lisa had no idea how long she lay soaking in the bath, but the water was cool when she climbed out to towel herself dry.

Lisa sighed dispiritedly as she slipped on the silk kimono-styled dressing robe that was chocolate brown and embroidered in pale ivory. The long bubble bath had eased the stiffness of her muscles, but it had done little to wash away the troubled light in her green eyes. Each day spent as Ann Eldridge was a risk.

Opening her closet door, she immediately turned away. She didn't feel like dressing even though she knew Mitzi was waiting downstairs for her to join her. The silk robe swished softly about her ankles as she walked barefoot to her bedroom door.

Maybe her aunt wouldn't stand on ceremony. A quiet evening spent lounging around was what Lisa dearly wanted and needed. She seriously doubted if Mitzi would object.

Her hand reached for the carved banister of the

staircase. Something—a sound, a voice—stopped her, her foot poised on the edge of the first step. At the bottom of the stairs stood Slade Blackwell, dark, arresting and vital. The sight of him paralyzed Lisa, and her hand clutched the loose fold of her robe together at the waist.

Insolently, his gaze slowly traveled the length of her. She reddened as she realized her action had drawn the clinging fabric more tightly over her curves, possibly revealing that she wore nothing beneath it.

Her skin seemed to burn from the appraising caress of his eyes, mocking yet suggestive. She released the robe immediately, spreading her fingers to try to relieve the sudden, elemental tension that claimed her.

"What are you doing here?" She finally broke the silence, her voice ringing with a challenge born of embarrassment.

"I don't think it's any of your business since I'm here to see Mitzi," he replied smoothly.

"Why?"

"I told you, it's none of your business." Slade continued to study her feminine shape with an arrogant unconcern that had to have been bred into him. The almost physical touch of his gaze was having disturbing effect on her senses, but Lisa was determined not to reveal it. Being dressed—or barely dressed—as she was, was enough of a disadvantage.

"Mitzi is my aunt and that makes your presence here my business," she retorted.

"The lawyer-client relationship doesn't recognize your right." His mouth twisted cynically. "*If* you have one."

274

"Where's Mitzi?" Lisa demanded.

"She misplaced her glasses and is off looking for them." He caught her gaze and held it. "Why don't you come down and entertain me?"

"I'm not dr—" The word "dressed" died on her lips. She was not usually so slow on the uptake. The entertainment he had meant didn't require clothes, as his throaty chuckle mockingly told her. "You're disgusting," she hissed.

But Slade appeared to ignore her insulting comment. His dark head was tipped slightly to the side, studying her with a seemingly new-found interest, puzzled and curious.

"There's something different about you," he drawled thoughtfully. "Maybe it's in your eyes, minus their sunglasses."

Lisa stiffened. He couldn't see the color of her eyes at this distance, not with the length of the staircase separating them. But his remark acted like a cold splash of ice water.

"There's nothing different about you!" she flashed defensively. "Tell Mitzi I'll be down when you leave."

Pivoting on her heel, she hurriedly retraced the way to her bedroom, trembling with delayed shock. That had been close, much too close.

Slade's appearance changed Lisa's mind about lounging around the house in her robe. In her room, she slipped out of the robe and put on a pair of pale yellow slacks and a blouse of a green and yellow print. She waited until she heard the front door close before venturing downstairs again. Mitzi was alone in the living room when Lisa entered it.

"You look better. How do you feel?" Mitzi walked to the wooden trolley cart and fixed Lisa a drink.

"Much better." Especially now that Slade was gone. Lisa settled into the orange- and rust-colored brocade chair. Slade's refusal to say why he had wanted to see Mitzi prompted Lisa to ask, "What did Slade want?" She didn't mention that she had spoken to him.

"He stopped over with some legal papers that needed my signature," her aunt explained.

"Oh?" Lisa took the drink her aunt brought her and sipped at it, wishing she had gotten a glimpse at those papers. "What kind of document was it? You did it read it before you signed it, didn't you?" she questioned, suddenly wary.

"I read it, but all that legal jargon is just so much mishmash. Who can understand it? If I wrote my novels like that, the readers would never be able to figure out the plot," Mitzi laughed with absolute unconcern.

"Do you mean that you don't know what you signed?" Lisa accused in astonishment.

"Slade explained it all to me," came the smooth assurance, which didn't reassure Lisa at all. Mitzi lowered her voice to a conspiratorial whisper. "I'm setting up a retirement fund for Mildred. Nothing very large, mind you, but something that will supplement her government pension when she reaches old age. She has been so loyal to me, and a friend, as well, despite her crabbiness. She's a regular skinflint, but I know she hasn't been able to put very much aside. This retirement program seemed a good way to help her without making it look like charity. Slade agreed when I mentioned it to him."

"I see." It sounded harmless. Lisa hoped it was.

Mitzi leaned back in her chair. "Tell me, what all did you see today?"

Lisa dreaded having to come up with more lies. She took a deep breath and tried to come up with a story that wouldn't trip her up.

"After breakfast, we took a carriage ride." Since that was one thing she had promised herself she would do. "The driver took us all around. As a matter of fact, we came right by here."

"I wish you had stopped for coffee. I would like to have met your friends. You are welcome to have them over anytime," Mitzi said.

"I thought about bringing them in," she lied, "but I knew you were busy with your new novel. By the way, how is it coming along?"

"Marvelously." Her aunt's face seemed to light up with excitement. "I'm getting to what I call the 'good' part. It's where the plot begins to thicken, if you'll pardon the use of a cliche." She began explaining the twists and turns of the plot, the element of suspense that was beginning to build, and the characters.

The rest of the evening Lisa adroitly maneuvered the conversation to focus on Mitzi's interests and avoided telling more lies about places she had supposedly seen. That night in bed, she questioned how much longer she was going to be able to get away with this deception. It seemed that only time would tell.

LISA LEANED OVER her typewriter when Slade walked out of his private office, pretending to read over the partially typed letter. He paused briefly beside her desk.

"I'm going to lunch now, Mrs. Eldridge. I'll be back shortly after one," he informed her.

After her near unmasking last night, Lisa took pains to avoid looking directly at him just in case some expression or gesture struck a familiar note. Even now when he was addressing her directly, she kept her head turned down, feigning a concentration in her work.

"Yes, Mr. Blackwell," she replied in a deliberately absent manner.

When he walked away, her green eyes followed him through the concealing veil of her sooty lashes. His day's calendar of appointments had indicated a business luncheon, but he wasn't carrying his briefcase. She breathed in deeply, knowing it meant it was still in his office.

From the reception area, she could hear him speaking to Drew. Hurriedly she began typing, removing the finished letter from the typewriter just as she heard the street door open and close. Slade was gone.

Lisa quickly separated the carbon copy of the letter from the original and set it aside. Taking the original and gathering up the other correspondence ready for his signature, she darted into his office.

The expensively tooled briefcase was on the floor behind the large swivel chair at his desk. Lisa shoved the papers on top of his desk and bent to open the briefcase. Her hands shook badly as she unsnapped the latch.

She felt like a thief and had to remind herself that Slade was the real thief. Still, her hearing was acutely tuned to any sound of invasion from the outer office.

Her aunt's file was not in the briefcase. Lisa rose in

irritation, looking at the endless stacks of papers and folders on his desk. She began riffling through them, searching for her particular needle in the haystack of papers.

"What are you doing, Mrs. Eldridge?" Slade's cold voice demanded.

Lisa froze for a panicked second, staring in disbelief that he could have approached so soundlessly. There was a ruthlessly hard look to his black eyes that made her toes curl.

Nervously she moistened her lips and tried to smile. "I brought some letters in for your signature." But that didn't explain what she was doing going through the other papers and his silence reminded her of it. "Your desk was in such a mess, I thought I'd straighten it."

"Thank you." Polite words without any sincerity. "But I prefer the mess," he stated icily. "Strange as it may seem to you, I know where everything is."

"I'm sorry." Lisa backed away from the desk, self-consciously aware of her foot bumping against his briefcase. A few moments earlier and she would have had a great deal more to explain. "I only meant to be helpful."

"In the future, confine your help to the outer office," Slade replied crisply, but apparently accepting her explanation. "Would you hand me my briefcase?"

"Of course." To give it to him, Lisa had to walk around the desk, her nerves leaping in awareness.

"It's nearly noon. Since you have the letters done, you might as well take your lunch break now." With case in hand, Slade courteously stepped to the side to let her precede him.

"I will," she agreed.

279

Any hope of going through his office at noon vanished as he waited expectantly in her outer office. Haphazardly she tidied her desk, gathered her handbag and spring jacket and led the way out of the building. In the street, they parted company with Slade issuing only a curt nod.

Lisa worked late, but Slade worked later. It was after six when she dashed into Mitzi's house. Her aunt was nowhere in sight, and Lisa was given a reprieve from explaining where she had been all day.

She had less than an hour to get ready before Slade arrived to take her and Mitzi to dinner. After undressing and bathing in record time, she reapplied her makeup and hurried to the closet.

Her choice of clothes was limited to the blue dress she had worn before and a satiny pantsuit in an unusual champagne shade, very nearly the color of her pale blond hair. A touch of vanity made her pick the pantsuit rather than wear something Slade had already seen. Lastly, she set the smoke blue sunglasses on the bridge of her nose, disguising the jewel green of her eyes.

At ten past seven, she hurried from her room to find Slade waiting at the bottom of the stairs. "I'm sorry I'm late." There was a hint of breathlessness in her voice—due entirely to the haste in getting ready, she was certain.

"That's quite all right." His hand took possession of her elbow, not letting her slacken her pace. "My car is outside." As he reached around her to open the door, his dark gaze skimmed her face. Her eyes were securely masked from his inspection by the sunglasses perched on her nose. "I see you're back to the sunglasses again."

"I did too much sight-seeing today." The story she had rehearsed for Mitzi sprang immediately to her lips.

"You seem to have a tendency to overdo things," Slade commented dryly.

You can say that again, Lisa thought. What had begun as innocent concern for her aunt had turned into a full-scale spying operation. It would be humorous if she wasn't so deeply ensnared in her own trap. But never in her life had she been half way involved in anything. It was always all or nothing.

The fragrant blossoms of the azaleas scented the dusk, their vibrant colors muted by the waning light. The bearded oaks cast dark shadows on the Lincoln Mark V parked in the driveway parallel to the portico entrance.

"I'll sit in the back. Mitzi can have the front seat," Lisa volunteered as Slade stepped ahead of her to open the car door. She intended to be a mouse in the corner that evening, observing, saying as little as possible.

"It's too late," he announced, more or less propeling her into the empty front seat and closing the door.

Turning in the plushy molded seat covered in a rich, midnight-blue velour, Lisa said, "Mitzi, I—" There was no one in the back seat. "Where's Mitzi?" she demanded of Slade as he slid behind the wheel.

"She's not coming." The key was in the ignition and being turned.

"What?" Stunned, Lisa stared at his boldly defined profile. "Why not?"

"Something to do with her heroine being in danger and she couldn't leave her novel until the hero had managed to rescue the girl." He shifted the car into gear, not sparing a glance in Lisa's direction.

"You put Mitzi up to this!" she accused in an angry hiss.

"I know you think I have unlimited power over Mitzi—" the look he flicked to her glinted with mockery "—but contrary to your belief, I have no control over the machinations of her writing. Nothing short of the end of the world could have dragged Mitzi away from the typewriter tonight."

"And I'm supposed to believe that?"

"I don't particularly care," he said with an expressively indifferent lift of his shoulder.

"Well, I'm certainly not going out alone with you!" Then Lisa realized the car was moving, its powerful motor purring almost silently as they glided through the narrow streets. They were easily two blocks from Mitzi's house. "You can turn this car right around and take me back," she ordered stiffly.

"No."

She grabbed at the door handle, but it wouldn't budge. "Unlock this door!"

"No."

Lisa was furious. She fumbled along the armrest, seeking the power lock control for her door. The seat moved with one switch; the window rolled down with another before she heard the click of the door.

As she reached for the handle, her arm was caught in a vice. She tried to twist away from the grip and it slid along the satin-smooth material of her long sleeve.

Then her hand was swallowed in the engulfing hold of his.

"Let me go!"

"You could at least wait until I've stopped the car," Slade taunted. "Or are you intent on breaking your neck?"

"Then stop it!" She was rigidly aware of the strength of his large hand. With the slightest pressure, he could break the slender bones in her hand and fingers, yet there was no pain.

"I can't stop here, I have a car behind me. You'll have to wait until I can pull over," he reasoned with irritating calm.

The street didn't widen until they turned onto Battery. Slade kept a firm hold of her hand until he had parked the car next to the curb. The instant he released her Lisa was out of the car in a flash, only to hear the motor switched off and his car door slam.

She darted into White Point Garden, hoping to lose herself in the dark shadows under the trees, but the pale, shiny material of her pantsuit was like a beacon in the darkness. He was at her side within seconds, capturing her wrist to slow her down.

She spun around. "I thought I'd make it plain that I don't want your company. I wouldn't go to heaven with you!"

"You're overdoing the dramatics, Lisa." His tone was dry with indulgence.

"If I am, it's because you drive me to it," she snapped. "You know very well that the only reason I agreed to this dinner tonight was because of Mitzi. That's why you manhandled me into the car and drove off without warning me in advance that she'd begged off. Whatever made you think I would agree to go out alone with an embezzler like you?"

"To talk."

"About what? What a low, despicable character I think you are?" Lisa strained against his hold on her wrist, trembling with the ferocity of her anger.

"I have a red-haired secretary who is better tempered than you are," Slade laughed. It was a low mocking sound.

For a split second, alarm kept her silent. "Take her out to dinner, then. I'm sure it really doesn't matter to you that she's married. All that regret about her ineligibility was just for Mitzi's benefit."

"You see right through me, don't you?" His remark was riddled with amusement.

"Yes, and I don't like what I see."

"That's a pity, because I like what I see." He loomed closer, his dark head shadowing her face.

Lisa retreated instinctively, remembering his avenging kiss in the study. He followed as she continued to back up warily until her shoulders were pressed against the rough bark of a tree trunk. Her breath was coming unevenly, yet she wasn't exactly afraid.

There were others wandering in the park, and not even Slade Blackwell would accost her in a public place. Not releasing her wrist, he brought his other arm up to lean a hand against the trunk near her head.

His nearness was having its effect on her senses, though. The musky fragrance of his shaving lotion was an erotic stimulant, wafting near her face in an enveloping cloud. There was a latent sensuality to his disturbing masculinity. His near-black eyes were lazily focused on her lips, moistened in nervousness. Lisa was left in little doubt as to what direction his interest was taking. Her pulse refused to behave normally, skipping beats when she needed most to remain calm.

"I've had time to think about our conversation—or should I call it confrontation—the other night." There was a decidedly caressing tone to his low voice. His thumb slid beneath the cuff of her sleeve to the inside of her wrist, rubbing her pulse point with disturbing results.

"What about it?" Lisa had to swallow the breathless catch in her voice.

"I've decided that it's mutually defeating to declare war on each other."

The lazy softening of his hard mouth into a smile was a bit too potent in its charm for Lisa to handle. She looked beyond him to the dark mound of a cannon, a relic of the Civil War permanently mounted in the garden. Its barrel pointed across the bay waters to the distant fortress of Fort Sumter.

"What are you suggesting?" *There,* Lisa sighed inwardly. She sounded much more in control of herself when she issued that question.

"That we effect a compromise."

"What kind?" The smoke blue lenses of her glasses shaded the green of her eyes, but they didn't lessen the sharpness of the look she darted at Slade.

"The kind that lets us join forces."

"Impossible!"

"Why is it impossible?" Slade argued smoothly.

"Why should we keep fighting one another? We'd both end up losing."

He still believed she was intervening because she wanted Mitzi's money. That was what he wanted, and he obviously believed it was the only thing she was interested in. Lisa hesitated. Perhaps this was another way of gaining the proof against him that she needed.

Slade noticed her hesitation and pressed his advantage. "It makes sense, doesn't it?"

"Perhaps," Lisa conceded, at least temporarily until she could think his suggestion through. She moved her wrist slightly against his hold. "Please, I'd like to walk." What she really needed was to get some distance between them so she could think clearly.

Obligingly Slade released her wrist and fell in step beside her when she pushed away from the tree trunk. But she didn't obtain the complete separation she desired. Vaguely possessive, his hand rested on the lower curve of her spine. The smooth material made his touch seem all the more sensuous against her skin.

She was much too aware of the man at her side, aware of him as a man. She had to remind herself of the character of the man beneath the tall, muscular physique. If she had needed any confirmation, she had received it a moment ago when he had suggested they work together to obtain Mitzi's money. She almost had to agree to go along with him so she could prove to Mitzi what Slade Blackwell really was.

Her attention shifted to the body of water glistening ahead of her in the twilight. The White Point Garden was located virtually on the tip of the peninsula of Old Charleston. Lisa's steps faltered, slowing almost to a stop as she stared at the water.

The surface was smooth and reflecting, giving no indication of the current flowing underneath. It reminded her of Slade. She had no idea what was going on inside his mind.

"The Ashley River," Slade quietly identified the body of water. "This is where the Ashley and the Cooper rivers flow together to form the Atlantic Ocean," he explained, voicing the whimsical tongue-in-cheek claim of the Charlestonians.

"I'm not interested in a geography lesson," Lisa returned impatiently. She turned to face him, tipping her head back slightly to see his features. "How do I know I can trust you?"

"How do *I* know I can trust you?" he countered.

"That's not an answer."

"The answer is we would have to trust each other."

"Honor among thieves and all that?" Lisa taunted sarcastically. "You don't know the meaning of the word honor."

"Do you?"

"I am not Mitzi's attorney bound by law to protect her interests," she reminded him.

"No, you're Mitzi's niece. Shall we begin comparing the blackness of the pot and the kettle?" Slade challenged dryly.

Her lips tightened grimly as she looked away. "You can't honestly expect me to forget your crude behavior the other night. No," she shook her head in agitation, "it would never work."

"You were the one who started the hostilities, Lisa."

"Because I slapped your face?"

"Didn't your mother ever teach you that you could win more friends with flattery? Or wasn't I supposed to catch the veiled insults you threw at me all that evening?"

"That was not an excuse for you to manhandle me," she snapped.

He was calmly and deliberately baiting her and, fool that she was, she was rising to snap at it. She breathed in deeply. She would not let him make her lose her temper.

"No, it wasn't an excuse, but—" Slade paused for effect "—it was only a kiss."

"Is that what you call it?" The retort was out before she could stop it.

"Issued in a moment of anger, I'll admit," he answered, revealing only amusement at her gibe.

"To put it mildly," Lisa snapped.

"You provoked that anger, to put it mildly," Slade mocked her.

"If that's the way you feel, why this sudden change?"

"With each of us tearing at Mitzi trying to convince her the other is no good, no matter which way it goes, we're going to end up putting doubt in her mind about each of us," he reasoned.

"And a third party could end up with all the money." Lisa followed the thought to its logical conclusion.

"Unless we come to an agreement," he added.

"Very well, tell me more about this agreement you want me to make," she breathed in decision.

"We'll discuss it after dinner." Slade smiled, the pressure increasing on the back of her waist as he turned toward the car. "I booked a table for seven-thirty. We're late, but I'm sure they'll hold our reservations for us. In the meantime, let's call a truce."

"A truce?" Lisa laughed in disbelief. "Are you serious?"

"Naturally I'm serious," he said, guiding her past a tall magnolia. "You need time to get used to the idea of trusting me."

"I doubt if I ever will," Lisa said, and meant it.

"You've made progress," he commented.

"Why?"

"Because you said 'doubt,' before you simply made it a flat statement that you never would." A glitter of arrogant complacency was in his look.

"A technicality," she dismissed the argument.

"Remember?" A dark brow arched in wry amusement. "My profession deals in technicalities."

"I'm afraid you're indulging in a bit of wishful thinking," Lisa denied a bit more sharply than she had intended.

Slade glanced at her as he reached to open the passenger door of the car. He didn't say anything, just let a faint smile touch the edge of his mouth.

CHAPTER SIX

CONTENTED, LISA DECIDED—that was the only word to describe the way she felt. The restaurant was sumptuously elegant yet relaxing at the same time, two qualities that did not necessarily go hand in hand.

The food had been excellent and her head was a bit fuzzy from the wine, but it was a pleasurable kind of fuzziness. She took another sip of the dry white wine in the stemmed glass. Soft music played in the background, gently romantic, setting the mood.

The table was small, intimately so with Slade sitting directly across from her. Lisa studied him openly, the intensity of her green gaze masked by the tinted lenses of her glasses. His roguishly thick mane of hair had a raven sheen to it, his eyes like black diamonds glittered with an inner fire.

His tanned features could have been chiseled in stone, yet they were so very male and so very compelling. Stone was wrong; no stone could ever possess the vitality that Slade had.

That vitality and charm had been working its magic on Lisa all evening. Slade's particular brand of charm was more potent than others she had known because it was so subtle. He didn't use an ounce of flattery, yet he made Lisa feel so good inside. It made him dangerous, but at the moment she was in the mood to flirt with danger.

It was crazy the way her mind was capable of dividing itself. One part of it was thinking about him, analyzing the things about him that set him apart from ordinary men. Another part was registering every word he said so she could make the appropriate responses when they were required.

The third part of her mind was noting other things about him. She liked the low pitch of his voice, smooth and rich like velvet. And she liked the way the corners of his mouth deepened when he thought something was amusing but didn't openly smile.

He said something dryly funny and Lisa laughed. "I was beginning to think you'd drifted away somewhere. You should laugh like that more often." A slow smile spread across his mouth, making an impact on her pulse.

"And you should smile like that more often," she returned, aware of the husky tremor in her voice, but not caring.

"We're beginning to sound like a mutual admiration society," Slade pointed out dryly, amused and mocking.

"Mitzi would be astounded," Lisa declared laughingly.

"I doubt it. Knowing Mitzi and her penchant for happy endings, she would find a romantically logical reason." Instantly something flashed across his face—a look of irritation or impatience, but Lisa couldn't be sure which. "Mildred mentioned that you'd barely returned to the house when I arrived. You were out sight-seeing with your friends?" The subject was deftly changed.

Lisa wondered why. Surely Slade didn't think she was becoming romantically attracted to him. Well, wasn't she, a small voice jeered. Wasn't she just a little bit curious what it would be like if he made love to her? She was afraid any answer she gave would be self-incriminating and she tried to ignore the questions.

"I was out with Peg and Susan for part of the day," she lied. "I browsed through the shops in the morning and the three of us went sightseeing in the afternoon."

"Where did you go?"

She hesitated for only a fraction of a second before she remembered a brochure she had seen. "Brookgreen Gardens. The statuary there is breathtaking. Unfortunately we got caught in the rush-hour traffic on the way back—that's why I was so late."

"There are some very fine American sculptors represented there," Slade agreed. "Which was your favorite?"

Was he testing her? Lisa wondered, then decided not. "They were all so beautiful it's impossible to pick one," she hedged.

"True. Brookgreen Gardens is very impressive, especially with its avenue of live oaks."

"Yes, isn't it?" Lisa smiled.

"Shall we go?" Slade asked unexpectedly. "I believe the restaurant is closing."

"What?" Lisa glanced around, surprised to see only two other tables occupied in the dining room. "Yes, of course."

As she reached for her handbag, Slade moved to the back of her chair. "It was a delicious meal. Thank you," she offered, rising as he held the chair out.

"My pleasure." But there was something distant in his reply.

The car was parked nearly a block away. Slade insisted that Lisa wait outside the restaurant for him to bring it around. As his long, smooth strides carried him away, she shivered slightly, feeling she had been abandoned to the cool of the evening.

Flames from the torches mounted on the building front flickered over the brick walls and the boarded, arched windows. Lisa shifted nearer to their light just as the sleek Lincoln drove up to the curb in front of the restaurant.

There was no indication of the chilling aloofness she thought she had detected in Slade moments earlier. She decided it must have been her imagination that made her think he had suddenly withdrawn. There was nothing cool about his attitude as he helped her into the passenger seat. In fact, his smile was quite disarming when he turned to her after sliding behind the wheel.

"Would you like to go directly back to Mitzi's or do you want to take a driving tour of Old Charleston by night?" Slade asked.

It was late and she would have to be up early to get to the office. The wisest choice would be to go directly to Mitzi's, but she heard her voice opting for the second choice.

"The driving tour."

She was crazy, she thought, settling back in her seat and smiling at herself. She disliked Slade yet she was dangerously attracted to him. She should feel wary instead of so contented.

"Why the smile?" He slowed the car as it turned a corner on to a rough, cobblestoned street.

"It must be the afterglow of good wine," Lisa sighed, confused by the change without really caring.

"I noticed it mellowed your temper."

"Yours, too," she countered, and glanced out the window.

The street they were on ran along the waterfront. On the opposite side of the docks were brightly painted old houses abutting each other. "How odd! Look." She pointed them out to Slade. "Each one is painted a different color."

He sent her a curious look. "That's Rainbow Row. I thought you'd been touring Charleston these past few days. How did you miss Rainbow Row?"

"Oh—" Lisa breathed in nervously, running the tip of her tongue over her lips "—I haven't toured Old Charleston yet. Mostly we've been taking other tours, like out to Fort Sumter and driving to the military academy."

"The Citadel?"

"Yes. I've been saving Old Charleston to see with Mitzi. She's used it and the Low Country of South Carolina so often as backdrops for her romances that I'm sure she would know all sorts of unique things about it. But tell me about Rainbow Row," she urged, wanting to get away from any detailed discussion about how she'd spent her time the past few days.

"The oldest house here dates from the 1740s. They're private residences, very much in demand. In the eighteenth century, this was the waterfront district. The different colors are a trademark, a means to set each one apart."

Passing the row of colorful houses, he turned at the corner. Lisa had the sensation of slipping into the past. With the buildings and houses shadowed by the night and few cars on the narrow streets, the modern touches seemed to be hidden from view, steeping the night in history.

Making another turn, Slade directed her attention to the house on the left. "The Heyward-Washington house, one of the places entitled to claim that 'George Washington slept here.' Thomas Heyward Jr. was one of the signers of the Declaration of Independence." Lisa had barely focused on the shadow-dimmed exterior when he pointed at something else. "Does that look familiar to you?"

"Vaguely," she admitted, wishing now the tour wasn't being made in the semidarkness. In the daylight she might recognize why it was familiar. Instead she had to ask. "Where have I seen it?"

"*Porgy and Bess,* the operetta. Cabbage Row inspired the setting for it. There used to be vegetable stands along the sidewalk, hence its name."

They drove down more streets, past more historic points of interest. It was a tour Lisa would have to make again by daylight. There was too much to see, but she was glad the first time had been by night. It had made the antique charm of the old section of the city come to life, its early glory more than just imagination.

She gazed silently out the window as Slade made another turn. She recognized the street, having walked it every day to his office. Her aunt's house was just off this street. Her gaze settled on a white mansion set back from the street, protected by lace grillwork and shadowed by massive guardian oaks, draped with Spanish Moss.

"Of all the mansions in Old Charleston, I think that one is the loveliest," she told Slade.

"Which one?"

"The one there," she pointed. "We're just approaching it."

"Would you like a closer look?" A half smile touched his mouth as he darted a questing look.

"Sure," Lisa agreed, thinking he meant that he would drive closer to the curb so she could have a better look at the mansion by night. Instead he turned the car in through the grillwork gates. "What are you doing?"

"You said you wanted a closer look," he mocked.

"Yes, but I didn't mean this close. Heavens, I walk by it every day—"

"You walk by it," his quiet voice immediately seized on her statement.

Lisa could have bit off her tongue. She blamed it on too much wine. She had been lulled into a false sense of security. She had to remember that Slade was still her adversary.

"Yes," she added with what had to be her millionth lie, "on my way to meet Susan and Peg. They usually pick me up at the corner." Even though his lean features were slightly shadowed, she could still see the twist of skepticism about his mouth. "We can't stop here," she protested as he stopped the car near the front entrance of the large white house.

"I know the owners very well," Slade insisted. "They won't mind if you have a look inside."

"There's no one home." The windows were dark, but it didn't bother Slade as he climbed out of the car and walked to Lisa's door.

"They're away, but they left the key with me," he explained, helping a confused and uncertain Lisa from the car.

"One of your clients?"

"More or less. I handle legal matters from time to time, but I've known them for years." His hand at her elbow guided her up the three steps to the door. Taking a key from his pocket, he inserted it in the lock and opened the door, switching on a light just inside the door before stepping back to let Lisa walk in first. "The house is closed up until fall, so the furniture has all been covered. But you can get an idea of the layout."

The oak floor of the foyer was polished to a high sheen. Ornate plaster cornices rimmed the ceiling. Light gleamed from the delicate crystal sconces on walls lined with paintings.

Still feeling like a trespasser, Lisa tentatively moved closer to inspect them. Her eyes widened at the first, a portrait of a man with raven hair and dark eyes, dressed in old-world clothes. Slade was just behind her and she pivoted to face him.

"The owners, they're relatives of yours," she accused.

"My parents," he smiled.

"Why didn't you tell me instead of letting me think that—" Lisa didn't voice the rest of her demanding question. She knew exactly how she would have ended it: something to the effect that the owners were more people he was systematically stealing from. For some reason she just didn't want to introduce that subject to their conversation. It was true, the wine had mellowed her somehow. It had taken the sharpness from her tongue and she didn't want to argue with him.

"Were you thinking the worst?" he mocked.

"Never mind. It doesn't matter." Lisa turned away, forcing the irritation she didn't understand from her voice. "Would you show me around?"

Despite the white sheets covering the furniture, there was a warmth to the house. Their footsteps echoed hollowly on the wood floors as they toured the rooms of the lower floor and followed the free-standing spiral staircase to the second. Yet the house didn't seem really empty.

"Don't your parents spend much time here?"

"Not any more—not since my father bought the farm," Slade admitted. "They spend all but the late autumn and early winter months there."

"He moved to the farm shortly after you joined the law practice, didn't he?" Lisa mused absently.

"Yes," Slade paused, his head tilting curiously. "How did you know?"

"Mitzi mentioned it to me, I guess." She shrugged, covering her slip with a lie. "Did you live here?"

"All my life." Slade started walking, his hand at her back drawing her with him.

"Why don't you live here now?" She looked at him curiously. "I mean," she laughed self-consciously, "it seems a shame for this beautiful old house to be empty for even a day."

"It's too big for one man."

298

"Yes, it's a family house," Lisa agreed, thinking of the numerous bedrooms meant for a brood of dark-haired, dark-eyed children. "Where do you live?"

"In the slave quarters behind the house," he told her. "We remodeled the building into a small bachelor apartment when I was in college. It's become quite popular to renovate the old quarters into apartments and rent them. Profitable, too."

"I suppose the next thing you'll do is invite me to your apartment. Every bachelor has a collection of etchings to show." Lisa said it in jest.

A roguish glint danced wickedly in his eyes. "Would you like to see my apartment?"

"Of course not." Her foot faltered on the stairstep. "It's just a standard bachelor line, isn't it?"

"So I've heard," Slade agreed. "But it's been so sadly overworked that no one uses it any more."

"That's good, because it's late, and I don't want Mitzi worrying about me. I'd better be getting back." *Before I end up in water over my head,* Lisa added silently. She was becoming much too friendly with Slade, the wrong kind of friendly. If she was going to be nice to him, it should be with the intention of getting information from him and not just to make small talk. He was making her lose sight of her goal.

"At least you have the advantage over me," Slade commented as they walked through the foyer to the front door. "You're on vacation and can sleep late in the morning. I have to be in the office first thing, which means getting up early."

"So do I." Lisa realized what she had said and rushed to cover it. "Not to be in the office, of course, but I'm meeting Peg and Susan first thing in the morning."

"Again? I thought you were here to visit Mitzi."

"I am, but she's in the middle of a book. It's silly for me to hang around the house every day waiting for her to finish. I might as well enjoy myself." She sounded more defensive than she wanted, but it couldn't be helped. "It is my vacation. Besides, I have the weekend to spend with Mitzi."

"Then you can act the dutiful and devoted niece, is that it?"

Her mouth opened to protest the tinge of sarcasm in his voice, but she caught herself in time. "I think I can play the role as effectively as you play yours as the loyal attorney."

The last light was switched off, throwing the mansion into darkness. Lisa waited at the steps while Slade locked the door. When he joined her, she started to descend the steps to the car, but his hand caught at her arm to stop her.

"I'm almost sorry the truce is over." He seemed to make the admission reluctantly.

Lisa agreed, but she wouldn't admit it. "You started it."

"You didn't waste any time making a retort."

"Did you expect me to turn the other cheek?"

"Would it have hurt you?" Slade countered.

His saturnine face was shadowed by the night darkness and Lisa couldn't see how much of his regret was mockery and how much of it was sincere.

"If you must know, yes, it would have," she returned sharply.

"We can't keep insulting each other if we're going to be partners."

"Who said we were going to be?" Lisa retorted. "I'm not convinced that I need you."

"Yes, you are. It just sticks in your craw to admit it." There was no mistaking the complacency in his tone. He was utterly sure of himself and Lisa.

"Maybe it's the other way around." She stubbornly resisted making the admission even though she knew she would eventually. Once Slade believed that she was on his side, he would confide exactly how he was obtaining Mitzi's money. "Maybe you need me more than I need you and you don't want to admit it."

"But I already have—when I made the proposal that we should work together," he reminded her. "What do you say? Are we partners?"

"I'd like to think about it." Now why did she say that? Lisa wondered. Did she want to make him sweat a little?

"What is there to think about? You know you've already made up your mind." He seemed to find her resistance amusing and futile.

"Maybe I have." Lisa tipped her head challengingly to one side, her silver blond hair shimmering in the faint light. "Maybe I've decided the answer is no. Did you think of that?"

He drew his head back, the angle faintly mocking, and she saw the corners of his mouth deepening. "If your answer was an outright no, you wouldn't have come with me tonight. You would have told me at the gardens to get lost. But you didn't. That means the answer is yes."

301

Lisa glanced away, her lips thinning. "You're very sure of yourself," she commented with irritation.

"No." His thumb and forefinger captured her chin and turned her back to face him. "I'm sure of you and the way your mind works."

His insolence was beyond belief, but it was the shiver of feeling evoked by his touch that claimed her. It rippled down her spine in tiny shock waves. Her throat was dry, incapable of speech.

Damn the wine, she thought. It was making her light-headed. The ground seemed unsteady beneath her feet, as if she was aboard a floating boat. Slade stood so tall and steady before her that she wanted to sway against his solidness and regain her equilibrium. It was the craziest sensation because she knew she was imagining all of it.

His gaze narrowed on her face, dark brows drawing together. His dark eyes seemed to physically touch each feature, inspecting, faintly caressing until they halted on her lips, softened in curious vulnerability. Slade bent his head toward her, then stopped as if waiting for a protest from Lisa.

There was a fevered awareness that he was going to kiss her and an equally shocking discovery that she wanted him to. This ambivalence toward him was insane, but she made not the slightest sound to stop him. His dark head began moving again, closing the distance until there was none.

The brush of his hard mouth against hers drew a tiny gasp, as her nerves tensed in shock. Lightly he explored the lips he had once plundered, sensually feeling his way. An eyebrow was quirked in puzzled surprise when he raised his head. Her lips were tingling with pleasure from his caressing kiss.

"It's crazy," she murmured, voicing the bewilderment she felt.

"Yes," Slade agreed, not needing to ask what she meant.

"I don't even like you," she added.

"I know."

His hand left her chin to spear his fingers through the spun silver of her hair at the back of her neck, tilting her head to meet his descending mouth. Her lips parted instinctively on contact, a golden storm of sensations racing through her body at his possession. There was nothing tentative in his kiss this time, and she felt the shuddering response she made to his demand.

Abruptly Slade drew away, frowning as he looked down at her. There was a hardness to the line of his jaw, a checked anger in his expression. Shaken by her reaction, Lisa turned away, trying to stop the leaping of her senses.

"We'd better leave," he said tightly.

"Yes," Lisa agreed fervently, wanting to conduct no more experiments in his embrace—if that was what she had been doing.

His hand was at her elbow, more or less propelling her down the short flight of steps to the car. He was still frowning when he helped her into the car and walked around to the driver's side. He reversed the car out of the driveway without saying a word. It was only a few minutes' drive to Mitzi's house, but the heavy silence made it seem much longer.

When he turned the car into the drive and stopped, Lisa didn't wait for him to get out of the car and walk her to the door, but darted out on her own. Her goodnight was lost in the slam of her car door.

Slade didn't follow as she rushed to the door, nearly running as if there was something that frightened her. The only problem was that Lisa was afraid of herself. At her aunt's door, she glanced back at the car. Slade was watching her, a thoughtful frown still darkening his face.

As Lisa entered the house, her aunt walked out of the study. Lisa struggled to appear composed. Mitzi glanced at the watch on her wrist, her expression registering astonishment.

"Is it that late already?" she murmured.

Lisa immediately seized on the remark to keep the subject away from herself. "Have you been working all this time, Mitzi?"

"I guess I have." The admission was made with a faint laugh of surprise. "I became so involved with the manuscript that I lost track of the hour. I hope you didn't think I was waiting up for you."

"For a minute I did think I was living at home again with mom mysteriously appearing whenever I came home from a date," Lisa smiled nervously, remembering how astute her mother was at reading her mind. She hoped Mitzi didn't possess the same prowess.

"How was your evening? Did Slade take you someplace nice for dinner?" Mitzi asked.

"It was very nice." Which was a safe answer as Lisa sought to avoid more personal questions. There was a great deal of her own emotional reaction toward the evening that she had to sort out.

"I'm sorry I had to back out like that at the last minute." The apology was sincere. And Lisa was convinced that her aunt's excuse had been genuine and not an attempt to manipulate the evening so she and Slade would be forced to be together.

"Slade explained why you couldn't come. I hope you managed to rescue your heroine," Lisa offered.

"Oh, I did." Mitzi's emphatic nod was cut short by the onset of a yawn. "You must be as tired as I am. It's time we both were in bed."

"Yes, good night, Mitzi." She walked to the stairs, relieved that she had avoided any discussion of Slade.

"Good night, Lisa," her aunt returned and started down the hallway to her bedroom on the ground floor.

Upstairs in her room, Lisa changed into her nightclothes and crawled into bed. She didn't switch off the light right away as she stared at the swirling cream satin of the canopy. Everything seemed suddenly very complicated. It was because of that kiss and the way she had responded to it. But more and more, it was because of Slade. She turned off the light.

The next day it was difficult to face him as Ann Eldridge. Lisa tried to be indifferently professional around him and failed miserably. Fortunately Slade was too preoccupied to notice or he would have seen how nervous his temporary secretary was in his presence.

He was bending over her desk signing some correspondence she had typed and that he wanted in the mail that day. Lisa found herself studying the way the overhead light gave a blue black sheen to his hair.

Her gaze slid to his profile, to the hard male line of his mouth. Only last night, it hadn't been hard and

305

unyielding when it covered hers. There had been a persuasive mastery to his kiss that her lips still remembered.

What was more important, she had let herself be persuaded to answer it. And it hadn't been an unpleasant experience. She only wished it had. It was so much easier to hate him than to be caught in conflicting reactions.

Her gaze shifted to the dark black of his eyes and found him returning her look with an absently puzzled quirk of his brow. Immediately, Liza glanced away, trying to cover the sudden confusion that brought a warmth to her cheeks.

"Is something wrong, Mrs. Eldridge?" he asked curiously.

"No, nothing," she rushed.

"Was there something you wanted to ask me?" Slade persisted.

"No. What could there be?" Lisa shrugged nervously.

"That's what I'm asking you."

Slade had been in a brooding mood all day. Because of that, this sudden interest in her made Lisa nervous and apprehensive. Perhaps he had noticed a resemblance between her and her other self. Lisa knew she had to be very careful.

"I assure you there's nothing." The letters were signed and she gathered them up to start folding them and putting them in their respective envelopes.

"If it's about your wages—"

"The agency pays me directly and will bill you later," she lied hurriedly. She wasn't going to accept his money when she was here to spy on him. "Was there anything else you wanted me to do?"

"Yes. Call Miriam Talmadge for me." Lisa paled at his clipped request. "Find out what time she expects her niece home this afternoon."

"Her niece?" Lisa repeated weakly, her face becoming even whiter.

"Yes, I believe that's what I said," he retorted impatiently.

"If—if Mrs. Talmadge should ask why you want to know, what should I tell her?" Her nerves were behaving as erratically as a jumping bean.

"Tell her it's none of her business." There was something savage in his snapped answer. Breathing in sharply, Slade immediately retracted his answer. "No, tell Mrs. Talmadge," he began, forcing himself to reply calmly to her question, "that I'll be over this evening to see Lisa—as well as Mrs. Talmadge," he added as a definite afterthought.

"All right," Lisa breathed, relieved that she was going to have advance warning of his visit.

Pushing back the tan sleeve of his suit jacket, Slade glanced at his gold watch. "If by some chance Mrs. Talmadge's niece should be there, put the call through to me and I'll talk to her. I'll be in Drew's office. If not, then pass the message on to me there as to when Mrs. Talmadge expects her back."

"I'll do that," Lisa promised, but Slade was already walking away, her compliance with his order anticipated.

After he had left her office, she toyed with the idea of speaking to him as Lisa Talmadge, pretending to be at her aunt's home. But there was too much risk that he might mention it to Mitzi, who would quickly deny that Lisa had been there.

Disguising her voice, she placed the call, informing Mildred of Slade's impending visit that evening, then crisply relayed the message to Slade that Lisa was expected home around six.

The knowledge that she would be seeing Slade that evening didn't make the day go faster. Instead it worked in the reverse, every minute dragging as she tried to guess his reason. Not knowing what to anticipate made her as skittish as a colt.

Her stomach was such a mass of knots that she was barely able to do justice to the meal Mildred had prepared. Every sound that came from outside of the house had her pulse skyrocketing, thinking it was Slade arriving.

"I don't know why Mildred didn't think to invite Slade to dinner," Mitzi sighed as she poured out the coffee and handed a cup to Lisa. "There was certainly enough food to go around, especially when you ate so little."

"I wasn't very hungry."

The cup was clattering in its saucer and Lisa realized that her hands were shaking. She quickly set the coffee on the table in front of the couch, clasping her hands together in her lap.

"I had a big lunch." The truth was she hadn't eaten anything. As as a result, she felt weak and trembling inside, but the thought of eating any of the small cakes on the coffee tray was repellent.

"You haven't told me how you and Slade got along last night." Mitzi settled back in her chair, her own coffee cup held steadily in her hands, a bright gleam in her brown eyes.

"Okay, I guess," Lisa tried to shrug away the question indifferently, but her aunt wasn't to be put off by her uninformative reply.

Clicking her tongue in mock reproof, Mitzi insisted, "Your answer is much too nonchalant, Lisa. It couldn't have been as bland an evening as that. Come now, what happened really?"

"I don't know what you mean," Lisa denied nervously. "We went out to eat. We talked, drove around a bit and he brought me home."

"No face-slapping? No fighting? Just a quiet little evening, is that it?" her aunt grinned knowingly.

"We argued, yes. Is that what you want me to say?" Lisa asked in agitation.

"But not all the time?"

Lisa rubbed her finger against the center of her forehead, trying to ease the throbbing pain. "No, not all the time," she admitted with a sigh.

"To be truthful, I didn't think you'd go out with him," her aunt commented.

"I didn't have much choice. He practically dragged me out of the house and into the car before I even found out you weren't coming along," she explained.

"That sounds like something Slade would do," Mitzi laughed to herself. "The two of you must have reconciled some of your differences after an evening together."

"I don't know." And that was the truth.

The doorbell rang and Lisa jumped. "That must be Slade," Mitzi announced unnecessarily.

As her aunt went to answer the door, Lisa rose from

the couch and walked to a window, lifting aside the curtain to stare outside. Without turning, she knew the instant Slade entered the room. She felt the touch of his gaze and tensed.

"Hello, Lisa." The greeting seemed to be forced from him, his tone clipped and taut.

"Hello, Slade." An artificial smile curved her mouth as she glanced over her shoulder.

The sharpness of his gaze seemed to thrust into her like a dagger, pinning her helplessly on its point. Relentlessly, he searched her expression, noting its strained tension. The vaguely angry frown was back on his face when he finally looked away. Released from his gaze, Lisa felt all the more confused about why he had come and why her heart was beating so wildly.

"We were just having coffee. You'll join us, won't you, Slade?" Mitzi invited, already reaching for the third cup sitting on the coffee tray.

"Yes." But the answer was given automatically without interest.

"You look troubled about something, Slade," Mitzi said, as she poured the coffee.

His dark gaze flicked to Lisa, ricocheting instantly away. "It was a rough day at the office. I guess I brought some of it with me."

That wasn't true. It had been one of the quietest days at the office, and Lisa wondered why he had lied about it. She stared at him, sensing his restlessness. Although he wasn't moving, she had the sensation of him prowling the room. It was as though they were on the same wavelength, except that Lisa didn't know the cause of his restlessness.

"Lisa, your coffee is getting cold," Mitzi reminded her.

"Sorry, I forgot." Then she wondered why she had apologized.

Her legs felt strangely weak as they carried her past Slade to the couch. She seemed to be caught up in his brooding mood, feeling the hidden disturbance as it grated on her nerve ends. His dark gaze was studying her, but she avoided meeting it.

Yet she was aware of his every move, of the coiled impatience in his controlled acceptance of the coffee cup. The muscles of her throat were beginning to constrict with the tension. She could only manage tiny sips of her lukewarm coffee.

"I didn't have an opportunity the other night to look at that review of your latest book, Mitzi," Slade said. "I'd like to read it."

"I'll get it," Lisa volunteered as quickly as she had the other time.

Her cup clattered noisily in its saucer as she set it down on the table and rose. But Slade's hand was on her forearm, stopping her with the punishing grip of his fingers.

"Mitzi will know exactly where it is," he said curtly.

"Maybe not exactly," her aunt qualified, "but I probably would have a better idea of where it is than Lisa. You two wait here while I look for it."

"Oh, no really," Lisa protested, a wildfire flaming hotly over her skin.

"Lisa," Slade muttered beneath his breath. In the use of her name there was a demanding order for her to stay.

"Come to think of it—" there was a decided twinkle

311

in Mitzi's eyes as she glanced at the two of them "—it may take me a little time to find that review."

Slade's piercing gaze never left Lisa's face. "I don't mind waiting, Mitzi."

CHAPTER SEVEN

WHEN MITZI HAD LEFT the room, Slade released Lisa's arm and took a hurried step away, turning his back to her. Lisa stared at the blackness of his hair brushing the rolled neckline of his ribbed, creamy yellow sweater, which complemented the tobacco-brown jacket of corduroy with light tan leather patches at the elbows.

"We both know you aren't here to read Mitzi's review, so why have you come, Slade?" Was that her voice that sounded so calm and nonchalant? It seemed impossible, considering the way she was trembling inside.

He slashed a black glance over his shoulder, brief and slicing. "It occurred to me that I was taking your agreement to our arrangement for granted. You avoided giving me a direct answer last night." Slade, too, sounded calm and controlled, yet the elemental currents crackling in the air seemed charged with high voltage.

"Did I? I thought I had," Lisa shrugged, intimidated by the rigid set of his shoulders.

Slade pivoted to face her. "You didn't and you haven't yet."

It was Lisa's turn to look away from his compelling

features, relentless in their demand for an answer. "Naturally, I agree to the arrangement. As you pointed out last night, it would be foolish and self-defeating for both of us not to join forces." Her attempt to be offhand came out brittle and defensive. "Is that direct enough for you, or do you want me to sign some binding document complete with the 'whereases' and 'hereinafters?'"

"Stop it!" he snapped out the words.

"Stop what?" Lisa turned on him roundly, more challengingly defensive than before.

"Stop being so sarcastic." A muscle worked convulsively along his lean jaw, the line of his mouth hard and forbidding.

"I can't help it where you're concerned," she restored. "It's instinctive."

"You managed to be civil last night," Slade reminded her.

"Last night I had too much wine," Lisa defended herself. It had been the crutch she had subconsciously used all day long to explain her reaction to his kisses.

"Was it the wine?" he taunted. "I've been wondering that myself all day long."

His admission caught her by surprise. She had been on his mind all day long? She was the reason for his moody preoccupation at the office? He had been going over in his mind what had happened the night before the same as she had. It must have been an unsettling experience for him as well. The knowledge quivered through her limbs, kindling an excitement she fought hard to control.

In one long stride, Slade covered the distance

314

between them, his hands spanning her slender ribcage. His touch sparked a flame that licked through her nervous system, making her insensitive to all but his nearness.

"I haven't had any wine today. Have you?" he asked with dangerous deliberation.

With a negative shake of her blond head, she gave him her mute answer. He slowly pulled her toward him. The hands on her ribs were firmly insisting, their searing warmth branding her skin. Her face was tipped upwards, her lips parting before he even touched them.

His questing mouth held no mercy, its fierce passion driving all resistance out of its path. The heady urgency he was arousing was more deeply intoxicating than any wine. Almost of their own accord, her hands slipped inside his jacket, sliding around the solidness of his waist.

Instantly his arms circled her, shaping her full curves to the hard contours of his body. The caress of his hands on her hips sent fires leaping high, consuming her with the scorching heat of their desire.

All men who had held her in her arms before were banished from her memory. None had ever lifted her to this towering peak that overlooked discretion and danger. The things she had resented about Slade, his strength and mastery, were the very things she now gloried in. She couldn't help shuddering in regret when he dragged his mouth from hers.

"What kind of a witch are you?" he muttered thickly against her temple, his breath warm and moist over her skin.

"A completely powerless one, I think." *Without*

315

resistance or defense, she thought silently. He could have seduced her and she wouldn't have been able to stop him.

His mouth punished her hard for telling such a lie. Only as far as Lisa was concerned, it wasn't a lie. Slade was the one who possessed the magic, trapping her inside the charmed circle of his arms while he wove a spell over her soul. She reveled in the addictive prowess of his long, drugging kiss, her need insatiable.

"Take off those damned glasses," Slade growled the demand.

It was the slap back to reality that Lisa needed. She twisted out of his arms, turning her back on him and taking a trembling step away. Her heart was knocking against her ribs, her breath coming in shaky gasps. She clasped her arms about her stomach, churning from the upheaval of her emotions, volcanic and frightening.

"I don't want to become involved with you, Slade, emotionally or physically," she declared, but much too weakly. "I want this to be purely a business arrangement." Eventually she would have to expose him, and she wanted to be able to do it without pain or regret.

"Do you think I don't?" His low voice sounded strangled by the savage control he was exercising over his reply.

"I don't know," she sighed with an aching tremor.

His hands touched the sides of her waist, then slid automatically under her arms to cup her breasts. Lisa's shoulders were drawn back against his chest. The hard pressure of his thighs left her in no doubt of his male need.

"I didn't intend for this to happen. In fact, it's the last thing I want." Even as he made the angry statement, he was forcing her head to the side, burying his mouth in the tangle of silver silk hair at the curve of her neck.

"Me, too." But delicious shivers were racing down her spine from his rough caress.

Her hands were clutching his muscled forearms, ostensibly to end his possession of her breasts. But she simply held on to him, inviting his intimate caress by not denying it. A wave of primitive longings surged through her—powerful, inescapable and dangerous.

"It's happened, so what are we going to do about it?" Slade breathed raggedly against the sensitive skin along her neck.

"Stop it."

"Can you?" he laughed cynically.

"I don't know." Lisa closed her eyes against the fevered ache in her loins that refused to diminish.

Tightening his hold, he molded her more fully against his male length. "I want you, Lisa." A hand slid to her hipbone.

"I know." How could she ignore the pressing force of his desire, any more than she could ignore the hollow throbbing of her own?

Abruptly Slade let her go, leaving her to sway unsteadily without the support of his body. Long, impatient strides carried him away from her until nearly the width of the room separated them. Lisa stared hungrily after him, not able to deny her desire now that he no longer held her in his arms.

He took a cigarette from the enameled box on the

317

coffee table and snapped a lighter flame to the tip. Exhaling an impatient, tasteless cloud of smoke, he raked his fingers through the thickness of his raven hair. The smoldering anger of his gaze burned her.

"What do you expect from me, Lisa?" he demanded with gritting control. "Besides a guaranteed share of your aunt's money," he jeered viciously.

"Nothing." Hot tears scorched her eyes, luckily hidden by the smoke blue sunglasses. "God, I wish I'd never met you!" she choked.

"Not half as much as I do," he growled. "Not by half!"

The just-lit cigarette was crushed in an ashtray, suppressed fury in the action. He was striding stiffly toward the door before Lisa could comprehend his intention.

"Where are you going?" she breathed in confusion.

"I'm leaving!" he snapped harshly. "Make my apologies to your aunt!"

Doors were slammed violently in his wake. Lisa flinched at each crashing sound, pain splintering through her, inflicting a million tiny wounds.

It was what she deserved, though, for so indiscriminately abandoning her pride and self-respect in the arms of a man who was a thief and possibly worse. There was no time to dwell on the humiliating aspects of her passionate response as Mitzi appeared in the living room.

"Gracious! Slade was really in a temper when he left," she declared. "I can't leave the two of you alone for five minutes but you're at each other's throats. What happened this time?"

"We—argued," Lisa answered tightly, her voice straining to sound natural.

"About what?"

"Does it matter?" she countered with undisguised bitterness.

"I suppose not," Mitzi sighed in reluctant agreement. "You two can't seem to see eye to eye about anything. If all else failed, you'd probably argue over the color of the sun. After last night, I'd hoped that—"

"Last night was a mistake." In more ways than one, Lisa could have told her. A fiery tear slipped from her lashes and she wiped it away with the back of her hand.

"Lisa, you're crying!" Mitzi was plainly astonished by the discovery.

"I always cry when I'm angry." *Or hurt or confused or frightened,* she thought.

Her aunt's expression became decidedly grim. "I am going to have a talk with Slade."

"Don't bother. He'd only laugh," Lisa declared acidly.

"Slade—"

"You don't know Slade," Lisa interrupted angrily, releasing the pent-up frustrations of her emotions. "You don't know what he's really like! How arrogant and demanding and sexy—" Oh, God, Lisa thought. Had she really said that last? She went red with shame.

"Well, no—" Mitzi tried to hide the laughter in her voice "—I don't think I know that side of him very well."

Lisa couldn't remember having felt so mortified in years, not since a teenage girl friend had confided

319

Lisa's infatuation to the very boy she had the crush on. She mumbled some unintelligible excuse and rushed from the room.

In her room, she locked the door, but no one came to invade her privacy. She cried out her misery and humiliation alone. But it was more than that that made her sob so brokenly with pain. It was knowing that she had found something precious and couldn't keep it.

But she refused to admit, even to herself, what that something precious was. With her head pounding and her body aching, she finally fell into an exhausted sleep some time after midnight.

The next morning, Lisa awoke with a start. She was late for work. Then her head sank back onto the pillow. It was Saturday and Slade's office was closed. Relief trembled through her in a shuddering sigh. She would never have found the composure to face Slade today as Ann Eldridge.

A glance in the mirror told her she would have difficulty facing anyone today. Her green eyes were parched and bloodshot from the gallons of tears she had cried. Her lids were puffy and swollen with dark smudges beneath her eyes. She could hardly stand to see herself.

She slipped on her sunglasses to conceal the ravages of last night's stormy collapse. Only when the worst had been hidden did she pull on brushed denim Levis and a white tank top. Her complexion was unnaturally pale, making the pink lipstick look gaudy. She rubbed it off with a tissue and ran a comb indifferently through her silver blond hair.

Downstairs the housekeeper gave her a sighingly

resigned look and said, "Mitzi is in the study working. Today is the day I polish the furniture, so if you'll be wantin' breakfast, it'll take me a while."

"Juice and coffee is good enough." Lisa still didn't have an appetite. Mildred nodded glumly, showing no relief that the request was small. "I'll get it," Lisa volunteered. "There's no need for you to bother, Mildred."

"Have it your way." Mildred shrugged and moved toward the living room.

In the end, Lisa had only a glass of orange juice before wandering aimlessly out of the back door into the garden. Listlessly she meandered under the large oaks, veils of moss trailing over the top of her hair.

Last night she had considered packing her bags and leaving—anything to escape Slade Blackwell. But that would mean leaving Mitzi to his mercy. Was she such a coward she would do that?

But if she stayed.... Lisa shuddered. She was supposed to be an adult, not without some experience regarding men. She should be capable of warding off unwanted attentions from a man. The problem was that they were not unwanted. All Slade had to do was touch her and she melted like a scoop of ice cream in July.

Never, not even in her worst nightmares, had she dreamed she might fall in love with a man who embezzled from rich, elderly women. She hadn't fallen in love with him yet; in lust with him maybe, but not in love.

But that was the risk she was taking if she stayed around him much longer, Lisa realized. And if she loved him, would she have the will to expose him before he destroyed Mitzi's future security?

She was so confused and uncertain. Nothing seemed as simple as it had when she arrived. A twig of an oak brushed her cheek and she snapped it off in irritation, twirling the tiny, green-leafed stick between her fingers agitatedly.

What was she going to do? How had she got herself into this mess? How was she going to get herself out of it? Was there a way out of it—one that wasn't filled with pain or heartache?

Sighing helplessly, Lisa tipped her head backward, gazing up into the massive branches of an oak tree. Far above her head she could see a man-made platform perched on the V of two limbs. She searched the fat girth of the main trunk, finding the slats of wood nailed to the tree forming a crude ladder to the platform.

It looked singularly inviting to be high up there in the tree, far above all her problems. The lofty treehouse offered a temporary escape, and Lisa took advantage of it. The boards nailed to the trunk were amazingly solid. Even if they hadn't been, she discovered that she hadn't lost her climbing skill. The platform, too, was sound, without a single indication of rotting wood.

Settling into a comfortable, cross-legged position, with her elbows resting on her thighs and her hands on her ankles, Lisa felt decidedly better. There was something uplifting about sitting in a tree. If Darwin's theory was true, she thought somewhat wryly, she was probably reverting to old ancestral habits!

322

The sensation didn't last long as she heard the crunch of footsteps in the graveled driveway. She tensed, a sixth sense warning her of the intruder's identity before she saw Slade. The minute he came into her view, he stopped, glancing upward to the treehouse where she sat.

Her heart somersaulted traitorously at the sight of him dressed casually in blue slacks and a print shirt that was opened at the throat. His hard features were expressionless as he gazed directly at her.

"Go away," she gulped tightly.

"I want to talk to you, Lisa," he said evenly.

"Well, I don't want to talk to you."

"Don't be childish," Slade scolded her for her pouting retort, "and come down from that tree."

"How did you know I was here?" She ignored his order.

"Mildred told me at the house that she'd seen you wandering around outside from the window. I've found Mitzi so many times in that treehouse that I guess I automatically looked there first."

"Mitzi? Up here?" Lisa repeated, finding it difficult to imagine her fifty-year-old aunt climbing the tree.

"Yes," Slade said dryly, "your aunt is remarkable in more ways than one. If you don't come down, I'll come up. You'll find that platform is a little cramped with two people on it."

He would climb up, Lisa knew it, and she glared at him angrily. He took a step toward the trunk and the crude ladder.

"I'll be right down," she muttered, and slid along the platform to the boards leading down the tree.

323

A few feet from the ground, a pair of hands took hold of her waist, ignoring her gasp of protest, and lifted her the rest of the way down. Lisa twisted free of the hold the instant her feet touched the ground. Her pulse was still racing even after Slade had let her go.

"What do you want?" she challenged coldly. But inside she was feverishly aware of him.

Slade stared at her for a long moment. "Mitzi told me you'd been crying."

His hand reached for her sunglasses and Lisa knocked it away, instinctively defending her identity. "She had no right to tell you that!" She couldn't deny the tears she had cried. Not even the tinted sunglasses could conceal all traces.

"Mitzi hasn't had many chances in her life to play mother hen. You can't blame her for springing to the defense of the little chick living in her house." He studied her thoughtfully. "Looking at you now, I can understand why she lectured me on my behavior. You look oddly vulnerable and in need of protection."

"You're wrong," Lisa denied. "You and Mitzi both are wrong. I can take care of myself."

"Can you?" Slade eyed her skeptically, his manner faintly arrogant and mocking. "It's funny, but you don't look like a hard-bitten little niece out after her aunt's money. You look like a little girl who's been hurt—"

"Will you get out of here?" she demanded hoarsely. "I don't need pity, least of all yours!"

"I'm not offering any."

Lisa turned away in agitation. "What are you doing here? Who invited you anyway?"

"I invited myself. I wanted to see you."

"Why?" she hurled bitterly. "Were you afraid after last night that I'd renege on our deal?"

"Frankly it didn't occur to me," Slade answered grimly. "Maybe it should have."

"Yes, maybe it should have."

His hands fastened on her upper arms, pulling her around to face him. Lisa hunched her shoulders away from him, recoiling from his touch that was both torture and bliss. She kept her face averted, unable to meet his compelling gaze.

"Let me go Slade!" The strangled words were ripped from her throat. "I'm not going to go back on our agreement."

His fingers curled deeper into the soft flesh of her arms, drawing her closer. Lisa raised her hands to wedge herself away from his chest, but one hand accidentally came in contact with naked skin where his unbuttoned shirt front opened at the neck. His body warmth seared through her like a branding iron, and the dark hairs on his chest tickled her sensitive fingertips.

"Last night—" Slade began tautly.

"I'm trying to forget about last night," Lisa interrupted in a throbbing voice. "I don't want to remember it even happened."

"I came over here this morning with the intention of apologizing and to suggest that we both forget about last night." There was a sensual note in his husky tone. "But I can't. It isn't possible."

His warm breath was fanning the top of her hair, letting Lisa know how close he was to her. Her gaze was riveted to the tanned column of his neck, and the pulse beating wildly there seemed to be in tempo with her own racing heart.

"I don't want to become involved with you." Her protest was almost issued in a moan of surrender. "It would complicate everything."

"Do you think I don't know that?" Slade argued grimly.

"Then leave me alone."

He offered the opposite. "Spend the day with me, Lisa. Mitzi's going to be working and she's already told me you aren't seeing your friends today."

"No." She shook her head. "I can't. I won't!"

"We won't talk about Mitzi or her money," Slade vowed. "We'll forget all about it. It'll just be you and me together."

The temptation to accept was almost irresistible. To have one day with Slade—to be just a man and a woman together—was a tantalizing thought.

"No!" The denial came in a tortured whisper, trembling with regret.

"You crazy, stubborn woman," he snapped in irritation. "You were human enough to cry last night. Can't you see that whether I like it or not, I'm falling in love with you?"

Lisa breathed in sharply, her head jerking up to stare dazedly into his face. His compelling features were set in grim, forbidding lines of determination.

"You can't mean it," she breathed.

His mouth twisted wryly. "Do you think it was easy for me to admit or accept?"

"I don't know." She wavered. "You can't love me," she protested uncertainly.

326

"That's what I've been saying ever since I left the house last night," Slade admitted, a rueful smile tugging cynically at the corners of his mouth. "But I know the worst about you, Lisa. Today I'd like to find out the best."

Yes, it was true for her, too. She knew the worst about Slade—that he was dishonest, an embezzler—but it didn't change the way she felt about him. The difference between Lisa and Slade was that she was afraid to pin the label of love on the emotion she felt. In her heart she was certain, but her mind refused to accept the verdict.

"It wouldn't change anything. It would only make it worse." She couldn't bring herself to accept his invitation.

"I don't know." He lifted an expressive brow in challenge. "I might find your company boring without any arguments to add spice."

Lisa held her breath for an instant, then released it in a long sigh. "No, I can't go."

"Why?" Slade demanded a reason.

"It's—it's too risky," she offered lamely.

"Why? Because you might find out you're in love with me?" he guessed astutely. "Is there a chance of that?"

Moistening her lips nervously, Lisa finally admitted, "Yes."

The smoldering light that leaped into his dark eyes took her breath away. "If there's a chance of that," he said tightly, "we can find out right here and now."

Her lips parted to protest, but his mouth opened over hers to silence her voice, devouring her lips with a savage hunger that brought sweet pain. Lisa sur-

327

rendered instantly to the fierce ecstasy of his kiss. Her arms slid around his neck inside his shirt collar, feeling the flexing of his muscles as he crushed her against his length.

The erotic stimulation in the molding caress of his hands drove out all questions about the wisdom of loving him. There was only here and now and the wonder of his arms around her. Her heart was singing a pagan song to accompany the primitive fires racing through her veins. The sensual probe of his lips as they explored hers had her quivering in eager response, needing to know him as intimately as he was discovering her.

His weight pressed her backward until the rough bark of the tree was rasping her shoulder blades and the bare skin exposed by the sleeveless tank top. A muscular leg was forced between hers as Slade pinned her arching body against the trunk. His hands slipped under the hem of her top, finding the heat of her bare skin and evoking a pleasure so piercing it was near torment.

Her breast seemed to swell in delight when his hand curved over the lacy cup of her bra. Lisa yearned to feel the nakedness of his hard flesh beneath her fingers. Lacking his expertise, her fingers fumbled with the few remaining buttons of his shirt. In her awkward attempt, she scraped her elbow against the rough bark and gasped at the sharp pain shooting up her arm.

Slade immediately straightened, pulling her with him away from the tree. "This is a hell of a place to make love to you," he laughed raggedly near her ear, nuzzling its lobe before dragging his mouth away.

Weakly Lisa rested her head against his chest, still quivering with a need that could only be satisfied in the consummation of their love. Unknowingly she whispered his name.

"Love me?" Slade roughly demanded an answer.

"Yes." And she closed her eyes at the frightening truth.

"And you'll spend the day with me?"

Lisa trembled. "Yes."

His arms tightened around her. "Do you have any idea how much I want you?"

"I think so," she nodded against his chest, her fingers spreading across his hard flesh in an unconscious caress. She knew how much she wanted him.

"It's so soon, though," Slade declared in agitation, rubbing his chin over the top of her head. Lisa could hear the frown in his voice. "Is there ever a right time and a right place?"

"I doubt it."

He captured her chin and lifted her head so he could study her face, his eyes darkened in seriousness. "Lisa, I want to spend the afternoon getting to know you—I don't mean physically, there's time enough for that later. I want to know about your family and friends, what you like and what you don't like."

"Yes." She seemed destined to agree with anything he said, but it wouldn't last forever. Maybe that was why she was clinging so tenaciously to those few moments they would share.

He gave her a hard, swift kiss. "It's not going to be easy to keep my hands off of you when you're in such a delectable mood, but I'll try," he promised in lazy arrogance. "As long as you don't provoke me." Clasping her wrists, he held her away from him. "Run into the house and let Mildred know you're coming with me. I'll have you back in time for dinner tonight."

"Should I change? I mean—" Lisa glanced down at the rumpled tank top and snug-fitting Levis.

"You're fine as you are," he assured her.

"All right," she nodded tightly. "Just give me five minutes to comb my hair and put on some lipstick."

"No." His grip tightened when she would have pulled free of his light hold to go to the house. Lisa looked back into his disturbing intent gaze. "No comb and no lipstick. I want you looking just the way you are—as if you'd just been kissed very thoroughly by me."

"Slade, what will people think?" She was faintly embarrassed yet thrilled by the possessive ring in his voice.

"They'll think we're in love," he informed her with more than a trace of arrogant satisfaction, "and that I've made mad, passionate love to you. I haven't, but I will."

"Oh, really?" Lisa had to challenge him. She had been much too agreeable.

"Yes, really." For an instant, he drew her against his chest as if to establish his mastery over her. "And if you don't hurry into the house with that message, I'll change the order in which I want to get to know you better." Then he released her.

"Damn you, Slade!" she breathed, standing motionless, loving him and hating him with equal desperation. "The first thing you should learn about me is that I don't like being told what to do."

"Very well." Amusement deepened the corners of his mouth. "I won't tell you what to do any more. I'll show you."

Taking her by the shoulders, he turned her around and pointed her toward the house. With a shove and a playful slap on her rump, he sent her on her way.

Entering the house through the back door, Lisa went in search of Mitzi. In the foyer, she heard the clicking keys of the typewriter in the study. Hesitating, Lisa decided not to disturb her aunt and began looking for the housekeeper.

After going through all the rooms but the study on the ground floor, Lisa continued her search upstairs. She found Mildred in her bedroom, polishing the chest of drawers.

"Here you are, Mildred." She was slightly out of breath. "I've been looking for you."

"I always polish the furniture upstairs first," Mildred informed her. "I don't know why I bother. Nobody hardly ever comes up here. I'm just wasting my time." She pulled out a drawer and ran a cloth around the edges and sides. "But it has to be done. So I do it first. That way I leave the downstairs till last and I have to do that. I can't put it off because somebody is always running in and out."

Lisa wasn't really interested in hearing Mildred's psychological methods of keeping house. "Slade is here and—"

"Yes, I know. I answered the door when he rang the bell. As if I haven't got anything better to do than run up and down stairs seeing who is at the door," she grumbled.

"Yes, well, I came to tell you that he's asked me to

spend the day with him." Not even the housekeeper's grouchiness could diminish the happiness Lisa felt at the prospect of spending an entire day with Slade. "I'll be back in time for dinner tonight."

"And I've got a casserole in the oven for lunch," Mildred grumped and opened another drawer. In alarm, she stepped away from it with surprising swiftness. "What is that thing in there?" she demanded. "It looks like some furry animal."

Lisa realized which drawer Mildred had opened and went white. "It isn't an animal," she started to explain but Mildred was already reaching a tentative hand into the drawer to touch it.

"It's hair!" she exclaimed in a mixture of bewilderment and irritation.

"It's a wig," Lisa identified it.

"A wig?" The housekeeper took it out of the drawer to examine it more closely. "You didn't have a wig when I unpacked your things. What would you want with a wig? And a red one, at that?"

The woman's attitude made Lisa feel as guilty as if she'd stolen it. "I . . . I bought it to play a joke on somebody." It was difficult to look the housekeeper in the eye and lie. "And I guess I always wondered what I'd look like in red hair."

"It's a waste of money if you ask me." Mildred sniffed in disapproval as she stuffed the wig back in the drawer.

Lisa inched toward the door. She didn't want to think about Ann Eldridge or anything about the reason she had come to Charleston, not today.

"You will tell Mitzi where I've gone?" she reminded the housekeeper that she was leaving.

"I'll tell her." The woman reached for the bottle of furniture polish, but it was empty. "Now I've got to make another trip downstairs. This just isn't my day," she complained aloud.

"Slade is waiting for me. I have to go." Lisa turned to leave the room, and Mildred was right behind her.

At the bottom of the stairs, Mildred spoke up. "I still don't understand why you'd want to buy a red wig when you have such beautiful hair."

"I told you I just did it for the fun of it," Lisa retorted impatiently, anxious to have the subject dropped before it infringed on her happiness.

"It's nothing to me how you spend your money," Mildred shrugged her slouching shoulders and turned down the hallway to the kitchen.

At that moment Slade rounded the corner, his dark gaze lighting on Lisa. "Your five minutes are up. Are you coming?"

"Yes." She almost dashed past Mildred to reach him and get him out of the house before the woman said any more about what she'd found in Lisa's drawer.

If Slade had appeared only a few minutes sooner, he would have discovered all about her deception. Lisa dreaded the moment when he would find out, not because she hadn't obtained the evidence she wanted, but because of what it would mean personally.

Outside, Slade helped her into the passenger side of the car. "I almost wish your answer had been no, you weren't coming," he said, pausing beside the car before he closed her door.

"Why?" She held her breath, her expression inscrutable.

"Because then I could have persuaded you to change

your mind all over again." A half smile curved the hard, male line of his mouth.

Lisa released the breath in silent relief as he closed her door and walked around to the driver's side. A little voice inside her head said she was being a fool, but she ignored it.

CHAPTER EIGHT

THE REST OF THE MORNING and afternoon was spent driving. As Slade put it, if he had to keep his concentration on the road, he would be less tempted to take back his statement that they would just talk.

They traversed the whole Low Country area of South Carolina located around Charleston, stopping at noon to lunch in a crowded restaurant and again in midafternoon for a cold drink.

Lisa didn't remember the last time she had told anyone so much about herself. But then they had both talked a great deal. The subjects had ranged from their childhood, their family and friends, to their work and hobbies, the kind of musing they liked and the books they read. Yet they both carefully avoided the subject of Mitzi Talmadge.

Myrtle Beach and the Golden Strand were far behind them now. Each rotation of the tires was taking them closer to Charleston. It was inevitable that the afternoon had to end. Staring at the Highway 17 sign at the side of the road, Lisa realized it and wished they were sixty miles from Charleston instead of six. Unconsciously she sighed in regret.

"What's wrong?" Perceptively Slade had caught the small sound and let his gaze be distracted briefly from the highway.

"Nothing," Lisa insisted, but she knew he would persist if she didn't divert his attention. "There must be a boom in baskets. I've never seen so many stands along the road selling them. Just look at them!"

"Surely you've seen them before?" he frowned.

"No, I haven't."

"But you had to come this way to get to Brookgreen Gardens." He was eyeing her curiously.

"Oh," she laughed self-consciously, "I guess we were talking so much we never noticed any roadstands. You know how it is when a bunch of girls get together. Peg, Susan and I are no different."

Slade nodded and Lisa knew she had covered her fabrication story of having been to Brookgreen Gardens and how she had missed seeing these stands.

"You mustn't have heard about our Low Country coil baskets." He slowed the car and turned off the road, stopping in front of one of the stands. "Coil basketry is an African art brought over here by the slaves. The skill and designs have been passed down from one generation to another, sometimes with new designs by new artists being introduced along the way. Come on and we'll take a look. We can't have your education neglected," he mocked gently.

With Slade at her side, Lisa inspected the roadside display. The baskets came in all shapes and sizes, some intricate in their designs, some plain, some with lids and some open.

An aging black woman sat in a chair to one side of the stand, a sweater around her shoulders. Her nimble fingers were busy creating the coiled base of another basket, but not too busy that she was unaware of Slade and Lisa looking over her display.

"Generally women make the show baskets," Slade explained, "and men make the sturdier work baskets that were, and in some cases still are, used for agricultural purposes."

He pointed out a large, very shallow basket, called a "fanner basket," used to winnow rice, which was once the main crop of the large plantations around Charleston because of the high water table of the Low Country. Lisa picked up a smaller basket to study it more closely.

"The craftsmanship is superb," she murmured more to herself than to Slade. "How do they make them? What do they use?"

"The show baskets use sweet grass sewn together with the split leaf of the palmetto palm. The dark stripes in some of the baskets are decorations made by long needles of pine straw." He showed her the stitches of the palmetto leaf that seemed to radiate out in a straight line from the center of the coil basket. "The work baskets use bulrushes and split white oak or split palmetto butt for more strength."

"The materials are found locally?"

"Once they were in great abundance, but that isn't as true today. Large tracts of land where the sweet grass and palmetto palm grew have been developed into housing or resort areas. It's becoming more difficult for the basket artists to find natural materials for their work because of it." He glanced at the basket in her hand. "Would you like to have that?"

"Yes, it's beautiful, but—" Lisa started to point out that she had no money with her.

"My first gift to you." Slade didn't let her finish as he

gently pried the basket from her fingers and walked over to the elderly artist to pay for it.

A few minutes later they were back on the road heading toward Charleston. Lisa held the small coil basket in her lap. Her first gift from Slade. He had said it as if it would be the first of many.

But whose money would pay for them? His or Mitzi's? She stared out of the window, wishing she hadn't thought of that. It spoiled her pleasure in the gift and, somehow, the day.

Neither of them spoke in the last half dozen miles to Mitzi's house. Lisa gazed absently out of the window, lost in her melancholy thoughts, and Slade had to concentrate on the traffic that got heavier as they entered the city limits of Charleston.

The scrolled wrought-iron gates were open to admit them to the driveway of Mitzi's house. Slade stopped the car in front of the portico and switched off the motor. Without a word, he climbed out of the car and walked around to Lisa's door.

"We're here," he announced unnecessarily as he opened it.

"Yes." Her reply was as instant as his comment.

They both seemed caught in the web of tension between them. Walking to the carved entrance doors of the house, Lisa attempted to brush it away.

"Did I bore you this afternoon?" She tried to be light and teasing, but there was an anxious note in the question.

"I don't know when I've been so—bored with a woman in my life," Slade mocked.

Lisa glanced away, a painful tightness in her throat. "Don't make jokes, Slade."

338

"Don't ask stupid questions, Lisa," he returned.

At the door she turned, her hand poised on the knob, straining for composure and wishing she didn't feel as if she was leaving him for good.

"Will you come in for a few minutes?"

"No." Slade leaned an arm against the jamb, effectively blocking her from entering the house immediately.

His dark head bent toward her and Lisa moved forward to meet him. The delicate violence in his kiss told her how great his restraint had been all day as he released the passion he had controlled. His desire wasn't satiated by the assault on her lips nor the feel of her pliant body arching to mold itself against the hard contours of his.

"I've been wanting to do that all day," he said, dragging his hard mouth from her lips to nuzzle the lobe of her ear. "That and more."

Her one free hand was exploring the rough texture of his face while the other still crazily held on to the basket. Eyes closed against the sweet torment of loving him and not knowing the culmination of that love, Lisa pressed herself closer to his length. She quivered with longing as he explored the base of her neck and the hollow of her throat, finding her pleasure points with seductive ease.

"Slade, I don't want you to ever let me go." The trembling plea was issued in fear.

His mouth broke off the burning contact with her bare skin as he crushed her in the iron circle of his arms. She felt the inner shudder of longing he tried to conceal.

339

"Come over to my apartment tonight," he ordered in a voice that was husky and raw.

"I—can't," Lisa denied achingly.

"Yes, you can." His arms tightened punishingly around her. "After dinner, you can leave Mitzi alone with her coffee. Or come after she's gone to bed—I don't care."

"No!" She shook her head, wanting desperately to agree.

"Damnit, Lisa—" Slade began angrily as if tortured, his need for her surpassing his endurance.

"I'm not a prude, Slade," Lisa answered shakily. "But I can't do that to Mitzi. She may be open-minded, but she would never approve of that."

"You're right." He breathed in deeply, fighting for control as he loosened his hold. "The mother hen would feel overly responsible for her adopted chick. If you spent the night with me, we could never convince her that she hadn't failed you somehow. It would be foolish to hurt her that way."

"Yes," Lisa agreed with sudden bitterness, "we don't want her thinking badly of us."

Inwardly she damned her aunt's money and Slade's greed for it. He claimed to love her, but not even for love would he risk losing his chance for Mitzi's wealth. It cheapened her feeling for him somehow.

"Tomorrow—" Slade began, sliding his hands caressingly along her spine.

Lisa knew she didn't dare see him or spend time with him Sunday. "Tomorrow I'll have to devote to Mitzi," she insisted. "Since I've been here, I've hardly been with her at all. I can't go running off again or she'll

340

think I've come here just to have free room and board on my vacation."

Slade seemed about to argue, then changed his mind. "Okay, I'll see you Monday. We'll have dinner and—" a tight smile quirked his mouth as he lifted his head to look at her "—we'll see what else."

"Yes," Lisa agreed with a strained smile, a terrible depression settling over her. "I'd better be going in." She firmly disentangled herself from his embrace and turned to the door. He didn't try to stop her. "Good night, Slade," she murmured, aware that he hadn't moved.

"Lisa." It was a husky demand to come back to his arms.

At the feathery brush of his fingers against the spun silver strands of her hair, Lisa wrenched open the door and bolted inside. Closing the door, she leaned against it, the pain of loving him choking her throat. Seconds later she heard the slamming of the car door and the starting growl of the engine.

The weekend dragged slowly by for Lisa. By Monday morning, the strain of being bright, supposedly untroubled company for Mitzi was beginning to show in her pale features. While Lisa was walking to Slade's office, she debated whether she was going to carry out her masquerade as Ann Eldridge for another day. The affirmative answer was inescapable. She had to find out the extent of Slade's treachery.

Drew followed her into the office when she arrived. "A redhead in basic black. I can't think of a more striking combination than that," he declared with a wolfish smile.

341

"Flattery will get you absolutely nowhere with me." She ran a perspiring palm over the hip of her black pantsuit.

The box-style jacket was a reversible green plaid. Lisa wished now she had chosen to wear that side out instead of the black. She would have felt less like being in mourning.

"Not even an acceptance of my lunch invitation?"

"No," she refused.

She was much too tense to make small talk over a sandwich, even if the noon hour was three hours away. Her taut condition was unlikely to improve.

"I don't think you're ever going to say yes," Drew sighed.

The outer office door swung open and Slade came striding in. Vitality radiated from him with the blinding force of direct sunlight, and Lisa was glad she was sitting in her chair. The sight of him made her weak, especially when he walked directly to her desk and flashed her one of his devastating smiles.

"Good morning, Mrs. Eldridge, Drew." He picked up the morning mail sitting in the basket on her desk and began glancing through it, a trace of the smile still curving the hard line of his mouth.

"Good morning, Mr. Blackwell." Lisa had to lower her gaze to keep from devouring him with her eyes.

Drew whistled softly. "Introduce me to her, Slade."

"To whom?" Slade tipped his head curiously at his close friend and associate, the half smile not leaving his mouth.

"To the girl who made your weekend so bright that it carried over to Monday morning. She must be

342

special to make you this cheerful," Drew declared, so intent on Slade that he missed the rush of color that rouged Lisa's cheeks. "I want to meet her."

"Not a chance." A rich, throaty laugh came from Slade, sending delicious shivers over Lisa's skin. "She's all mine and I intend to keep it that way."

When Slade disappeared into his office, Drew turned to Lisa, his eyes widening suggestively. "I get the feeling Cupid has struck. I swear I saw a whole quiver of arrows sticking out of his back. I don't know who's luckier, Slade or the girl."

A warm glow brightened the green of her eyes. "Both, I hope." It was almost a silent prayer that it could be so.

"Slade's caught the golden ring and you've turned me down for lunch," Drew shook his head. "I couldn't feel more left out if I was locked in a tower with the key thrown away."

"Your turn will come," Lisa offered.

"Yeah," he agreed glumly. "In the meantime, back to the 'blue Monday' salt mines!"

Drew had barely left Lisa's office when Slade walked back in from his, carrying a stack of papers and folders which he dumped on her desk.

"Here," he said. "You can file these this morning, Ann," he added, using her supposed given name unconsciously before turning to reenter his office.

"What about those contracts you said last Friday had to be typed first thing this morning?" Lisa reminded him.

He paused at his door, a recklessly indifferent look carved in his compelling features. "Forget it," he shrugged with uncharacteristic disregard for the contracts' importance. "Typing isn't one of your favorite things, and the day is too beautiful to be clouded by drudgery. The contracts can wait till another day."

Her mouth opened in disbelief, but Slade was already closing his door, not seeming to realize how unlike himself he was behaving. Yet it left Lisa in little doubt that he really loved her. With a happy smile, she turned toward the stack of filing to be done.

Black letters seemed to leap from the tab of one of the folders and her heart stopped beating for a split second. "Talmadge, Miriam," the letters spelled.

With shaking fingers, Lisa pulled the folder out of the stack, staring at it almost in dread. It was what she had been waiting for—to have Mitzi's file in her possession. She closed her eyes weakly, wishing it hadn't happened.

The telephone rang shrilly in her ears. Lisa hesitated, then quickly slipped the folder in a desk drawer and answered the phone. When she had transferred the call to Slade, she ignored the closed desk drawer. Picking up the stack of papers and folders, she carried them to the metal cabinets, setting them on top of one of them and systematically began filing them in the proper place.

She had not completely mastered the filing system. She still relied heavily on the guess and search method. In consequence, an hour later there was one-third of the stack yet to be filed when Slade emerged from his office.

"I'll be gone for about twenty minutes if anyone's

344

looking for me," he told her, still with that contented light burning in his dark eyes.

"Yes, Mr. Blackwell," she nodded.

With the closing of the door, she walked back to her desk, sat down in her chair and stared at the desk drawer. She clenched her hands tightly in her lap, then tore them apart to reach for the telephone, finding a reason to stall the inevitable for a few more minutes.

When she'd left the house that morning, she hadn't said where she was going nor how long she would be gone because she hadn't been sure she would come to the office. She dialed Mitzi's number, fabricating another story in her mind as to why she wouldn't be home until early evening.

"Talmadge residence." The call was answered on the second ring.

"Mildred, this is—" she began.

"Lisa, is that you?" It was Mitzi who was on the phone instead of the housekeeper.

"Yes, it is," Lisa rushed nervously. "I was cal—"

"I'm so glad you called," Mitzi interrupted her again. "Exactly sixteen minutes ago I typed those six magic letters."

"What?" she asked blankly.

Mitzi laughed. "'The End.' I've finished my new novel!"

"That's wonderful," Lisa agreed with forced enthusiasm.

"It's heavenly!" her aunt gushed. "And it calls for an immediate celebration. Where are you? I'll meet you for lunch at some frightfully swank restaurant."

Her heart sank. "Well, actually, Mitzi, I'm—"

"Oh, no, don't tell me you can't make it." Mitzi sounded genuinely crushed. "If you're with your two friends, bring them along. We'll make a party of it."

"No, no, they can't make it." Lisa rubbed her hand across her forehead, feeling the beginnings of a headache start to pound in her temples. She just couldn't disappoint her aunt. "But I can meet you at noon. Where would you like to celebrate?"

Mitzi suggested a restaurant that was fortunately within walking distance of the office, and Lisa agreed. Her aunt sounded quite jubilant when Lisa hung up, while she sighed dispiritedly. She opened the desk drawer to take out Mitzi's folder and Drew walked in. She closed the drawer with guilty swiftness.

"Aha! I caught you doing your fingernails, didn't I?" he accused with mock anger. "If you don't have lunch with me, I'll tell Slade."

"You're out of luck. He isn't here," Lisa retorted with false brightness.

"Where did he go?" Drew grimaced.

"He didn't say. All he told me is that he would be back in twenty minutes." She shrugged, and rose from the desk to return to the filing.

"Well—" Drew breathed in deeply and shoved his hands in his pockets "—I guess I'll keep you company until he comes back." He wandered over to the cabinets where Lisa worked. "What are you doing?"

"Filing. Want to help?" she offered.

"No, thanks," he smiled, and eyed her lazily. "So you won't give in to my blackmail and have lunch with me?"

"No," Lisa repeated her earlier refusal.

"It's just as well, I suppose. Considering the benevolent mood Slade is in, he'd probably send you out for a manicure if I told him I'd caught you doing your nails. Not that they need doing." He caught one of her hands and refused to let it go. "Everything about you is beautiful, Ann, including your nails. No wonder you can't type," he said, touching the rounded length of one of her nails.

"Now you know my darkest secret." Lisa firmly pulled her hand from his grasp just as Slade returned.

"No holding hands during office hours," he scolded laughingly. "Her husband is going to show up here one day, Drew, and you're going to be in trouble."

The telephone rang, interrupting Drew's reply. Lisa started toward her desk, but Slade waved her away. "I'll answer it." He picked up the receiver. "Slade Blackwell," he identified himself briskly, and Lisa turned back to the cabinet, resisting the desire to gaze at him. "Hello, Mitzi, how are you?"

Lisa froze, the folder in her hand poised above the open cabinet drawer, her fingers tightening whitely as they gripped the stiff paper.

"It goes here," Drew whispered, indicating a spot between two file folders already in the drawer. She shoved the folder between them.

"You did?" Slade was speaking again. "Congratulations....Lunch today?"

He seemed to hesitate and Lisa pivoted quickly toward him. "You have an appointment for lunch, Mr. Blackwell," she reminded him, hoping she didn't sound as panicked as she felt.

Slade glanced at her briefly, then smiled suddenly at

the mouthpiece. "She's meeting you at noon? Of course I'll be there, Mitzi."

"What about your appointment?" Lisa accused frantically when he hung up the telephone.

"Who was it with?" He glanced at the day's calendar with remarkable unconcern. "Art Jones? Call him up and change it to another day."

"*She* is going to be there." Drew stressed the feminine pronoun suggestively.

Slade flashed him a glittering look, his dark eyes sparkling with an inner brilliance. "I'm not inviting you along, Drew. It's bad enough that her aunt is going to be there, without having you, too."

"Nobody wants to eat lunch with me," Drew declared with mock exasperation.

"Too bad," Slade chuckled quietly. "Did you want to see me about something, Drew, or are you here just to give Ann a bad time?"

"No, there's something I want to discuss with you. That is, if you think you can concentrate on business for five minutes and forget your girl," was the teasing answer.

"Mr. Blackwell?" Lisa heard herself asking for his attention.

He turned, absently curious. "Yes?"

"I have a dental appointment over the noon hour," she lied. "Would it be all right if I left a little early?"

"Of course."

A few minutes past the appointment meeting time, Lisa walked into the restaurant. Her silver blond hair fell soft and loose about her shoulders; the red wig was tucked safely away in her bag. Her jacket was reversed

348

to the green and black plaid side, not going well with the smoke blue sunglasses perched on her nose.

A movement at a far table caught her eye. Having seen Lisa enter the restaurant, Slade was rising to meet her. Lisa's steps faltered as he moved toward her. She wasn't attempting to feign surprise at seeing him there. Her momentary uncertainty was caused by the panic racing through her veins. She managed to force it back and smile as they approached each other.

It wasn't really too difficult to smile warmly, not with his heart-disturbing look fanning the fires of her love. Slade halted, letting her cover the last few feet that would bring her to his side. Tall and darkly male, he stood before her, commanding all of her senses.

Unmindful of the other patrons in the restaurant, his dark head bent toward hers, stealing Lisa's breath in a hard kiss that was frustratingly brief for both of them. When he straightened, she swayed toward him and his arm curved around her shoulders to guide her toward the table.

"Hello." His low, belated greeting was husky and caressing. "You didn't expect to see me here, did you?"

"No, Mitzi didn't mention you would be joining us," Lisa could say truthfully.

The smoldering light in his eyes seemed to physically and lovingly touch each of her features, making her want to melt under the fiery glow. The possessive curve of his arm added to the boneless sensation.

"Sunday was the longest day of my life," Slade offered for her hearing alone.

"For me, too," Lisa admitted softly. They were nearly at the table where Mitzi waited, and Lisa had to tear her gaze from its adoring inspection of Slade's ruggedly handsome face. "Hello, Mitzi." But her voice still echoed the velvet quality induced by the magic of Slade's nearness. "I'm sorry I'm late."

"I didn't mind waiting, although I think Slade did." There was a knowing and pleased gleam in her aunt's eyes as she studied the two of them together.

Lisa flushed warmly as she sat in the chair Slade held out for her. Bending forward, Slade pushed her chair to the table, his face relatively close to her hair.

"Do you know something?" He took the chair to her left, a faintly bemused smile on his mouth. "You wear the same fragrance of perfume that my secretary does."

Lisa stiffened, every muscle tensing, every nerve alert to the danger of comparisons. "Really?" Her response was much too cool.

"Jealous?" he mocked laughingly, not seeming to care how much of their new relationship he was revealing to Mitzi. "You needn't be. It explains how you've seemed to haunt my every waking moment with the suggestion of you."

"It's a popular fragrance, sold at most cosmetic counters," she assured him.

"It suits Lisa well, though," Mitzi inserted. "Adult and evocative without being too cloyingly sweet."

"Speaking of suiting Lisa, I like your outfit," Slade complimented. "I would never have chosen green as your color, but you look beautiful in it."

"Thank you," Lisa responded nervously.

"Of course green is her color," her aunt spoke up. "Why shouldn't it be, with those—" The waiter appeared, opportunely for Lisa, with glasses and a chilled bottle of champagne.

"Champagne!" Lisa was delighted to interrupt Mitzi and keep her from remarking on the green of her eyes. "We really are going to celebrate the completion of your book!"

Minutes later the three of them were lifting their glasses as Slade toasted, "To your newest book. May it be the most successful one yet. Congratulations."

For a time the conversation was focused on Mitzi's new book, its plot and characters, and Lisa was able to relax. When Slade refilled the glasses, Lisa automatically reached for hers to take a sip of champagne, but Slade stopped her.

"Wait." His hand moved to the inside pocket of his suit jacket. "I don't mean to steal your thunder, Mitzi, but we have something else to celebrate."

Puzzled, Lisa didn't understand what he meant until she saw the velvet ring box in his hand. She breathed in softly when he snapped it open to reveal the rainbow brilliance of a diamond ring.

"I didn't intend to give this to you until tonight," he told her huskily, "but when I found out we'd be having lunch together, I couldn't wait. Give me your hand, Lisa."

She was too overcome with joy to speak or move. Happiness radiated from the shimmering tears in her eyes as she gazed at him. There was an equal depth of feeling in the glowing darkness of his own eyes. Smiling, Slade took hold of her left hand and drew it over to him. Immediately a deep frown was carved into his face.

351

"What is this?" he demanded.

Blinking in confusion, Lisa looked down at her hand, paling at the sight of the golden wedding band on her third finger. She had forgotten to switch rings. Quickly she tore it from her finger.

"It's a friendship ring the girls gave me this morning," she lied desperately. "It was too small to wear on my right hand."

She couldn't tell whether Slade believed her or not. The gold ring seemed to burn a circle in the tightly closed palm of her right hand, but she was afraid to put it in her bag for fear Slade would glimpse the red wig hidden inside.

"I'll take it to the jewelers for you and have it made larger," Slade offered, watching her closely.

"That isn't necessary," Lisa refused, and hurriedly slipped the gold band into her jacket pocket. "I can do it."

"Hurry and put the ring on her finger, Slade," Mitzi urged. "I want to see it."

Her hand was shaking badly as he slipped the diamond ring on her third finger. It never occurred to her to refuse it. When Slade smiled at her, all masculine and virile, Lisa knew that she loved him no matter what.

"Do you like it?" he asked.

"It's beautiful," she smiled.

"It's stunning, is the word!" Mitzi exclaimed, reaching for Lisa's hand to examine the ring more closely. "The two of you have made me the happiest woman in the world. I should have known something like this would happen when the two of you struck sparks off each other the instant you met."

"Didn't I tell you that's what she'd say?" Slade mocked.

"When is the wedding to be?" Mitzi wanted to know, still admiring the ring.

"Soon," Slade promised with typical self-assurance. "Very soon."

A toast was proposed by Mitzi, followed by more talk before they gave their luncheon order to the waiter. But all the while Lisa was plagued by stirrings of unease.

There was nothing in Slade's attitude to make her feel that way. She still received the touch of his hand and the warm caress of his gaze. The problem seemed to be solely her own—a guilty conscience.

After the meal was served and the dishes subsequently cleared, neither Mitzi nor Slade seemed inclined to bring the luncheon gathering to an end. Lisa was intensely conscious of the passing time, aware that the minute hand of her watch was inching near the one-thirty mark. And Ann Eldridge was supposed to have only an hour lunch break.

Twice she tried to make excuses to leave, but each time Slade used his persuasive charm to see that she didn't. Being newly engaged, Lisa could hardly reveal how eager—how anxious she was to leave, and she finally had to wait for one of them to make the first move.

Seconds ticked rapidly away before Slade glanced absently at his watch and sighed. "It's nearly two o'clock. As much as I hate to leave you, I have to get back to the office."

"I understand," Lisa assured him, smiling with relief.

353

Rising from his chair, he rested a hand on her shoulder, saying his goodbyes first to Mitzi before glancing down at Lisa. "I'll see you at seven tonight if not before."–

"Yes," she agreed, lifting her head to receive the brushing kiss from his mouth.

There was no hope of beating him back to the office, not when she had to change into Ann Eldridge somewhere along the way. So she lingered for several more minutes with Mitzi before resorting to the much-used pretext of meeting Susan and Peg as the reason she couldn't return with Mitzi to her home.

"Run along," her aunt insisted, not raising a single objection to the news that she would again be denied Lisa's company. "I know how eager you must be to show off your engagement ring to your friends."

"Yes, I am," Lisa said, agreeing with the excuse and hurrying from the restaurant.

CHAPTER NINE

THIS TIME LISA did not overlook any minor details like rings when making her hasty change of identity. She was secure in that knowledge when she, Ann Eldridge, walked into the office. But that didn't stop her from quailing under the piercing look from Slade.

"Do you realize it's past two o'clock?" He stood beside her desk, tall and imposing.

"I'm sorry. I know I was late, but I didn't realize it was that time already." She apologized profusely, and began the speech she had been rehearsing since leaving the restaurant. "My dentist was running late in his appointments. Then, just as I got in the chair, an emergency came in—some little boy had his permanent front teeth knocked out and the doctor tried to save them. I shouldn't have waited, but they didn't think it would take very long. It turned out that it did and I'm late. If you want me to, I'll stay on later tonight to make up for it."

"There's no need for that." Slade appeared to relent slightly after hearing her explanation.

To reach her desk, Lisa had to walk around him. She did so reluctantly, depositing her handbag in a lower desk drawer before sitting in her chair and attempting to assume a professional posture.

"I'm glad you're so understanding about this." She smiled nervously. "When you gave me permission to leave early, I never intended to take advantage of you this way."

"I'm sure you didn't," he responded smoothly. "I came back only a few minutes ago myself."

Lisa felt the tension mounting to a screaming pitch. "Did you?" The brightness of her reply was forced. "It seems we both overextended our lunch hour."

"And both of us had cause. You, with your troubles at the dentist, and me," Slade paused, "I became engaged this noon."

"Really? Congratulations! That's wonderful news, Mr. Blackwell." She had never felt so small in all her life.

"Yes, it is." A complacent smile curved his mouth.

Having made this announcement, Lisa expected him to leave her, but he didn't. He continued to stand beside her desk. Her poise would splinter soon if he didn't go.

"Was there anything else, Mr. Blackwell?" She tried to prod him into leaving. "Will you be taking the rest of the afternoon off? Or did you want something?"

"There is one thing—" Slade paused.

"I'd like to buy my fiancée an engagement present. I wondered if you would have a suggestion."

"I have never met her so I really wouldn't know what to suggest." She could hear the breathless quality to her voice that revealed her inner agitation.

"What did your husband buy you for an engagement gift? Maybe that will help me," he said.

Lisa swallowed nervously. "He...he didn't have

enough money to buy me anything. He could barely afford the ring when we got engaged." She hated all these lies. They were tearing at her soul.

"You said your husband was in construction, didn't you?" Slade seemed to tower above the desk. Despite his seeming interest in the personal life of Ann Eldridge, Lisa felt increasingly uneasy.

"Yes, that's right," she murmured and began moving papers around on her desk to give her trembling hands something to do.

"What company does he work for? I'm familiar with a great many of them here in Charleston," he said.

Lisa wouldn't have been surprised if he knew every single one—which made it impossible for her to make up a fictitious company.

"I've forgotten what firm it is," she pleaded ignorance.

"You've forgotten." His gaze narrowed. "What would you do if there was an emergency and you had to get in touch with him? How can you explain forgetting the name of your husband's company?"

"I don't know." Lisa faked an indifferent shrug and struggled to bluff her way out of the corner. "If it's a dire emergency, I'll find a way to contact him."

"Is that how you explain it?"

"Yes." Her voice sounded small.

"Then I would like you to explain what this—" he reached down and opened her desk drawer, revealing Mitzi's file folder lying on top of the other papers "—is doing in your drawer."

"That folder?" Her throat was dry and her heart pumped wildly in fear. "It was among the stack of

357

papers you gave me to be filed. I didn't get that one filed away before I left this noon, so I put it in my drawer rather than leave it lying out."

"I see." he murmured.

"I'll, er, file it now," Lisa stammered. Her hand was shaking as she picked up the folder and walked to the filing cabinets.

Slade followed leisurely to watch, his continued presence in the room scraping her nerves raw. She didn't know how much more she could stand.

"Did you have time to eat anything for lunch?" he asked unexpectedly as she went through the file drawer to find the proper place to put Mitzi's folder.

"No, I didn't," Lisa lied, "but that's all right. I should watch my weight anyway." She immediately regretted the allusion to her shape as his gaze skimmed her figure, setting off sensual shockwaves that vibrated her taut nerve ends.

"I've been meaning to compliment you on the outfit you're wearing. It's very attractive." Slade lightly traced the pointed collar of her jacket, his touch paralyzing her as if it was lethal. "It would be more striking in green, though, to match your eyes."

When he began to run his finger down the buttoned front of the jacket, Lisa regained control of her muscles and flinched from his touch.

"Please, Mr. Blackwell, don't do that." Her protest was breathy with alarm.

"'Don't do that, Mr. Blackwell!'" His angrily sarcastic mimicry of her protest startled Lisa.

The words were still ringing in her ears when her arm was caught and she was yanked roughly against

358

him. The breath was knocked from her lungs by the unyielding contact with his muscular chest.

She never had a chance to regain it as her lips were crushed against her teeth by the brutal assault of his mouth. For unending moments Slade plundered the softness of her lips, savagely ravishing them until she had not the strength to resist if she had found the will.

When he was finished wreaking his anger on her, he let her go. Lisa reeled backward, her hands seeking the support of the sturdy metal cabinets. But Slade wasn't quite through with her. He followed her, arms stretched against the cabinet on either side of her, trapping her there to face his proud fury.

"What kind of a fool do you think I am?" he snarled.

"Slade, let me explain." Her heart was hammering in her throat and she could hardly breathe. Her legs were still shaking from the raging anger in his kiss.

"Just because I didn't see through your charade in the beginning, did you think I'd go right on being blind, Lisa?" A muscle twitched convulsively in his jaw, indicating how very tenuous his hold was on his temper.

"You don't understand," she protested.

"I understand very well. When I saw that wedding band on your finger today, all the pieces began to fall into place." His voice was flat and hard, riddled with contempt and disgust.

If Lisa had been given a moment of warning, some little sign that she was about to be unmasked, she might have been better able to defend herself. But no, Slade had let her tell more lies, given indications that he believed them, then pounced like a sleek panther on

359

an unwary prey. She was completely at his mercy—or his lack of it.

"I—" she began, intimidated by his sheer masculinity and the ruthless set of his hard jaw.

"No more lies, Lisa!" Slade slashed away her attempt to explain, looming closer to her as if he would silence her forever.

Lisa flattened herself against the filing cabinet, the metal cool to the hands she spread against its surface. Her left arm was seized and twisted upward by steel fingers.

"Where is my ring?" he accused.

The pain he was causing her was more than just physical. There was the mental anguish of his slicing voice, wounding her heart with its ability to hurt deeply. When she didn't answer immediately, he increased the pressure on her arm, unaware of how fierce his grip was.

"In my pocket," she answered, biting back the cry of pain.

"It never had a chance to be warmed by your skin before you were slipping it off," Slade muttered savagely. Swiftly he made the change to sarcasm, lifting her left hand to force the gold wedding band into her view. "You slipped it off to put on this." His upper lip curled in a sneer.

"Give me a chance—"

"No!" The denial seemed to explode from him as his free hand fastened itself around her throat. His glittering look was darkly menacing, intensified by the coldly ruthless line of his mouth. "You've had your last chance."

But Lisa wasn't really frightened. She seemed to know instinctively that no matter how great his anger was toward her, Slade would never harm her physically. He didn't need to, not when he could cut her heart into ribbons with words.

The door to the reception area opened and Drew came sauntering into Lisa's office. He came to an abrupt halt at the sight of them, his mouth opening for a speechless second.

"Slade, what the hell are you doing?" He demanded in a voice that sounded positive he was seeing things. A disbelieving frown creased his forehead. "Ann—"

"No, not Ann." Slade's hand left her throat to grab a handful of the red wig.

Gasping in pain, Lisa caught at his wrist to stop him. "Slade, it's pinned!"

"Then unpin it and take the damned thing off!" He released her completely and took a step away, anger vibrating from him even as he remained motionless.

While Lisa shakily removed the hairpins that secured the wig to her scalp, no one uttered a word. Drew was stunned and confused, especially when silver blond hair tumbled to Lisa's shoulders. There wasn't any satisfaction in Slade's angrily grim expression at the completion of the task. He took the wig from her unresisting fingers.

"Here." He turned to Drew and tossed him the scarlet-haired wig. "You always claimed to be partial to redheads. Take it and get out!"

In reflex action, Drew had caught it. Now he stared at it, not quite able to take in what was going on. "But—" He looked back at Slade and frowned.

361

"Out!" was the acid command.

Glancing uncertainly at Lisa, Drew finally turned and hesitantly retreated to the reception area, closing the door quietly behind him. Slade's attention returned to her, but Lisa sensed that Drew's interruption had given him a measure of control he hadn't previously had.

He stared at her, assessing her with narrowed eyes. "The wig was an excellent red herring, Lisa, if you'll pardon the expression," he jeered. "I never suspected for an instant that Ann and Lisa were the same person, but that's what you counted on, wasn't it?"

"Yes." It was foolish to deny it. Lisa lifted a weary hand to brush the hair from her face, letting it stay at the back of her neck and pressing her fingers against the throbbing tenseness that was there.

"And your lying green eyes," he snapped. "Equaled only by the falsehoods that come so easily from your lips."

For the second time she was hauled roughly against him. Her heart fluttered a warning before his mouth closed over hers to kiss her long and hungrily—and angrily. Her lips were parted by the bruising urgency of his. For a few delirious moments, she thrilled to the passion of his love, deepening the kiss with a fiery response of her own.

His arms circled her to hold her in their vice, while her own hands spread over his muscled shoulders. Just when she thought Slade loved her enough to forgive her for deceiving him, he broke off the kiss. Her eyes fluttered open to see the self-disgust and contempt that thinned his mouth. The pain to her heart was swift and stabbing.

A moan of protest came from her throat as she rested her forehead against him. "No matter what else you think about me, you must know that I love you, Slade."

Violently she was thrust from him, long impatient strides cleaving a distance between them. Several feet away he stopped, muscles rigid, to glare over his shoulder.

"Do you really love me?" Slade taunted cynically. "Or is it simply convenient to love me?"

"No," Lisa denied in a choked voice. "It isn't convenient to love you."

Not when she was faced with the dilemma of either keeping silent about his unethical if not illegal use of Mitzi's money or exposing him. If she didn't love him, the choice would be much easier to make. In fact, there probably wouldn't even be the need for a choice.

Slade turned his head away, tipping it back to stare at the ceiling. "It's amazing how I could have been so blind not to see it before now," he sighed bitterly, lowering his head with a grim shake. "Everything clicks into place now like the pieces of a puzzle, fitting perfectly. No wonder you didn't have any secretarial skills. You aren't a secretary. The agency people have never heard of you, have they?"

"No," Lisa admitted.

"And I opened the door for you when I mistook you for one of their girls," he muttered with a sharp edge of irony. "There's nothing wrong with your eyes, either. You only wore those sunglasses to hide their color, didn't you?"

"Yes, there's nothing wrong with—"

"And your two girl friends, you invented them to

363

explain your whereabouts during the day to Mitzi so she wouldn't wonder where you were spending your time. You don't have any old college friends in Charleston, do you?" Slade accused.

"None that I know—"

"Which explains why you were so unfamiliar with the sights of the city," he interrupted coldly. "You haven't seen anything, not even Brookgreen Gardens. That's why you didn't remember the basket stands along the highway. Because you'd never been anywhere close to them."

"Okay, so I haven't," Lisa retorted in a frustrated spurt of defiance.

His needle-sharp words were painful. She couldn't continue to endure being the whipping boy for his anger. It wasn't in her nature to keep getting hurt without trying to hurt back.

Pivoting, Slade faced her, his hands on his hips in proud challenge, his dark gaze relentless searching her face. "The day I found you in my office supposedly straightening my papers, you were really going through them, weren't you? What were you looking for? The Talmadge folder?"

"Yes." Lisa tossed back her head, blinking at the tears that burned her eyes, refusing to shed one of them.

"Why? What did you hope to gain?" he demanded.

"I wanted to find out what you were doing with Mitzi's money," she answered truthfully and without apology.

"My God!" Slade muttered, cursing savagely beneath his breath.

"What did you expect me to do?" Lisa stormed. "Let you steal every dime of it?"

The tears nearly escaped to form a waterfall down her lashes. She barely managed to check their descent in time, glancing quickly away from him to open her green eyes as wide as she could and swallow the lump in her throat.

"And what did you find out when you got your greedy hands on the folder?" He was snarling, his teeth bared in challenge.

"Nothing!" she breathed in a rush. "I never had a chance to do more than open it!"

"And that's the way it's going to stay!" Slade declared. "Because you're through. Your charade is over and I don't want Lisa Talmadge in this office!"

Lisa gulped in a deep breath, held it for an instant and expelled it in a long, shuddering sigh. She couldn't meet the steel black quality of his eyes and glanced away. She should have known it would end like this.

"Do you know what's the matter with you, Slade Blackwell?" It was a taut challenge, flung out in the despair of heartbreak.

"Yes," he replied grimly. "I foolishly thought I could expect trust from someone like you."

Trust! Someone like you! The accusation hurt unbearably, because it came from Slade and because he didn't have the right to cast the first stone.

She was caught in the grip of an impotent kind of anger. Too many conflicting emotions had become trapped inside and had to be released. It was a jumbled assortment that came out, half love and half hate, a coin whose two sides had joined to make one.

"That isn't what's eating you," she denied with a

vigorous shake of her head. "No, it's your precious male ego. You can't stand it that I managed to fool you even for a few days. It's too damaging to your fragile male pride to be taken in by a mere inferior female. All you can think about is that I made a fool of you!"

He took a threatening step toward her, then checked himself. His glittering eyes scanned her pale features. Slade seemed to control his temper with difficulty.

"What are you trying to prove, Lisa?" he breathed raggedly. "That you can get under my skin without any effort?"

"No," Lisa answered tightly. "I just want you to admit what's really bothering you."

"You want to know what's really bothering me?" His jaw hardened into bronze. "I'm trying to figure out how I got myself engaged to a greedy little bitch like you."

Lisa recoiled as if he had slapped her face, the blood draining from her cheeks and her stomach muscles tying themselves in a nauseous lump. Shaking fingers searched frantically through the pockets of her jacket until they found the hard gemstone of his ring.

"That's easily remedied." Her voice was hoarse, the wounded cry of an animal in intense pain. "You can take your ring back and you won't have to wonder any more!"

In that fleeting moment when she had taken her attention from him, Slade had crossed the space that separated them. The diamond ring was stripped from her trembling hand and her left was captured.

"I am not taking it back!" he snapped, and began twisting the plain gold band from her third finger. Lisa struggled to free her left hand from his bruising grasp,

366

but he was too strong for her. When the finger was bare, he roughly pushed on the diamond. "This ring is going on and it's staying on."

"No."

"Dammit, yes!" He gave her a hard shake that rattled her teeth. "When you leave here, you're going to march yourself straight to Mitzi's house and pretend that nothing has happened. Because nothing has. Nothing has changed."

"Hasn't it?" Lisa retorted bitterly.

"No, it hasn't," Slade informed her in a steely voice. "And when I get there tonight, you're going to pretend to be the happy bride-to-be that Mitzi expects to see."

"Why?" she breathed in protest.

"Because we're going to be married and you damned well better get used to the idea," he declared. "The only thing that's different now is I've found out about your lies. I don't know—maybe you're incapable of the truth. But you are going to be my wife, make no mistake about that."

"What—" Lisa hesitated, daring to hope "—about Mitzi's money?"

"You don't need to worry about that," he jeered. "Once we're married, what's mine is yours and what's yours is mine."

Lisa flinched, hurt. "Is that why you're marrying me?"

"Don't put that question in my mind," Slade ordered crisply. "Or I'll start asking myself if that's why you're marrying me."

"Slade—" she began earnestly.

"No!" He released her, breathing in deeply as he moved away. "No more talking, not until I've had a chance to think a few more things out. Go on back to Mitzi's." His mouth quirked cynically. "I'm sure you can come up with some story to explain why you're returning sooner than you planned."

"That was unnecessary," Lisa stiffened in resentment.

"I'll see you at six," Slade said, ignoring her comment with autocratic ease. "You be there."

"I will," she answered as curtly as he had given the order. "You have my word on that."

"I don't want your word," he snapped. "I just want you there."

Lisa stared at him silently through a mist of proud tears, then walked to the desk to retrieve her bag from the drawer. She could feel his gaze watching her every move, but he offered not one word of parting when she walked out of the door into the reception room.

Drew was sitting on the edge of the receptionist's desk when Lisa emerged. His searching look was echoed by the receptionist, curiosity gleaming on both their faces.

Lisa guessed that they were bound to have overheard some of what she and Slade had said. Neither of them had given much thought to the volume of their voices at times. Her gaze bounced away from them as she started toward the street door. Drew straightened from the desk.

"Ann—" he began uncertainly.

Lisa turned, meeting his questioning gaze directly. "The name is Lisa Talmadge."

"Talmadge?" he echoed in disbelief, but Lisa was already walking out the door onto the street.

CHAPTER TEN

LISA TWISTED HER HANDS nervously and stopped pacing as Mitzi entered the comfortably furnished living room. She had come to a decision, a difficult one that was already beginning to give her cold feet.

"Sl—" Her voice broke shrilly and she started again. "Slade will be here at six, Mitzi."

"Yes, you mentioned that before," her aunt replied with amused patience.

"Yes, I know," Lisa nodded, looking away in agitation. "If you don't mind, I'd like to speak to him alone for a few minutes."

"Well, of course you can," was the laughing response. "I'm not so old that I don't remember what it's like to be in love and wanting to be alone with the person you love."

"I don't mean it that way exactly," Lisa faltered, and breathed in deeply to try to control the clamoring of her nerves. "I want to be alone with Slade, but I want you to be in the next room."

"The next room?" Mitzi was plainly astonished by the request. "Whatever for? You surely don't think you're going to have to call me for help?"

"No, I—I want you there to listen." Lisa's gaze ricocheted from her aunt to the intertwining of her fingers.

"To listen?" Mitzi was even more astonished. "Why?"

"I don't know how to say this exactly, Mitzi, but—" She paused in agitation, ripping her fingers apart to run a hand over the side of her forehead into the pale blonde of her hair.

"Just say it," her aunt urged.

"I'm afraid Slade is—stealing from you." The accusation clawed its way out of her throat.

"What?" Mitzi's mouth remained open for several seconds before she frowned. "Is this some kind of a joke?" she breathed in a short laugh.

"I wish it were," Lisa declared in torment, "but it isn't."

"Whatever gave you this ridiculous idea?" was the frowning demand.

"I suspected he might be when I first came here. When I confronted him with my suspicions, he admitted it." Tears filled her eyes and Lisa had to turn to the window, blinking furiously to keep them at bay while she swallowed to ease the burning tightness in her throat.

"I don't believe you," Mitzi returned slowly, emphasizing the negative contraction.

"I didn't think you would." Lisa glanced sadly over her shoulder, gazing at her aunt with troubled green eyes. "That's why I tried to get proof."

"Proof?"

Lisa rushed on, not wanting to explain about Ann Eldridge and the lies she had been telling since her arrival. "I don't blame you for not believing me. That's why I want you to listen at the door. I'll... I'll get Slade to admit it again."

370

"Lisa." Mitzi walked to her niece, lightly taking Lisa by the shoulders and intently searching her face. "You really believe this, don't you?"

"Yes." It was a stiff little sound, teeth clenched to keep the pain in her chest from escaping in a sob.

"But at noon—you took his ring? You said you'd marry him?" Her aunt frowned.

"I'm afraid I really do love him, Mitzi." Lisa tried to smile, her chin quivering uncontrollably. "Isn't that the pits?" She tried to laugh at her foolishness, but it came out in an anguished sound.

"I'm sure there's some mistake," Mitzi insisted. "Slade—"

The doorbell rang and Lisa stiffened. "He's here." She looked frantically at her aunt. "Will you listen?"

Mitzi pursed her lips thoughtfully, then nodded a reluctant agreement. "But you've made some kind of mistake about Slade, Lisa, I'm sure of it."

"I wish you were right," Lisa sighed brokenly.

With a comforting squeeze of her shoulders, Mitzi let her go. "I'll answer the door and send Slade in here. I'll be outside."

Cowardlike, Lisa wanted to call the whole thing off as her aunt walked from the living room to the front door. But she was doing it for Slade as well as Mitzi. Breathing in deeply, she wiped the moistness from her lashes and faced the door when Slade entered the room.

He paused a few feet inside the living room to stare at her, a black shuttered look to his dark gaze. His saturnine features were carved in an aloof mask, hard and withdrawn. Yet Lisa's pulse leaped at the sight of

him, tall and vital. Nothing could diminish that aura
of virility that surrounded him, magnetically attract-
ing her to his presence.

"I see you're here," Slade observed curtly.

"I told you I would be," she reminded him defensively.

"Yes—" he exhaled a cynical breath of amusement
"—but your lying tongue has told me many things
these past few days." Lisa flinched at the cutting
gibe and he turned away, muttering, "I need a drink."

Long, impatient strides carried him to the drink
trolley. He paused as he added ice cubes to a glass to
let his dark gaze rake Lisa's rigidly erect form.

"You look as if you could use a drink, too," Slade
noted in uncomplimentary fashion.

"No," she refused.

But Slade began pouring her one anyway. Her green
eyes skittered a look to the door where she knew Mitzi
was listening. Breathing in shakily to find courage, she
walked stiffly to the drinks' cart.

"Slade, we have to talk," she said nervously.

"Here." He thrust a glass toward her, ice clinking
against the sides.

"I don't want it," Lisa refused again.

"Take it," he snapped. His temper hadn't improved.
It was only more tightly leashed.

Reluctantly she accepted it rather than let herself be
sidetracked by an unimportant argument. The cold
sides of the glass seemed to echo the chilling tempera-
ture that numbed her heart.

"We have to talk, Slade," she repeated.

"Yes," he agreed grimly, and took a long drink from

372

his glass. "Bob Turner is back." His gaze sliced to her. "I know you haven't met him, but I'm sure Drew told you about him. He's the third member of my legal team. I've arranged the schedule so that we can leave tomorrow for Baltimore. That will give me a chance to meet your parents before we're married."

"Slade—" Lisa tried to interrupt. That wasn't what she wanted to talk about at all.

"I'd like a private ceremony," he continued without so much as a glance to acknowledge her attempt, "with just the immediate family present. I imagine you would prefer to have it conducted in Baltimore where your family is. I can't see any reason why it can't be arranged to take place within a week."

"Stop it!" Tears welled in her eyes, the shimmering pools intensifying the olive green darkness of her pupils.

"I'll stop nothing!" The shuttered look lifted briefly to reveal the anger that still blazed within. "We will be married, Lisa."

"That isn't what I want to talk about," she protested. "There are other things."

"Such as?" Slade taunted.

The shutters were closed again. The tears threatening to flow from her eyes had been noticed, but they didn't soften his hard features.

"Such as Mitzi," Lisa choked.

"What about Mitzi?" He swirled the liquor in his glass, watching the spinning ice cubes. "She'll be invited to the wedding, of course."

"You know that's not what I want to talk about," she hurled in a tormented whisper.

373

"No, it's never what you want to talk about when you mention Mitzi, is it?" Slade taunted acidly. "It's always her money. I told you this afternoon not to worry about it any more. Once we're married it'll take care of itself. I'll handle it from now on."

"How much—" It was difficult to get the words out. "How much have you taken from Mitzi already?"

"What's the matter, Lisa?" His lip curled sarcastically as he lifted the glass to his mouth. "Are you afraid I'll cheat you out of your share?"

Lisa paled but refused to let him avoid the question. "How much?"

Downing the rest of his drink, Slade glared at the empty glass. "Is the money that damned important to you?"

"Isn't it to you?" she countered.

"Dammit, Lisa!" The glass was slammed onto the trolley, bottles rattling loudly at the suppressed violence in his action. "I—"

"I'm sorry, Lisa." Mitzi's voice came from the doorway, bubbling with inner laughter. "I couldn't stand out in the hallway another minute." Lisa turned with a jerk, staring at her aunt in dismay. "I can't make up my mind if I was listening to a tragic comedy or a comic tragedy!"

Slade turned on Lisa, towering above her in an icy rage. "You arranged for Mitzi to be outside listening?" he accused savagely.

"Yes," she admitted weakly.

"Lisa came to me this afternoon with this nonsense about you stealing from me," Mitzi explained, with an indulging smile at her niece. "I tried to convince her

374

how ridiculous the idea was, but she simply wouldn't listen to me. So I agreed to listen outside. I never heard such silliness in all my life!"

"I was trying to do what I thought was best," Lisa defended tightly.

"Best for whom?" Slade challenged, his mouth thinning whitely in anger. Abruptly, he turned away. "Never mind, don't answer that. I can guess."

"Lisa is certain she's doing it for your own good." High amusement laced Mitzi's voice. "I don't know what game you're playing, Slade, but I think you should put the poor girl straight. It's tearing her apart."

"I'll bet," he jeered, rubbing an angry hand across the back of his neck.

The telephone rang and the housekeeper's shuffling footsteps could be heard in the hall as she went to answer it. Lisa gazed achingly at Slade's taut figure. She knew that he thought she had exposed him simply to get into Mitzi's sole favor. And it hurt.

"It's for you, Mitzi," the housekeeper called with sighing patience.

Her aunt glanced briefly at Lisa, giving her an encouraging smile that said everything would be all right. Lisa wished she could believe Mitzi as her aunt left the room.

At the closing of the door, Slade sighed, "I can't believe you actually did this, Lisa."

"What else could I do?" she cried in frustration. "I couldn't let you go on stealing from her!"

"No, you couldn't do that!" he hurled sarcastically. "There might not be anything left for you!"

"What does it matter, Slade?" Lisa protested. "She doesn't believe me."

"Thank heaven," he muttered.

"Even if she did, she'd forgive you. I don't know how much you've taken, Slade, but give it back. Mitzi loves you almost as much as I do. She wouldn't turn you in, not if you paid back all the money you've taken."

"What?" Slade turned, frowning as he stared into Lisa's entreating green eyes.

"I can help. I can find a job here in Charleston and earn—" She didn't have a chance to complete her offer as Slade fluidly crossed the space to capture her shoulders.

"What are you saying?" he demanded, eyeing her warily. "I thought you were after Mitzi's money."

"No, I only pretended—"

"You mean you lied about that, too!" His frown was starting to change into a disbelieving smile.

"You have to understand, Slade," Lisa tried to explain. His touch was playing havoc with her senses, making it difficult to think straight. "I was trying to protect Mitzi." She stared at his shirt collar, aware of his dark gaze inspecting her face. "I let you think I was after her money, too, hoping you would make a slip and give me proof that you were stealing from her. I knew Mitzi wouldn't believe me without proof because she cares about you too much. It never occurred to me that I might begin to care for you." His shoulders were shaking. Lisa couldn't look up, afraid to see tears staining his proud face. "Let alone fall in love with you. Give the money back, Slade. We don't need it."

A low rolling sound started. Lisa flinched, closing

her eyes at what she thought was a groan of suffering and hopefully remorse. Then it exploded into chuckling laughter, deep and throaty and riddled with amusement. In disbelief, she looked up to see Slade's head thrown back, a smile splitting his male lips.

"I don't see anything funny about that!" she breathed with a trace of temper.

"Don't you?" The glittering warmth of his gaze inspected her indignant expression, laughing and bright. "Oh, Lisa—" he sighed in what sounded very much like contentment "—I haven't taken a cent of Mitzi's money."

"Thank goodness!" she shuddered in relief.

"What's more—" he curved a finger under her chin and tipped her head up "—I never had any intention of taking her money."

"But—" Lisa frowned with bewilderment "—you said—"

"I never said I had," Slade reminded her gently. "I let you believe it because you were already so convinced that it was true."

"But you wanted us to join forces!" Lisa stared at him, wanting desperately to believe what he said, but unable to ignore the lingering doubts.

"Because I thought you were after Mitzi's money. I've become very fond of your aunt these past few years. She seems like my own. I was trying to protect her from you. And all the while, you were trying to protect her from me."

"Oh." It was a tiny sound that slowly curved her mouth into a smile. "Oh, Slade!" She began to laugh, too, at the sheer ridiculousness of the whole thing.

377

His arms circled around her, holding her close as he joined in her laughter. The warmth of his body heat melted the chill that had encased her heart. Lisa felt alive again, deliriously alive and happy.

"What a pair of liars we are!" Slade chuckled against her hair.

Lisa raised her head, leaning against him. "But I've never lied about my feelings," she told him, lost in the enchantment of his spell. "I never lied about loving you, Slade."

"And I never lied about loving you," he said as he lowered his mouth to hers.

What readers say about JANET DAILEY

"The books of Janet Dailey bring joy into an otherwise turbulent world."

B.J.S.* St. Catharines, Ontario

"When reading a Janet Dailey novel I feel like I'm reading a letter from a dear friend."

S.V., Inver Grove Heights, Minnesota

"I wait to buy each new Janet Dailey book as soon as it comes out."

R.G., Des Moines, Iowa

"The only complaint I have of Janet Dailey's books is that they end."

A.M.W., Belford, Ohio

*Names available on request

LaVYRLE SPENCER
SWEET MEMORIES

a special woman…a special love…
a special story

Sweet Memories is the poignant tale of Theresa Brubaker and Brian Scanlon, separated by Brian's Air Force officer training, but united in spirit by their burning love.

Alone and unsure, Theresa decides on a traumatic surgical operation that proves devastating for both her and Brian, a proud sensitive man whose feelings of betrayal run deep. Through the tears and pain, Theresa emerges from her inhibitions a passionate, self-confident woman ready to express her love.

SM-1R

Harlequin Temptation

The sensuous new romance-fiction series about choices...dilemmas...resolutions...and, above all, the fulfillment of love.

These are the novels that ask your heart to decide. Because in every woman's life there comes a moment when her heart must choose her destiny.

Each of the four monthly **Harlequin Temptation** romances provides 224 pages of involving, satisfying reading entertainment for only $1.95.

Available wherever paperback books are sold or through Harlequin Reader Service:

In the U.S.
P.O. Box 52040
Phoenix, AZ 85072-2040

In Canada
P.O. Box 2800, Postal Station "A"
5170 Yonge Street
Willowdale, Ontario M2N 5T5

TEMP-1-R

Harlequin Celebrates

Thirty-Five Years of Excellence

...and our commitment to excellence continues. Indulge in the pleasure of superb romance reading by choosing the most popular love stories in the world.

Harlequin Presents

Exciting romance novels for the woman of today— a rare blend of passion and dramatic realism.

Harlequin Romance™

Tender, captivating stories that sweep to faraway places and delight with the magic of love.

HARLEQUIN SUPERROMANCE™

Longer, more absorbing love stories for the connoisseur of romantic fiction.

Harlequin Temptation™

Sensual and romantic stories about choices, dilemmas, resolutions, and above all, the fulfillment of love.

Harlequin American Romance™

Contemporary romances— uniquely North American in flavor and appeal.

Code: 35-1

Yours FREE, with a home subscription to

HARLEQUIN SUPERROMANCE.™

Complete and mail the coupon below today!

FREE!

Mail to:
Harlequin Reader Service

In the U.S.
2504 West Southern Avenue
Tempe, AZ 85282

In Canada
P.O. Box 2800, Postal Station "A"
5170 Yonge St., Willowdale, Ont. M2N 5T5

YES, please send me FREE and without any obligation my **HARLEQUIN SUPERROMANCE** novel, LOVE BEYOND DESIRE. If you do not hear from me after I have examined my FREE book, please send me the 4 new **HARLEQUIN SUPERROMANCE** books every month as soon as they come off the press. I understand that I will be billed only $2.50 for each book (total $10.00). There are no shipping and handling or any other hidden charges. There is no minimum number of books that I have to purchase. In fact, I may cancel this arrangement at any time. LOVE BEYOND DESIRE is mine to keep as a FREE gift, even if I do not buy any additional books.   134 BPS KARJ

NAME _____ (Please Print)

ADDRESS _____ APT. NO. _____

CITY _____

STATE/PROV. _____ ZIP/POSTAL CODE _____

SIGNATURE (If under 18, parent or guardian must sign.)

SUP-SUB-11

This offer is limited to one order per household and not valid to present subscribers. Prices subject to change without notice.

Offer expires December 31, 1984